IT ENDS WITH VIOLENCE

SAINT VIEW PSYCHOS #3

ELLE THORPE

WWW.ELLETHORPE.COM

v3.

Line edits: Studio ENP

Proofreading: Barren Acres Editing

Original cover photography: Wander Aguiar

Original cover design: Elle Thorpe Pty Ltd

For the curvy women.
You deserve to be the main character.

1

BLISS

*S*creams were the first indication that something was wrong.

Screams that drowned out the low, sultry music.

Screams that cut right through my chest with fear and panic.

In an instant, Psychos turned from a room full of lust and sex into a swirling storm of chaos with me at the center.

"Bliss! Get out of here!" Rebel shouted in my face, but then she was gone, lost to the swarm of people rushing for exits in various forms of undress.

I stumbled a foot in her direction, instinct telling me to follow her even though my brain wasn't cooperating. The crowd pushed me, sweeping me along with a force I was too shocked to fight.

We'd been having a good time.

Nash's birthday had been everything I'd promised him it would be. Sexy. Fun. A roomful of people ready to party, and a much smaller one with just me and him, no barriers between us.

Until my mom had let it slip about Nash's past.

About how he'd used women. Pimped them out and made money from them.

I'd given my body up to Nash tonight. Let him have me in a way no other man had. My heart had cracked wide open and let him in.

I thought he'd felt the same.

But he wasn't the man I thought he was, no matter how much my mother tried to persuade me he wasn't like her abusive husband, Jerry, who'd sold her to any person willing to pay. Her assurances the women had all liked Nash and he'd treated them well didn't fly.

It was all too raw. Too wrong and too far away from the life that had become mine when my father had given me a home in Providence.

Gunshots rang out. Piercing blasts of noise, one after the other that froze me to the spot in terror.

"What's going on?" a man shouted above the din, his eyes wide and flickering erratically.

"It's the cops!" a woman yelled back. "They're shooting! They're shooting everyone!"

Everything stopped.

People I loved were in this club.

One in particular who I'd seen slip from the room and out into the parking lot when Nash's hands on my body had become too much for him to watch.

I was mad at Scythe. He'd put me in a shitty position with War when he'd admitted to being the one who'd killed his father. Then I'd had the displeasure of meeting his 'fiancée' while I was wearing nothing but his T-shirt.

But earlier, Rebel had accused me of being in love with him.

In that instant, I knew it was true.

"Scythe," I whispered.

He was out there somewhere, in the thick of the shooting and screaming and chaos. All I could think about was getting to him. I launched into action again, pushing toward the gunfire while everybody else ran in the opposite direction.

I sprinted through the coatroom and out the other side, pumping my legs as fast as they would go. Through the open doorway that looked out into the parking lot, pandemonium reigned. Guns popped, motorcycle engines roared, men shouted, women cried.

My gaze collided with his, right as he was tackled to the ground, mere feet in front of me. His head cracked off the concrete with a sickening thud.

"Scythe!"

A team of burly, uniformed men pinned him down with brutal punches and kicks to every inch of his body.

Prison guards.

It took me a moment to work out why they would be attacking the man I loved. Until I remembered Vincent's confession of a prison escape, and it all made horrifying, sickening sense.

They'd found him. They were going to drag him back to prison and I'd never see him again. Or worse, they'd kill him right here in front of me. I'd been so worried about War finding out and killing him that I hadn't even considered Scythe's past catching up with him. "Stop," I screamed helplessly. "Please!" I threw myself at them, barely getting a fingertip to one of the guard's uniforms before strong arms wrapped around me, holding me back.

I fought against them, my heart breaking and tears rolling down my face while they attacked Scythe's lifeless body.

"Bliss, stop. We have to get out of here."

Nash.

I sank back into the warmth and comfort of his embrace but shook my head, unable to tear my eyes off Scythe. "We have to help him!"

"We can't. Not now. There's too many of them."

I shoved him off me, whirling around to face him. "We have to!"

He gripped my arms, fingers digging into my biceps painfully. "Dammit, Bliss. We've got a club full of drugs and a parking lot full of cops offloading bullets. I let you go and you're either going to get shot or arrested. He wouldn't ever forgive me if I let anything happen to you, and neither would I. You're coming."

I shouted Scythe's name as Nash lifted me off my feet and dragged me back through the club to my office.

He threw open the door and stopped in the doorway, his mood changing instantly. "I should have fucking known."

His voice was laced with so much disgust I stopped fighting him and took in what he saw.

My mother with my safe open, loading all the drugs into her purse.

My heart broke all over again. Things had been going too well with my mother around, and she'd somehow managed to convince me she really had turned over a new leaf. She'd had me believing when she swore all she wanted from me was a fresh start.

Obviously, she'd just been biding her time, waiting for her chance to strike.

"You were just waiting for your moment, weren't you, Kim?" Nash snarled, storming across the room and snatching the bag she was filling. "Once a junkie, always a junkie."

I expected her to wilt in on herself, to turn and flee, seeing as she was so very busted.

The last thing I expected from my spineless mother was for her to straighten her shoulders and square off with Nash. She snatched the bag back from his hands. "Those cops are going to be in here any minute now." Her gaze darted between me and Nash. "Go, Bliss. Get out of here. I'll clear this out and hold it for you until this all blows over."

There was a sincerity in her gaze that I wasn't sure I'd ever seen before.

She held the look, her eyes burning with a surety that was unmistakable.

She wasn't raiding the safe, she was protecting me.

I swallowed hard. I couldn't run away. That was what Bethany-Melissa would have done.

Bliss didn't let those she loved go down for something she was responsible for.

Bliss stayed and fought. "Mom, I—"

"Everybody get on the floor!"

The lights inside the club lit up in a blinding flash. Nash spun around, only to be met by a wall of riot police storming the building.

None of us got another word out.

Two burly officers zeroed in on Nash and body-slammed him to the floor. A moment later, another shoved me up against my office wall so hard my teeth cracked together and stars swam in my eyes. He spat words in my face, each one undecipherable in the storm of noise.

Through everything, all I could see was my mother and the fact she never wavered.

Not even when the officers snatched Jerry's gun and a full bag of drugs from her fingers, then placed all three of us in handcuffs.

2

BLISS

There were only two holding cells at the Providence police station, one for males, and one for females. Because I hadn't tried resisting arrest and had kept silent in the back seat of the car I'd been driven in, I was allowed to walk beside the police officer who escorted me to the female cell.

Nash was given no such special treatment.

I bit down on my lip to stop myself from crying out when he was hauled in between the two officers who had tackled him to the floor. He fought them every step of the way, twisting and turning in their grip and yelling my name right up until the moment they slammed his cell door shut.

"Step back please, miss." My officer eyed me warily and then sighed with relief when I moved back so he could lock me in.

The door closed in my face, only a small glass window allowing sight of what was going on outside the four walls.

Nash stared at me from behind the glass window on his holding cell.

Don't say anything, he mouthed slowly and deliberately.

I nodded.

Are you okay?

I nodded again. Physically, I was. But all I could think about was Scythe's head hitting that concrete and the dazed look in his eyes as men had closed in, intent on hurting him. I had no idea where they'd take him, but I was almost certain it wouldn't be a hospital.

And War...

A new torrent of fear flooded me. He'd said he was coming to Nash's party late. Had he been caught in the gunfire? He couldn't have been arrested because he would have been at the little window with Nash. Was he one of the bodies lying dead in the Psychos' parking lot?

A sob welled up in my throat.

This wasn't how tonight was supposed to end. The things I'd gotten mad about didn't even seem important anymore. It didn't matter what they'd done. Or the secrets they'd kept.

I wanted my guys.

All three of them.

I flinched at an officer blocking my view and rapping a baton across the window. "Incoming."

Relief coursed through me when the door opened again and my mother was shoved in.

I wrapped my arms around her, catching her mid-stumble. "Oh my God. Are you okay?"

She scowled at the officer as he closed the door

behind her but then focused on me. "Not my first time being arrested."

It was mine. And I didn't like anything about it. My palms sweated, and my heart raced too fast.

"She fresh meat? Barely dressed fresh meat at that."

I jumped at the voice behind me. I hadn't even realized there was anyone else in the room, but a woman about my mother's age blinked sleepily at us and sat up from where she'd sprawled out across the wooden benches that lined the cell walls. My mother scowled at her with a fierceness I could only fake, and the woman shrugged and went back to her nap.

Mom pulled me over to another bench, and we sat, side by side, so close our arms pressed against each other.

"You didn't say anything, did you?" Mom asked, dropping her voice so it was barely above a whisper.

I shook my head.

"Good. When they ask, you tell them the club is mine. The drugs are mine. And so is the gun."

I shook my head. "I'm not letting you take the fall for this. I knew this was a possibility when I took over. Nash warned me about getting in over my head, but I didn't listen—"

"Bliss, there was a potential murder weapon and enough drugs in that safe for you to go away for years. Probably a lifetime. Is that what you want?"

I swallowed thickly. "No. But—"

"But nothing." She squeezed my fingers. "I know you won't understand this, and I'm glad you don't, but I'll be safe here. Three meals a day. A bed to sleep in. No Jerry." She forced a wobbly smile. "It'll be like a holiday."

The sad truth of it broke my heart and fed my guilt. "I

should have come back earlier," I whispered. "I should have got you out. I was such a child. So naïve."

She dug her fingernails into my arm, hard enough that I let out a yelp. "I'm a grown woman, Bliss. And your mother. It was never your job to rescue me."

Maybe so, but I wasn't going to just roll over and let her do this without a fight either. "Don't you admit to anything."

"You can't stop me, Bliss. If it comes down to you or me, which I'm pretty sure it will since it's our names on Axel's will, I'm going to confess."

"I have no priors. My sentence won't be as harsh as yours would be. Nash will look after you if I tell him to. You won't have to go back to Jerry."

She pressed her lips together but didn't argue any further.

I eyed the telephone in the corner. "Nobody says anything until I get us a lawyer."

I strode to the phone and picked it up before she could argue, punching in the number of the one person I knew had the contacts we needed. "Dad? I need help."

3

VINCENT

*L*ights flashed behind my closed eyes, but every time I tried to open them, the pain was near unbearable. My feet trailed uselessly along the ground, my skin ripping and tearing on the rough concrete. My arms and shoulders ached from being pulled along like I was a sack too heavy to carry.

I didn't care where they'd taken me or how hurt I was. Revenge for all of that could come later.

All I cared about was Bliss and whether she'd made it out.

"He awake?"

I stopped trying to open my eyes, knowing I needed information if I wanted to get the upper hand. Despite the urge to try to walk and stop the damage being done to my feet, I forced my head to go elsewhere, where the pain didn't exist.

Look after them.

Scythe's voice in my head was quieter than I'd ever heard him.

No. Not quiet.

Resigned.

Full of defeat and a knowledge that through the damage done to him, he hadn't been strong enough to hold on.

There'd been too much rage. Too much turmoil.

Enough to cause a shift in personality.

"Nah. Wouldn't be surprised if he's dead."

"He's not dead," a third voice stated, this one up ahead of us somewhere, deeper and more menacing. "He's not dying when I've spent this long looking for him."

I knew that voice all too well.

Tabor. Warden of Saint View Prison.

The man was good at his job. I could give him that respect. It had taken me longer than I'd wanted to figure out a way to escape.

But I'd done it once.

I could do it again.

His gaze crawled all over me. It burned my naked body, my clothes stripped at some point when I truly had been unconscious and not just faking it.

I knew his game. It was meant to make me feel weak. Helpless.

But I'd given up those emotions a long time ago.

He gripped my face, fingers tight around my jaw, and jerked my head up.

I felt more than saw his grin. "He's awake."

Pretend time over.

I lunged toward him, but pain and something else made me sluggish. What should have been a sudden, quick movement that ended with me snapping his neck, became a stumbling, pathetic, almost zombie-like lurch.

Tabor's laughter rang around me, echoing in the bare, cold room. He tilted his head condescendingly and studied me with cold, dead eyes. "Good to see you, Scythe."

Jesus. Someone order a psych evaluation to the creepy room because this guy is more unhinged than we are.

"Vincent, actually." My lips stung from bleeding cuts.

Tabor raised one eyebrow. "Ah. The less murderous personality."

Why do I always get the blame for all the killing?

"I wouldn't say that," I countered. "I'd be quite pleased to kill you right now if my hands worked."

See? It's not just me who likes knives.

Tabor sniggered. "Sorry about that. But you didn't really think I'd be stupid enough to not drug you, did you? This time I stabbed it squarely in your thigh myself."

"The heights of your stupidity know no ends, Tabor. So yes, I'd assumed."

Anger flickered behind the dead black of his eyes.

You're getting to him. This is so fun! Tell him he's not fooling anyone with that comb-over. We can all see he's going bald. Ooh! Wait, I've got a better one. Tell him you slept with his mama! Guys like him HATE when you diss their mamas!

Tabor eyed something above my head and motioned to his goons.

They snapped cuffs around my wrists and ankles, and whatever drug he'd injected me with meant I could do little about it. Every time I tried to move, my head was overcome with fuzzy dizziness, and the urge to vomit was strong. My limbs were weak, my legs barely holding my weight, and my arms pulling heavily on the cuffs when they hooked them over my head.

"Talk," Tabor demanded.

I blinked at him. "Did you have a topic in mind?"

You could tell him about our fifth birthday party. Or when I lost our virginity. You never said thank you for that by the way. Oh, Maisie Waterstone. I wonder what she's up to these days.

Being the dominant personality for a while clearly hadn't made Scythe any less irritating.

Tabor set up his phone, hitting the red record button on his screen before setting it down on a wall ledge. "I want to know every detail of how you and Heath Michaelson escaped my prison."

"I'm a solo act."

"Bullshit. You might have escaped at different times, but you two were tight."

I honestly didn't know how Heath had done it. I'd seen him on the outside, when he'd still been on the run and hiding with his partners, Mae, Liam, Rowe, and Rowe's little boy, Ripley. When I'd first escaped, I'd sat in their yard, watching them from a distance, making sure they were safe, knowing there had been other threats that followed us out into the real world. But we hadn't talked about our escapes. Once those threats had been eliminated, and Heath's name had been cleared, I'd kept my distance, missing them all terribly but knowing the cops were probably watching them for any sign of me.

Heath and the family he'd found for himself was everything I wanted. I'd thought Mae was the perfect woman.

Until I'd met Bliss.

Now I understood that Mae was perfect for Heath, Rowe, and Liam.

Bliss was perfect for me.

And Nash and War?

I wasn't sure I had an answer for that. I'd seen everything that had happened since Scythe had taken control. He been too weak this time to fully push me out, or maybe my need to know Bliss was okay had kept me hanging around, present enough to be aware of what was going on.

I'd developed a fondness for Nash and War. They took care of Bliss like I'd wanted to. And they'd accepted Scythe in a way that he and I both craved.

But there was something more between War and Scythe that I didn't feel.

Something I felt guilty over taking away from him, because I'd felt the depth of his feelings.

Scythe stayed suspiciously quiet over that thought. For once.

"I don't know how Heath escaped," I said again. "But I simply walked right out. Very easy to do if you have an access card and a code. I'm sure you know how terrible your cameras are. Though with the amount of staff who were fired after the riot, I'm pretty sure there was no one manning them anyway." I tilted my head, mimicking his posture. "Question is, Mr. Tabor, how come it took you so long to find me?"

He didn't like the slug to his intelligence. So he sent a fist into my stomach.

Pain vibrated through my midsection and knocked

the breath from my lungs. Another hit followed, then another, until I was groaning and gasping.

The ringing of Tabor's phone put a halt to his attack. He glanced over at it, shaking his fingers, the knuckles scratched and bleeding. "Oh, for fuck's sake."

One of the other guards who'd been standing back, watching the assault with a leering grin, jerked his head in the direction of the phone. "You want me to cancel the call, boss? Or answer it and tell 'em you're busy?"

To my surprise, Tabor shook his head, stalking across the room and snatching the phone up from the ledge. "You here?" he barked down the line.

Whatever the person on the other end said, Tabor didn't look particularly happy about it. He spun around, facing the wall. "Yeah, yeah. I know what I promised. I'm not going to back out on it. He's still alive. You'll get your shot."

He hung up, and Tabor motioned at one of his friends. "Get the door. Vincent has a visitor."

"How lucky for me," I mumbled around coughs and splutters that I couldn't seem to stop. My stomach spasmed, squeezing with pain.

"I suspect you'll think otherwise when you see who it is."

I already had an inkling. It had to be War. He and Tabor were the two men who wanted me dead. The thought they'd been working together saddened me, more than angered me, which was interesting.

I almost sighed with relief when it was another man entirely who walked through the doorway, his head held a whole lot higher than the last time I'd seen him.

"I hope you've changed your pants since our last

encounter, Caleb," I said quietly. "I don't enjoy the smell of urine."

Scythe sniggered. *I'm rubbing off on you. That was almost clever.*

I paid for it in the form of a slap across the face from the man who had once been engaged to Bliss. Vile human that he was, I didn't know how Bliss had ever seen anything redeemable in him.

"Who's the one pissing his pants now?" Caleb taunted, getting up into my personal space, brave now I was tied up in a way he hadn't been any other time our paths had crossed.

"Clearly not me, because I'm not wearing any."

That only angered Caleb further. A second slap cracked across my face. And then another. And another. His blows rained down until he was out of breath, his chest heaving with exertion and excitement.

His fingers clenched into fists by his sides, and he let out a bellow of frustration, a scream that echoed around the empty room. "I hope she was worth it. Her stupid slut cunt. Was it worth your death?" He ripped his shirt open, the little white buttons tearing and popping off, rolling away on the dirty concrete floor. "Her name is on my chest. In my skin."

He was right. I took in Scythe's handiwork, Bliss's name carved into Caleb's chest in crude letters that had scarred over. They were huge, arcing the full width of his chest in recently healed, angry red slashes.

Scythe practically crowed with pride. *I want her name tattooed on me like that.*

I did too. There was a beauty in the mutilation. Or

perhaps it was just beautiful to me because it was her name, and everything about her was beautiful.

Caleb pulled a gleaming knife from a holder on his hip and waved it around in front of my face, tauntingly slow. "I'm going to enjoy telling her all about how you bled out in this pathetic hole. About how you begged and cried for my mercy, and how I denied it. I'll tell her all about it once she's my wife and I own her."

He dragged the blade along my chest, blood welling in its wake.

I'd barely been holding on to consciousness before his attack. It was all I could do not to fade out into the black.

It's hurting me to see you like this, Vinny boy. You just gonna let him kill you? You gonna leave Bliss when she's this close to falling in love with me? Or you. Maybe both of us. I don't know. But we're never gonna find out if you tap out like a pussy now. Fight back!

The darkness inside me stirred, riled up by Scythe's encouragement and Caleb's threats.

I wanted to let it loose. With everything inside me, I wanted a blade between my fingers and to let the darkness do its thing.

But there was no knife in my hand. Nobody was coming to help me. I had nothing left in me to help myself.

When Caleb's blade stabbed through my skin again, Scythe's shouts to fight back quieted, and my life blood dripped from my body in a steady stream of red.

4

BLISS

"*B*ethany-Melissa Arthur. You're up." The officer stared at me expectantly, impatience written across her makeup-free face.

I stood quickly, not exactly sure what I was 'up' for but knowing I didn't get the luxury of arguing about it. I took a step, but my mom tugged fiercely on my hand.

I stopped and gazed down at her.

Her eyes were bright and full of unsaid warnings.

I nodded once and then pulled away, focusing on the officer. "Do you know anything about my friends? War Maynard and Vincent Atwood. Were either of them brought in?"

She acted like I hadn't even spoken. I didn't know if that meant she had no knowledge of War and Scythe or if she did and just wasn't willing to tell me.

The worry swirling around my stomach intensified. The lack of information gave my head too much room to run wild, and none of the things I imagined were good.

"Where are we going?" I asked the woman, changing

tactics as she slapped cuffs on my wrists again and motioned for me to follow her. The metal bit into my flesh painfully, but I ignored it, knowing it was merely a discomfort compared to what Scythe was probably going through right now.

"Your lawyer is here."

A tiny kernel of relief sparked to life. Someone on our side. Someone who could get me answers on where Scythe and War were. "Is she good?"

"He," the officer answered. "And yes, he's good. You must have some money if you can afford Liam Banks."

My heart sank. I didn't answer, knowing my father had no money, and now, neither did I. Everything I'd had stashed in the safe had been confiscated, along with the drugs and the gun.

This was bad. So very freaking bad. This expensive lawyer was probably only here because my father's name still meant something, and his dwindling bank account wasn't yet public knowledge. They probably knew each other from the club and played golf on weekends. I hadn't heard of him, but all my father's friends golfed, with their trophy wives watching on, sipping cocktails handed to them by uniformed staff on minimum wage.

This was an expense my family couldn't afford. Another hole we were digging for ourselves, but one I had no power over.

I needed a good lawyer. Nash and my mom needed good lawyers. And Scythe and War probably did, too, wherever they were. We'd have to work out how to pay this man later.

The officer opened a door, leaning on it and motioning me inside with her free hand. "Go on."

I nodded my thanks at her and entered the little inter-rogation room. There was nothing but a desk and two chairs inside, one of those occupied by a surprisingly young man, sinfully good-looking, and dressed in an expensive suit.

"Bethany-Melissa?" he questioned, standing to greet me with a smile that only made him more attractive. If that were even possible.

"Bliss," I said quietly. "Please call me Bliss. I hate Bethany-Melissa."

He scribbled my name on a yellow legal pad and nodded. "Right. Got it. Bliss. Your father called me and filled me in on the basics. There was some sort of commotion at your club, is that—"

I couldn't stand the not knowing any longer. I didn't care what they did to me. I just needed to know Scythe and War were alive.

"Can you find out where my friends are, please?"

He frowned. "I don't have any knowledge about anyone other than you."

"You can find out, though, right?"

His frown turned into a sympathetic smile, but then he looked down at his papers again. "I was only hired to represent you—"

My frustration, stress, and worry all bubbled up and spilled over. I slammed my hand down on the table. "Then as my lawyer, you work for me. I don't care what happens to me. But I need to know if War and Scythe are okay."

Liam's head jerked up. "Did you say Scythe?"

Shit. I squeezed my eyes closed at my slipup. I'd let emotion get the better of me and gone and used the wrong name. Though it hardly seemed to matter anymore, after everything that had happened.

"It's a nickname," I explained. "His real name is Vincent."

Liam sat back in his chair, folding his arms across his chest. "Is this a joke?"

"If it is, it's not funny."

Liam studied me for another long moment, perhaps trying to discern if I was in fact pulling his leg, though I had no idea why he would think I was. Then he leaned forward and grabbed his cell phone from the table.

Bewildered, I watched him scroll through it until he finally turned it around so the screen faced me. "Is this your friend? Scythe?"

On the screen was a photo of Scythe, or more likely Vincent, sitting beside a muscled, dark-haired, tattooed man I didn't recognize. Both of them were in prison issue uniforms, but they smiled at the camera, a genuine affection between them.

Suspicion rose its ugly head, and I jammed my lips together, not knowing who I could trust. For all I knew, Liam Banks was working with the cops to have Scythe thrown in jail again.

Liam seemed to read the mood and pulled back the phone, scrolling through it again. "I know him as Vincent, though I'm aware of his alter ego." He showed me another photo, this time a group shot, though the tattooed man from the first photo was right in the middle. This time he was in regular clothes. Liam stood beside him, smiling widely, his arm around a gorgeous, curvy blonde woman, who was noticeably pregnant. A third man and a small boy rounded out the happy family shot.

"The boy in the photo is my son, Ripley." Liam pointed out each person in turn, the group standing in front of a cabin in the woods, trees surrounding them and thick green grass beneath their feet. "This is my family. Mae, Rowe, and this guy here? His name is Heath. I don't know if Vincent ever mentioned us to you, but Heath was in jail with Vincent. They were friends, before they both escaped. Mae is the prison teacher, and Rowe is a guard."

"Why are you telling me all this?" I asked curiously.

Liam put the phone back down and leveled me with an honest gaze. "Because if we're talking about the same person, which I assume we are, since you haven't denied it, he's very important to my family. He saved Mae's and Heath's lives while inside the prison, and Ripley's outside it." He swallowed. "I owe Vincent everything, so if there's anything I can do to help him..." He eyed me carefully, "Or the people he loves, I'm going to do it."

Something inside me broke at the compassion in Liam's voice. And the dam of tears and worries I'd been holding back all cascaded over me.

Liam let me cry, only reaching across the table to squeeze my hand in support. "Tell me everything, Bliss. Every detail you can think of." He grinned. "I'm really good at my job. Like, really fucking excellent. I got Heath off death row, so whatever is going on with you is going to be a cakewalk. From what your dad said, it should be a pretty simple case."

"I had a lot of money, drugs, and a weapon that was possibly used in a murder stashed in the safe at my club."

Liam's pen paused mid word. "Your father did not mention any of that."

I grimaced at him.

He let out a long breath, straightened his legal pad, and then picked up his phone again.

"Who are you calling?" I asked. "More lawyers?"

"My girl. To tell her not to wait up, because I'm going to be a while."

I wanted to burn that motherfucking police station down. Or storm it with my guys behind me, guns blazing.

Whatever it took to get Bliss back.

But the bullet that had taken a chunk out of my bicep had other plans.

"Would you fucking sit still already, asshole?" Gunner complained, peering at my bloody wound by the light of an iPhone. "I need to see if the bullet is still lodged in your arm."

"It's not," I ground out. "Just fucking stitch it and quit being a priss about it."

Gunner sighed. "You should go to the hospital."

"Like that's happening when they have my girl."

I'd watched the cops drag her out and put her in the back of a squad car. Hawk, Gunner, and Aloha had held me back, shoving me down on the ground and pinning me with their knees in my back to stop me from running back in after her. Nash and Kim had also been hauled away, both of them seemingly uninjured.

But Vincent. Or fuck, Scythe. I didn't fucking know what to call him anymore. He'd barely been conscious when he'd been dragged into the back of a van marked Saint View Prison.

The things we'd said as we'd fought in the parking lot still echoed around my head.

Him admitting he'd been the one to put a bullet in my father's head.

Him claiming my father had driven the car over the cliff himself and that the bullet to the brain was an act of mercy.

And me, hating him all the more because of the way he made me feel.

I'd never had trouble taking a life. When it came to club business, it was just that. You played with fire, you got burned.

Bang, and it was all over.

But I'd never had to kill someone I cared about. Someone I probably fucking loved. I pushed the thoughts away, because I knew for sure I did love Bliss, and she needed me now more than ever.

Whatever had happened between Vincent and me was over.

Not willing to wait any longer, I snatched the needle and thread from Gunner's trembling fingers and stabbed it into my arm. The pain lanced through me, but it was pale compared to everything else I'd lost tonight. A bit of blood from a flesh wound wasn't going to kill me. I just needed to stitch it up and get to Bliss.

I gritted my teeth through the rest of my clumsy

stitches and tilted a whisky bottle over the top of them, spilling brown liquid over my handiwork and hoping it would ward off infection.

All it did was remind me of the night Vincent and I had poured our drinks on each other and used our tongues to clean them off.

I squeezed my eyes shut tight against the too-fresh memory. It had been only days ago. I'd been fucking happy. Pressed between his hard body and Bliss' softer one.

I wanted that back.

And I fucking hated him for ruining it.

I yanked my shirtsleeve down and tugged my cut back on over the top. "Good enough."

Before any of the guys could object, I peeled away into the early morning light.

By the time I parked in front of the Providence Police station, the sun was almost fully up, splashing pinks and oranges across an otherwise gray sky which suited my mood better. Boots thumping on the concrete, I launched myself up the handful of steps and shoved open the glass door that led to the station's reception area.

On instinct, I glanced over at the seats to my right. That was where Bliss had been sitting the very first time I'd seen her. Now it was occupied by a guy about my age but dressed a whole lot nicer in an expensive suit. He had his phone pressed to his ear and two fingers pinching the bridge of his nose while he talked. "No, no, you don't need to worry. Go back to sleep, okay? You need it to grow that baby. But give Rowe the phone first. I need to talk to him."

The mention of a baby immediately had me thinking

about Bliss's belly rounding with my kid, and my heart picked up the pace. I'd never once been careful with her. I knew she was probably on some sort of birth control, but I couldn't remember if we'd even discussed it. Completely irresponsible, but I couldn't bring myself to care. Fuck. I wanted her knocked up. I wanted a part of me inside her.

I wanted everything we had together to be permanent because Scythe had shown me exactly how easily it could all go away.

"Bliss Arthur," I said to the bleary-eyed cop behind the desk. "She was brought in from the Psychos' raid. Has she been charged?"

The woman typed something into the computer, then turned back to me with a bored expression. "Nothing's been processed yet. Take a seat and wait if you want."

A muscle ticked in my jaw. "Nash Sorensen? What about him?"

She shrugged. "He's here. Awaiting questioning."

I bit my lip. I didn't want to ask about Vincent, but I had to fucking know if he was okay. "Vincent Atwood?"

The woman sighed heavily, fingers dragging slowly across the keyboard. "Nobody by that name has come in."

I stopped. "Where did they take him then? To the hospital?"

The woman shrugged. "You can call them and ask."

The guy in the suit paused his conversation. "Actually, I already rang the hospital, and they have no record of him either."

She blinked at him. "Who are you again?"

"His lawyer."

A sinking feeling came over me. And the lawyer looked as concerned as I felt when he went back to his call. I gripped the reception desk tighter to keep myself anchored. "I watched guards kick and beat the shit out of him and load him into a van. He should be here."

The woman lost her patience. "Sir, I can only tell you what I've already told you. There's no one by that name here—"

I slammed my palms against the plexiglass. "Then where the hell did they take him? Straight to the prison?"

"Sir, settle down, please."

My heart slammed against my chest, panic pulsing through my blood. This wasn't right. They weren't following protocol. I'd watched them put Vincent in that van with my own eyes. If they'd gone rogue...

I felt sick at the thought. "I'm not going to fucking settle down until someone tells me he's okay!"

"Security to the front desk, please."

I groaned, holding up my hands in surrender and backing off. "No need for that. I'll behave. I swear." I sat my ass down in a seat beside the lawyer and rubbed a palm across my forehead.

The lawyer ended his phone call and stuck his hand out to me. "Liam Banks. Vincent is a family friend of mine, and I'm representing Bliss. She's okay. Facing some pretty hefty charges, but don't worry, I'm good."

I nodded. "Can you tell her I'm here? War Maynard."

He smiled. "You saved me a phone call. You were next on my list. She was worried about you." He stopped, his gaze dropping to the bloodstains on my T-shirt. "Am I going to be lying to her if I tell her you're okay?"

I shook my head. "I'm fine. Just get her out. Please."

I needed her out from behind those bars and here

with me. I needed to see her for myself, so I could know for sure she was fine.

She was all I had left. My dad was gone. Vincent was gone.

I wasn't losing her too.

6

NASH

$\mathcal{M}$inutes ticked by into hours. There was no external window in the holding cell. I had no watch, and my phone had been confiscated on arrival, so I had no way of knowing if those hours had turned into days.

It felt like it.

And still, I sat there, moving only when footsteps sounded in the corridor outside, checking if it was Bliss returning to her cell.

She'd been taken hours ago.

Kim not too long after.

But nobody had come for me, and the waiting was driving me insane. Eventually, sleep worked its way inside my head, shoving out all the adrenaline and leaving only fatigue in its wake. I didn't dare close my eyes for fear I'd miss seeing Bliss through the dirty, scratched window.

That was the only thing keeping me going.

But eventually, when the corridor remained empty, my body had other ideas.

Footsteps woke me, and anger instantly rose at the realization I'd let sleep get the better of me. I rushed for the door, peering through the window, only to have the officer thump a fist on the other side. "Stand back!"

I did as I was told, backing up and perching on the edge of a bench so they could open the cell door.

"Nash Sorensen. You're free to go."

I blinked. "Sorry, what?"

"You're out."

"I haven't even been questioned."

"No need. Got a full confession from the woman you were with. She said you had nothing to do with it. So unless you want to argue with that..."

Dread filled me. "Which woman?"

"Do I look like I keep a diary of names? Get moving."

I pushed to my feet, anger slowly filling me. Bliss was too damn noble for her own good. This was exactly what I'd been worried about when I'd told her not to say anything.

I knew she'd try to protect me and her mom.

I had been going to tell them that the entire thing was on me. The drugs. The money. Even the fucking gun, though I had no idea where the hell that had come from. I was one-hundred-percent sure it wasn't a legally registered weapon.

I hadn't even gotten the chance. She'd beat me to it. But I couldn't just walk out of here and leave her behind to sacrifice herself. I scuttled forward to catch up with the officer leading me back out to the processing room so I could retrieve my things. "Wait, Officer, there's been a mistake..."

A flash of auburn in the waiting area had the words drying on my tongue.

The officer paused, hand on the door. "What sort of mistake?"

Bliss turned around, spotting me on the other side of the glass. I scanned her body. No cuffs. Just a scratchy-looking gray blanket, wrapped around her shoulders, and pure relief in her eyes at seeing me.

"Never mind," I murmured.

He opened the doors, and Bliss hurled herself across the room at me.

Nothing had ever felt as sweet as her pressed against my chest, my arms wrapped around her. I tilted her chin up, claiming her mouth like a dying man who needed her kiss to save him.

"What happened?" I whispered, linking my fingers between hers and holding on so tight I was sure it would cut off the circulation to her fingers, but she didn't complain.

She shook her head. "I don't know. I called my dad, and he sent a lawyer." She dropped her voice again. "I was in the middle of telling him everything when an officer walked in and said I was being released."

"Much the same thing happened to me, except no dad to send a lawyer." I gave her a rueful grin, so fueled by relief my head spun.

The cop interrupted, shoving paperwork at us and stabbing at the bottom of it with his finger. "Sorensen, sign here. Arthur, you're here."

Bliss and I shuffled over in unison, me unwilling to let her go for even a minute.

Bliss bit down on her plump bottom lip, letting it slip slowly from between her teeth. "My mom…"

I glanced at her sharply and shook my head. "Not here."

Her eyes were filled with tears. We both knew that there was only one way Bliss and I were walking free right now.

After a lifetime of shitty behavior and always putting herself first, Kim had finally become a real mom and sacrificed herself for her child.

We collected our few things, and after signing some more paperwork, we were released into the waiting room.

I tensed as a big body swooped in, grabbing Bliss from my arms, but relaxed when I recognized War's MC cut. I couldn't see his face, he was too busy burying it in Bliss' neck. He hauled her right up off her feet, walking her a few steps away to have his own reunion with her.

I wasn't even jealous. After everything that had happened in the past twenty-four hours, they deserved a moment together. Bliss would want it as much as he did, and I just wanted whatever made her happy.

But she was quick to move away, her worried gaze darting between me and War. "What's happening with Vincent?"

"You mean Scythe," War said quietly.

I blinked in confusion, but it meant something to Bliss. Her mouth dropped open. "You know?"

He gave a curt nod.

"War… I can explain…"

He shook his head. "I don't even care." He pulled her

in again, inhaling the scent of her hair. "All I care about is that you're here with me." Then he glanced over her at me. "With us."

I nodded in agreement.

War stepped away when a frazzled lawyer in a suit appeared. "Bliss," the man said quietly.

"Liam, what's going on? This is Nash, by the way."

I reached a hand out to the man who shook it firmly with a mumbled, "Hey, man," before turning back to Bliss, his expression serious. "Come outside. We need to talk."

Bliss, War, and I all exchanged glances. When a lawyer said we need to talk, it never meant anything good.

Bliss cleared her throat. "Whatever you need to say, you can say it in front of them."

Liam jerked his head toward the roomful of cops. "Maybe not in front of them, though?"

We walked out into mid-morning sunshine, which gave me a better idea of exactly how long we'd been held without charge. War took a pack of cigarettes from his pocket, lit one, then offered me the pack. Even though I'd given them up, I took one, figuring that if you couldn't have a smoke after a night like we'd had, then when could you?

Liam declined War's offer as the four of us formed a huddle outside the lawyer's expensive car. "First, as the two of you probably already worked out, Kim confessed to everything in the club being hers. Her name is on the ownership paperwork along with Bliss', but with her full confession and prior history, it was easy enough for me to convince the cops that Bliss was merely an employee and had no knowledge of what her mother was doing off the books.

Bliss' eyes filled with tears again. "I can't let her do this."

"I spoke to her, and she said you'd say that. She said to tell you it's what she needs. I'm going to represent her at her trial, pro bono, and I promise, I'll get her into a good rehab program within the system. She'll be well looked after."

"The gun, though, Liam. What if it...?"

He shook his head. "They already ran the ballistics. It's not a match for the weapon that killed Axel, or any other unsolved incidents in the system."

Bliss let out a long sigh of relief. "So, no murder charge."

Liam nodded in agreement. "No. The drug charges aren't going to be pretty though. I want you to be prepared for that, but if you're willing to give up your dealer, we might be able to get those downgraded too."

"We don't know his name," I filled Liam in. "He's always concealed his identity when she's met with him."

"Which I always thought was a weak move." War blew a smoke ring slowly into the air above Bliss' head. "But now it seems smart."

Liam cracked his knuckles and steeled Bliss with a serious expression. "If you want to help your mother, find out who he is. If we can go after the big fish, they might let the little fish go."

Bliss tucked a strand of hair behind her ear, determination settling over her pretty features. "I'll get his name."

Liam squeezed her arm. "Good."

"Did you find out anything about Vincent?" Bliss asked hopefully.

War shifted slightly, turning away, but I could tell he was still listening.

Liam's mouth flattened into a concerned line. "Only that he's not here, and he's not at the hospital. I've got Rowe trying to find out if they've taken him straight to the prison. I would have had Mae look into it too, but she's pregnant, and I don't want her stressing out about this. Go home and sleep. More than likely, Rowe will come back with a confirmation that he's at the prison. I'll call you as soon as I get it."

Bliss clutched my hand. "What if he's dead?"

Her big-eyed gaze darted between me and Liam, and then over to War who stared silently at the ground.

We couldn't lie to her.

So nobody said a word.

7

BLISS

*L*iam got in his car after promising again that he would call me as soon as he had an update on Vincent. The minute he disappeared from sight, my knees buckled. I'd been holding it together, but with only Nash and War left behind, I could let my guard down.

War slipped an arm around me, keeping me upright. "You're wiped. You need sleep."

I shook my head stubbornly. "Not until we find Scythe."

But Nash was just as stubborn as I was. "We will. But none of us have slept. We're no good to him wrecked."

"I can't go home without him." The thought left me cold.

War tightened his grip on me, and Nash squeezed my hand. "Come back to my place," they said in unison.

War exchanged a look with Nash. "Both of you come back to my place."

"We aren't all going to fit on your bike," Nash complained.

Both mine and Nash's cars were still at Psychos, but I couldn't bring myself to go back there yet. There would be a lot of work to be done once I did, but I couldn't even think about it. I stifled a yawn and fought the urge to rub at my eyes. They were as gritty as sandpaper. "I'm too tired to be on a bike right now anyway." I knew the moment I got on behind War, wrapped my arms around his waist, and snuggled into the warmth of his back, I'd be a goner. Sleep would take me, and I'd end up splattered on the gravel road halfway to War's compound.

"I'm calling an Uber." Nash pulled out his phone and stabbed the app with his finger. "War can follow us on his bike."

I nodded my thanks, but War shook his head.

"I need to be touching her. I've spent the last few hours sure you were going away for life. My bike can stay here." He scrubbed a hand over his face. "Now that the adrenaline is faded, all I want to do is curl up and sleep. Doesn't mix well with riding."

Nobody argued, and the Uber arrived within minutes.

All three of us crawled into the back seat, me pressed between the broad shoulders of the two men. If the driver spoke to us, I didn't hear him. The car was warm, and Nash and War at my sides were comforting. I laid my head down on Nash's shoulder, while War's big hand covered my thigh, gently massaging it with his fingers, his touch soothing.

The overwhelming sense of safety was a warm blanket, and I was only minorly aware when we stopped, and

Nash scooped me up from the back seat, cradling me to his chest.

I didn't bat at him to put me down.

I didn't squawk about how heavy I had to be.

I let him carry me up the steps to War's cabin and place me in the middle of the bed.

I didn't remember it being this comfortable. The sheets felt softer than the last time I'd been here, and I burrowed beneath the covers, exhaustion overwhelming.

War's and Nash's quiet voices floated around me, but I wasn't coherent enough to register their words. Right before sleep took me, Nash lay down facing me, his soft lips pressing briefly to my forehead.

While War tucked himself in behind me, fitting his body to mine, his warmth permeating through my clothes.

Safe between two of the men who held my heart, I finally let myself drift off.

---

*I*t was dark when I woke, and it took me a long moment to work out where I was. I blinked several times before I could make out anything but shadows, and lifted my head, squinting at my surroundings.

An arm tightened around me, and the room came into focus simultaneously.

War's cabin, the blinds all still open but near complete darkness outside them, only a smattering of stars breaking up the inky blackness peeking between trees.

I felt more than saw the tumble of arms and legs I was

in. I tried to sit, but someone's heavy leg pinned me down.

"Where are you going?" War mumbled.

"Bathroom."

"No. Too warm. Too soft." That was Nash' s voice, scratchy with sleep.

"It'll be wet too if you don't let me get up."

They grumbled and groaned but let me shove their heavy bodies off mine.

We'd slept the entire day away, but I still felt like a truck had hit me. I dragged my feet along the wooden floor to War's bathroom and closed the door behind me. I did what I needed to do and then washed my hands in the little sink, while staring at my reflection in the mirror above it.

I looked rough. My hair stuck up at all angles, my makeup was a trainwreck of smudged mascara and worn-off lipstick. My teeth felt furry, and I was sure my breath didn't smell like roses.

"Shower," I murmured to my reflection.

Without bothering to check with War, I twisted the faucets and set the shower to running. Steam immediately billowed around the small room, and I stripped off my clothes, dropping the sexy but now filthy piece I'd worn to Psychos on the tile floor.

I knew I'd never wear it again, despite how much I loved it. It held too many memories. Some of them, like the things I'd done with Nash before everything had gone to shit, were good. But the bad tainted it.

I'd need to get a new outfit to wear to the next party we threw.

If there ever was another one. I had no idea how I

would even go about that now. No cash. No drugs. The entire thing was so royally screwed, and all of it was because of the stupid decisions I'd made.

Nash had warned me not to get in over my head, and I hadn't listened. Worse, I'd dragged my mother and everyone else down with me.

I stepped into the hot water spray, suddenly feeling like I didn't deserve it. Not when Mom was probably having cold showers in Saint View Prison.

Not when Scythe was probably lying hurt somewhere, while I was sleeping soundly in a comfortable bed.

I turned the hot water all the way off and bit down on my lip when the cold water sprayed across my body.

My automatic instinct was to jump out of the way, but I forced my feet to stay planted, and I took the full brunt of the now freezing water. It ran over my body in a constant stream, chilling me all over.

Sometime later, a knock at the door caught my attention, and I dragged my gaze in that direction.

"Bliss? You okay? You've been in there for a really long time."

I didn't say anything. I didn't deserve War's concern. Goosebumps covered my flesh, and my nipples were so tight they hurt. Each drop of water was a tiny, freezing needle, but I still didn't let myself get out from beneath the spray.

The door opened, and War stuck his head in. "Hey, just checking you haven't..."

He pushed the door open wider and stared at me huddled beneath the freezing water.

"What the fuck are you doing?" He stormed across

the space and twisted the water off. "You're practically blue!"

He reached for the hot water, but I batted his hand away. "No!"

The word came out sharp and hard.

He froze.

I'd never spoken to him like that.

"Bliss," he said quietly. "You need to get warm."

I shook my head, forcing my feet to move even though my entire body was so cold it hurt to do so. "I don't deserve it."

"And you do deserve a case of pneumonia?"

I didn't answer. My teeth chattered together too violently to get anymore words out. The open bathroom door let in a draft that was chilling me to the bone.

War grabbed a towel from the rack by the door and wrapped it around me. Then pulled a second, twisting it around my hair.

I stood silently, too cold to move, while War swore quietly beneath his breath.

I couldn't stop the shaking. Full-body trembles that shook me all over and made every muscle ache. It went on so long even with War drying me off that after a while, I couldn't tell if it was solely from the cold or if it was some delayed form of shock.

"Nash, get in here," War bellowed.

War's tone signaled something was wrong, and Nash stepped into the bathroom a moment later.

He took one look at me and blanched. "What the hell happened? Her lips are blue. She needs to be back in the shower. A hot one."

I shook my head, the hate and guilt inside me

drowning out the common sense that begged me to listen to him.

I didn't want soft, kind, and gentle. I needed rough. Hard. Cold.

But Nash wasn't having it. He ripped the towel from my naked body, and in two steps, had me up in his arms again.

"No!" I screamed.

He stopped, indecision playing all over his face.

"I can't," I begged. "Please. It hurts more than the cold does."

Some flickering of understanding dawned in his eyes. He changed directions and carried me back to War's bedroom, laying me down and covering me with blankets.

He pulled his shirt off, then undid his pants, stripping right off until he was completely naked too, and then got beneath the covers with me. Despite myself, I reached for him.

He blanched at my freezing touch, and I quickly pulled away, but he was right there, following me in, gathering my cold and aching body to his warm, solid one. "War," he gritted out. "Get in."

War stripped his clothes off, no care about the fact Nash was seeing him naked. He stalked around to the other side of the bed and slid in behind me. "Oh, holy shit, Bliss! You're like ice. Why the fuck did you do that to yourself?"

I didn't answer. It might not have made sense to them, but it made sense to me. Even now, with the two of them wrapped around my body, and safely cocooned in a snuggly bed, my limbs slowly thawing out, I knew I didn't deserve it.

"Hit me," I whispered.

Nash froze. "What the fuck, Bliss?"

"Hit me," I begged again. "Please. I don't deserve the kindness. What's happening to my mom, and to Scythe... I can't lie here and have the two of you take care of me. It hurts too damn much."

"Nobody is fucking hitting you," War growled. "Over my dead body."

"I need it," I begged. A bigger pain to take away the one that ached so deep over what I'd done.

"Not a chance," Nash agreed. His fingers trailed up and down my arms, and while I'd loved his touch just hours ago, now it was too soft. Too gentle.

I slapped his hands away. "Stop it. Stop being nice."

He stared at me, complete and utter bewilderment all over his face.

And then he slammed his lips against mine.

Hard.

Hard enough that they stung.

He pulled away, uncertainty in his eyes.

But it was exactly what I wanted. "More. Make it hurt."

He groaned, doing it again. His stubble scratched and bit at the soft skin around my mouth, but every tiny prick of pain took away the ache. This—his hands on my body, his lips ravaging mine— this was a pain I wanted.

He opened his mouth, deepening the kiss, his tongue meeting mine and controlling me in a way I hadn't known I'd needed.

His featherlight fingers turned demanding, sinking

into the curve of my hip and holding me tight to him as his dick thickened.

"Fuck, sorry," he muttered.

"Don't be." I reached between us, taking hold of his erection. "War..." I twisted, looking over my shoulder at the man spooned in behind me.

"Yeah, baby girl. I'm still here. Tell me what you need."

Hard. Fast. Not to think. Not to feel.

"Don't be gentle."

I pumped Nash's dick while War kissed a path down my shoulder. I opened my mouth to complain, but then the kisses changed to bites. Strong sucks and pulls of my flesh underneath his teeth that would leave a trail of hickeys, showing everyone exactly where he'd had his mouth.

Surrounded by their warmth, I slowly began to thaw. Wetness pooled at my core, and a needy heat spread its way from between my thighs across my entire body. I pressed my breasts against Nash, and he responded by lowering his head and sucking my freezing nipple into his mouth. I searched for War's mouth to kiss, giving Nash better access at the same time.

War kissed me, sinking his tongue past my lips without any sort of hesitation or warning. All the while, I kept up a steady rhythm on Nash's dick, his precum sliding through my fingers and coating my palm.

War's solid cock nudged my backside, and I wiggled, moving so the tip of him prodded my ass.

"Bliss..."

"I want it," I whispered to him. "I want you there."

He groaned. "You aren't ready."

"I don't care." I arched back toward him.

But he dug his fingers into my hip. "Wait."

He rolled away, but I didn't want to wait. I couldn't. I needed them inside me, punishing me for the mistakes I'd made.

It was the only way I'd feel some relief.

I hooked one leg over Nash's thigh, bringing us closer together, and guiding his cock toward my entrance.

He closed his eyes, hissing my name when he sank inside the wet heat of my pussy. He was big and solid, and the stretch to accommodate him only made me crave him more. I ground on him, taking his entire length and enjoying the scratch of his coarse hair across my clit. He drew back, and I whimpered at the loss of him, before he slammed back home, seating himself fully once more.

"More," I begged. "War…"

I didn't know where he'd gone, I'd been too distracted by getting Nash's cock inside me, but now came the crack of a lubricant bottle being opened and the cool gel spreading between my cheeks.

So full of Nash, I groaned at War's touch to the puckered star of my ass. He rubbed me there, building me up until I was panting, and moaning, and desperate to come.

"Not yet," Nash murmured. "You want it to hurt? This is how we make it hurt. No hitting you. Just not letting you come until whatever the fuck you're trying to bury is long gone."

"Yes," I moaned, breathless.

I wanted it. Them edging me until it was agony.

Nash pulled out, and the loss of him was devastating. But War maneuvered me over onto my belly so I was facedown on the mattress, his knees forcing my legs wide, his fingers spreading my ass cheeks open.

Nash lay beside me, his hand snaking beneath me to rub my clit.

I was sure I was dripping on his hand. Pleasure zoomed from the sensitive little bud of nerves, sending arousal gushing through me.

War's tongue lapped it up.

I cried out at the first touch of him, his tongue in my most intimate of spaces, but it didn't prepare me for him licking higher, tonguing my ass.

"Oh!" I screamed, the sensation too good and so dirty and forbidden all at once.

His palm slapped my ass, making it jiggle. His lips and tongue kissed away the sting.

Nash worked my clit at a constant pace, and when I ran out of air with my face smothered by the mattress, I twisted to look at him.

His free hand stroked his impressive cock, so slowly it was practically torture to watch. Clearly wanting to prolong the agony some more, he fingered my pussy, searching for my G-spot.

My eyes rolled back when he found it.

War took the opportunity to press one finger up inside my ass, matching the tempo Nash set, until I was grinding back against him, begging for more.

They weren't giving it to me, still too busy trying to edge me into oblivion.

I took matters into my own hands, forgetting all about the fact I'd agreed to let them withhold an orgasm as the punishment I'd asked for.

I straddled Nash, impaling myself on his cock, desperate to find my finish line. Too lost to the pleasure, I'd forgotten all about making it hurt.

But they hadn't.

Nash gripped my hip with one hand, steadying my movements.

I switched tactics. "War," I groaned. "Fuck me. Please."

His fingers disappeared, only to be replaced by the head of his cock. He nudged my ass, coating it in the lubricant before pushing forward just a fraction.

I groaned. He was so much bigger than his fingers, or the plug Nash and I had practiced with. I was so full from Nash, and my ass was so tight around War's cock, I didn't see how it could possibly work. I dropped my head to Nash's chest. "I don't know if I can."

War slapped my ass again.

A fresh burst of arousal spread through me. "Oh God."

"Tell me to stop."

"No," I moaned.

"You said you don't know if you can."

All I knew was that I didn't want it to end. "I can," I groaned. "War, please, I need to come."

My pussy spasmed around them, the beginnings of my orgasm lighting up inside me.

War's palm dragged down my naked spine, pushing all the way in, until I was complete, two men fully seated inside my body. "You should see yourself right now, Bliss, so full of both of us. Fuck, baby. You don't even know how beautiful you are. You're so tight."

I could barely breathe for the pleasure. It was blinding and deafening, to the point nothing else existed. Nash moved cautiously, setting a rhythm that took me a moment to catch on to. But once I did, War found himself too, and the three of us moved like pieces of a clock, all wound around each other, working toward a common goal.

One that was ready to blow my mind.

I pressed my hands into the bed either side of Nash's head, arching my back, chasing down the angle my orgasm so desperately demanded. He lifted his head, sucking one breast that dangled in his face, while pinching the nipple of the other. I bounced on his cock, faster and harder, taking over and setting the pace, letting War keep up with me now.

War slapped my ass, then leaned over me, grabbing my hair and pulling it back roughly, increasing the arch in my back. "Enough of the punishment. Come for us, baby girl."

A shout of pleasure welled up from somewhere deep inside me, my scalp prickling deliciously from his grip on my hair. I slammed my hips down, grinding, taking what I needed for the good feelings to morph into great ones.

Turned out, War's permission was all I needed.

The orgasm roared down on me, and I screamed out my release, not knowing or caring if anyone outside could hear. There was no controlling it. It was a wave of pleasure, crashing over me, and taking out everything in sight, as destructive as a tsunami, as blinding as a fire. It rained down, over and over, my body shaking and pulsing, muscles trembling, my tongue letting loose a babble of indecent noises.

War and Nash came with me, Nash groaning, grabbing my face and pressing his lips to mine, his tongue quick to claim entrance and stay there while he rode out his orgasm. War muffled his, his mouth pressed to my back while telling me the entire time how much he wanted me, how much he treasured me, and how he'd never get enough of the sight of me.

We collapsed on the bed, a sticky, sweaty mess.

Demons slain.

At least for tonight.

8

BLISS

There was no food in War's cupboards. I'd searched through all of them as quietly as I could, not wanting to wake the guys, even though we'd all fallen back asleep and I hadn't woken until early the next morning. The refrigerator was just as empty as the shelves. Not a strip of bacon, an egg, or a bottle of milk in sight.

My stomach loudly protested. I couldn't remember the last time I'd eaten. All we'd done since leaving the police station was have mind-blowing sex that had seemed to cancel out the need for food with the complete and utter exhaustion it had brought with it.

War raised his head to squint at me. "Your stomach is loud enough to wake the dead. I can hear it from here."

"I'm starving," I admitted. Then grinned, feeling more like myself after hours of deep sleep. The punishing sex had lifted a little of my guilt and cleared my head. "And it's the sort of hungry your dick in my mouth isn't going to fix."

War sniggered. "As tempting as it would be to find out, I'm pretty starving too."

"Your cupboards are bare, Mother Hubbard."

War squinted. "Who's Mother Hubbard?"

Nash piped up, his voice muffled from beneath the covers. "Isn't she that celebrity chef?"

I stared at them. "Are you serious? From the nursery rhyme. Old Mother Hubbard, went to the cupboard, to fetch her poor dog a bone…"

Nash poked his head out of the blankets. "Hey, War. Bethany-Melissa from Providence just rocked on up to your cabin."

War grinned and got up, strolling across the kitchen bare-ass naked to kiss the top of my head. "We didn't have parents who read us nursery rhymes, baby girl."

"Oh." I hadn't always either, but the nursery rhyme jogged an old memory of my dad sitting on the floor of my bedroom with me, not long after I'd moved in with him. The house was huge, a mansion by anyone's standards, but especially those of a five-year-old girl who'd rarely spent time anywhere but a tiny trailer house.

I'd been terrified of it. Of the tall ceilings and large windows that cast shadows once the sun started going down. Of the winding staircases that led up multiple levels, each one scarier than the last with their endless halls, rooms, and silence.

But he'd been patient with me. Sitting quietly, singing me nursery rhymes, and reading me stories from across the other side of the room. By day, I'd have nannies while he was at work. But by night, it was always him, waiting for me to accept him. Each night I'd shifted closer, until one night, I'd crawled into his lap to look at the pictures in the book he'd read.

I still remembered the shocked way he'd stopped reading, and then the contented sigh he'd given when he'd wrapped his arm around me and continued on with the story.

I could relate to poor Mother Hubbard and her lack of food. But that had been the first night I'd called my father 'Daddy', and from then on, everything had changed.

Nash and War hadn't been as lucky.

War peered over my shoulder at the empty refrigerator, though his hands seemed more interested in feeling me up. His palm landed on my bare thigh and slid up to cup and squeeze my bare ass.

Nash groaned at the flash of my skin, and War lowered his head so his lips brushed my ear. "I'd rather eat you for breakfast anyway."

I nudged him out of the way with my hip because if I gave him even an ounce of encouragement, I knew I'd find myself spread out on the kitchen counter with his head buried between my thighs.

And I really did need food. "Food, War. Real food."

He grumbled and let me go. "Get dressed then. Both of you. Grab whatever you need out of my closet, and we'll go up to the clubhouse. There'll be food there, and prospects to cook it."

I rewarded him with a smile, and a lingering look at his dick, just to tease him. I scuttled away to his drawers, taking out sweatpants and a T-shirt for Nash and another set for me. I didn't even have a bra here or shoes that weren't heels. War's clothes weren't too bad a fit for me, since he wore his sweats big, but there was no chance of me being able to wear his shoes.

"Sweats and heels it is," I muttered, wincing as I put them back onto my feet.

War frowned. "What size are you?"

"Eight."

"I'll have something more suitable up at the club-house when we get there."

I wasn't going to refuse because my toes were already protesting. The short walk through the woods from War's cabin to the main clubhouse was going to be a recipe for a broken ankle.

War motioned for me to throw him some clothes, too and he pulled them on there, in the middle of his little kitchenette. "I need to make a couple of calls," he announced, picking up his phone and taking it out to the front porch.

He closed the door behind him, keeping the warmth in the cabin while I made my way into the bathroom to scrub my face with water. I tried to tame my hair with the comb I found in War's top drawer, wincing as it made it about an inch through my hair before getting tangled. I gave up and went out onto the porch with it still stuck in my hair.

War spun around at the door opening, took one look at my problem, and chuckled down the line. "Queenie? Can you add a brush to that? Bliss' hair is a disaster."

I flipped him the bird, and he grinned, saying goodbye to Queenie and pocketing the phone.

"You and Nash ready to go?"

Nash appeared in the doorway, tugging on the shoes he'd worn to Psychos, which were far too fancy for his current attire, but at least he wouldn't roll his ankle. "I could eat a horse," he complained.

"Same," I agreed.

War nodded, slinging an arm around my shoulders. "Let's go then."

Nash fell in at my other side, his fingers brushing mine uncertainly.

But I knew what I wanted.

I threaded my fingers through his.

War glanced down and grinned. "Probably a good thing Vincent isn't here, since you don't have a third hand…"

But the joke died on his lips before he'd even finished it. My worries over where exactly Vincent was lit back up in full force.

War looked away.

An awkward silence settled over us, thankfully broken quickly by Queenie's joyful greeting as we walked through the open doors of the clubhouse. "Sugar! I brought everything you need to feel human. Here." She thrust the care package into my arms, which included a pair of size eight ballet flats that I gratefully slipped on, much to the relief of my feet.

"Don't stretch 'em out," Siren huffed, glaring at me from the far side of the room. "And I want them back."

Queenie leaned in and nudged me with her elbow. "Sorry, sugar. She was the only size eight I could find."

Great. Just great. There was nothing I loved more than Siren's wrath early in the morning. It was bad enough that I was rocking up at the clubhouse wearing War's clothes. Though War didn't reciprocate Siren's claims on him, I still felt like I'd done something wrong.

"Knock it off, Siren," War snapped at her. "If you needed a pair of shoes, Bliss would be the first person to give you one. Don't be a fucking bitch."

He was right. As much as I didn't like the woman, I would have always given up something of mine to another woman who needed it. But if War had spoken to me like that, I probably would have cried.

Siren didn't seem bothered though. She just glared at him and then went back to the bike she was fixing.

War disappeared into the kitchen, presumably to find a prospect to make us some food, and Queenie drew Nash into a conversation. He knew everyone here, because they were all Psychos' regulars, so he was almost as at home as War was.

My manners, drilled into me by my father and nannies, demanded I go over and thank Siren for the shoes, even though she was being unpleasant about it. I wandered in her direction and nodded at Gus, Siren's dad, who was eating cereal from a bowl while watching Siren fix a bike.

"Is that yours?" I asked her curiously, trying to offer an olive branch. I didn't need enemies within War's club. Not if I was going to be with him.

She glanced up at me from her position, squatting on the floor. "Yeah. What's it to you?"

I ignored the barb. "It's gorgeous."

Siren glanced up at me, her expression suspicious like I might have been poking fun at her.

I wasn't.

Siren huffed, clearly unsure of what to do with the unexpected compliment. "Yeah, well, she's a lot prettier when she's running right."

"You'll get her fixed up," Gus said around a mouthful of breakfast cereal. "Taught my baby girl everything I know. She knows her way around a bike better than half the men in my club."

Siren preened under his praise, and to her credit, she really did look like she knew what she was doing. She had oily parts spread out on a light-colored drop sheet, protecting the concrete floor. Amongst them were a variety of tools, none of which I knew the names of. It was the first time I'd seen this side of her. Every other time I'd seen her, she'd been in skirts that showed half her ass and tops that barely covered her nipples. Those outfits were a far cry from the tight, ripped, dirty jeans and cropped Guns N' Roses T-shirt she wore today.

War wandered back out from the kitchen, wrapping his deliciously thick arms around me and resting his head on my shoulder. I tensed, and as predicted, any warmth Siren may have been developing for me instantly disappeared in War's presence. Even Gus shot War a disapproving look.

All War did was tighten his grip on me.

The roar of a motorcycle engine outside interrupted the awkwardness between us, and Hawk stormed in a moment later. He stopped in the doorway, his gaze narrowing in on War. "Where the fuck have you been?"

War stood up straight at the hostility in Hawk's voice. "In my cabin."

"Your bike ain't here, and you haven't answered your phone in over twenty-four hours. I was out searching for you, you asshole! You go and get yourself a gunshot wound and then disappear. We found your bike outside the cop station but no sign of you. I thought that Scythe caught up with you and you were lying with your throat slit somewhere. You're a fucking asshole, War." Hawk turned his wrath in my direction. "A fucking pussy-whipped asshole at that."

War had been contrite at Hawk's dressing down, but the moment he turned his anger on me, War's entire demeanor changed.

He dragged me behind him and faced off with Hawk, the two of them going chest to chest. "Don't you fucking talk to her like that. Show some respect."

Hawk sneered. "For what? Your cunt of the week? She was all shacked up with Scythe this entire time. You can't tell me she didn't know who he was and what he'd done. How do you know she wasn't involved in your old man's death too?"

I gasped. "I didn't have anything to do with that!"

At the same time, War growled, "Back off, brother."

Hawk snorted. "Don't call me brother when you clearly chose pussy over all of us. You're still so blinded by her, even when the facts are slapping you right in the face. She was sleeping with the enemy, War!"

"So was I," War roared back.

A shocked silence settled over the room, all eyes trained on their prez, his chest heaving with anger.

War's hands shoved against Hawk's chest. "Is that what you wanted me to admit? That I got down on my knees for him, took his cock in my mouth, and blew him until he came? How I swallowed everything he had? Or did you want to hear about how much I fucking liked it? You want to blame her for sleeping with Scythe and not knowing, then blame me too, because I didn't know either."

Hawk's eyes blazed. "Is that why you didn't kill him when you had the chance then? 'Cause you're fucking in love with the faggot?"

What? Killed him when he had the chance? What the hell did that mean? "War? What is he talking about?"

Hawk laughed cruelly. "Oh, you didn't tell her?"

"Shut up," War hissed at him.

But Hawk was having none of it. His handsome face was twisted with hate, all of it aimed in my direction. "That's why we were at Psychos when the raid went down. It had to be done, Bliss." He said my name like it tasted bad. "An eye for an eye. We went there to kill Scythe, but War pansied out."

My mouth dropped open, and I stared at War. "Is that true? You were there to kill him?"

War's teeth clenched together. "He killed my father. He knew the score."

I had too. This was exactly what I'd been worried about when I'd found out what Scythe had done in the name of 'work.' But after seeing the way he and War were together, I'd tried to convince myself they could work it out. I'd seen the attraction between them.

Some stupid part of me had hoped that if Scythe was important to me, then maybe War could let the grievances between the two of them go.

For me. Because I needed both of them in my life and didn't want to choose.

I was an idiot.

Nash clamped a hand down on my shoulder, his tall, solid presence at my back reassuring. But inside, my heart was breaking for what felt like the hundredth time in days.

"So what now?" Hawk asked, dragging his gaze away from me. "Nothing has changed as far as I'm concerned. We find the bastard and end him. You with us, War? Or you with them?"

I begged him with eyes filled with tears.

War glanced between me and Nash and the rest of his club. "There's no sides. Not until we get him free from whoever took him." His gaze settled on me. "Once he's free, then I'll decide his fate."

9

WAR

The look of betrayal on Bliss' face killed me. The funny thing was, for all Hawk's hate toward her, he wore an identical expression of hurt.

I was damned if I did and damned if I didn't. I was bound by club and blood to avenge my father's death.

I was bound by the way my heart beat for Bliss and the feelings I had for Vincent not to.

Somebody had to lose. I already knew that somebody was going to be me.

"What's your plan then?" Hawk demanded.

"Bliss' lawyer has contacts within the prison. We're waiting for him to get back to us on whether Vincent was taken straight there."

Bliss stared at me with a frost that I'd never seen in her eyes before. "I'm not telling you anything unless you swear to me you won't hurt him."

I couldn't do that.

"What are you going to do with that information then?" Hawk sneered. "Whether he's in the prison or not, they have him. You're gonna need people to get him out. You got people who can do that?"

Bliss frowned, like she hadn't considered it, but I knew Hawk was right. The only way Vincent was getting out of whatever the hell mess he'd gotten himself into, was with me going in after him.

Not just me. Me. Hawk. And the rest of my crew.

Fuck. I needed to decide. Was I picking Vincent, Nash, and Bliss? Or was I sticking with my brothers? The family I'd always known.

Something deep inside me already knew the answer.

I would have killed Vincent last night if I was going to. I'd had the chance, and I hadn't taken it. Because I couldn't stand the thought of losing him anymore than I could stand the thought of losing Bliss.

"Screw her contacts," Hawk shouted, eliciting a ripple of agreement from the other men who'd gathered to find out what the commotion was. "We find him, kill him, and dump his body at the bottom of the cliffs," Hawk declared, eyes blazing. "Just like he did to our prez. Army didn't deserve to go out like that."

There were cheers of agreement from the other men, and Gus pumped a fist in the air, while Siren clapped. "Justice for Army and Fancy!"

"Hear! Hear!"

I held up my hand for silence, but when the shouting continued, I realized my grip and that control I'd once had on these people had already slipped. "Shut the fuck up for a second!"

Everybody settled, their eyes turned to me.

Hawk's threats to throw Vincent's dead body off the cliff face had jogged something free in my brain. Something I hadn't really considered when he'd said it, because I was too blinded by anger and adrenaline. But now, I wondered if any of it could have been true.

I hoped like hell it was.

I cleared my throat. "Before Hawk leads you all off on a fucking witch hunt, you need to know what Vincent—Scythe—said to me when we argued outside Psychos."

I steeled each of them with an evil eye until they all shut up. "He said Army drove that car over the edge of the cliff. Not a brake light to be seen. And when he trekked down the path to the car, Army was in a bad way, metal speared through his chest. He said Army begged him to end it."

"Bullshit!" Hawk sneered. "You believed that?"

I pulled up the email I'd been sent on my phone weeks ago and scanned over the details. I'd read them briefly before, but I'd been so blinded by grief I hadn't really taken them in. The details hadn't seemed important. He'd been shot in the head, lost control of the vehicle when he'd died on impact, and then that vehicle had gone over the edge of the cliffs, taking my mother, strapped into the passenger seat, along with it. It was a miracle she'd made it out alive, and in those early days, that's what I'd chosen to focus on.

But now, I wondered if the details supported Vincent's version of events.

Hawk started to run his mouth again, but I glared in his direction. "Last I checked, I'm still the prez. So shut your fucking mouth and wait."

His jaw went tight, but he did it.

I went back to the email, checking for the detail that

would prove Dad had been alive and well when that car went over the cliff.

"There!" I shouted, the tiny print on the email giving me hope. "Penetrating trauma to the chest. And a gunshot wound to the head were both noted on the body. Testing confirms the shot was point-blank." I stared at Hawk over the top of my phone. "Unless Scy…" I couldn't call him that. He was Vincent to me. "Unless Vincent was sitting on Fancy's lap when that car went over the cliff, there's no way he was the cause of the accident." I glanced at Bliss. "He was telling the truth when he said it was a mercy killing."

Relief flooded me, though when I looked at Hawk, he still scowled.

But it was Gus who stepped forward, folding his arms across his barrel chest. "So, what? You think Army was suicidal? Even if he was, 'cause God knows the action we saw fucked us up for a long time after we returned, he loved Fancy more than life itself. He would have never taken her with him."

That was true. My dad hadn't been like most men in his position who had a different club slut on his dick each week. He'd loved my mother so whole heartedly; his gaze had never strayed. The only woman in his bed, ever, was her.

I couldn't see him taking her over that cliff, knowing he'd be killing them both. Not unless… "Maybe she wanted to die too."

Gus shook his head. "I don't buy it. Not for either of them. There were no signs they were depressed."

Nash cleared his throat. "There's another option."

We all looked at him expectantly.

But I couldn't think of one. "There were no skid marks on the road, the police confirmed that for me twice, which was why I was so sure he'd been shot by a sniper as he drove. Even Vincent said there'd been no brake lights."

"What if he had tried to brake?" Nash asked. "What if he'd tried but couldn't?"

As the cold, hard weight of that settled over my shoulders, there was only one thing I knew for sure.

Cutting someone's brake lines wasn't Vincent's style. He liked weapons.

And if Nash was right, we were only getting further from working out who really killed my father.

10

BLISS

*P*sychos' parking lot looked like a bomb had hit it. Yellow crime scene tape had been put up around the entire perimeter of the parking lot and building, and the cops hadn't bothered removing it after they'd finished their investigations. Now it blew tattered in the cold breeze that whispered of winter coming.

I got out of War's club van and took in my own club with a sigh of defeat. Bits of garbage were strewn across the blacktop, and bullet holes peppered the crazy clown logo painted on the doors. I pressed my finger into one, shuddering at the disturbing thought that I could have been standing on the other side. Any of us could have been.

I ripped another section of tape off the doorway and unlocked the doors, pushing my way inside. I sighed at the mess in the foyer and beyond. Chairs and tables overturned. The pool table with a huge rip down the middle of the green felt. Bottles and glasses smashed all over the floor, the liquid sticky beneath our feet.

"Fucking pigs," Nash muttered. "There was no need for them to do this."

I tried to give the cops the benefit of the doubt. "It was probably protocol to search for more drugs."

"And they needed to destroy the place in order to do that? They're just a bunch of stuck-up cunts who think their shit don't stink because they're from Providence." Nash toed at a shard of glass and moved it out of the way. "This pisses me off. I bet if the club had been on the other side of the border, they would have gently picked things up, dusted them off, and placed them exactly where they'd found them. Not torn through the place like a wrecking ball."

There was no denying that was the truth. But there was no use crying over spilled milk. Though I couldn't deny that cleaning all of this up was overwhelming and depressing. It only got worse when I walked through the coatroom and into the other side of the club, where we held the parties. If anything, the carnage in there was even worse. My beautiful office was near completely destroyed.

Nash clenched his fingers into fists. "I spent weeks doing up this room."

And I'd spent weeks loving it. Weeks. It hadn't been long enough for all the effort he'd put in.

"I'm sorry," I whispered.

He whirled on me. "Don't start that shit again. This isn't your fault."

I nodded, not wanting to argue, but I needed a minute.

Nash was angry. War was too.

It was all too much. I didn't think either of them were in the right frame of mind to fuck my worries out of me like they had the day before, so I excused myself and headed for the bathroom to splash some cold water on my face.

To my surprise, the bathrooms were mostly as we'd left them, only the tops of the toilet tanks askew where the cops had searched them for drugs.

Very thorough of them.

I turned on the faucet, letting the cold water run into the sink for a moment before cupping my hands and letting them fill. When the water was overflowing, I closed my eyes and brought my hands to my face, splashing the cool liquid over my too-hot skin.

I straightened, wiping the water from my eyelids with my fingers and looked at myself in the mirror.

Two women stood either side of me in the reflection.

I widened my eyes, then opened my mouth to scream, only to be cut off by a hand hastily slapped over my mouth.

"Now, now," Jezebel crooned in my ear. "No need for screaming."

The fact she and her friend had snuck up on me without so much as a squeak, and now had a hand over my mouth, certainly felt like something to scream about.

The other woman was dark-haired with tanned skin. She was tall and lithe, and if she'd been wearing a leather catsuit, she could have absolutely starred in a Batman movie. Her brown eyes stared me down in the mirror, her sharply angled features familiar, and yet I was sure I'd never met her.

"Let her go, Jez. She isn't going to scream, right, Bliss?"

This version of Jezebel was nothing like the woman I'd met a few days prior. Decked out all in black, she had an air of menace about her that hadn't been there when we'd had breakfast at Scythe's kitchen counter. She'd been sweet, chatting with me about her florist business and which sorts of greenery she liked to pair with roses.

But today, despite her light-blond hair and pretty features, a danger lurked in her eyes. Metal glinted in her free hand, and my heart picked up the pace when I realized it was a knife.

I should have known that any woman Scythe's mother picked out for him would have a penchant for knives. Scythe and Jezebel were two peas in a pod. A perfect match by his mother's standards, clearly.

I shook my head quickly, answering the dark-haired woman's question about whether I was going to scream or not.

She raised an eyebrow. "You sure? We aren't here to hurt you. We just want to know where my brother is."

Brother?

I widened my eyes, finally understanding exactly why the woman looked so familiar. I put my fingers to Jezebel's hand over my mouth, and she let me drag it down. But I only had eyes for the woman who so clearly Scythe's sister that I was shocked I hadn't immediately recognized her.

"Fawn?" I asked, recalling Scythe's sister's name.

She shook her head, scrunching up her face. "God, no. Fawn is probably off somewhere kissing puppies and painting rainbows." She stuck her hand in my direction. "Ophelia."

Scythe and Vincent's older sister.

I took it tentatively. "Bliss. Nice to meet you..."

Except it wasn't. Not under these circumstances.

A thumping came from outside the door. "Bliss? You okay in there? You're taking forever." The bathroom door swung open, War poking his head in behind it.

Ophelia whipped a gun from her back pocket faster than I'd ever seen anyone move. Apart from Jezebel, who yanked me to her chest and hovered the knife over my throat menacingly.

"What the fuck?"

War's shouts brought Nash running. He skidded around the corner to stop in the doorway with him. They both stared at me in terror, their gazes flickering back and forth, assessing the situation. War went for the waistband of his jeans, where I had no doubt he had a weapon stashed, but Jezebel edged the knife a little closer to my neck. "I wouldn't."

War's arm dropped to his side in defeat.

The two women had the upper hand, and we all knew it. It was hardly surprising, considering their families.

"War, right?" Ophelia asked, her hands steady on the gun. "And you must be Nash. I've heard all about both of you from my mother. And you too, Bliss. I'd like to say she spoke highly of you..."

I bristled. What on earth had I done to make the woman not like me?

Like Ophelia could read my mind, she shook her head. "Oh, don't take it personally. She just doesn't want Vincent marrying you and quitting the game. I kind of ruined that for him by getting out myself. And Fawn is such a bunny rabbit, she couldn't even hurt a fly, so

Vincent was really the only one Mom had to carry on the business."

I stared at Jezebel in the mirror. "But you…"

She shrugged. "I like knives as much as he does, so she likes me."

Ophelia waved her free hand around. "But that's all beside the point right now. Because apparently, my brother is missing. I assume you all want to find him?"

Nash and I nodded quickly.

War didn't move, his gaze alternating between the gun Ophelia held on him and the knife at my neck.

Ophelia narrowed her eyes at War. "Even you, biker boy? I heard your club had a meeting with my mother. And not long after that, there was a…let's call it a distur-bance, at this here very establishment. That wouldn't have had anything to do with you, would it?"

War gritted his teeth. "I want to find him more than anyone. We have…unfinished business to discuss."

Ophelia cocked her head, assessing him. "Does that business involve you trying to kill him?"

"I haven't one-hundred-percent decided either way, to be honest."

Ophelia's sudden and abrupt laughter filled the bath-room, bouncing off the tiles. "You know what, War? That's fair enough. Because I'm thinking about killing him myself. You know I was lying on a beach in Spain, tanning my tits when I got the call about all this? I swore I was never coming back here, and yet, here I freaking am, bailing out my little brother and getting sucked back into my mother's web of drama." She clucked her tongue against the inside of her cheek. "If I lower this gun, are you going to work with me so one of us can kill my brother, or are you going to be a pain in my ass and go for your gun? Truly, this would be a lot easier if we work together."

"I'd be a lot more inclined to say yes if you tell your girl there to get that knife away from Bliss' neck."

Ophelia shot a glance toward me and Jezebel. "Let her go."

Jezebel groaned with what I was pretty sure was disappointment, but her grip on me loosened, and I scuttled across the bathroom into Nash's waiting arms. War pushed both of us behind him.

Ophelia raised an impatient eyebrow. "We good?"

War nodded. "We're good."

Ophelia lowered her gun. War's hand inched ever so slightly toward his weapon.

I grabbed his fingers, lacing mine through them and pushing my knuckles into the side of his thigh. I gave the tiniest shake of my head.

I wasn't going to let him pull a gun on Vincent's sister.

The violence had to end. And Ophelia was right. We could get Vincent back quicker if we worked together.

The shrill music of my ringtone pierced through the quiet truce, all eyes turning toward me. Grateful for the distraction and a chance to lower the simmering tension, I snatched it from my pocket gratefully. I didn't recognize the number, but I answered it anyway. "Hello?"

"Bliss, it's Liam Banks. Your lawyer."

"Tell me you found him," I begged. I put my hand over the speaker and whispered to the others. "It's Liam."

Jezebel mouthed, "Who?" at Ophelia, and she shrugged.

Nash, ever the gentleman, filled them in. "Bliss'

lawyer. He's a friend of your brother's too. He's been investigating where he was taken after they nabbed him outside the club the other night."

I was vaguely aware of relief filling me at them all getting along for a moment, but I was more interested in what Liam had to say.

Liam cleared his throat. "I couldn't get anyone at the prison to talk to me over the weekend, but Rowe was back in at work today, so I had him investigate."

"Is Vincent there? At the prison?"

"No, not from what we can tell. I've got Rowe here. He wants to talk to you, so I'm putting him on speaker."

"I've got Vincent's sister and…" I didn't know what to call Jezebel, but I sure as hell wasn't going to call her his fiancée. "His family friend here too. As well as War and Nash."

Another voice came down the line. The prison guard, Rowe, I presumed. "That's probably good, because I think we're going to need an army if my assumptions are right."

A shiver rolled down my spine at the dead tone in Rowe's voice.

"Tabor, our warden, has been very conspicuously missing ever since Vincent was taken from Psychos. He hasn't come to work, and his crew of favorite guards also happened to call in sick today. All five of them."

"Fuck," War muttered. "That had to have been the guys I saw shoving him into the van."

"I agree," Rowe said on the other end of the line. "I know that prison back to front. I know every nook and cranny and I searched them all. I asked everybody I thought might have even the slightest scrap of information. But there's nothing. Vincent isn't at the prison."

"Which is a whole lot worse." There was little emotion in Ophelia's voice, other than a steely, cold determination. "Wherever they do have him, there aren't cameras to make sure the guards and Tabor are playing by the rules."

"So, guard," Jezebel butt in. "What other options are there? This guy Tabor...his house?"

"Doubtful. He's got a wife and kids. I can't imagine he's bringing home someone as dangerous as Vincent. I checked the files of the other guards, and they were all similar."

"This is going to be like searching for a needle in a haystack," Nash murmured. "We've already wasted so much time."

Rowe cleared his throat. "Maybe not. While I was in the office, looking through the files, I noticed several sets of keys were missing. One was for the van, which I expected, because Liam told me they'd used it to take Vincent. I checked the pegboard to see if they'd been returned, and they hadn't. So wherever the van is, we'll probably find Vincent."

"Has it got any way of tracking it?" War stared shrewdly at the phone.

"No. The prison doesn't have enough funding for anything high-tech like that. But what they do have is an old training barracks. It hasn't been used since there was a gas leak there about eighteen months ago, but when I was first employed, all new recruits were sent there for a month of training. It was used for prisons all over the state, and neighboring ones, so there were army-style rooms of bunks where you could sleep if your commute was too long. I drove in each day, because it was only an hour away."

"And the keys to that place were the other set missing?" Hope lit up my voice.

"You got it," Rowe answered.

"What do we do?" I asked. "We can't call the police, can we?"

Everybody stared at me like I was a moron.

"Okay, fine, I deserved that. But what do we do? We can't just sit around, waiting and praying they let him go."

"No fucking way," Jezebel muttered.

"Liam, Heath, and I want to go check it out," Rowe said determinedly through the speakers. "But there's only three of us, and at least five guards, plus Tabor potentially at this location, and I don't like our odds alone."

"I've got guys." War straightened, crossing his arms over his broad chest. "We'll get him."

Ophelia held up a finger. "Ah, excuse me if I don't jump for joy over that plan, considering the last time you were with my brother you tried to kill him."

"What the fuck?" Rowe asked, but everybody ignored him.

"That was in the heat of the moment," I tried to explain on War's behalf. "War and Scythe are..." I clamped my lips shut, knowing it wasn't my place to say.

Ophelia wasn't convinced that easily. "Whatever you all are to my brother, it isn't enough to make me trust you. You can come, but just the three of you. With Liam, Rowe, and Heath, that's six, and Jezebel and I make eight. We'll have the element of surprise, so that should be enough."

"Bliss—"

I cut War off with a glare. "Warrick Maynard, don't you even think about telling me I'm not coming."

Jezebel sniggered. "Warrick? Damn. I'd go by War too."

He shot both of us dirty looks but shoved his hands in his pockets. "Fine, but you stick with one of us."

Ophelia linked her arm through mine. "She can stick with me. It'll be a good chance for me to get to know my future sister-in-law."

She smiled at me, and there was a sincerity in it I hadn't expected. "Your mom wants Jezebel to be that person."

Ophelia sniffed. "My mother doesn't care about my brother. I do. He and Jez would probably stab each other in their sleep."

Jezebel picked at the chipped black polish on her fingernails, like she didn't have a care in the world. "Highly likely. I get nightmares sometimes and wake up with my pillows slit and feathers everywhere."

All of us stared at her. I didn't know about the others, but that was a disturbing image.

"What?" She shrugged.

"Okay, on that truly terrifying note, I say we fall out," Rowe said. "We'll meet you all at the freeway turnoff, and you can follow me in. We'll conceal the cars about two hundred yards before the driveway and go in on foot."

"Oh good." Jezebel linked her fingers together and stretched them over her head. "I haven't got my steps in yet today, so I hope it's a good walk."

I inched a little closer to Ophelia, who seemed less crazy.

She gave me a reassuring smile. "Hey, she's basically Vincent's clone. You like him."

I liked him because he liked me. I knew he wouldn't try to kill me.

I wasn't sure if I could say the same about Jezebel.

11

CALEB

I smacked a hand across Vincent's face, enjoying the sting on my palm as it connected with his cheek. "Wakey, wakey, asshole."

The other man stirred, greasy hair stuck to his grime-smeared face.

I slapped him again, just because it was fun. "You're not dead yet. So wake up."

A surge of power rose at seeing him, once so tall and mighty, staring down at me like I was the worthless scum on the sole of his shoe, now hanging from shackles above his head, his naked, cut and bruised body as helpless as a newborn foal.

Hate rushed in on top of the power, swirling and combining into a lethal mix that went straight to my head.

I'd waited a long time for this. When Tabor had found me, dirty, piss-covered, and barely conscious at the police station, after Vincent had tortured me for a second time, he'd promised me this day. He'd promised I would get to hurt Vincent the same way he'd done to me.

I'd degrade him. Make him feel so small and worthless that not even a fat slut like Bethany-Melissa would want his dick.

It was all that had kept me going the last few weeks, knowing I was going to get my revenge, and get my wife back.

She would come crawling back on her slut knees, begging my forgiveness once she saw what I was capable of.

I'd sink my dick inside her, take her in just the way I knew would make her scream. Then I'd do what I should have done that night up on the bluffs.

Leave her dead for ever defying me.

I poked the tip of my knife blade into the skin of Vincent's chest and watched a tiny trickle of blood roll down over his pecs.

He stared at me through his strands of grimy hair, but he didn't say a word.

I dug the knife in a little deeper and dragged it down toward his nipple.

Still, he made not even the tiniest of sounds.

My fury grew, remembering the way I'd cried and screamed and how he'd taunted me for it. I wanted to do the same to him. So I'd cut him until I had that satisfaction of hearing him beg me to stop.

I brought the knife back to my starting point and made a curved line that ended halfway down the first one, and then an identical curve to end at the bottom.

A perfect B.

Frustrated by the lack of response, I ripped my own

shirt off with my free hand and thumped a closed fist against my chest. Right above the angry red scars that spelled out 'Bliss' across my pecs. "You remember this?" I asked him. "You remember writing that slut's name in my skin while you laughed at me?"

I moved in closer, sneering into his face. "Who's laughing now?" I made a new line on his chest. A single vertical slash, followed by a horizontal one, representing an L. I forced my laugh right in front of him so my breath would wash over him, in the same way he'd done to me. "We're going to have matching scars, friend. Bonded forever over that stupid cunt."

"He should have killed you," Vincent murmured so softly I wasn't sure I'd heard him correctly.

I had no idea what he was talking about. "Who?"

"Scythe."

I laughed with joy, pure delight filling me at the realization. "You're so fucking delirious with the pain you don't even remember your own nickname? I heard her call you that, you pussy. It was your pathetic nickname that got you here in the first place. Probably should have gone with something less distinctive, don't you think? Vin. Vinnie. Vince, even. But no, you had to be tough and go with Scythe. Tabor knew exactly who you were as soon as I mentioned it."

Vincent didn't say anything.

I got to work on the I, and then the first S. I moved the knife as slowly as I could go, scraping each letter out in the hopes of him crumbling. My anger soared when he didn't.

"What's it going to take?" I hissed at him. "Tell me!"

The final S was done with sharp, erratic movements,

messier than the other letters because he refused to break.

The door to the room swung open, and I spun, bloodied knife still clutched in my fingers.

Tabor stopped just inside the door, his gaze shifting to the knife in my hand, and then slowly traveling over to Vincent, suspended from the ceiling by chains, his body slick with both dried blood from the fun I'd had yesterday, and the new, brighter blood from my artwork across his chest just now.

Tabor turned a sickly shade of white. "What the hell have you done?"

I glared at the older man. "Exactly what I said I was going to."

"You never said anything about mutilation! He looks like he's been part of some satanic ritual. You were just supposed to beat him around a bit. I can't take him back to the prison like that! He needs a hospital!"

He shouldered past me, storming to stand in front of Vincent, who merely lifted his bloodshot eyes to meet Tabor's. Tabor pushed two fingers to Vincent's bloody neck, checking his pulse, before he swore.

He spun around and glared at me. "You've gone too far." He pulled his phone out and brought up a contact.

"Who are you calling?" I asked, wiping Vincent's blood off my knife and onto the leg of my pants.

Tabor turned around, ignoring me, and pressed his phone to his ear. "Perry? It's Stephen Tabor. Listen, I need you to get together a med kit with as many surgical supplies as we have. Tapes, gauzes, whatever that stuff is you use for stitching wounds. And then I need you to bring it to—"

A gurgling moan cut off his instructions.

He fell to his knees, hard on the concrete floor, before slumping forward. His phone clattered from his fingers, bouncing away into the shadows, though Perry's concerned voice still came through the speakers. "Stephen? Stephen? What's going on? Are you there?"

"He'll die if you don't do something," Vincent said through cracked lips. "You got him right in the jugular vein, Caleb. He has approximately two minutes before he bleeds out."

I blinked, trying to understand what he was saying, then looked down at my blood-smeared hands.

They were empty of the knife.

"You did this," I hissed at Vincent. "It wasn't me."

Vincent twisted his hands in the shackles. "When I was a child. Or a teenager, I guess. Thirteen or maybe fourteen, I wanted to make the cross-country running team at school. I trained hard, every day, running miles and miles."

"So?" I snapped. I couldn't drag my gaze away from Tabor, lying helplessly on his side, his body twitching and spasming while blood pooled beneath him at an alarming rate.

"I'd never been part of a club. I'd tried out for many. Chess. Debate. Football team. Lacrosse. I never made it in. But running was something I really enjoyed, and I wanted a spot on that team more than I'd wanted anything."

I lifted my gaze to meet Vincent's. "Did you make it?"

"No. I didn't. I tried out. But I wasn't fast enough. I came in eleventh, and they only took the fastest ten."

I sniggered. "I was on the team all four years. Made state in senior year."

Vincent ignored that. "When I came home that afternoon and told my mother I hadn't made it, she patted me on the shoulder and said, "We can't all be good at everything, son. You may not be good at chess, or lacrosse, or football, or running."

Vincent's gaze suddenly turned sharp, like the memory had focused him.

A chill ran down my spine.

"You know what she said then? After listing all the things I wasn't good at?" He rattled his chains as his voice picked up volume. "She said I was good at killing. At ending a life quickly, and cleanly, so that nobody ever saw me coming or leaving." He ran his tongue over his dried, cracked lips. "So don't insult me by saying your sloppy kills have anything to do with me." He jerked his head toward Tabor on the floor. "He's dead by the way."

Tabor's eyes were fixed and staring. His chest had stopped moving.

My fingers shook. There was so much blood. It reached my shoe, spreading around and beneath the expensive white sneaker. I stumbled back a step, knocking into a pile of pallets, then skittered toward the door.

The blood crept closer with every step I took. Its red fingers reaching, clawing their way across the room, seeking me out.

"Run, little Caleb," Vincent whispered softly. "Show me how fast you are and run."

12

WAR

*A*t Jezebel's and Ophelia's insistence, we gathered in the Psychos' parking lot as darkness fell.

Liam, the lawyer, met us there with two other guys who introduced themselves as Heath and Rowe. Liam looked different tonight, his suit replaced by dark distressed jeans and a black hoodie. Heath paced the parking lot while we waited for the others to arrive, about as happy as a caged tiger. Rowe watched him from a spot leaning against a wall, his gaze silently tracking the bigger man. I still wasn't entirely sure why they were sticking their necks out for Vincent, but they were as determined as the rest of us to find him and bring him home.

Ophelia and Jezebel pulled up in a sleek black sedan, and Rebel had shown up out of nowhere, just in time to jump into Nash's Jeep with me and Bliss.

Nash seemed like he'd wanted to kill her, but in true Rebel fashion, she'd taken no shit from anyone and had stubbornly put her seat belt on and waited for Nash to start the engine.

"He's my friend too, Nash. If we're going on a rescue mission, I'm in."

It was no wonder she and Bliss got on so well. They were both as stubborn as each other. They sat in the back seat of Nash's Jeep now, their fingers clutched around each other while Bliss stared out the window.

I hated this distance that had cropped up between me and her. I knew it was my fault and that the only way to fix it was to bring Vincent back. Alive.

But it had been almost three days since we'd seen him last, and there was a low roiling terror somewhere deep within me that said we were going to be too slow. Too late. And that all this mission was, was a body retrieval.

I glanced back at Bliss from the passenger seat and hated what I saw. Her fingernails bitten down and ragged. Her eyes rimmed with red and bloodshot.

I caught her eye, but she turned away again.

She may as well have stabbed a dagger through my chest.

My phone buzzed, and I glanced down at the screen, tapping on the preview to open the entire message when I saw it was from Gus.

I checked into the reports on your dad's car. There's no evidence of the brakes being tampered with, son. I'm sorry. I know that's not the news you were hoping for.

I stared at it for a long moment, willing the letters to rearrange and say something different. Something that proved Vincent's excuses were valid and that he really had done Army a kindness in executing him.

They didn't.

Another text came in before I could put my phone away.

War, I know you don't want to hear this, but this can't be ruled a suicide. We can't let the idea catch steam. Your old man's name would be ruined. He'd be seen as weak, and that reflects straight back on you. On your club. None of the guys are going to stand for that. After your little announcement this morning, you're already going to be struggling to hold the men's respect, especially Hawk's, and, son, you need Hawk by your side if you're going to ride out this storm. If he's not with you, he's against you. I don't know that your men won't follow him. Do you? Someone has to die for Army's death. The guys want it to be Scythe. Give them what they want, and all your problems go away.

I canceled out of the message and shoved the phone deep in my pocket.

Somebody else's phone jingled from the back, and Bliss plucked her purse from the middle seat to find it. "Dad? Is everything okay?"

I held my breath, because I knew she couldn't take another hit right now. She went quiet for a moment, listening, and then she sighed heavily. "You might be right. Can I think on it?"

I wished I could hear his answer, but she finished the call a moment later.

"Everything okay?" Rebel asked.

I was grateful, because I'd wanted to ask the same thing but knew what sort of response I'd get if I had.

Bliss sighed again. "My dad thinks I should sell Psychos."

I spun around, not caring that she was mad at me. "You can't sell Psychos."

"Can't I?" she asked. "What good has owning it done? Look how many people it's hurt."

"Bliss..." Rebel reached out to clutch Bliss' hands again. "You can't be serious. It was Axel's baby. You can't let some stranger take over."

"You or Nash could run it," she said quietly. "I think my dad is right. I tried and I failed. Maybe it's just time to admit that I don't belong here."

"No," Nash ground out. "I'm not buying it."

"Me neither," Rebel said adamantly. "The fact I haven't got a dollar to my name hasn't got anything to do with it either. Even if I had a million dollars, Psychos is your place, Bliss. It's Axel's legacy."

Bliss turned away again. "Someone from the realtor's office is coming out in a couple of days."

"And then what?" I asked sharply. "What happens when you sell it? What do you do?"

"I go back to Providence."

The silence that settled over the four of us was so filled with awkward, loaded tension the back of my neck prickled.

But nobody said anything.

If Bliss had made her mind up, that she was leaving Saint View and Psychos, and all of us, then she'd made her mind up. All I wanted for her was whatever made her happy. If that wasn't Psychos and Saint View, and me and Nash and Vincent and Rebel? Then there was nothing I could do about it.

I'd stand there, with everything inside me dying, as she walked away.

"Looks like we're here," Nash said stiffly, putting on

his indicator and following Liam's car off the freeway. "Rowe said it wasn't far past the turnoff."

I pushed aside everything happening with Bliss, and Gus' warnings about the club, and focused on the task ahead. We had no idea what we were walking into. We were hoping it was just Tabor and his five guards, which should have been okay if they were spread out around the property. We had five guys, plus Jezebel and Ophelia, who were downright disturbing with their arsenal of weapons and the sheer ease with which they'd handled them. Plus Bliss and Rebel, who weren't to be discounted. Rebel ran her fingers idly over her brass knuckles, and while Bliss was unarmed, there was no doubt her depth of feeling for Vincent would have her doing whatever needed to be done in order to save him.

As Rowe had instructed, we parked beneath some low-hanging trees, switching off our headlights as Jezebel and Ophelia pulled up behind us. We all got out, but I only had eyes for Bliss, who had her arms wrapped around herself, like she was trying to keep herself together. Nash and I both moved to flank her, Rebel sticking close as well.

Far down the hill, lights cast a glow around a huge, dark building.

Rowe took the lead, since he was the only one of us who'd been here before. "There's lights on. There shouldn't be, not with this place being shut down years ago. Somebody is down there, so I'm going to assume we're in the right place."

Ophelia twisted her head to one side, something in her neck popping audibly. "Let's get this show on the road. Split up into pairs, and we'll go in from all sides. Jezebel and I will take the front entrance."

Jezebel jumped up and down on the spot, like a boxer getting ready for a match. She grinned, clearly enjoying every minute and desperate to get into the action.

"Bliss is with me," Nash said before I could say the same thing. "We'll get the right-hand side."

"Heath and I will take the left." Rowe rolled up a sleeve, checking with Heath at the same time.

Heath nodded.

I glanced at Rebel. "You should go with Liam. I'm good alone."

"No chance in hell. I know you have my back. You're stuck with me. Liam can go with his people. I'll stick with mine, thank you very much." She nodded fiercely, her brass knuckles glinting in the moonlight. "Let's go find your man."

I swallowed hard at the sudden ache in my throat.

I'd been trying so fucking hard to block out my feelings for Scythe. There was no space in my body for them, and yet they appeared out of nowhere, as fast and hot as they'd come the last time I'd seen him. "Fine. Keep up."

She mumbled, "You fucking keep up," beneath her breath, and the four groups set out in different directions, all of us sticking to the woods, rather than taking the easier route down the gravel road.

It was slow going, picking our way along the steep descent into the gully where the prison training camp sat. Headlamps or flashlights wouldn't have gone astray. We both had our phones, but I didn't dare turn the flashlight function on for fear of being spotted.

Rebel fell a few steps behind me, her shorter legs not

covering the same distances my longer ones could. I stopped to wait for her, and she grabbed the back of my hoodie silently, which was reassuring, knowing I wouldn't lose her in the darkness. Having to call out to her was the last thing I wanted to do.

My palms sweated, despite the cool night, and adrenaline coursed through my veins, pumping me up and making me want to run down this hill at full speed, just to get on with things.

Scythe was behind the walls of that building, mere yards away, and it was all I could do to stop myself from going in, gun drawn, ready to kick down doors and take out anyone who stood in my way.

A crash behind me froze me to the spot, and the roaring of my blood in my ears drowned out everything else. I spun, lifting my gun, before I realized Rebel no longer held the back of my hoodie.

"Ow, fuck," she whispered from the ground.

I squinted down at her, while my heart tried to thump its way out of my chest. "What happened?"

"Twisted my ankle, I think."

"Fuck. Can you walk?"

"Yes, help me up."

I grabbed her hand, hauling her to her feet, but almost instantly, she dropped back down. "Ow, stop, no. Walking is bad."

I squatted, grappling around in the dark to find her. "I'll carry you back to the car."

But she shoved me away. "Like hell you will. Two people I care about a lot are down there, about to enter that building. They're expecting us to be coming through that rear entrance to back them up. I'm not going to be the reason they die when we don't take our guard out. You keep going. I'll get myself back to the car."

Maybe I should have argued. Hell, I loved Rebel like a sister, I really wanted to pick her up and make sure she got safely back to the car.

"People you love are down in that building too, War. Just go. I'm used to looking after myself."

She was right. I dropped a kiss on the top of her head. "Don't fucking die out here, kid."

She waved me away, and without her to worry about, I doubled the pace I'd been moving at, until I was at the edge of the woods and catching my breath while I surveyed the scene.

The building was freaking massive up close. Several times the size of Psychos or my compound. It was a long rectangular wall with a single entrance in the middle, manned by a very bored-looking guard who leaned against a wall, watching something on his phone.

That was good. Rebel's stumble had been high enough not to alert him to our presence. The others had probably already made it inside, and if this guy was still chill enough to be standing around watching a movie on his phone, then I had to assume no guards had called in a warning that they were under attack.

He was though. I moved silently from the shadows at one corner and plastered myself to the wall once I reached the building. I stopped, waiting for the guard to give a shout that indicated he'd seen me, but nothing happened. In the mottled light cast from his phone, the man grinned and let out a snort/laugh at whatever he was watching.

My fingers clenched around my gun as I let the anger

I'd been keeping a lid on boil over. This asshole had been one of the ones who'd attacked Vincent at Psychos. I remembered his short, stocky build. I didn't care who he was outside of work, he could die if it meant getting to Vincent. I crept toward him, inch by inch, imagining the bullet I was going to put right through his brain with each step.

The door behind him gave way, and he tumbled back with a shout of surprise.

I froze.

From inside, another man emerged, his chest bare, his legs covered by dark pants, sneakers on his feet. He sprinted forward for the cover of the trees, much like I had a few minutes earlier. He was little more than a dark, blurring shadow, until he hit a patch of moonlight that covered his body in a silvery glow. It lit up the blood soaked all over his torso and pants and shoes.

For half a second, I thought it was Scythe.

But the man's fair hair made that impossible.

The guard shouted something, stumbling to his feet and giving chase, all while shouting for help into a walkie-talkie.

I didn't know where his help was coming from, but I wasn't sticking around, standing here like a pussy, waiting to find out. I ran for the open, now unguarded entrance, and slipped inside.

Instantly, my skin chilled over with goosebumps. It was colder inside the old building than it was out in the night air, and cold damp clung to the dirty cinderblock walls at my back. I edged down a hallway, carefully placing my steps and straining my ears for any sign of somebody else coming.

A groan of pain came back to me instead, and every hair on my body stood on end.

I knew that voice.

I'd heard him groan in pain before.

I'd also heard him groan in pleasure.

My hurried but careful footsteps turned into a sprint. "Vincent!" Smart or not, I couldn't help the agonized shout that fell from my lips.

"War."

His voice was quiet. Weak. But it was there, on the other side of the door. I shouldered my way through it, stopping dead on the other side.

"Holy fuck," I whispered, frozen to the spot.

The unseeing eyes of the man dead on the floor, surrounded by a pool of his own blood, a knife buried in his neck, didn't faze me.

But Vincent, hung from the ceiling like a slaughtered animal, had bile rising up my throat and my stomach churning.

"War," he said again.

That was enough to unlock my muscles. I rushed to his side, lifting him so the weight was off his arms.

He shook his head. "Keys in Tabor's pockets."

I let him go gently, his groan of agony ripping through me. I knelt, ignoring the blood beneath my knees, to pat down the dead man. The set of small handcuff keys were buried in his pocket.

I straightened with them clenched in my fist and hurried back to Vincent.

Something stopped me from putting them in the lock.

It was right there. The little hole that just needed the key in my palm to free him.

My fingers trembled.

Vincent slowly raised his eyes, until his gaze locked with mine.

The keys fell from my fingers, and like my hand had a mind of its own, it moved toward my gun. The cold, hard steel welcomed me home and whispered loving promises of how good it would feel to unload a bullet into this man.

"I could kill you now," I said quietly. "Nobody would know. I could say I came in here and you were already dead." The shaking in my fingers turned into a full-body tremble I couldn't control.

The gun begged me to pull it. To press the trigger. To let it do its job.

Vincent watched me silently, sweat and blood glistening all over his chest, crude letters carved in his skin that spelled out Bliss' name. "But you won't."

The surety in his voice caught my attention. Despite how weakened his body appeared, his voice was strong. Sure.

More sure of anything than I'd ever been in my life.

"How do you know?"

"Because you love him."

I froze. "Who?"

"Scythe."

What the fuck kind of delirious mind game was this?

"He says to tell you he loves you too."

I crumpled beneath his words. He didn't sound like the Vincent I'd fallen for. Something was off. Different. But his words still meant something.

"Could you get me down now, please? I'd really like to check in with Bliss. It's been much too long."

I didn't ask questions because he was right. I wasn't going to kill him. I somehow doubted I ever could. If I'd been going to, I wouldn't have hesitated that night outside Psychos. I wouldn't have been so wholly devastated by the thought of his betrayal.

I did love him. And Bliss too.

I plucked the keys from the floor again, fitting my arm around Vincent's back so that when I stuck the keys in the handcuff lock, he dropped into my arms. I lowered him to the floor, feeling sick over the wounds that covered his entire body, head to toe. I went to work on his ankle cuffs when footsteps down the hall caught my attention.

Despite his condition, Vincent's head whipped to the side.

This time, I didn't hesitate in taking out my gun.

So when Bliss and Nash rounded the corner of the door, they were staring right down the barrel when, hyped up on adrenaline and fear, I instinctively pulled the trigger.

13

CALEB

*F*rom behind a grove of trees, I slowed my breathing, making it quiet in the night air. My skin was scratched and torn from running through the woods at pace with no care to the low-hanging branches and brambles that bit into my flesh.

She was pretty.

The pixie-like woman with the short hair, trying in vain to pull herself up the steep incline. Even from a distance, lit only by the silvery moon shining onto the clearing she was trying to maneuver through, her pert nose and big eyes drew me in.

So did the thrill of watching her, without her knowing I was even there. Still full of hyped-up power from stabbing a knife into Tabor's neck, and watching the curve of her small tits, my dick went hard. They could be bigger. I liked a proper handful, and she didn't have even close to that, but still, something about her was intriguing.

"Honestly, Bliss. Being your best friend needs to come with a danger warning," the woman muttered. It carried on the still night air, her sweet tones sinking their way inside my skin.

She was tainted though. Dirty from associating with Bethany-Melissa, but my dick didn't seem to get the message. It strained in her direction, urging me on.

Fucking Bethany-Melissa's sweet bestie would do me the world of good and have the double bonus of really getting under that slut's skin. There were multiple cars here now, and I'd seen people slipping into the building as I ran from it. Bethany-Melissa was probably in there right now, on her knees, sucking the blood off that psychopath's dick.

My fingers clenched unconsciously. I'd put that blood there. Scythe should have been left to bleed out and rot, like I had when they'd left me to die on the bluffs.

But I was a survivor.

I hadn't had anyone to rescue me. I'd had to rescue myself.

Bethany-Melissa's sexy little friend looked like she could use someone to rescue her too. All injured and pathetic like she was.

I was more than willing to be the one to save her.

Because then she'd owe me.

And I always collected on what I was owed.

14

BLISS

The gunshot cracked through the silent room, earsplitting as a firework going off in your face. Nash dragged me down to the floor at the same time War screamed my name.

"Jesus fuck, War!" Nash shouted, searching me all over, and then himself. "Thank God you're a lousy shot."

"I wasn't trying to kill you, dumbass."

"Sure felt like it!"

I would probably need therapy to process that later, but right now, there was only one man I had eyes for. "Scythe!" It was a half shout, half sob as I scrambled out from beneath Nash and scurried across the floor to Scythe's side. He was beaten and broken, but beneath all that, he was still the man I'd fallen for. I grasped both his cheeks in two hands, staring into his chocolate-brown eyes.

I knew before he even opened his mouth.

"Vincent. Not Scythe."

Tears filled my eyes and spilled over. And then I was nodding, pressing my lips to his in the gentlest of kisses.

"I missed you," he whispered.

I was too overcome to speak, because I'd missed him too. I loved Scythe, but I'd fallen for Vincent's soft ways first. I loved them both. All I wanted was for them to be alive.

He was.

"We need to get him out of here and to a hospital." I finally dragged my gaze away from Vincent's and let it roll over him, assessing each of his injuries. I gasped when I got to his chest, the crude letters carved there that dripped with fresh blood.

"Oh my God," I whispered. "Caleb? He was here?"

"You just missed the pleasure of his company." Vincent shifted, wincing in pain.

This was all my fault. "I'm so sorry."

"Why?"

"He mutilated you!"

"Your name in my skin would never be a mutilation, Bliss. I like it."

I had no idea whether that was completely insane or almost romantic. Maybe it was both.

Nash and War moved in, War pulling off his hoodie and tugging it over Vincent's head. He helped him get it on then draped Vincent's arm over his shoulder, Nash moving in to get his other side.

"What are we going to do about...?" I eyed the dead body on the floor.

"Nothing." War put his arm around Vincent's waist, offering more support. "He can rot in Hell."

But Nash was more practical. "Are your fingerprints on that knife?" he asked Vincent.

Vincent smiled, just the corner of his mouth flickering. "No. Only Caleb's."

War let out a hoot of laughter. "I know I called Nash a dumbass before, but wow, Caleb really takes the cake."

"Leave it all for the cops to find," I decided, not caring what happened to Caleb. He deserved everything he got. "Let's go home."

I followed behind the three men toward the rear exit, War and Nash mostly carrying Vincent despite his weak protests that he could walk. My heart swelled up at seeing the three of them like that.

The three men who owned my heart. The three men who set my soul on fire. The three men I couldn't choose between because nothing felt right without all of them.

We emerged into the fresh air outside the building, and shouts went up from the small group huddled there, waiting on us.

But for the first time that evening, they weren't shouts of warning. They were of pure joy.

"Ophelia?" Vincent asked.

The tall woman who looked like the feminine version of her brother grinned and strode over. Without pause, she went right up to Vincent and wrapped an arm around his neck, hugging him close. "You could have dressed up for me, little brother. That hoodie barely covers your junk."

"I'll try harder next time."

She kissed his cheek and stepped back. Heath took her place, staring down at Vincent with unconcealed emotion in his eyes.

Vincent's gaze darted to Liam and Rowe, and then back to Heath. "What are you all doing here?"

Heath shook his head. "You think Mae would have ever forgiven us if we'd let her favorite student die?"

"You didn't tell her, did you? The baby…"

"No, we kept that one to ourselves. She thinks we're playing poker. We're just really fucking glad we didn't have to tell her you were dead."

"Sorry to be a bitch," Jezebel drawled. "But he's bleeding everywhere while we're all just standing here having a reunion."

She wasn't wrong, I was antsy to get going myself, but Vincent wouldn't budge. "Ripley? Is he okay?"

Heath clapped a hand to the back of Vincent's neck, holding him. "He's good, my friend. He's really good. He misses you though. Talks about you all the time. So don't be a stranger, okay?" Heath eyed Nash, and War, and then me, but his words were directed to Vincent. "When the heat dies down, maybe you can introduce us properly to your family."

Vincent paused at that, then said quietly, "Ripley's birthday is coming up. Does he still like Spider-Man?"

Rowe cleared his throat. "Always."

Vincent nodded. "Go. Get home to them."

Liam and Rowe hugged Vincent quickly and then disappeared into the woods. It was only then, when their big bodies cleared out of the way, that I realized three guards sat huddled on the ground. Jezebel, armed with a gun in one hand and a knife in the other, stopped the three men from moving.

"Vincent's call what we do with these three," Ophelia announced, taking up her position beside

Jezebel, training her weapons on the huddled group of men.

"Who knows about this?" Vincent asked them.

"No one," a dark-haired man assured quickly. "Tabor wouldn't let us tell anyone because, well…"

"Because, escaped prisoner or not, what you all did here to him is wrong?" My anger rushed out in a spew of sharp words.

The man nodded.

"We were just doing our jobs. Please," one of them sniffed. "I have kids."

My heart clenched at the thought of leaving anyone fatherless, even if that father was a scumbag. It hit too close to home, after not having a father for my first five years. War went tense beside me, and I knew he had to be feeling it too, his own father gone.

"Let them go." Vincent didn't stop his slow, staggered walk to pay any attention to the guards. "They're going to forget the last few days ever happened. They're going to forget my name entirely. I'm just a harmless prisoner who escaped, never to be seen again, and forgotten at the bottom of the pile of paperwork. Isn't that correct?"

They nodded.

It made me nervous though, knowing they could go back on their word and straight to the cops. I stared down at the men. "You know who he is, right?"

More nods of heads.

"You know what he's capable of then. Don't try his patience by going back on your word, because if he has to come find you, it won't be to deliver a warning."

"Nicely said, Bliss." War grinned at me.

"Very Saint View of you," Nash agreed.

I straightened, pushing back my shoulders, fighting back a smile. "Let's go." Then something struck me. Liam, Rowe, and Heath had already left, but we were a person short. "Where's Rebel?"

War cursed low under his breath. "She sprained her ankle. She was going to make her way back to the car."

"You just left her?" Nash accused.

"You ever tried arguing with that woman?" War said defensively.

He was right. I could imagine exactly how it would have gone down. Rebel could have been lying near dead on the side of the road and she still would have made a joke and called War a wimp if he'd tried to help her. She was stubborn and independent, and she cared about other people more than was good for her.

Which meant we needed to look out for her all the more.

"Caleb was in these woods," Vincent said quietly.

Fear gripped my throat.

In unison, all four of us yelled her name.

Silence echoed back. Nash offloaded Vincent's full weight onto War and strode to the edge of the woods, with me hot on his heels.

"No, no, no," I whispered, searching the dark woods ahead of us. If Caleb had hurt her, I'd never forgive myself. I'd brought him into their lives, and one after the other, my people had been hurt by him.

With no care now about being caught, we pulled out our phones, switching on the flashlight functions.

"Rebel!" Nash shouted.

"Christ Almighty, Boss Man," a small voice called

back. "Quit your hollering. It takes a girl a minute when she's gotta hop, you know."

Relief flooded me. Nash jogged toward her voice and came back to the clearing with our little pixie friend hoisted easily into his arms.

She eyed Vincent's torn-up legs and feet. "You do all that just so you didn't have to walk back up the hill?" She grinned. "Same."

The laughter that surrounded us was music to my soul.

All the pieces inside me that had been jumbled and scattered for the last few days fit themselves back into place. I had my guys and my best friend. Everybody was alive.

It was easy to ignore the puzzle pieces that were missing.

Axel's killer.

Psychos.

And the fact I'd lost a small fortune of drugs that a dealer would be wanting payment on any day now.

15

NASH

"*M*issed a spot on the floor over there, Boss Man."

I glared at Rebel, sitting on a chair with her bandaged-up foot resting on a box of wine coolers I hadn't put away yet. Her crutches leaned against the wall, right by the bucket of hot, soapy water I was using to clean the floor. A job that was normally hers.

"You're enjoying this a bit too much," I griped. "How many more days are you on those things?"

"A month."

My mouth dropped open. "Are you serious? For a little sprain?"

She sniggered. "What, you don't want to mop floors that long?"

I didn't actually mind the floors so much. It was more the fact that between her and Vincent being off work, and Bliss playing doctor, I was struggling to get Psychos back into shape by myself. The bank accounts had been frozen in the aftermath of the raid and still hadn't been released, despite Kim's arrest, so I'd used my own money to replace all the broken bottles of alcohol and repair the pool table.

Not to mention the smarmy real estate guys who kept dropping by, hoping to talk to Bliss about selling the business. They were a complete and utter waste of my time, and today I'd flat-out refused to let them in. They'd hung around in the parking lot like vultures though, talking into their cell phones like they were making important deals.

"Don't stress it, Nashy. The ankle is all good. I'll be back on the floor by the end of the week."

I scrubbed harder at the spot I'd apparently missed. "I'd kiss you if I wouldn't much rather kiss Bliss."

"So go home and kiss her."

"She hasn't left Vincent's side in days."

"She's your girl too."

My heart clenched. She was. But he needed her more right now.

There was no doubting it was hard though. We'd had such a good time together the night of my party. Giving in to my feelings for her was the best decision I'd made in probably my entire forty years.

Only now, I was a drug addict who'd been sent to rehab against his wishes. Vincent needed her, so I hadn't begrudged her sleeping in his room. But it had sucked going home to my lonely house when all I wanted to do was run back to her.

I wasn't sure she felt the same. Her hanging out with Vincent felt a little like avoidance.

I still remembered the look of disappointment in her eyes when Kim had let it slip about my past. My stomach churned with hate and disgust for myself every time anyone brought up my days of pimping women out to men for sex. I never let myself think about it. I'd completely erased it from my everyday thoughts because anytime one snuck in, it floored me that I could have ever done something like that.

We'd been young. Stupid. Desperate. Axel and I had been sleeping on the streets for weeks, trying to find work, but nobody would give us a chance. We'd gotten jobs at Psychos eventually, but the pay had been so bad there was no chance of making ends meet without something to supplement it. All it had taken was a few whispered words from Jerry, and a shove in the wrong direction, and I'd been making a living doing the same shit he'd done.

Taking a cut of something that wasn't mine to take.

Ruining lives.

I wanted to think I would have stopped of my own accord. But the truth was, it had taken going to jail. I'd taken the hit for both me and Axel, leaving him to buy and run Psychos with the money we'd been hoarding away.

I didn't regret it. Getting sprung had been the first steps to better lives for both of us.

But what about the women we'd left behind? I never let myself think of them. Except now, ever since Kim had brought them up, it was all I could think about.

"Penny for your thoughts, Boss Man. You went all frowny face and serious for a second there."

"Do you think I'm a good person?"

She paused, studying me. "Little early in the day for deep and meaningfuls, isn't it?"

"That sounds an awful lot like you avoiding the question. Which makes me think I wouldn't like the answer." I shoved my mop back into the bucket. "Fuck."

Rebel reached out and grabbed my shirtsleeve, a frown etched between her eyebrows. "Hey. What's all this about? Nash, you're the best man I know. And I don't say that just because around here, most men are assholes and I have little good to compare you to."

I groaned. "You're making it worse."

"Okay, fine." She sat back in her chair and held up a hand, pointing to her index finger. "One. You gave me a job when nobody else would."

"And look how that turned out? This place wouldn't run without you. I should really be thanking you for ever agreeing to take the job in the first place. Hell, there's nicer places you could have gone."

"But none of them had you watching out for me. Which brings me to number two. I've never had anyone care about me the way you do. You're like the big brother I never had. You and Axel both, but you especially, Nash. All the girls here feel that way about you. You don't talk to my tits."

"Because you have none."

She sniggered. "There's that brotherly love again. You don't 'accidentally' grope anyone. Nobody is afraid to be in a storage room with you for fear of your wandering hands. Hell, I can waltz around Psychos in my birthday suit with a complete lack of fear, because I know that if something does happen, you're going to be there to back me up."

A soft glow of warmth flickered in the cold depths of my gut. I wanted this to be a safe place for women. I knew the men who visited here weren't always angels, and

Rebel had learned how to defend herself so well I'd never truly been concerned about her. But she was right. I did love her like my sister. She'd popped up out of nowhere one day, refused to tell us anything about who she was, or where she'd come from, but said she'd work twice as hard as any man. And she had.

"You know what I did in my past, right?" I asked.

"Everybody knows, Nash. We all still like you. Because even then? When you made some questionable decisions? You did it in the best way you could. This is Saint View. Questionable decisions are what we know. Hell, I've made some. Many, probably. People who live in glass houses and all that."

Bliss might have been born here, but she hadn't grown up here. She didn't know the daily struggle it was to even keep yourself alive when there'd been no path paved for you, other than ones you didn't want to take.

Rebel bossed me around from her throne for the rest of the day, and I drove her home afterward. She twisted in her seat before she got out and punched me in the arm. "Midlife crisis ends here, Nash. Stop beating yourself up over things that happened in a different lifetime. You aren't him anymore."

She got out and slammed the door, and I watched her until she made it inside, even though it was still light out.

I needed to see Bliss. To explain everything and make her understand why we'd done what we'd done. I headed toward Vincent's place but slowed when I drove past a different familiar house.

Before I could really think about it, I'd parked the car and gotten out, hesitating only briefly then crossing the overgrown lawn and banging on the door that desperately needed a coat of paint.

A baby cried inside, and there were cars parked in the driveway, so I knew they were home, but when nobody came to the door, I banged on it again, harder this time, and just kept going.

The door opened a crack, and a set of big blue eyes stared back at me.

"Hey."

The door suddenly swung all the way open, the woman on the other side pulling her robe closed tighter over her bare skin. "Nash? What the hell are you doing here?"

Her name was Lucy. The last time I'd seen her had been the day I went to prison for pimping her out.

I ran a hand through my hair, while the child in the background screamed some more. Lucy hurried over to the playpen in the corner of the room and picked up the skinny toddler, holding him to her chest to soothe him.

He looked just like her, his blue eyes peering at me curiously. "You have a son," I commented.

Lucy nodded. "Two. The older one is next door. My friend is watching him while I work. This one is supposed to be sleeping."

"Bitch, I ain't payin' you to chitchat!" a man shouted from somewhere within the house.

Lucy dropped her gaze to the floor. "I'm working, Nash. I need to go."

She went to shut the door, but I grabbed her hand. "Are you okay?"

Her big eyes filled with tears. "Doesn't really matter, does it?"

Fuck. She so wasn't okay. "It matters to me."

Her mouth pressed into a firm line. "If it mattered to you, you wouldn't have left us. Me. Rhiannon. Stella. None of us are okay, Nash. None of us have been okay for a long time."

They were the women I'd pimped. "I went to jail."

"We know. And that sucked. But we were all counting the days until you were out, and until you came back for us. Things were good when you were around. You actually paid us what we're worth. You vetted the men and made sure they all knew the rules. You never hit us or forced us. It was always our choice, you just supported it."

The man shouted again, and Lucy glanced over her shoulder nervously. "This is what we're left with. No regulation. Scraping by with men who hurt us because we have kids now, mouths to feed, and everything is ten times harder than it was back then." She looked me over, her stare hard. "I heard you're with Axel's fancy sister now. Probably won't be long until you move to Providence and forget all about us here in Saint View, right?"

I opened my mouth to respond, but she cut me off with a shake of her head. "I don't blame you, Nash. I wouldn't want to remember us either."

When she shut the door, I didn't stop her. I wanted to make things better for them, but all I knew was one route and I was trying to be the sort of man Bliss could be proud of. I couldn't see her happily showing me off to her family and friends, telling them all what a great pimp I was.

So I turned around and got back into my Jeep, and did exactly what Lucy had said I would. I drove into Providence.

16

BLISS

*L*ittle Dog barked insistently at the front door, her tail wagging furiously. I hadn't heard anyone knock, but Little Dog could hear someone coming well before I could, and I didn't want her waking Vincent when he needed to rest. So I dumped a pile of cut-up vegetables into the soup pot and wiped my hands on my apron.

I passed her in the entryway, patted her fluffy head, and noted that she was standing solidly on all fours now. She'd had her bandages removed a few days earlier, and the vets were pleased with her progress. "Good girl," I murmured. "Who's out there? Is it your cute boyfriend dog from next door? I've seen the way you two eye each other through the fence."

She gave nothing away, licking my hand before I used it to open the door.

I frowned at the man standing on the step. "Hey, sorry. Did you knock? I didn't hear you."

Nash shook his head. "I didn't. I was standing here

debating whether I should knock or turn around and go home."

I opened the door wider. "I think you should come in."

He trudged through the doorway, kicking his boots off in the entryway and hanging his coat on the rack. He scratched Little Dog behind the ears and, satisfied she knew him, and he'd given her enough attention, she trotted up the stairs again, probably in search of a warm spot beneath Vincent's blankets. Or a window in which to peer over the neighbor's fence longingly at her unrequited love.

I motioned for Nash to follow me into the kitchen and picked up my knife again, going back to the carrots I'd been chopping.

"Cooking?"

That one question spoke volumes to the awkwardness that had crept its way in between us recently, because it was pretty clear I wasn't doing a magic show. "Soup for dinner. Lots of meat and vegetables." I nodded toward the stairs where I'd left Vincent. "He needs it."

"How's he doing?"

I smiled. "So much better."

Nash leaned on the counter, watching me. "Good. I'm really glad."

He said the words, but they sounded mechanical, and he watched me with the disconnected gaze of a man whose head was somewhere else entirely.

"Everything okay?" I paused in my chopping to study him. "How are you going with the mess at Psychos?"

"Psychos is fine. Getting there. We'll be able to reopen

next week like we thought. But we haven't talked about what Kim told you that night. About my past."

I sighed, resuming my attack on a potato. "What is there to talk about, Nash? You did what you did. We can't change it now."

"But what you think of me matters."

I'd been ignoring the elephant in the room, and it had been easy when Vincent was missing. All my attention had been taken up by worrying about him, and then over keeping War from trying to kill him.

With Vincent safe in the bedroom above our heads, and his and War's feud at a shaky standstill, there was room for me to consider how I felt about Nash's actions again.

I didn't like what I felt. I'd watched my mother live in fear at the hands of a violent man who cared only about what she could bring him financially. She'd been a piece of property. Just a thing that made money.

Barely even human.

The thought that Nash had treated women the same broke something inside me that I didn't know if I wanted fixed.

It must have been written all over my face.

Nash bit his lip and nodded. "I should go."

I didn't want him to. And yet, at the same time, I did.

My heart hurt too much. But it also felt like he was the only one who could fully repair it.

When I didn't say anything, he turned around and walked to the door.

I let him go, hating every minute but not knowing how to call him back when I knew what I knew.

He reached the door and put his hand on the knob. He twisted it but didn't pull it open.

Then suddenly, he spun around, storming back into the kitchen, his face full of anger, and all of it directed at me. "You know what, Bliss? No. I know you were born in Saint View. And I know that the things you saw colored the way you see things that happen there. But your story isn't mine. And you don't get to judge me for it. You got out. You got to grow up in Providence with a father who loves you, money in your bank account, and food on your table. You might look at what I did and see me just trying to make a buck at someone else's expense. Or you could learn the truth." His fingers wrapped around the countertop, his knuckles white. "I took care of those women, just the same way I looked after you when you were a little girl. I took them from pimps who hurt and abused them, and I made sure they were safe. No man hurt a woman on my watch. And I paid them all every cent they were owed. I couldn't give them jobs that weren't opening their legs for men willing to pay for it. I didn't have those means back then. So I made it as good as I could for them." His face was full of agony. "I did the best I could, Bliss. The best I fucking could, with what I fucking had. I'm sorry for it. I wish I'd known another way. I wish I'd had the brains or the money or the education to offer them more, but I didn't. I did the best I could so no one would hurt them the way..." He swallowed thickly. "I'd been."

It was true. Everything he'd said. I was born into this life, but enduring five years of it wasn't the same as an entire life. I'd been given opportunities that he and Axel and Rebel never had.

Nash had delivered me to a man who would have

never hurt me. Nash hadn't had anyone to do that for him. My breath hitched, and my eyes flooded with tears.

He held a hand up. "Don't. Please don't."

"Nash..." I knew it was a common story. Not very many kids made it out of Saint View Trailer Park without experiencing some form of abuse.

I'd always thought Nash one of the lucky ones.

I knew now that he wasn't. He just hid his wounds better than those of us who wore them on our sleeves. He stood there, with wounds as deep as mine, but always putting on a brave face. That was who he'd been, ever since Axel had died. The solitary man, always alone, always having to look after himself because there was no one left to have his back.

Not anymore.

I moved in to stand in front of him, wrapping my arms around his torso and pressing my chest against his.

He froze, not moving at first, until slowly, his muscles thawed, and his shoulders slumped in defeat. He circled his arms around me, and his body shuddered, releasing the rest of the tension. My tears brimmed over. I sobbed for the little boy he'd been, the one who hadn't had a big brother and his best friend watching out for him.

"I'm so sorry," I whispered into his shirt. I really was. For everything he'd experienced. For slipping back into my Providence snob mode and not even considering that he'd been one of Jerry's victims as much as me and my mom. I was ashamed of myself for not immediately giving him the benefit of the doubt, because I knew him. I knew his good heart. I knew his kind soul. And I knew that if there'd been any other way, he would have done it differently.

His arms tightened around me. "Sorrys aren't enough, though, are they? They're just words. I said the same thing to one of my old girls, and it made me realize how very cheap talk is. I don't say that to make you feel bad. But it's the truth. She's suffering. Her and all the women I used to watch over." His voice grew hoarse. "I just fucking left them, Bliss. Like they meant nothing."

My heart split down the middle at his pain. "*Shh*," I comforted, not knowing what else to say. So many heart-breaking stories came out of Saint View. Mine, Nash's, those of the women he'd once been associated with... They were all just a handful in a bucket of thousands.

"I want to help them," he murmured. "I have to. I can't just keep burying my head in the sand and pretending this isn't a problem I helped create. It's on me to fix it."

"Us," I whispered. "It's on us."

But I didn't know where to even begin.

I didn't want to say that and add to the burden he'd already placed squarely on his shoulders. But there was one thing I could say, that would maybe make a differ-ence to him. "We're okay, Nash. You and me. We're okay."

When he didn't instantly respond, doubt crept in, and I quickly added, "If you want us to be, that is."

He gazed down at me, his blue eyes glassy with emotion.

I gave him the tiniest of nods, an encouragement he'd been needing. He slowly lowered his mouth to mine, touching our lips together in a tentative kiss that still held all the stress he'd been carrying. All I could think about was getting him to let it go.

"I promise," I whispered, between presses of his lips against mine. "We'll find a way to help. For my mom, and all the women like her who Jerry took advantage of. We can build something better."

He pulled back to gaze into my eyes, and in them I saw everything I needed to know about who he really was.

He was still the man who'd rescued a scared little girl and given her a better life.

He tugged me tighter, brushing his lips across my forehead. "I'm in love with you, Bliss."

I closed my eyes, basking in his words. They were words I'd wanted to hear from him ever since I'd run through the door of Psychos wearing a ballgown and searching for my brother. Now they found their way to my heart, winding their way around it and stitching the broken parts back together.

"I'm so in love with you," I whispered back. "I think I have been since I was five years old."

His smile lit a fire low in my belly that spread out through my body, taking a pleasant heat with it. He found my lips again, no hesitation in the kiss this time, just his sweet self, bared wide open after spilling his soul at my feet.

I knew how impossible those words must have been to say. So now I kissed him back with everything I had, wanting to mend him the way he'd fixed me so many times before.

My lips parted, and he drove his tongue into my mouth eagerly, searching and exploring like it was the first time he'd kissed me. There was no holding back now, everything between us had been said, so I kissed him back with the freedom that came from saying your truth and letting someone else in. I felt his trust in the way he clutched me to him, his heart beating beneath my hands. And I made a silent promise that I would always take care of it, and of him. His hands slid up my sides, and over my arms to my face where he cupped my cheeks and whispered that he loved me, over and over again, until I laughed at how many times he'd said it.

He leaned back, grinning. "You laughing at how much I love you, woman?"

I kissed my fingertips and touched them to his lips. "I might be."

His fingers dug into my hips, and he hoisted me up onto the kitchen counter.

I squealed but immediately opened my legs, making room for him to stand in between.

He stepped in, fingers running over the frilled edges of the apron I'd tied on earlier. "This is really sexy."

It was the kind that tied around the waist and only covered your lap. Perfect for wiping your hands on but not great for protecting you from spaghetti sauce splashes. It had been fine for cooking soup though.

Now Nash toyed with it, like it might just be fine for other things.

"You like my apron?" It was hardly attractive. It looked like something my grandmother would have worn.

He leaned in, brushing his lips along my jaw and up to my ear. "Mmm hmm. It would look better if that was all you were wearing though."

That fire he'd lit inside me traveled lower, settling between my thighs.

He raised an eyebrow. "You didn't protest?"

"Why would I?"

He groaned in the crook of my neck. "I'm going to

strip these clothes off you, so all you have left is that apron."

"And then?"

His eyebrows shot a mile high.

I stifled a laugh.

He kissed his way along my jaw to my neck, sucking the sensitive spots there until that heat turned into a beating pulse behind my clit.

"Then I'm going to lay you out on the kitchen table and fuck you until you forget about laughing and start thinking about screaming."

Yes.

He peeled my cardigan off my arms, dropping it on the floor, and I helped him along by yanking off the T-shirt I'd worn beneath it, leaving me only in my bra. Nash immediately went for my breasts, taking two handfuls and swiping his thumbs over my nipples. I leaned back on my hands, dropping my head back to give his lips better access to the swells of my breasts and my cleavage. He tongued my skin, kissing and licking a trail that dipped into the valley and sucked at my nipples through the fabric of my bra.

I closed my eyes, basking in the touch of him.

I'd never have enough of this man. This man who'd held himself back for so long but was now willing to give me all he had. His fingers snapped the clasp on my bra, and the material fell away in one easy tug.

He attached his mouth to my nipple, sucking it between his teeth and flicking the sensitive tip with his tongue while his other hand found my fly beneath my apron, undid the button, and drew the zipper down.

"This is so unsanitary," I murmured, supporting my

weight on my hands and lifting my ass so he could yank my jeans and panties down.

"Wait 'til I have you dripping on the countertop." He pulled back and grinned at me. "Don't worry, I'll lick it off."

As promised, he'd gotten me completely naked except for the flowered apron with the ruffles on the edges. He lifted it, licking his way up my inner thigh. The first swipe of his tongue through my folds was enough for me to forget my own name. All worries about sanitary cooking surfaces flew right out of my head.

I'd spray the counter down later. After I'd come on it.

Nash's tongue moved around my pussy with the experience of a man who knew what women liked. He started slow, licking and kissing around the outside, before he took up an assault on my clit.

The little bundle of nerves sang his praises in the form of rippling pleasure that surged right through me. His talented tongue set up camp there, but his hands roamed all over me, massaging my thighs, sliding over the softness of my belly, before coming back up to take full handfuls of my breasts.

I loved the way he pinched my nipples, rolling them between his warm fingers. My eyes fluttered closed as I pushed up into his touch and widened my legs, completely unashamed to give him full access to the body I once hadn't liked.

There was no room for thoughts like that anymore, when there were three guys hell-bent on making sure I knew exactly how much my body turned them on.

I'd never felt more like a queen than I did when one of them was going down on me. After a lifetime of men who'd never wanted to, and body insecurities, the way they didn't hold back was everything I'd read about in romance books.

None of it had seemed realistic.

Until them.

"Eyes on me, Bliss," he demanded. "I want to see your face when you come on my tongue."

I focused on him above the planes of my tits and belly, and the ridiculous apron that would have made me giggle if I hadn't so desperately needed to orgasm.

I wrapped my legs around his shoulders, linking them behind his head, letting him know exactly what I needed.

Him. Right there. For as long as I could stand it. I reached a hand down to grasp the short length of his hair for good measure.

He groaned. "Fuck, Bliss. Harder."

He thrust two fingers up inside my slick core, and I bucked against the sweet intrusion, the stretch too delicious to lie still. Even if he hadn't said anything, I wouldn't have been able to let him go. I pushed down on the back of his head and bucked against his fingers and mouth.

Nash groaned his approval right onto my clit, and the vibrations sent me wild. I moved with him, rolling my hips so his fingers hit my G-spot every time, until I was sure I was going to pass out.

He pressed a fingertip to my ass, edging the tight hole and eliciting a gasp from me. It wasn't a surprise anymore, to be touched there, but how much I liked it still shocked me.

"God, Nash! More."

I ground down until sparks exploded somewhere inside me. My orgasm rolled through me, bringing with it the most intense pleasure. He worked me through it, thrusting his fingers into me until I came down the other side.

So gradually it was almost agony, he withdrew his fingers from my body, and I let go of the vise-like grip my legs had on him.

Realization rushed in. "Oh my God, Nash. I'm so sorry. I shouldn't have done that."

"Wrapped your thighs around my head and held me to your sweet slit like you couldn't get enough of what I was doing? Are you insane? Do that every time. Every day. Fuck. Do it again right now."

He was dead serious. He grabbed my legs, draping them over his shoulders again, and I laughed, kicking him away.

"Go away. I'm all orgasmed out."

He raked his gaze over me, slowing over my breasts and then lower between my legs. "That sounded like a challenge."

He leaned over me and kissed me hard before I could protest. I fell into the kiss, losing my head all over again.

He flipped me to my stomach, and I gasped at the cold marble counter on my nipples and belly. My feet touched the floor once more, but Nash bent over me, kissing my mouth when I twisted my head to the side, and then kissed his way down my spine.

One hand remained on my upper body, keeping me in place the same way I'd held him where I'd wanted him.

The tables had turned, and now it was all about how

he wanted me. A fresh wave of arousal gushed through me, soaking my core.

"Spread your legs, Bliss. I want to see exactly what I'm doing to you."

I widened my stance, my breath switching to short pants of excitement.

"Reach beneath you and touch your clit."

I hesitated, knowing exactly how sensitive it already was.

Behind me, Nash licked his thumb and rubbed it over my ass again. "Do it, Bliss. You can take it."

He had eons of experience over me, and everything inside me wanted to submit to him completely. He grabbed my hand and guided it beneath my thighs. I took over and moved it the rest of the way, so I was touching my clit.

Already sensitive from my earlier orgasm, I let out a cry of pleasure so intense it almost hurt.

"Every time I fuck you like this, this is where I want your fingers, Bliss. This here..." He pressed into my ass. "Is mine to play with. And this..." His cock notched at the entrance to my pussy. "Is mine to fill."

My pussy spasmed, painfully empty and aching for him.

"Yes," I whispered. "God, yes, Nash. Please."

He thrust into me, his dick sliding in without resistance because I was so ready for him. He pulled out inch by inch, then thrust in again, groaning. "Fuck, Bliss. Your body is amazing." He kissed my spine. "*You're* amazing."

I knew exactly how big he was, but I wanted him so bad, and he knew what he was doing to make the thick, solid length of him pleasurable instead of scary.

Like they had a mind of their own, my fingers picked up the pace on my clit, slow rubs becoming frantic desperation as another orgasm built inside me.

Nash gripped my hips, pulling back and then slamming himself inside me. My entire body jolted with each hard thrust, my pussy desperate for more.

"Harder," I moaned.

"God, I love you." He held on, driving home, time after time, until I couldn't take another second.

We both came together, his perfect cock filling me to the brim. I lost track of everything but the pleasure cascading through me, this second orgasm even stronger than the first. I rested my head on the hard counter, enjoying the feel of him on top of me.

Eventually, he stood straight, slowly withdrawing his dick from inside me.

I was too out of breath to move, even though I knew I needed to clean up. "Just give me a second," I said sleepily.

He kissed my shoulder. "Stay there all fucking day if you want to. Nothing beats the sight of my cum seeping out of your cunt."

Warmth spread across my skin. "We probably should have used a condom."

His fingers trailed through the mess between my legs and then back inside me. "I'm not sorry," he whispered. "I kind of hope you get pregnant."

I jerked, pushing up on my hands and twisting to look over my shoulder at him. "You what?"

There was no remorse in his face, just a cheeky shrug. "What? I can't help it. I'm forty. I want kids and I want them with you. I'll wait 'til you're ready, but I'm done holding back. I'm all in, Bliss. I want to be your man. Your husband. The father of your babies."

I blinked at the rush of words. "Sorry, can you say all that again? I think I had a stroke."

He chuckled and leaned in to kiss me. "You heard. I'm not taking it back. So don't ask me to."

As if I would have. I wanted everything he'd just said too. The thought of having his baby filled me with a joy and longing that was so intense it was practically palpable. A baby we could parent with the love and kindness he hadn't had.

But Nash wasn't the only man who held my heart. I caught his hand. We'd all been so irresponsible with birth control. But I already knew my body wasn't made for pregnancy. I was too fat. Doctors had told me that time and time again, at every medical appointment since I'd turned eighteen. They were all friends of my father's and knew my situation with Caleb. There had been a lot of, "You'll be wanting babies when you and Caleb are married, so you need to lose the weight now."

I hadn't even tried.

Part of me knew that it was because I hadn't wanted Caleb's babies.

But I did want Nash's. And War's. And Vincent's.

I bit my lip at the mess I'd made for myself. "War and Vincent…"

Nash kissed my cheek. "I know what I'm signing up for, Bliss. I don't care. I just want you. If you're a package deal, then I'll learn to love them too."

17

REBEL

On a desk chair that was doubling as my wheelchair, I zoomed around Bliss' office, checking things off my to-do list. I'd already straightened up the furniture that had been shoved aside by the police, and I'd picked up everything off her shelves that had been rifled through and thrown on the floor. Now I was up to repair work. Armed with a tube of putty, I diligently patched bullet holes in her dusky-pink walls.

"You do realize you aren't supposed to be slapping that stuff on with a kitchen spatula, right?" War leaned against the doorway, watching me work.

"Didn't have the right tools, and I'm nothing if not resourceful, Warrick."

He frowned at my use of his full name. "What do I have to do to get you to stop calling me that?"

"It's your name."

"Only by law."

I spun around and raised an eyebrow in his direction, sass levels at an all-time high. "Just think of it as your punishment for abandoning me out on that hill when we went to save Vincent."

He groaned. "I told you I was sorry!"

I sniggered at him. Truth was, I was incredibly fucking bored, and picking on War was the only thing keeping me sane today. Without work, I had no idea what to do with myself. My ADHD demanded I do anything other than rest, so I was here, working in whatever capacity I could, until everything went back to normal.

A door opened somewhere nearby, and I glanced over my shoulder toward War. "Who's that?"

War took a half step back into the corridor, his smile widening at whoever he saw. "Hey, baby girl."

"Don't come down here, Bliss!" I shouted. "I'm not done with your surprise."

But War had a look in his eye. "Nuh-uh. Come down here right now, because I need your lips on mine."

"Oh, gag me with a spoon," I complained as my best friend appeared in the doorway and put her arms around her man.

One of them anyway.

I continued making immature vomit noises while they kissed with zero care that I was sitting right there. War grabbed the back of her head, holding her tight to him while he kissed her deeply. Bliss melted into him like he was the sun and she was a popsicle.

I had to look away before she started dripping on him.

Truth was, I was jealous as hell of Bliss and all the nasty, kinky, dirty sex she was having. I could do without the relationship side, but it had been way too long since anyone had looked at me with even a remote scrap of interest, let alone the way War, Nash, and Vincent lusted after her.

"Where's my freaking harem when you need 'em?" I muttered to myself, going back to my walls. But the unre-quited tingling inside me didn't dissipate. "War?" I asked louder. "Is Fang seeing anyone right now?"

At least the question got his tongue out of my best friend's throat. "Seeing anyone?"

"Yeah, you know, like, dating?" Bliss grinned. "You've heard of that, right?"

"Sure. But Fang is..."

"Hot as fuck?" I supplied.

"I think you're the only one who thinks that, Rebel." War turned back to Bliss, putting his hand to the back of her neck to draw her in again.

I couldn't stand another PDA. "Is everybody else blind? He's tall. Solid..."

"Scariest man I've ever seen in my life?" Bliss supplied.

"With a face only his mother could love," War added.

Irritation rolled up my spine. "You're an asshole. He's your friend. If Bliss spoke about me like that, I'd have to get my knuckles out."

"You're adorable," Bliss added in quickly.

She was right. I was.

War shrugged off my accusations. "Kid, Fang is the first one to tell you that he's nothing to look at. It doesn't matter. He could still get his dick sucked by any old club slut, but he chooses not to because he knows they're all scared of him."

"That's...sweet?" Bliss asked as a question more than a statement.

But it just made my heart hurt. A feeling I didn't like all that much. It set off an alarm bell in my head. If I was the only one Fang was fucking, then a bond would form. No matter how much I liked the tree trunk of a man, and the things he could do to my body, I wasn't getting tied down. So now I had to take him off my rotation.

Men were fine for sex, but anything more than that would end in tragedy. I'd seen my mother do it too many times before. I'd scraped her off so many bathroom floors and held her while she cried and threatened to kill herself over the latest man who'd left her high and dry. For as long as I could remember, that had been our routine, me parenting her.

It was what happened when you were birthed by a thirteen-year-old. You grew up together, and if you were as unlucky as I was, you became the more mature one by the time you were about six.

"Rebel?" Bliss snapped her fingers in front of my face.

I pulled my attention out of my memories and back into the room. "Yeah, sorry. What?"

"I came in here to get you for a meeting with Nash. We need to make some decisions about Psychos."

"Not just to dry hump your boyfriend, then?"

Bliss' cheeks went pink. "That was an added bonus."

War pushed her up against the doorway and ground his pelvis against hers. "Nobody told me dry humping was on the menu. Mmm."

I spun my office chair around, so I didn't have to watch, and grabbed my clipboard from the desk, adding two more points. Sand the walls. Buy paint. I drew some little love hearts on the paper, just to kill time while they slobbered all over each other like dogs in heat.

"I thought you were just coming to get Rebel," Nash called dryly, his footsteps echoing through the party room as he approached. "Now I see you were just coming to come."

"Didn't quite get that far." War grinned, stepping back and holding a hand out to Nash. "Hey, bro."

Nash pulled him in for a one-armed hug, and Bliss took the opportunity to scoot away from War and perch on the edge of her desk beside me. "Sorry," she whispered. "We haven't seen each other much lately with me taking care of Vincent."

"War hasn't been over doing that too? Aren't he and Vincent...you know...sorta together as well?"

Bliss shook her head. "Not anymore, apparently."

I frowned. "They were good together. He okay with that?"

"Right now, all I care about is that they aren't trying to kill each other and that nobody is in any danger."

Nash caught the end of our whispered conversation. "Except, I'm worried someone is in danger." He stared at Bliss.

She blinked. "What, me?"

"Yeah, you. Have you forgotten that you owe a small fortune to a drug dealer and now we have no way of paying for it?"

My stomach gave an unpleasant lurch. "We hadn't paid up front for the product the cops confiscated?"

Bliss shook her head. "Only for about a third of it."

"Fuck," War swore. "How much do we need?"

"More than I even want to think about," Bliss replied with a heavy sigh.

Her phone beeped in her hand, and we all watched her check the screen.

She groaned. "Great. Just great. That's Axel's landlord reminding me we only have thirty days to clear out his house." She buried her face in her hands. "I'm not going to lie, guys. I don't know what to do about any of this. So if anyone has any ideas..."

Nobody said anything.

The silence was deafening. Bile churned in my stomach, a sick feeling creeping its way up into my chest. Psychos was my home. I didn't have a husband and kids. All my friends were here. If I didn't have Psychos, then what did I have?

It was a confronting thought to have, but I refused to let it bury me. "We'll ask for an extension. A payment plan. And then we'll throw the parties without the damn drugs and just encourage irresponsible drinking instead."

War sniggered. "We could do a themed shot night? All Cocksucking Cowboys and everyone could come in assless chaps..."

I snorted on a laugh at the idea of everyone walking around in nothing but assless chaps. They were supposed to be worn over jeans, but at a Psychos' party, jeans were never part of anyone's attire.

"We could do Sex on the Beach cocktails and dump a load of sand in the middle of the party room for everyone to have sex on..." I threw in with a laugh.

Bliss spluttered on nervous laughter. "Oh God. There'd be sand in every nook and pussy..."

We all cringed at that, and I chimed in with the story of how I'd had sex once with a random guy beneath the piers on the beach that ran the length of Saint View and

Providence. I provided them with all the graphic details about an elderly woman walking a dog and stumbling across us, and how the woman told me I should seek Jesus, while the guy just continued pumping into me.

I did a great impersonation of the woman's high-pitched screech and lecture, while everyone rolled on the floor laughing.

Later, in the Psychos' parking lot, I waved off Nash's, Bliss', and War's offers of a ride home, explaining I'd already booked an Uber to come collect me. Bliss frowned at me, but I didn't like feeling like a bother. They all had things to do...probably each other...and I was too independent to rely on other people's generosity too much. Nash had already driven me home a couple of times, much to my discomfort.

I never wanted to be a burden, the way I'd been to my mother for my entire life.

I leaned against the wall, using my crutches to support my bum ankle, and flicked through my social media while I waited for my Uber. It was a never-ending roll of disappointment. An old high school classmate with a husband, three kids, and a swimming-pool-sized mortgage. Some family I didn't particularly care about. A couple of guys from War's club. I tapped the 'memories' button, and it brought up a bunch of past posts that either I'd made or been tagged in on this day in years gone by.

A photo of me and Axel, our arms around each other, floored me. The pain punched through me as sharply as if someone had hit me with a closed fist.

I'd been doing good since the funeral, trying hard not to think about him. But now, seeing that photo, his face smiling at me from the image, just reminded me how fucking unfair this life was. He'd been too young to die.

Losing him had made me consider ending it as well.

It would have solved a whole lot of problems.

Instead, I went and let Fang fuck the desire out of me. Now I couldn't even do that.

My head filled with dark thoughts, until a black car pulled into the driveway. I hobbled over to it, and the driver lowered the window.

"You the Uber?" I asked. I hadn't bothered checking the description of the car when I'd had the app open.

The man behind the wheel was young, like most Uber drivers, but the car was abnormally nice for the ride-sharing app. I'd been picked up in hundreds of different cars, but not one of them had been a BMW.

And not one of the drivers had been wearing a sharp, expensive-looking suit. Before he could get a word out, I laughed at my own stupidity. "You aren't the Uber driver, are you?"

He gave me an all-American grin. "Nope."

"You're the guy trying to get Bliss to sell this place, aren't you?"

He paused for a second, then nodded. "The boss sent me around."

"That his car?"

"Sure is."

"Nice. But you're out of luck. My boss just left. And she's changed her mind about selling." It was a lie, and maybe Bliss would be cranky with me when she found out, but I couldn't let her sell Psychos. It had been Axel's baby. That had to mean something to her, the way it meant something to me.

The man raised his eyebrow. "That's a shame."

"For you, maybe."

"I would have got her a good price. I'm good at my job."

It was my turn to raise a brow in his direction. "That so? Awfully cocky of you to say."

He shrugged. "Not cocky when it's the truth." His gaze raked over me slowly, before returning to my face. "What do you do here?"

"Serve drinks."

His gaze darted toward the building again. "Topless?" He gave that cheeky grin again.

It was one I probably should have slapped off his face. Except that was exactly what I did, and I'd never been ashamed of my body. "Sometimes I'm fully nude."

He groaned and stuck his hand through the window. "I'm...Callum."

"You forget your name for a second there?" I asked, sassing him because he was cute.

"I was still thinking about you nude waitressing."

We both laughed, but then another car pulled in, and a woman called out. "Uber?"

I gave her a thumbs-up. "Be there in a second."

Callum stuck his hand out the window, his phone held in his fingers. "Can I get your number?"

I shook my head. "Nope."

He clutched a hand over his heart. "Don't tell me you have a boyfriend?"

"Nope. I just don't give out my phone number."

"Can I ask you out on a date now then?"

"Don't date."

He nodded. "To be honest, I don't either. That was just my way of getting you into bed."

I put my hands on the doorframe and leaned in. "That so?"

He grinned. "You wouldn't be disappointed…"

My spine tingled at the idea of getting naked on the back seat of this man's expensive car and letting him fuck the worry right out of me. With Fang out of the action, I was now a bed buddy down, and this guy looked as good as any.

The Uber driver beeped her horn impatiently.

On a whim, I held my phone out to him. "Give me your number. Maybe I'll call you if the batteries on my vibrator die."

He laughed and punched in his number. "I hope you do. We could have fun together. You're cute. And funny."

That was me. Queen of the funny or awkward story, told always when things got too tough. Queen of picking up random men when I didn't want to think about my life anymore.

Right now, I really didn't want to think about how completely and utterly fucked my best friend was. Or that she might be closing the one place that had ever felt like home.

18

BLISS

*I*t was another five days before I answered my phone. But when I finally did, my father sounded furious. "Bethany-Melissa Arthur."

Vincent looked over sharply from his position sprawled across his bed. His torso was bare, because having anything on it rubbed on his wounds. But other than that, he was healing well and itching to get back to work. But he frowned at me now. "I don't like him talking to you like that."

I waved off his overly protective concerns, but of course he didn't budge. So, I got up and paced away to the door, opening it, and then closing it behind me. "Hey, Dad," I tried again, faking a chirpy voice in the hopes of defusing his anger. "How are you? Vincent is doing a lot better if that's why you're calling."

"I'm glad to hear that, but you know it isn't. The realtor called. They said you missed your meeting with them. Again."

I leaned back against the wall. "I know. Sorry."

My father's voice softened. "I told him you were ill and rebooked for next week. Don't miss this one, okay? Did you find the paperwork they asked for?"

I hadn't. The email was still sitting guiltily in my inbox because I hadn't decided what to do. My gut was saying to sell the business. Which was why I kept making appointments with the realtor.

My heart kept saying not to. Which was why I kept missing said appointments.

I didn't know where the paperwork they wanted was. Definitely not in my possession. But going through Axel's house was probably the place to start.

I'd been dodging that, choosing to play nurse with Vincent for the best part of a week instead. But I also had the email from Axel's landlord, stating that since the cops had finished their investigations, we had thirty days to get his stuff out before they got new tenants in. I'd already wasted a lot of those in avoiding the place.

How anyone could want to live in a house that someone had been murdered in was beyond me. But it was probably the case for more houses, especially in Saint View, than anyone knew.

"I'll find the stuff, Dad."

"Good. Family dinner on Sunday night? You can bring Nash if you want." He paused and then cleared his throat. "Or Vincent... Or...War, did you say his name was?"

I tried to hide my laughter. "Yes, it's War."

He sighed. "Bethany-Melissa, don't laugh at me. I'm trying to understand, but I don't. Are they all your boyfriends?"

Oh Lord. Even I didn't know the answer to that. If I

didn't understand exactly what we were, then there was little hope for my sixty-year-old father. "We haven't exactly put a label on it. But I would like for you and Nichelle and the kids to get to know them. All three of them."

"They're all important to you?"

"Very."

I imagined him staring out the window of his office that overlooked the spacious backyard and swimming pool in the house he could no longer afford. His eyebrows would be furrowed together, and he'd be shaking his head in confusion over the daughter who had apparently shunned traditional relationships to shack up with a couple of thugs from Saint View and a rather intense man with a house in Providence.

"They aren't jealous of each other? You...spending time with each of them, I mean?"

A blush heated my cheeks. I understood my father's curiosity, but we were dancing dangerously close to talking about my sex life, and that was one conversation I would have much preferred not to have now. Or at any point in the future for that matter.

I took the easy way out and changed the subject. "So, Sunday at six? I'll bring dessert. Something full of chocolate and horribly unhealthy."

"Your siblings will be thrilled. See you...all four of you...then."

I smiled softly as I hung up. He might have been the aging CEO who hadn't been able to move with the times quickly enough to save his business, but he was trying to understand this. It only made me love him that little bit more. Not many men his age would have even tried.

A bit of guilt seeped in over missing the meetings he kept setting up for me. I had a feeling his own business failings were playing into that, and he was trying to get me out before Psychos dragged me under. He was probably right. Without the drugs and the parties, Psychos wasn't a business that I could afford to keep losing money on. Maybe that meant selling it and moving on. Finding some other way to help my family. What I'd been doing so far certainly hadn't helped anyone much, even if I had fallen in love with the place.

I wandered back into Vincent's bedroom and sat on the edge of his bed.

He instantly moved his hand into my lap, and I threaded my fingers between his. His hands were so much bigger than mine. I felt tiny around him and War and Nash.

His thumb brushed the back of my hand. "I'll come with you. To Axel's house."

I glanced up at him. "You're so supposed to be resting."

"I'm rested. If I lay here any longer, I might…"

"Might what?"

He got up off the bed and padded barefoot across the carpet to his closet. "Never mind. Let's go now."

He pulled open the closet door and stepped inside so I could no longer see him. It was weird and abrupt, even for him, but he was right. I needed to quit sticking my head in the sand and get this over and done with.

We met again at the bottom of the stairs, Vincent pacing anxiously back and forth across the entranceway.

"Are you okay?" I picked up my purse from a rack by

the door. "I'll be fine by myself. Or I can call Nash or War to come with me if you aren't feeling well."

"Let's go."

Okay then.

He opened the driver's-side door to my car and waited for me to get in before stalking quickly to the other side. He slipped in, placing his hands on his thighs. His shoulders were suddenly rigid, his spine ramrod straight.

I wasn't going to ask again if he was okay, even though tension radiated from him in waves. On the drive from Providence to Saint View, I pondered everything I'd said in the last hour, wondering what it was that had sent him into this weird, tension-filled silence. I analyzed every word, but by the time I parked in front of Axel's house, I still had no answers.

Seeing the dried blood on the front porch obliterated all worries about whatever Vincent was upset over.

My throat suddenly felt tighter than if hands were around it, squeezing the life out of me.

Did nobody care? That a man had been murdered right here, his blood still clinging to the old wooden porch while people walked by on the street on their way to the bus stop or to meet friends?

I stumbled out of the car and hurried up the steps, Vincent hot on my heels. I clamped my teeth together, pressing them tight until my jaw ached while I fumbled with the front door key. It had been in the package of Axel's things I'd picked up from the police, and I'd added it to my key ring so I wouldn't lose it. But now my fingers wouldn't work, and I dropped the set twice until Vincent covered my hand with his and guided it toward the lock.

I don't know why I was surprised when the door

opened and I got my first glimpse into Axel's home. But I ignored all his belongings and rushed straight for the kitchen, opening the cupboard beneath the sink and rifling through it, shoving bottles and cans out of the way until I found what I was looking for.

Without a word to Vincent, I stormed back outside, rubber gloves on, scrubbing brush and cleaner in hands. I yanked the lid off the bottle, pouring the entire contents onto the bloodstains covering the porch, before dropping to my knees with the scrub brush.

The liquid frothed up, forming a lather, and I worked it harder, scrubbing at the dark stains that was all I had left of my brother.

My eyes stayed dry. I'd cried too much, and I was more sick of tears than anything. If I never cried again for the rest of my life, I would be happy.

Vincent came back out to the porch, and my scrubbing turned frantic. "Don't try to stop me."

He dropped down on his knees, his own scrub brush clutched in his fingers. "I wasn't going to."

I glanced over at him, his forearms flexing with the effort of scrubbing the blood off. He didn't have to do it. In fact, he probably shouldn't have, the motion had to be hurting the wounds on his chest. But just like he wouldn't have been able to stop me, I wouldn't have been able to stop him.

We scrubbed silently, side by side, only the scraping sounds from our brushes and cars driving by on the street to be heard.

Sweat dripped down my face, and my arm ached by the time I rocked back on my heels, surveying our work. "It's not much better, is it?"

Vincent shook his head sadly. "Bloodstains don't come out easily. These have been here for a long time."

It was my fault for not coming earlier.

I stood stiffly, dropping my brush and taking my gloves off. A numbness spread through me, but I welcomed it because it took away the sting. "Forget it. Come on, let's go find what we came here for. I'm taking anything that looks to be personal or sentimental, but the rest can stay. The landlord can give it away or throw it out. I can't be here in this house, surrounded by his things, but knowing he's never coming back to them." I turned sad eyes on Vincent. "I hate this."

His fingers wrapped around mine. "I hate it for you."

He pulled me toward the door, and I followed him, drawing strength from the warmth of his touch.

The front door opened into a small living area with a couple of couches pointed at a big-screen TV which was by far the most expensive thing in the room. The rest of it was mostly cheap, functional furniture—a couple of stools at a breakfast bar, a coffee table bare of anything but a used coffee mug, a rug that looked like it could use a deep clean. Vincent tugged open the drawers on the TV unit but only found a PlayStation and a handful of games.

"Take that, if you want it," I told him.

He shook his head. "No, thank you. We could take it to Psychos though. I bet it would get some use there. We could use the TV there as well."

I nodded and left him to pack it up while I wandered through the rest of the house. I paused at Axel's bedroom, the bed a mess of crumpled sheets, the scent of dust in the air. A pile of clothes spilled out of a laundry basket on the floor, which I bypassed, not knowing if they were clean or dirty. There was a chest of drawers that held nothing more than sloppily folded T-shirts and shorts, so I moved on to the closet. It was scarce compared to the closet full of clothes I'd seen Vincent take from this morning. It took me less than a minute to poke through the hangers of jeans and jackets. His shoes were thrown in haphazardly but held nothing of interest either.

Vincent came back, holding a pile of papers. "I found these in the kitchen. It could be what you need."

I took it from him, leafing through the first few pages of the thick pile, then nodded. "This is good. There's some stuff with Psychos' logo on it. We can go through it at the house. I don't want to be here any longer than we have to. There's nothing else here anyway."

Vincent followed me, hefting the TV into his arms even though I frowned at him because he wasn't supposed to be doing any heavy lifting. He'd packed the PlayStation and its associated controllers, cords, and games into a laundry basket, and I dumped my pile of papers onto the top so I could carry the whole thing in my arms.

"What's that?" Vincent asked, nodding toward a red envelope corner that had poked out of the pile. It stuck out like a sore thumb among the otherwise white and cream papers.

I wriggled it out, and for a second, a tiny smile lifted my mouth. It had Axel's name written on the front and a message on the back, confessing the sender's undying love. "A Valentine's Day note, by the look of it. Cute that he kept it."

"Are you going to read the inside?"

"Should we?"

Vincent turned over the envelope. "I don't normally advocate for breaching someone else's privacy and reading their mail. I'm sure that's actually a crime. But…"

"But we've all come to realize I know almost nothing about my brother's life, and right now, anything that could provide some insight might help?"

He nodded. "He's not here to get upset with you either. So that's an added bonus."

I traced a finger over the loopy letters. "The writing is childish. I'd bet it's from high school. No grown woman still puts hearts over her I's." Still. I was dying to open it, if only to know my brother a little better, so I was glad Vincent wasn't going to judge me for it.

"No postmark," I commented.

"All the more reason to read it. If Axel had an ex-girl-friend who lived locally, then that's someone the police should have investigated, don't you think?"

I did. Instead, they'd wasted all their time searching for gang-related motives where there clearly were none. I slipped my fingers inside the torn edge of the envelope and plucked out the single sheet of paper within. I unfolded it, and the same neat but young-looking writing on the front of the envelope covered the page. I glanced at Vincent uncertainly because the further we went into this, the worse it sat with me.

He gave me a single nod of encouragement.

I gazed down at the paper and read it out loud so he could hear.

"Axel. You can't keep ignoring me. What we did…It meant something to me. I know it meant something to you too."

My stomach flipped. Everything after Axel had hairs

standing up on the back of my neck. This was nothing like the cute love note I'd been expecting. I read it again silently to myself. "What do you make of that?" I asked Vincent.

"Unrequited love. Could be a motive for murder."

"Do you think?"

"Could also just be an ancient schoolgirl crush. We have no way of knowing how old that letter is. And you're right, that writing looks like a high schooler. I'm going to assume your brother wasn't in the habit of dating high schoolers when he was nearly forty."

The thought made me sick. "God, I hope not!"

"So it's probably ancient history, but that doesn't mean we should ignore it. His past relationships should be investigated."

I groaned. "Rebel has insinuated that he was a manwhore. He probably had a little black book of hundreds. What are the odds the useless Providence Police Department would have investigated each and every one of them?"

"They might have considered it but come to the conclusion that a more recent relationship would be more likely."

"Or just decided that investigating his death wasn't worth the effort." It was the sad truth. "We should at least ask Nash if he had any relationships that ended badly." I shoved it back into the pile and then picked the whole thing up again. "We can drop this all at Psychos on the way home. No point taking it home first and having it clutter—"

Vincent let out a tiny noise, and I looked up at him sharply. He turned away quickly, moving toward the door with the TV, but not before I saw the sweat beading across his forehead and the paleness of skin.

I hurried to catch up with him, his longer legs covering more ground than mine did. He got to the car first but leaned so heavily on it I dropped my basket and ran the rest of the way to his side, grabbing the TV from his grip before he could drop it. "You are not okay!"

He breathed heavily, and I knew he was really feeling it when he let me shove him inside the car. I watched him tilt his seat back and close his eyes. I stood there so long, he eventually opened his eyes again and said, "I'm fine. The corner of the TV caught my stitches. It hurt a tad."

"A tad? It hurt enough that you nearly passed out."

"Like I said, it hurt a tad."

Typical Vincent to downplay his pain. I was sure that in his old line of work you had to get used to it, but his threshold seemed unusually high. He hadn't complained once about his injuries since we'd found him. He'd stubbornly refused any sort of painkillers. This was the first time I would have even known he was injured if I hadn't seen the state his body had been in when we'd found him.

His color started returning, so vaguely satisfied I wasn't going to have to call an ambulance, I went back to putting the things in the rear of the car. I hid how heavy and awkward the TV was, biting down on my lip, and shoved the basket of video games and paperwork in after it.

"Home," I said, getting in behind the steering wheel. "This stuff can wait."

He didn't argue, which only worried me more.

Back in Providence, I didn't think twice about leaving

a TV in the back of my car. I probably didn't even have to lock it, but I did anyway, leaving everything we'd grabbed from Axel's place where it was so I could focus on getting Vincent back up the stairs and into bed.

I jogged around from my side of the car to his, draping his arm over my shoulders so he could use me as support.

He stiffened when I wrapped my arm around his waist, and I glanced up at him in confusion. "Am I hurting you?"

He shook his head. "No."

We moved together through the entryway and up the wide staircase to his bedroom. He let go of me immediately, kicking off his shoes before lying down.

"What can I get for you? Soup? A drink? There's always the painkillers you haven't touched."

"I don't need any of those things."

The way he said it, and the fact it was Vincent with his literal ways, made me think he did need something after all, just not the things I'd offered. I reworded my question. "What do you need?"

But he rolled over and closed his eyes without answering.

I stood there for a long moment, waiting for him to say something, but he didn't. I closed the door quietly, more worried about him now than I'd been with his body cut to shreds.

19

VINCENT

The tension in my body was near unbearable. It seeped its way into every muscle, every sinew, every vein, spreading around like a disease I had no control over. It hurt a thousand times more than the crude stitches across my chest, disturbed from their healing by the unfortunate poke from the TV.

It's not the TV making you feel that way. You do know that, right?

Scythe still hadn't gone away. It had been days, and normally by now, his voice in my head would have faded, but if anything, it had only gotten louder. To the point where he was downright chatty.

It was the most unpleasant few days of my life.

Again. Not me that's making you uncomfortable, Vinny-boy. You don't really need me to spell it out for you, do you?

I squeezed my eyes shut and tried to sleep, but he was as loud as a cheer squad.

It's called horny, V. HORNY. You need to get laid.

"I've gone this long without sex," I muttered. "I'm just tired."

That why your dick's hard, too?

I really hated Scythe.

Things have changed, V. The line between us isn't as strong as it used to be. You know it. I know it.

"No. I'm still the dominant. You'll fade. You always do."

That was before Bliss. I can't go now. Just the same way you couldn't. I have double the reason to hang on, because I have War too.

He was wrong. He would fade. This was just one of the ways he tortured me, always getting in my head, confusing me. When my head swirled the way it did right now, he had the chance to take over and push me out.

He was trying to trick me, and if I let him, he'd win. Maybe for good. Scythe couldn't be trusted. Not for a minute.

You're so dramatic. If I could, I'd roll my eyes at you.

"I'm sleeping."

Just trust me on one thing. The way you feel right now has nothing to do with me or your injuries. We both know you've had worse. It has everything to do with the way you want Bliss. Just think of it as the sexual awakening most of us had as teens. You're just a decade late.

I ignored him, and his voice finally quieted. But the relief I'd expected didn't come. If anything, it only got worse when downstairs Bliss started singing along with the radio. Her sweet, albeit out of tune, voice carried up the stairs, sounding nothing short of perfect to my ears.

I closed my eyes again, breathing deeply, trying to

find some sort of meditative state where I didn't think about her constantly.

About the soft smiles she gave me every time she walked in to place her hand against my forehead, checking for a fever.

About the way her sweater pulled tight over her breasts and the gentle swell of her belly and thighs.

About everything I'd seen her do with Scythe and War, even if I only had a secondhand account of it through Scythe's memories.

About how I'd heard everything she'd done downstairs with Nash just a few nights ago when she thought I was sleeping.

I turned my face into my pillow so it smothered the agonizing groan of pain it was to have Bliss but not really have her. Not in the way a man wanted a woman who seemed so perfect she had to have been made just for him. I thumped the mattress a few times for good measure, taking my frustration out on something soft that wouldn't injure me any further than I already was.

The door cracked open, and Bliss rushed in, kneeling on the other side of the bed. She put her hand to my hair, smoothing it back. "Hey. Wake up. You're having a nightmare."

The problem was the nightmare wasn't when I was sleeping. It was the everyday torture of being around her and wanting her in a way I didn't quite know what to do with except it felt like a need that would take control if only I let it.

Her warm hand touched the skin at the back of my neck.

I gave in and let the desire take control.

In a split second, I had her on her back, her wrists pinned to the bed and my legs straddled either side of hers.

Beneath me, her eyes went wide, and her mouth formed a little O of shock. "What are you—"

"I want to kiss you."

She paused, searching my eyes, no hint of fear at the fierce way I held her. "Okay, but you're going to hurt yourself."

"I'm already in agony for wanting you. Because that was a lie. I don't just want to kiss you. I want every inch of your body, Bliss. I want all of you, and it's torture to lie here with my body on fire because of it. I was hoping getting out of the house today would do something to quell it, but it didn't. It only made it worse."

She sighed. "Vincent, let me go."

I let go of her wrists instantly and moved off her so she could sit up. But I hated it. I hated that she didn't want me the same way she'd wanted Scythe. He was charming, I knew that. Confident. He picked up on the cues she gave whereas I could only wait to be told. My head swirled, a confusing mess of emotions and feelings that hurt physically as well as emotionally.

"Lie down."

I did as she said, because I always did. She'd wanted me to rest, so I'd done it because she seemed to like taking care of me.

She straddled me the same way I'd done to her a moment ago.

My breath stalled in my lungs at having her center right over the bulge that tented my pants.

Bliss leaned forward slowly, placing her hands either

side of my head so our lips were inches apart. "I've waited a really long time to hear you say you want me, Vincent."

Vincent. Not Scythe.

She sat back and took her sweater off, letting it drop to the floor beside the bed.

There you go, big boy! You're at home plate! You're gonna swing and hit a home run!

I really needed to get some tablets that would silence him.

Rude.

But even Scythe stopped running his mouth when Bliss pulled off her T-shirt, leaving her only in a cream bra that barely contained her breasts. My gaze drew down her body, sweeping over the curve of her cleavage before moving lower to her belly and her skirt rucked up around her waist.

I pressed my fingers into the blankets, wrapping the fabric around them to anchor me to the bed.

She reached down and covered my hands with hers, slowing unfolding each finger from the covers and then bringing my hands up to rest on top of her thighs. She leaned in again, this time, her lips brushing over mine in a kiss so soft I barely felt it. "Touch me."

Her words opened up a storm inside me, one I'd so desperately wanted to lose myself in for as long as I could remember. No other woman had ever made me feel the way Bliss had. Nobody had made me want them like she did.

I slid my hands up her thighs and out to her rounded hips, stroking my fingers over the skirt. "I don't know what you like," I said simply, the honest truth because that was all I had to give. "What if you don't like it?"

It was a deep need, this feeling of wanting to please her, take care of her, and make her feel good. I knew War and Scythe knew what to do, but I couldn't read social cues like they did. I relied on people telling me or showing me what they needed from me.

Bliss knew.

She slid her hands up her hips and waist, giving my hands a path to follow. She inched them around to her back, unsnapping the clasp on her bra, but let me catch it when it fell open and draw it off her shoulders and down her arms.

Her breasts fell into her hands, heavy and full, over-spilling her fingers. She watched me, her eyes hooding as she ran her fingers over her nipples. She squeezed them and played with them until she was unconsciously rocking over my erection.

I took over, replacing her hands with mine, a shot of pleasure spearing through me when she kept up the rocking but closed her eyes and threw her head back. A little sound of pleasure escaped from her and my erection spasmed. Without thinking about it, I raised my hips to meet her, only to be frustrated that I wasn't met by her warm center but my pants and her underwear.

"Too many clothes," I muttered, abandoning her breasts to raise her skirt higher so it settled around her waist, out of the way. Her panties shot another explosion of lust through me. Lacy cream to match her bra. Practical but somehow still sexy enough to keep my attention, with little patches of sheer lace that showed everything she had behind the barrier.

I had the sudden urge to kiss the skin I could see through it.

"Take these off." I tucked my fingers into the sides of her panties.

She smiled. "You want me naked?"

"Please."

She lifted her leg off me to stand at the side of the bed and shimmied out of the panties and skirt. She instantly moved to resume her position on top of me, but I grabbed her wrist, holding her in place.

"Stop. Just let me look at you."

A blush spread across her entire body, and I chased it with my gaze, watching it spread over her chest and the swells of her breasts as well as creep up her neck and into her cheeks.

She shivered.

"Are you cold?"

She shook her head. "Not at all." She studied me. "What do you want, Vincent?"

"To make you feel good."

She smiled softly. "Then touch me here." She took my hand, guiding it to the junction of her thighs. "Feel how good you already make me without even trying."

My fingers came away slippery with her arousal.

I brought them to my mouth and tasted her. Her juices exploded on my tongue, and I instantly craved more. I rolled to my side, so I was on the edge of the mattress, and hooked my arm around her thigh. "Spread your legs." Then I looked up at her face. "Please."

Her fingers brushed through my hair. "You don't have to keep saying please."

"It's polite."

"You don't have to be polite when you want to lick my pussy, Vincent."

She widened her legs, then pressed lightly on the back of my head, guiding me to exactly where I wanted to be. I darted my tongue out, the tip just barely protruding into the top of her slit and flicking the little bean hidden there.

"Oh!" Her fingers tightened in my hair.

"Tell me you like it." I needed to hear her say it because I didn't trust myself to understand her otherwise.

"I like it. Do it again."

I pushed my tongue in once more, rubbing it over the same spot that she seemed to like, because she gasped again.

I kept doing it. Over and over, each lick of my tongue gliding over the little bud then deeper, tasting the arousal between her folds. Each stroke brought a sound of pleasure to her lips.

"Oh. Oh. Ohhh."

I tightened my grip on her thigh, hugging it while I buried my face deeper and deeper between her legs. I wanted more. To explore her fully.

I dragged her up onto the bed. "I need to lick all of you."

"Will you let me do the same to you?"

I swallowed hard. "Yes."

She nodded. "Take your pants off."

My heart hammered against my chest, but I did it, pulling the gray sweatpants down, exposing my erection.

Her gaze narrowed in on it, then slowly rolled back up my body. "Your shirt too."

I sat and pulled it off, folded it neatly, and added it to the pile of clothes on the opposite side of the bed.

She smiled and shook her head. "Trust you to fold the clothes as you take them off."

It just made sense to me. Then they wouldn't get wrinkled. "I don't want to talk about folding the clothes."

She smiled again.

Heat surged through me. "I don't want to talk about clothes either. Especially when we aren't wearing any."

It was the first time I'd been naked with a woman. Until Bliss, I'd never had any desire to do so. I understood now why Scythe and other men liked it so much. Her body did things to mine, and she wasn't even touching me. The taste of her on my tongue was fading, and I wanted it back. "I want to lick your little slit again," I said. "And more."

She nodded, pink in her cheeks. "Can I...do something?"

"Anything."

"You shouldn't say that."

But I meant it. She could do anything to my body because it no longer felt like mine. I was hers. Wholly and totally, and if she wanted to touch me, then I wanted her to do it too.

She spun so she was facing my feet and straddled my head.

I groaned when her wet, pink pussy opened up above me.

I wrapped my arms around both her thighs, clamping her into place, because I didn't want her moving. "Why didn't you do this before?" I licked her opening, teasing it with my tongue.

"Because I'm clearly a very stupid woman."

She wasn't stupid at all, not in the least, but I was too busy licking my way through her center to answer.

She dropped forward onto all fours, her hands sinking into the mattress either side of my thighs. I spread her ass cheeks, giving me full access to every intimate part of her, wanting to taste every inch because I'd seen how much she liked it when War and Scythe did it.

Before I could, warmth wrapped its way around my erection, and I froze. "What are you doing?"

The warmth went away. "Licking you. Do you want me to stop?"

Arousal leaked from my tip. "No."

She let out a little laugh, and the wetness of her mouth returned.

I let out a hiss at how good it felt, her tongue flicking along the veined underside before pulling back to then engulf me with her whole mouth, the head of me pressing against the back of her throat.

I closed my eyes, reveling in the feeling while I speared my tongue up into her gaping channel, licking away every ounce of her arousal only to find more and more of it the longer I did it. Her juices coated my lips, my chin, my nose. I would have bathed in it if it had meant I was making her feel good.

"More," she moaned, her words coming out in stuttered, incoherent gasps rather than full sentences. "Fingers. More. Fuck me." She lifted off my face and reached between her thighs to plunge two fingers up inside herself.

I watched in fascination as they disappeared inside her body, only to come out gleaming before she did it again.

After three times, she grabbed my hand, moving it to her core to take over while she rocked herself over my face.

I pushed two fingers inside her.

"Oh God!" she screamed, then shoved her mouth down over my dick, sucking and working me thoroughly, her voice muffled.

I added another finger, loving the way her body stretched to accommodate them and how her thighs around me shook. I found her clit again, licking it frantically. The walls of her pussy spasmed and pulsed, and she pulled off my erection to arch her back.

"Yes!"

Her legs trembled, and her body clamped down around my fingers.

"Keep doing that," she moaned.

So I did, until she flopped down hard on my chest and stomach, her legs still splayed out around my head.

"Oh shit, Vincent! Your chest!"

Pain pierced through, but I couldn't have cared less.

I didn't want her to move.

Ever.

She tried to get off me, but I pinned her there with one heavy hand to her lower back, and the other clutched around her thigh. I raised my head to continue licking her wet core, and her little whimpers turned into cries of need once more.

"I want to see you," she moaned, licking at my cock again. "Let me go."

I didn't want to, but I did.

I was rewarded with her spinning around and sinking down onto my cock.

The pure pleasure that rocketed through my body was like nothing I'd ever known before. She lifted off, then dropped back down, the pleasure intensifying with every movement. I dug my fingers into the fleshy parts of her hip, the instinct to thrust up to meet her taking over.

She dropped forward, placing a kiss to my chest just below my stitches. "I'm sorry."

"I can't even feel it, Bliss. Not when I'm inside you."

She kissed her way all around my wounds, her lips taking away the sting, until she got to my mouth. Her face hovered over mine, and she smiled. "Hey." Then she leaned down and kissed me, her mouth gentle and sweet.

It was slow and tentative, not at all matching the way our lower bodies moved. Her tongue pressed inside my mouth, and I closed my eyes and kissed her back because it had been far too long since I'd gotten to kiss her.

I grasped the back of her head, pushing my tongue into her mouth, wanting her to taste herself on my lips.

"Touch my clit," she murmured against my lip. "I want to come with you."

I moved my hand between us and slowly rubbed her clit until her eyes closed.

She rode my erection, rocking her hips and meeting my thrusts from below while she kissed me.

The world spun around me until all I could see was her and the rounded fullness of her pretty face, the heavy fall of her breasts, and the slow curves of her hips and behind. She was the most perfect thing I'd ever seen, and all I could do was mutter, "Mine."

Not Scythe's.

Mine.

She nodded. "Yours."

It was the word that sent my body over the edge. Everything inside me tightened, heat and pleasure coiling at the base of my spine before spilling inside her body.

She groaned, clamping down on my erection like she had my fingers, her slick juices coating both of us. Her pussy fluttered, drawing my orgasm out, until we were both spent.

She pulled off me this time and rolled onto the bed beside me, deftly avoiding my injuries. She placed her head on my shoulder.

I tightened an arm around her. "I would have dragged you back on top of me if you'd gone any farther than right here," I said quietly, inhaling the scent of her hair.

She sighed contentedly. "I'm too boneless to go anywhere. Pretty sure my legs couldn't hold my weight."

She looked down our bodies though, at the sticky, sweaty mess we'd created. "I need to get up and have a shower though."

I twisted onto my side, cradling her like she was the most precious thing in the world. Because she was. I drank in the sight of her glistening breasts and shining pussy. My cum seeped from inside her onto her inner thighs, and without even thinking about it, I swiped my fingers through it and then up inside her again.

"Oh," she moaned, pressing against me. "What are you doing? I can't come again, I'm exhausted."

I shook my head. "I want it inside you. Always."

She went pink, turning her face into my neck. "That shouldn't sound as hot as it just did."

"You said you were mine." My fingers were still inside her. I had no intention of moving them.

She shifted up onto an elbow, her gaze searching mine. "I am yours. But you know I'm also Nash's and War's and..."

I swallowed hard. "Scythe's."

She nodded.

I shook my head. I knew Nash and War wouldn't give her up for me, just like I wouldn't give her up for them. They made her happy, and that was all I wanted for her. I wouldn't ask her to choose.

But Scythe was a different story. If he was here, then I wasn't. He was always there in the back of my head, just waiting for his moment to take over. But now that I'd had her, in all the ways that a man could want a woman, I knew I couldn't give her up. I'd fight. Harder than I ever had before, because tasting her once was never going to be enough. "He's gone," I lied.

Bliss bit her lip and pulled away. "Okay."

You're an asshole. It doesn't have to be like this.

But it did. I watched Bliss pad her way into the bathroom, my essence deeply planted inside her.

I was stronger this time. Enough that I could ignore his tricks and taunts.

I wouldn't give her up.

20

BLISS

*S*unlight peeked around the edges of the blackout shades in Vincent's bedroom. I rolled away from the heat of his body and drew a blanket tight around my naked shoulders. I was deliciously sore from hours of sex with him. He'd been insatiable, taking me several more times through the night, always waking me and politely asking permission, which I'd given up readily, my body aching for him in the same way.

Making up for all the time we'd lost while Scythe had been in control.

My heart gave a pang, thinking about him. It was something I didn't know how to fix. I wanted Vincent. I'd wanted the man since he'd first walked into my life.

But having Vincent here meant Scythe wasn't. I'd sworn black and blue that I hated Scythe, but I didn't.

I was in love with him.

The thought he might not come back broke my heart in two.

I wanted to be with Vincent, but he was the one who

was keeping Scythe away. And maybe I just needed a minute to process that. I got myself a coffee and stood with it at the huge floor-to-ceiling windows, brushing aside the drapes so I could see out into the landscaped yard.

With Vincent out of commission, the grass was overgrown. Weeds poked through the soil in the plant beds, and there were piles of leaves that needed raking from the last of the fall season.

I put my coffee mug in the dishwasher and went upstairs to get dressed. I found a pair of sweatpants and a T-shirt, threw on my trainers, and jogged back downstairs, suddenly excited over the prospect of getting my hands dirty and a full day of work to keep my confused mind busy.

In the back garden shed, I found the lawn mower, edger, and an array of gardening tools. I got right to work on the weeds, wanting to give Vincent time to wake up before I started the lawn mower up. I pulled on a pair of too-big gloves and got busy, joyfully yanking weeds out and throwing them in a compost bin.

That took me a while, and by the time I was done, it was midmorning. I glanced up at Vincent's bedroom window. "I know you were up all night giving me multiple orgasms, but nobody should sleep 'til noon." I checked the fuel level on the lawn mower and pulled the cord.

I grinned at the roar of the engine, and after a little fiddling to set the cut level, I was off. I shoved in my AirPods and walked up and down the yard, watching the uneven lengths of grass fall away to leave behind nice, short blades. It was oddly satisfying, and when I reached the side of the house that led to the front lawn, I just kept going because it was so soothing. Lady Gaga sang in my ears, and I grooved along with her, swaying my hips and ass to the beat as I pushed the mower along. A white van parked up on the road in front of the neighbor's house, and for a second, I thought it was War in his club van, but when no tall, handsome biker got out, I quickly lost interest in favor of mowing another line.

It was the lawn mower's fault I didn't hear the van door open.

It was Gaga's fault I didn't hear the man's boots on the ground behind me.

All I felt was the terror when he clamped one arm around my middle, one hand over my mouth, and dragged me backward, shutting me inside the vehicle before I even got a chance to scream.

21

SIREN

*E*verything would be fine. There was absolutely no need to panic. Promises and agreements meant something in this world, and they couldn't be gone back on without a fallout that nobody would want.

Especially not War.

I repeated it over and over in my head as I puttered around the cabin that would one day be mine. Or maybe we'd build something bigger. We'd definitely need a couple of extra bedrooms once kids came along.

But I liked War's cabin, and it would be the perfect little love nest once he woke up to what was right in front of him.

My molars ground together, but nobody liked a woman with frown lines, so I made a conscious effort to relax my face and went back to silently chanting my mantra while I cooked. All of War's favorite things. Loaded potato skins for a starter. Steak for the main course .

Chocolate mousse, whipped cream, and me for dessert.

I used to cook for him all the time. I knew what he liked, both on his plate and in his bed. Before she died, my mother had drilled into me the ways to keep a man happy, and good food and good sex had been at the top of her list.

It had worked just fine until Bliss had come along.

There'd been other women, of course. I wasn't naïve enough to think that a man like War wouldn't have some wild oats to sow. But he always came back to me. He knew the rules and how this had to play out between us. He could go do his thing, but I would be the one on the back of his bike. As the son of the prez, that seat was a throne. Whoever sat there would one day be queen.

It had been promised to me since I was a tiny baby.

But now Bliss was fucking the whole thing up.

At first, I'd thought her completely harmless. Just another pussy he'd stick his dick into before he came back.

But it hadn't happened. And every time I saw the two of them together, some little part of me died.

He looked at her the way he was supposed to look at me. Since she'd come along, he hadn't even fucked any of the other girls, and everybody was talking about it in hushed whispers behind my back.

It was downright embarrassing. And worse when my father cast me disapproving glares whenever War and Bliss were around, like it was my fault he'd gone and gotten himself a girlfriend from outside the club.

I stabbed a long-handled spoon into the sauce I was making and flinched when the hot liquid sprayed up and sizzled on my skin. I didn't even like cooking, but it was time to take back what was mine.

I checked the time and blanched at how late it was getting. War was due back from a 'business trip' as the men all called their illegal runs. I'd asked Hawk to give me the one-hour heads-up, and though it had cost me a blow job, he'd agreed. That was less payment than I'd been expecting, but I knew he was no fan of Bliss and War either, so that had probably played into it.

I trotted into War's bedroom and stripped out of my clothes. Quickly, I lathered on a pretty-smelling lotion, studying my body in his mirror as my hands traced over every inch of exposed skin. Tight, high tits. Flat, toned stomach. Tanned and waxed all over so I was silky smooth.

I pinched at the skin on my hips and was satisfied I hadn't put on any weight. No man wanted a fatty, my momma had always said. She'd been a tiny stick figure of a woman, and I'd spent my entire life on a diet to try to emulate her appearance.

War should want me.

He shouldn't be passing me over for a woman who couldn't even look after herself.

I put on a silky robe and tied it around my waist before letting my hair out to cover the marks on the back of my neck that Hawk had left there during the blow job payment. "Suck his dick like this, and you'll have War back in no time," Hawk had uttered as his dick had slammed into the back of my throat and my eyes had watered. "Just be the little slut we all know you are."

He'd been right. It was the best I had to offer.

The roar of a motorcycle engine outside had me

hurrying back into the kitchen, checking everything was ready, and fluffing up my hair.

His boots thumped heavily on the front porch steps, and then the door swung open. "Bliss? Whatever's cooking in there smells amazing."

"Hey, baby," I murmured, ignoring the jab that came from him assuming I was that other woman. I couldn't let that in. I just had to be better than her. "Welcome home."

War stopped in the doorway. "Siren?"

He wasn't pleased to see me. I could tell just from the way he said my name.

"What are you doing here?"

"Whatever you want me to." I tugged the tie on my robe, letting it fall aside and expose my naked body beneath.

War didn't even look down. "You need to leave."

A stab of hurt poked through my steel defenses. "I made you a meal. All your favorites. I thought you'd want a good home-cooked meal and sex after being away last night."

He sighed. "I do. I feel like shit for saying this but I think you already know. I don't want those things from you, Siren. I'm with Bliss. If anyone is giving me those things, it's only going to be her."

Irritation crept up my spine, but I shoved it away, knowing men didn't like women who weren't soft and gentle. I walked over to him, dropping the robe on the floor as I went. "Baby, you're the prez. You get to take any woman you want. I'm here, offering. Where is she?"

I grabbed the sides of his cut and dragged him in, pressing my naked body against his chest.

He stepped back like I'd electrocuted him. "Get your clothes on and leave, Siren. Please."

I'd been here once before, sent away by his fat bitch. I wasn't doing it again. I slammed my hands onto my hips. "No. I've been really good about whatever you're doing with her, but I've had enough. People are starting to talk. You owe me, War."

His eyes narrowed. "Excuse me? I owe you? For what? You've been given everything you've ever wanted your entire life because you're Gus' daughter. That doesn't extend to me."

"You know very well it does. We're promised. We have been since we were babies."

He ran his hand through his hair. "I'm calling that off."

My mouth dropped open. "What? You can't."

"Says who, Siren? Our parents made some sort of stupid pact twenty years ago. We went along with it as teenagers because back then, we were too powerless to stop it."

"I never wanted to stop it!" I threw myself at him again, desperate for him to look at me the way he had when we were younger.

He shook his head. "Maybe I didn't either. But I'm grown now. So are you. You don't want me when I want somebody else."

I shook my head. "It doesn't matter. I know what my role involves, and I know it's not your fidelity. You owe me a marriage, War. A title. All the guys expect it. They're never going to accept an outsider with their prez! You know this!"

A silence fell over us. "I love her, Siren."

I threw up my hands in frustration. "What do I care about love? I don't need that from you."

He shook his head. "Bliss is going to be my old lady, Siren. I'm not changing my mind."

He picked up my robe and handed it to me without so much as a glimpse at my nakedness. "You need to leave." He moved toward his bedroom but then he stopped, one hand on the doorway. Without turning around, he added, "When Gus leaves to go back to his chapter, I think you should go with him."

He disappeared into the bedroom, leaving me gawking at a closed door.

Slowly, anger boiled inside me, bubbling up, each one bringing with it new hate for the woman who'd stolen my man.

I wasn't giving up without a fight.

Not after everything I'd done to get here.

22

BLISS

I wrapped my arms around my knees, fighting back the uncontrollable shivers. Cold seeped up through the metal floor of the van, spreading through the rest of my body. I was tense all over, muscles aching from hours of being in the dark without enough clothes on.

My throat ached from screaming for the first few hours I'd been locked inside, but I'd given that up when it had become clear nobody was searching for me.

I squirmed against my restraints, but every movement only made the knots tighter, until the splintering rope cut the skin around my wrists and ankles. I'd managed to shrug out of the hood they'd shoved over my head to drive me here, but the restraints weren't budging.

Voices from outside the van set my heart pounding again. I screamed out for whoever it was to help me.

The driver's-side door opened, and a man got in without glancing at me. He whistled cheerfully as he started up the engine, like he was completely oblivious to my pleas for help.

Anger stirred inside me. I'd sworn off crying, so fury was all I had left. "You asshole," I seethed. "You piece of cowardly scum! You can't even look at me!"

The man put the van into first gear, and we moved forward with a jolt. With one hand on the steering wheel, he changed the radio station until it was playing golden oldies. He sang along with the tune, his voice deep and rich.

I took in every detail I could about the man, my brain confused with fear. "Where are we going?" I asked quietly, giving up on screaming again to avoid permanent damage to my vocal cords.

I didn't expect an answer.

"You'll see. It's time for a reunion."

I didn't know what he meant by that, but I wanted to keep him talking. "You could have at least let me get dressed up to meet whoever it is," I complained. "There's still grass clippings all over my shoes, and I probably reek of sweat."

He chuckled. "He won't care. Reeking of sweat comes with the job."

His voice was so familiar. Too familiar. The voice of my dealer.

I should have realized earlier. I kept coming back to the white van outside my neighbor's house, and my initial reaction to it, when I'd assumed War had been behind the wheel.

It was someone from his club. I'd always suspected it, but now I had proof.

And I was pretty sure I knew exactly who it was.

"War trusts you, you know," I said bitterly.

Gus glanced over his shoulder. "What makes you think War isn't the one who set this entire thing up?"

A few weeks earlier, I might have fallen for that. My self-esteem had been so low after Caleb that I could have easily believed that everything between me and War had been fake and leading to this moment.

But Gus had waited too long to play that card. He'd waited until three men had put me back together, stood me on my own two feet, and then planted themselves firmly behind me, always having my back.

Bliss had a backbone that Bethany-Melissa never could have dreamed of.

Gus must have seen the disbelief in my expression and sniggered. "Fine. I wouldn't have fallen for that one either. Boy is so pussy-whipped by you, it's embarrassing."

I ignored him. "You aren't going to get your money by dragging me off into the middle of nowhere to kill me, Gus. I thought you were smarter than that?"

His eyes darkened in the rearview mirror. "Oh, sweetheart. Aren't you a precious sunflower? You think I'm taking you somewhere to kill you?"

"Aren't you?"

"Not at all. Like you said, that would be pretty silly of me, wouldn't it? Hard to get my investment back if you're dead. No, no. We have other plans for you." He spun the steering wheel, and the van bumped over the uneven ground. "We're almost there. Play nicely and you can be delivered back to your pretty house in Providence within the hour."

"And if I don't? You already said you aren't going to kill me."

He shrugged. "If you don't, I do kill you, then I go through this whole process again, with Rebel, or your pretty stepmother, or maybe even your little sister, until one of you agrees to pay back the debt you owe, Bliss. *You*. Don't act like I'm the bad guy here. Nobody forced you to take product you couldn't keep safe."

He was right. I'd made my bed, and now I was going to have to lie in it, no matter what options he presented me with tonight. My stomach lurched at the thought of Verity sitting in the back of this van, cold and terrified because of something I'd done but then hadn't had the guts to set right.

I did owe Gus this money. It would be cowardly of me to back out of our deal now.

I straightened my shoulders as much as my restraints would allow and steeled myself mentally for whatever was about to come.

"We're here," Gus announced a moment later. He parked the van and then squeezed between the two front seats, bending over so he wouldn't hit his head on the roof. He crouched in front of me and started untying my restraints. "You ready to make a deal and get your business back on track? I don't have to remind you of the alternative, do I?"

I forced myself to nod. "I'm ready."

"Good girl."

War had said that to me once, and I'd practically thrown myself on top of him with desire. When Gus said it, my skin crawled.

He grabbed the handle and slid the door across.

Cool night air and the brightness of another car's headlights hit me in the face. I blinked a few times, trying to clear the spots from my eyes.

Jerry's laughter turned my blood to ice. "Look who it is. The daughter I never wanted."

I fought the urge to vomit and snuck a glance at Gus. "What is he doing here?"

"Well, that's rude. No, hello Daddy for me?" Jerry sneered.

Bile rose in my throat. "You aren't my father."

His eyes narrowed and his slimy gaze raked over my body, so disgustingly slow. "No, sweet cheeks, I'm not. Which is all the better for me, because I'm fucking horny now that you got your mama put away."

"You so much as touch me and I'll—"

"You'll do nothing but take it," Gus interrupted. "Remember our deal?"

I widened my eyes at him. "How does this pay off my debt to you?"

"I bought you," Jerry said, delight in his voice. "For the exact price of your debt. And all it cost me was my rainy day stash of cash and a couple sluts for his club back east. So now you owe me instead. You'll come work your sweet cunt on my blocks until you've paid back every cent you owe. And when you aren't busy with your legs open for men on the streets, you'll service my every need. Just like the good little slut your mama was."

I shook my head, panic clawing at my throat. "No chance in hell."

"Should have thought about that before you let your mama take the fall for you, shouldn't you? Someone has to take her place. If it's not you, Gus supplied me with a

list of viable alternatives. I believe you know all of them."
He started listing names, stabbing at his fingers as he
rattled them off. "First there's Rebel, the best friend. No
tits, but I hear she's a firecracker. I bet that applies to in
the sack as well. Second, there's the stepmommy.
Nichelle. Pretty name for a street whore, isn't it?" He
licked his lips. "There's always sweet Verity..."

Hate surged within me for the two vile men who
stood in front of me.

I refused to feel that same hate for myself. Which was
exactly what I would feel if one of the women I loved was
hurt because of poor decisions I'd made.

"What's it to be, daughter dearest?" Jerry taunted.
"And don't go thinking you can run to your boyfriends...I
know all about them. Did a little digging after they left
me for dead on my steps a few weeks back. I wanted to
make sure I had something to hold over their heads if
they ever came for me again. Vincent's on the run from
the po-po, huh? Escaped from Saint View Prison,
maximum security?" He gave a slow clap. "I have to
admit, I was impressed. I'd hate to have to turn him in.
Takes a lot of skill and smarts to be able to pull off something like that. Would be a shame for it to all be in vain,
because you can't play by my rules." He stepped forward,
grinning at me like the Joker, and put a hand on my
breast.

I flinched away, but he only grabbed me harder,
twisting my nipple fiercely. "Ready to pay your penance?"

Knowing I had no other choice that I could live with, I
dropped my gaze to the ground and nodded.

Jerry let me go. "Go home and get cleaned up. I don't

like my sluts dirty. You start on Friday night. Don't be late or I'll go looking for a replacement. You understand?"

I understood.

I'd stepped right back into my old life. The one that had always been destined to be mine before my brother had diverted the course.

But destiny didn't work like that. I'd been born for this world. Thinking I could escape it was a fool's errand.

I left Bliss a few blocks from the house where I'd snatched her and turned the van around, whistling along with the tune on the radio. In my mirrors, I laughed at her pathetic form, shoulders slumped as she trudged along the dark streets. I tapped the thick envelope of cash inside my jacket pocket and gave myself a pat on the back for killing two birds with one stone. I'd gotten the money I'd been owed. And I'd humiliated my daughter's rival, which was really just a bit of fun for me. But I would happily tell Siren and get some daddy-daughter bonus points for it. No matter how grown she was, she was always going to be my princess.

My phone rang, connecting through Bluetooth to the car's speaker system, and I glanced at the name on the display. "Speaking of... Hey, sweetheart. What are you up to?"

Muffled sobs came down the line.

I gripped the steering wheel tighter. "Talk to me. What's happened? Where are you? Are you hurt?"

If anyone had so much as laid a finger on my daughter, I would kill them. She was the only family I had left. Her mama was dead, and though Army hadn't been my blood relation, he was the only one I would have considered a brother. There were bitches who'd come crying to my doorstep with swollen bellies, claiming their bastard spawn were mine, but Siren was the only child I recognized.

She was the princess to my throne, and once she married War, she'd be untouchable.

As her father, so would I.

"He..." She sobbed some more.

"He what? Who?" My muscles coiled tight, ready to fight.

"He's not coming back, Daddy. I tried. I swear, I did everything I could. He doesn't want me."

I shook my head, realization dawning. "Of course he's coming back. Men like War need time—"

"He's in love with her!"

I paused. "He said that?"

"Yes!"

"Fuck."

Siren's wails grew louder. "What am I supposed to do now? Everything I've done is so he and I could be together. If he knew what I—"

"Stop. Don't you say another word. There are ears everywhere at that club." I sighed, running a hand through my hair.

War was a sentimental sap like his old man had been. Army had fallen hard and fast for Fancy. He'd walked around like a stupid, lovesick fool and shirked all his responsibilities. She'd been the one who'd come between me and my best friend and why I'd been forced out to start my own Slayers chapter.

Army had always chosen Fancy over me. Now his kid was choosing pussy over my daughter, disrespecting me and the entire club by going outside the agreement his father and I had made.

I wasn't having it.

"Where's War now?" I ground out the question between gritted teeth.

Siren sniffed into the phone. "His cabin, I think. I was there, too, but he called Aloha to come pick me up. I refused and walked back to the clubhouse."

She'd always been stubborn and headstrong. Even as a little girl with dirt on her nose, she'd never thought twice about shoving her hands on her hips and glaring at me when I'd gone out to work on a bike without her. Her blond pigtails had been so fucking cute and at complete odds with the fierce kid she'd been.

She was still mine to protect though. Always had been.

"Wait in my room at the clubhouse. I'll deal with War."

"What's the point?" she wailed. "He's made up his mind!"

But she didn't know the cards I held. Neither did he.

I cut off her squawking by hanging up and gunning the engine on the van, pushing the vehicle faster until the looming iron gates of the compound could be seen through the darkness.

Fang nodded at me from his sentry post and opened the gates so I could drive through. I bypassed the clubhouse and took the track through the woods that led to War's private cabin.

My lip curled at the sight of it.

I'd built the motherfucking thing. Slaved over every log and nail. I'd had to give it up when it had been 'suggested' I go start my own chapter. Property was easily lost when nobody wanted you around.

I parked up out front and took the steps two at a time to slam my fist against War's door.

He opened it, took one look at my face, and his expression instantly darkened. "Siren's been in your ear already, huh? Didn't take her long to go tattle."

He turned around, leaving the door open so I followed him inside.

"She called. Cryin'."

War nodded. "I told her she was never gonna be my old lady."

My fingers flexed into fists. "That's not the deal we made."

He crossed his arms over his broad chest and glared at me. "We never made any sort of deal. You and my dad might have thought you could play matchmaker for your own personal gain, back when you were friends, but he ain't here no more, and now it's me calling the shots."

"So, what? You're just gonna make some fat bitch from Providence your old lady? While she's shacked up with the Psychos' bouncer? While she's fucking Nash Sorensen? Where's your backbone, War? You want a woman who's sleeping around on you?"

"As opposed to Siren who was sucking Hawk's dick just two nights ago?"

I glowered at him. "You show her the respect she deserves, and she'll be faithful to you. You know how it is. Put a ring on her finger and she's yours forever. You can still fuck whoever you want, but give my daughter the respect she deserves by putting her on the back of your bike."

War opened the refrigerator and took out a beer, cracking off the top. He didn't offer me one. "Go home, Gus. I've been on my bike for two days straight and I'm done with this conversation. I'm gonna have a drink, a shower, and then I'm going to see my girl."

He turned his back, effectively dismissing me.

Cheeky fucking brat. I still remembered when he was in diapers.

"Your girl has a problem," I threw at him.

War spun around. "What's that?"

"She's got a big drug debt, doesn't she? Cops raided the place. Took her product. Now she's got no way of paying it."

War took a sip of his beer, eyeing me over the top of the bottle. "What would you know about that?"

It was time to play my ace card, even if I'd technically sold it to Jerry. "It's me she owes the money to."

War swallowed thickly. "You're Axel's dealer? Since when is your chapter into drugs?"

"Since your old man pushed us out of guns. Gotta make a living somehow. Axel's been a client of mine ever since he started running those parties at Psychos. Bliss took over the contract when he died."

"So cancel her debt."

I strolled over to the coffee table and picked up a

motorcycle magazine from the neat pile stacked in the center. "I could," I bluffed. "For a price."

War shrugged. "Fine. Just so happens we just sold a big shipment. What does she owe and I'll pay it out. You take cash or check?"

I shook my head. "Neither. You know you can't take club money like that, and your cut ain't gonna even touch the sides of what she owes. But in any case, I'm not interested in your money. All I want is a favor." I held my poker face steady, knowing full well that Jerry had already paid out Bliss' debt. War obviously didn't know that, and I was fairly sure Bliss wouldn't tell him what she'd agreed to do to pay her way out of the hole she'd got herself into.

I was more than happy to be paid for her debt twice.

"Get on with it, old man," War bit out.

"I'll forget all about her debt if you renew the deal your father and I made and marry Siren. Fuck Bliss on the side all you want, but Siren becomes your old lady. It's the respect she deserves after waiting this long for you. You and I both know it. It's what your guys are expecting too. They're already iffy on your presidency, do you really want to give them further reasons to go against you? Your father left all of this for you, but you're on the knife's edge of losing it. Siren is a good girl. She knows her place and the role of an old lady, especially old lady to the prez. She'll help you."

War opened his mouth to respond, but I held up a hand. "Take a couple days to think it over. I think you'll see I'm right."

I opened the refrigerator and took a beer from the

shelf inside. "Thanks for the beer. Let me know what you decide. But, son? I know what your dad wanted you to do. He knew this world a thousand times better than you do. Might do well for you to actually listen for once."

24

BLISS

*O*n my lonely walk home, I plotted all the ways I
could kill Jerry.

Firebomb his trailer. Run his car off the road, or
better, mow him down while he stood on the sidewalk.
Push him off the side of a boat because I knew he couldn't
swim.

While each gave me a small hint of glee, there was an
easier option.

Tell Vincent what he'd done. What he'd threatened to
do to the women in my life and to him. Telling Nash or
War would probably end in the same result.

But with every step I trudged, each one bringing me
closer to the home I'd made and the men who were probably wondering where I was, reality sank in.

I couldn't ask them to take a life for me. Not even
one as pathetic and cruel as Jerry's. Especially not after
everything Vincent had gone through recently. He was
barely healed from the last time he'd tried to fight one
of my battles. We were barely off the cops' radar. I

wasn't going to put any of us back on it. I still needed to sleep at night. I had a conscience that wouldn't allow the words, "Can you kill for me?" to come out of my mouth.

I'd find another way out. I didn't need rescuing.

War's bike and Nash's Jeep were both parked in front of the house, and I stood in the shadows at the edge of the property, staring at the lawn mower which still sat in the same place I'd left it. I had no idea how I was going to explain any of this to them. I'd been gone for hours without a word.

My ringtone broke the silence around me, but it was muffled and far away. I patted my pockets on instinct, but I already knew I didn't have it. Through the darkness, half buried in grass clippings, the screen light flashed.

I hurried across the lawn and plucked it up, hitting the answer button when I recognized Vincent's number. "Hello?"

There was silence for a moment, then Vincent cleared his throat. "Where are you?"

His voice had a deadly low tone that sent shivers through my body, each and every one of them centering inappropriately between my thighs.

I forced a fake cheerfulness into my voice. "Hey! I'm just out front. I'll be in in a minute."

The line went dead, and within seconds, the front door slammed open and all three of them shouldered their way out the door. All I could do was stand there and let a tidal wave of man engulf me.

After the day I'd had, I didn't even want to fight it.

Nash got to me first, grasping my chin and tilting it so his gaze could search my face. "Where the hell have you been? Vincent called me hours ago when he couldn't find you."

I moved away from his touch, not wanting to look him directly in the eye while I lied. "I went out. With a friend."

They all stared at me, clearly waiting for more information.

"Sarah from my old daycare center," I explained. "She was over this side of town, so she picked me up." I held up my phone guiltily. "I just found my phone outside on the lawn. It must have slipped out of my pocket when I was mowing the lawn. I didn't even notice."

Nash moved in and pressed a kiss to my hair. "You scared the shit out of us."

"Sorry," I whispered, hating every syllable. I hated lying to them, but the truth wasn't a viable option either.

Vincent didn't say anything. He just watched me quietly.

We let War and Nash walk away, but Vincent and I lingered behind. I reached a hand out to him and squeezed his fingers. "You mad at me too?"

He didn't say anything. His fingers just tightened around mine.

I swallowed thickly. Vincent might have been an extremely literal person, and sometimes, he didn't pick up on tone or actions like other people did, but he wasn't stupid. And I was almost certain he knew I was lying. I had the sick worry that he might have even known I was lying to protect him.

I changed the subject. "Did you all eat dinner? I know it's late, but I'm hungry."

There were shouts of agreement from the kitchen, so I pulled away from Vincent, not wanting to see the confusion in his expression. I went straight to the pantry and started taking various things out. "We could do burgers? Maybe a pasta?"

War moved in behind me. "What if I want Bliss on a platter? Is that on the menu?"

"I'll take a serving of that," Nash called out from the dining room table. He made a show of sweeping his arm across the tabletop, like he was sending imaginary plates and cutlery flying. "Right here."

Vincent remained quiet.

War glanced over at him, and his smile fell. "None for you, huh?"

Vincent folded his arms across his chest but didn't say anything.

War shook his head. "This is so fucking weird."

"War," I said quietly.

But War shook his head. "What? It is weird. One minute he's cracking jokes and crawling into bed with us, and now he's just…" He turned his back, but not before I saw the hurt on his face.

He missed Scythe.

I had feelings for both Vincent and Scythe which had softened the blow, but Vincent didn't have the same feelings for War that Scythe had. Even I could see the difference. That electricity that had crackled between War and Scythe was completely gone now.

Nash and I exchanged a glance, the awkwardness palpable.

War put down the package of pasta he'd been holding. "I'm gonna get out of here for a bit. I need a minute."

I didn't want him driving when he was upset. We all watched him leave, the front door slamming behind him.

"Go after him," Vincent said quietly. "Please."

I glanced at Nash who nodded as well.

"War!" I ran through the house and out the door, but he was already on his bike, tires spinning as he peeled out of the driveway.

I spun around, ready to sprint for the entryway where I'd last seen my car keys. Vincent was standing there with them already in his hand. He tossed them to me.

I nodded at him and hit the button on the key fob that unlocked the doors, before diving behind the wheel. I caught up with War two streets away at a red light and relaxed a touch. With him in my sight, I could get some relief from the sinking feeling in my stomach that everything I had was about to implode, beginning with him. When the light turned green, I followed him back into Saint View. But to my surprise, he didn't take the turnoff for the compound. Instead, he continued straight, and a few blocks farther, he turned left at a sign for the hospital.

He stopped his bike, and I parked in the space beside him, lifting a hand in a wave through the windshield.

He came over to the driver's-side window and leaned down, surprise on his face, like he'd been off in his own world and hadn't noticed me behind him the entire way. "What are you doing, baby girl? You follow me here?"

I motioned for him to step back so I could get out.

He held the door for me, and I took his hand. "You visiting your mom?"

"If they'll let me in at this hour. Might have to sneak in."

"Can I come with you?" Something inside me kept urging me on, pushing me to stick by his side.

He didn't say anything, but his fingers entwined with mine, and he tugged me toward the brightly lit entrance. Silently, I trailed him through the mostly empty corridors, my heart hammering when we got to the nurses' station. War turned around and put a finger to his lips to silence me. On his cue, we ran past the empty desks and slipped inside the same room Fancy had been in the last time I'd been here.

I shut the door quietly behind us, and we stood at the end of the hospital bed, gazing down at the woman who looked so incredibly peaceful she could be dead.

"Is there any point in me even coming here anymore?" he whispered to me. "She's been like this for weeks. She's as gone as Scythe is." His helmet dropped to the floor at our feet, and he engulfed me in his arms. His lips dropped to my hair, and he inhaled a shaky breath. "I don't know how to be around him. Vincent. Scythe... A week ago he and I...fuck." He pressed his face into my neck. "I fucked up so bad with him, Bliss. The last things I said to him, that night before the guards beat the shit out of him? They were horrible. I was hurt and angry...I don't want that to be the last things I ever get to say to him."

I gazed up at him. "Say it to Vincent. It might get through to Scythe."

War shook his head. "Oh my God, this whole thing is insane. We're talking about them like they're two different people!"

"I think even to them, they are."

Agitated, he ran a hand through his hair. "It's probably for the best that he's gone."

I gawked at him. "I love Vincent, so I'm torn in a

different way, but how can you say that? You never want to see Scythe again? You're just going to forget about him like what the two of you had didn't happen? I still see him in Vincent, but I don't think you do."

"If he's not around, my club can forget who I was with him."

I shook my head sadly. "And then what? You just go back in the closet? Pretend that side of you doesn't exist?"

He ground his teeth. "It doesn't. Not without him. This is better for everyone. The club will get what they want. Their straight-as-a-ruler president, who likes to fuck women in front of them all, just so everybody knows he's never getting a boner over any of them."

I hated the thought of it. Of him being someone he wasn't because people he called family didn't accept him the way he was. "You're the prez, War! Since when do they get to dictate who you love? They want you to marry Siren too. Are you going to do that?"

I'd thrown the accusation out there in the heat of the moment, not really meaning it because I knew how War felt about me. It was warm, and sweet, and everything that was good.

All of that disappeared in his cold silence.

I jerked my head up. "War?"

War swallowed thickly, then dropped his lips to mine. "I don't want to lose you the way I lost my parents. And the way I lost him."

I clutched his arms tighter, my fingers digging into his biceps. "Why would you?" I whispered, my stomach sinking because I already knew the answer.

"Bliss..." His face was a mess of devastation.

My throat swelled with the words I knew he was going to say. "Just say it."

He said them slowly, like he hated every word and was forcing each one between his teeth. "I'm marrying Siren."

From the bed, and the tiny frail woman in it, came a croak, barely louder than a whisper but full of fury. "Like hell you will."

25

SIREN

I shoved my hands on my hips and surveyed the room again, my fingers itching for something else to clean. I'd already picked up every item of clothing from the floor and tossed them into a laundry basket, made the bed, tidied the side table, and dusted the lamp, all while ignoring the stack of magazines with naked women on the covers.

"The walls," I muttered, grabbing my cleaning cloth and scrubbing at the range of marks that had probably been there for decades. "God, I don't even want to know what's touched these."

My father's room at the clubhouse had been disgusting, but I cleaned when I was stressed, so I'd been grateful for the distraction.

Someone banged on the door. "Siren! You coming outta there? I got a job for you," Hawk called, his voice slurred.

"Does it involved me sucking your dick?"

He laughed, and the door moved, like he'd slumped

against it. "Sucking it. Riding it. Whatever you want, baby."

I rolled my eyes. Hawk was hot and dynamite in bed. But he was the vice prez. He'd always have to answer to War, so what was the point in me hanging out with him? He wasn't going to get me where I was going.

I refused to even consider that War had been serious when he'd said we were done.

My father would talk him around. I just had to wait for him to get home.

"Fuck's sake, Hawk," someone else grumbled from outside. "Get outta the way."

Speak of the devil. I dropped the cleaning cloth and flung open the door. My father stood on the other side, glaring at Hawk who threw me a wink and mouthed, "Later."

I ignored him and grabbed my father's arm, yanking him inside the room and slamming it behind him. I turned big eyes on him, all doe-like and innocent because that was how I always got my way with him. "Well? Did you talk to War?"

He walked to the mini refrigerator in the corner and pulled out a beer. He pressed a kiss to the top of my head. "I told you I'd take care of it. And I did. Have I ever let you down?"

I squealed and clutched his arm. "He agreed?"

He nodded. "You'll be his old lady. I made him an offer he couldn't refuse."

Everything inside me collapsed in release. War was everything my mother had wanted for me. She'd spent my entire childhood telling me stories about how one day, War would be mine and we'd rule the club together, joining the Saint View chapter with our own, the way it was always meant to be. War's dad hadn't been able to see the sense in a merger like that, but my father was smarter. He'd had Mom teach me how to cook and clean for War, how to always be ready for him, whenever he wanted me, and how to please him. All the things she'd done to nab my father.

I'd done them all. After she'd died, I tried even harder, because I couldn't let her or my father down.

I'd really thought I'd screwed it all up when War had sent me packing, but now everything was back on track and how it was supposed to be. I threw my arms around my father and hugged him tight. "Thank you, Daddy."

He patted my back roughly. "Of course, princess. You know I always take care of you."

A cheer went up from the men in the common areas of the clubhouse, so loud and boisterous I stepped out of my father's arms to crack open the door and peer out.

"What the hell is that all about?" Daddy asked, pulling the door wide. "Sounds like someone's team just won the Super Bowl, but it ain't football season."

I followed him back down the hall where everyone stood in a tight group, jumping up and down or hugging, wide grins from ear to ear on every person.

Queenie went over to the speakers and cranked up the volume, swaying her ample hips in time with the music that blasted through the speakers. Reba McIntyre crooned the song "Fancy," and everyone sang along at the top of their lungs.

I grabbed a drunk Kiki as she passed by on the way to the bedroom with Ice. "What's happened?"

She clutched my arms and spun me around. "Didn't you hear? Fancy's awake!"

I froze. "What? I thought the coma..."

Kiki shook her head and shouted. "It's a miracle! War just called and said she's awake and talkin'. Isn't that a miracle, Siren? I thought she'd kicked the bucket for sure."

So did I.

Ice bellowed for Kiki to hurry up, and she wriggled her eyebrows at me with a grin and hurried after him, leaving me standing there in shock.

"Well, that's not fucking good," my father muttered.

I shot him a sharp glance, warning him to keep his big mouth quiet. "Don't even think that in here," I hissed beneath my breath. He should have known better, considering he'd given me the same warning not long earlier and I hadn't even been around the other club members.

Realizing we were drawing suspicion, I plastered on a fake smile and rushed in to join the celebration, hugging Queenie, who had tears pouring down her face.

"I can't believe it!" she said over and over. "I prayed, you know. Every day, that the good Lord would let her come back to us."

I nodded.

She gave me a boisterous hug that near cracked my smaller frame, but when she pulled back, she gave me a stern look. "What are you doing here, girlie? You should be by your man's side. He's gonna need you now."

She was right. If I was going to be War's woman, then I needed to be by his side now. Everybody here would expect that of me. I pushed away the swirling nerves inside me and squeezed Queenie's hand. "I'm on my way now, just wanted to see if any of you had a message for Fancy. I can pass it on for you."

Queenie's eyes overfilled with tears again. "You just tell that sleeping beauty that I can't wait to see her. I'm gonna go start cooking so she has a freezer full of meals when she gets home from that hospital. All her favorites. Nothing but the best for her."

I swallowed thickly and nodded.

The women would do that for me once I married War. They'd love me, the way they loved Fancy. And War would love me the way Army had loved his mom. It was all within my reach. So close I could feel it on my fingertips.

I slipped outside to my bike and grabbed my jacket and helmet from the saddlebags. The engine roared beneath me, and I let the vibrations rumble up through my body, shaking loose the worries that this was not how the plan was supposed to go. That didn't matter. I could swerve. Pivot. None of that was worth thinking about right now when my man needed me by his side.

The ride to the hospital sent cool night air gusting into my face. It cleared the cobwebs, leaving me with a better focused mind and only one goal.

Be there for War, in whatever way he needed me. He might have sent me away from the hospital before, but now it would be different. Fancy was awake. He wouldn't be so upset, and he'd want me there to hold his hand and make him feel better.

I just needed to get to him.

I pushed the bike harder and faster, taking turns at breakneck speed, my mother's voice insistent in my head that I give my man whatever he needed, because that was how I'd get to keep him.

The hospital loomed ahead, and nervous excitement coursed through me. I spotted War's bike parked near the entrance, but there was no sign of him.

I squeezed my bike into the parking spot beside him, taking care not to scratch my paint on the little white hatchback on the other side.

It took a second to register, but when it did, my heart sank. The car was familiar. I'd seen it around the compound and always with War's fat side chick behind the wheel.

No. No. No. Lots of people drove little white hatchbacks.

I got off my bike, cupping my hands around my eyes to peer through the glass. The back had a huge TV and a laundry basket full of something I couldn't see in the shadows, but on top was a folder of paperwork, the Psychos' logo proudly displayed on the front.

The sinking in my stomach turned into a pit.

This bitch was not here. Not now. War's mother waking up was huge. A monumental moment that I needed to be by his side for. Not her. I glanced up at the window to Fancy's room. I'd stood down here, watching War keep vigil over her so many times, that I knew exactly which one it was.

The vision in the window was a punch to the gut.

War with his back to the window.

Bliss right by his side, her hand lovingly touching his shoulder, reassuring and overly familiar.

Rage boiled up inside me, hot and fierce and angry.

I knew what I had to do.

This woman was more than just a bitch who sat on his dick from time to time. I could have handled it if that was all it was.

Bliss was more than that. She was a threat to everything I wanted. He'd proved that when he'd picked her over me, time and time again.

I stared up at them through the window, both so innocently naïve to me watching them from the shadows.

I knew how to take care of my problems. I'd done it once before. I could do it again.

From the storage compartment on my bike, I pulled out the tools I'd used just a couple of days ago to fix it. I hadn't had a chance to put them back in the garage yet and now I was glad because they were exactly what I needed.

It was all too easy to break into Bliss's car and make a few adjustments. Just little ones she'd never notice.

Army and Fancy hadn't.

Not until their car was sailing gracefully over the cliffs without working brakes.

Bliss would be no different.

And when War cried his little heart out over losing yet another person he loved, I'd be there to pick up the pieces.

26

WAR

"You idiot," Fancy scolded, while medical professionals hurried around the room, checking monitors and writing notes on clipboards. Another group of nurses rushed in, each of them with big smiles on their faces and cheerful greetings for my mother who had just woken up from the dead.

She scowled at all of them, weakly brushing away their attempts to check her temperature, blood pressure, and who knew what else. The entire time, she glared at me, in much the same way she had when I'd been busted for breaking her beloved flower vase. I could get a D on a test or get busted sneaking out to parties with no repercussion, but break something my mother loved, and I knew to run.

I felt like running now. Except I couldn't because I had to tell her that she was going to have to spend the rest of her life without my father.

The urge to run only intensified when I looked at

Bliss and heard myself saying I was marrying someone else. The words may as well have cut all the tendons in my legs because I couldn't move, even though the room felt like it had no air.

Concentrating on Fancy seemed the more pressing matter in the moment, so I picked up her hand. "Just let them help you, Mom. You've been in a coma."

"So I've been told."

I bit back a smile at her feistiness, even if was as scratchy as sandpaper. Apparently even knocking on death's door couldn't quell that. "Just rest."

"I'll rest when you find your brain. You aren't marrying Siren."

I swallowed, my smile falling. "I have to."

"Says who?"

I glanced at Bliss, and my heart fucking broke all over again. Because instead of the hate she should have had for me after I'd just told her she couldn't ever be more than a mistress, she had her hand gently on my back and her face full of concern. Not for Fancy. But for me.

I didn't deserve her love. Not even an ounce of it, and yet she was there, caring about me even when I'd done everything so fucking wrong. "I made a deal."

Bliss frowned. "You mean your dad made a deal."

I shook my head. "Gus is your dealer."

"I know."

Shock punched through me. "You know?"

"Yes. I had the displeasure of his company earlier where he decided to lay his cards on the table."

I wanted to drag her into my arms and hold her so tight she could never leave. Except I knew I didn't have the right after what I'd agreed to do. I shoved my hands deep into the pockets of my jeans. "Well, you don't need to worry about him anymore. He's wiped your debt, as long as I agree to marry his daughter."

Her mouth dropped open. "That's insane. You aren't doing that. You aren't throwing your whole life away for me."

I couldn't contain it anymore. Before I could even remind myself to keep my hands in my pockets, I grabbed her wrists, pulling her closer. "I'd do it a hundred times over to keep you safe. Don't you know I have no life without you in it? You know what the alternative is? He kills you, Bliss. You think he'd just let a debt that big slide? That's not how men like him work." I paused, the truth choking me until I said it. "That's not how men like me work!"

She shook her head and opened her mouth, but I put my hand over it, silencing her. "I'd rather marry Siren and give you up, but know you're safe, than have you dead and buried next to your brother."

I waited for the acceptance. The resignation that I was right. Any minute now she was going to realize there was no other way, and then she'd walk. She wasn't the type of woman to accept the tiny scraps I'd be able to throw her way once I was married to Siren. I didn't even want that for her. I could share her with Nash and Vincent because they loved her like I did.

I didn't want her to have to share me with a woman I didn't even like anymore.

She'd see that. She'd nod her head and walk out of my life.

Fire burned in her eyes, and she dragged my hand

down off my face. And then shoved me in the chest. "You idiot!"

It was the second time in the space of ten minutes a woman had called me that. I'd been called worse, but damn.

"There is another way," she insisted.

I shook my head. "There isn't."

She sighed, complete frustration in the exhale of air. "He played you, War. I'd already made a deal with him, and the debt had been cleared."

My eyes widened, and for a moment, I just stood there, mouth flapping and trying to find words. "What? How? Your dad?"

She swallowed thickly, irritation flashing in her eyes. "No. Not my dad, War. Me. I know you think I'm still the girl from Providence who needs a man to look after me and protect me from this world. But I'm not. See me for who I am now, not the woman I was when I first came to your clubhouse, a scared, timid mouse. Trust that I can handle Gus. Because I can."

"I like this one," Fancy croaked from her bed. "Marry her."

A tiny smile appeared on Bliss' lips, and she leaned in and picked up my mother's hand. "I'm Bliss. It's really lovely to meet you. Even if your son is a bonehead."

Fancy chuckled. "Indeed. But he's a good one. I can see you already know that."

Bliss squeezed my mom's fingers and nodded. "I do indeed. I'm hoping he's now going to realize he doesn't have to marry someone else, because I kinda want to keep him. With your blessing, of course."

Fancy nodded. "He can marry any woman. As long as it's not that conniving bitch, Siren."

"Geez, Mom. Tell me what you really think of her."

My mother silenced my smart-assery with a dangerous look. "All she cares about is your title, just like her momma did. This stupid deal was made a lifetime ago when Gus and your father were drunk and I was too pregnant to stop it. You know how he is. Honor above all else. That's all that stops him from cancelling it. He might put on a gruff front, but your father knows what it is to feel true love." She smiled. "I taught him that. He wants that for you, son. I know it. I'll talk to him."

She lifted a hand and pushed it through her limp hair. "I must look awful. Don't let him see me like this, okay? Where is he? At the clubhouse? Did you already talk to him? Just call back and tell him I passed out again or something and to come in the morning when I've had a shower."

Bliss glanced at me, smile falling from her mouth.

A gut-wrenching pain twisted my insides. "Mom..."

"Mmm? Bliss, do you have a mirror in your purse?"

Clearly not knowing what else to do, Bliss nodded and riffled through the bag on her lap. A tear dropped off her cheek, and she quickly wiped it away with the back of her hand.

Mom stared at her, her shrewd eyes missing nothing, despite being unconscious for longer than anyone should be. She turned to me slowly. "Why is she crying?"

"I'm sorry," Bliss mumbled beneath her breath.

It wasn't her fault. I was the one being a pussy and not saying what needed to be said. "Mom," I murmured, taking her hand. "I need to tell you something."

Maybe it was the tone in my voice that gave it away. The forced smile on my face, or the way I had to swallow too hard to just to form words. But she caught it.

She held up a hand. It was a strong, forceful gesture without a single tremor. "No. Whatever you're about to say, no."

I gripped her hand harder. "Mom, Dad didn't—"

"No, War! Call him. Tell him to come down now. I was joking before. It doesn't matter if he sees my hair all messed up. He won't care. He never has. It was me who was always so insistent on wearing makeup and being pretty for him. He always told me I didn't need it. So just tell him to come down now."

A shot of grief rolled through me. "Mom, listen."

She squeezed her eyes closed. "No."

I needed to just rip the Band-Aid off before the grief and anger engulfed me again. "He's gone, Mom," I shouted. "Please. Just let me get this out. He didn't make it, okay? He's gone. He's been gone for weeks."

If I hadn't already been dying inside, her wail of pain would have done it. A wall broke, and the tidal wave of emotion crashed through. It ripped from deep within her, the sound filled with a pure grief that was devastating to everyone who heard it.

"He tried to brake," my mother sobbed. "I remember. He tried, but there was something wrong with the car." She turned watery eyes on me. "We went over the cliff, didn't we?"

I nodded. Her story matched everything Scythe had claimed. It only made my heart hurt more because he wasn't here either. Anger boiled up within me. I was so sick of losing people. So fucking sick of my heart hurting all the damn time. I reached out for Bliss, grasping for her desperately.

She was there instantly, her fingers tight around mine. All we could do was watch my mother cry for the man she'd lost. He might have been a hard old bastard, messed up from the war he'd seen and unsupported by the country he'd come home to, but he'd been hers. Ours. And somebody had taken him too soon. Well before my mother had had her fill.

Slowly, her wails became sobs, and then after another moment, she drew in a breath and composed her face into the emotionless mask I was more accustomed to. Hard as rock, like nothing could touch her. "You'll make them pay, War."

"The Slayers will get what's coming to them," I agreed.

She twisted her head, focusing her green eyes on me. "Siren was working on my car that day."

I froze. "What do you mean? Dad always worked on your car."

"It wasn't long before we left for dinner that night. Everybody else was at the clubhouse, but I forgot my lipstick, and we were going out to celebrate our anniversary, so I wanted to look extra nice. I went back to our cabin while everybody else was having drinks, and Siren was there, packing tools back into her bag. I thought it was odd at the time, but she said Army had asked her to do a tune-up on my car because he'd been too busy." Her bottom lip trembled, but she bit down on it for a moment before it could turn into anything more. "He'd been gone for a week on a gun run, and I just let it go because I was happy he was home. I opened the door and found the lipstick, and by the time I'd applied it, Siren was gone and your father was back, ready to take me out. We took my car because he'd been riding for a week straight and he wasn't as young as he used to be..."

She trailed off into sobs again, no longer able to hold it together.

Everything inside me hardened. Despite the tiny skirts and full-face makeup, Siren knew more about mechanics than any guy on my crew. Most of them tinkered, but apart from me and Hawk, the rest of them were all first-generation riders. They hadn't grown up with bikes shoved in their faces at every opportunity, like Hawk and I had. Me, Hawk...and Siren. Club brats from day one.

"It could be a coincidence," Bliss said quietly. "Or an accident."

I shook my head. "Siren knows cars and bikes, Bliss. If she was working on that car the day it had a fatal malfunction, she either knew about a problem and didn't say anything, or..."

"Or the conniving little bitch did it on purpose to get me out. With me and your father gone, and you set to marry her, the two of you would have taken over. She would have gotten everything she and her skank of a mother had always wanted. I watch enough crime shows to know you need means, motive, and opportunity. She's got all three." There was no sign of tears in Fancy's eyes anymore. Just cold, hard anger. She yanked out the IV in her arm with a vicious tug. "I'll kill her myself."

"Mom!" I grabbed at the sheet and used it to press against the mess she'd made of her arm, while Bliss ran to the door to call in a nurse.

Mom thrashed and fought with me, twisting and turning in the bed, while she screamed, "I'll kill her! I'll kill her!"

I pinned her to the bed as nurses rushed in, one of them with an injection of something that she stabbed right into Fancy's upper arm.

"Wait! What is that?" I asked.

Fancy went limp beneath me, the fight draining out of her and her eyes closing. That sent a fresh wave of panic through me.

But Bliss put a steadying hand on my arm. "Just a sedative, I'm sure, right?"

The nurse nodded, looking a tiny bit afraid of me. "Don't worry. It's common for patients in your mom's situation to wake up feeling disoriented and confused. They say all sorts of crazy things. She's still going to have a long recovery, so its best she rests for a while. Why don't the two of you go home and get some rest too? It's very late."

I just nodded, the fight draining out of me under the weight of everything else. I didn't bother telling the nurse that my mother hadn't been confused and disoriented at all. She'd been sharp as a tack, just like she always was.

They didn't need to know that when she shouted about killing a woman, she meant it literally.

27

BLISS

*W*ar stormed through the hospital corridors, his fingers tight around mine. Nurses called out to us, asking what we were doing here at this hour, but he ignored them all, and we were outside before security could be summoned.

The night was dark around us, but lights illuminated the path to the parking lot. War didn't pause. I half jogged to keep up, until we reached the spots we'd parked in.

"War..." I said softly, not even knowing what to say but hating the anguish pouring off him.

He thrust a helmet at me and then swung his leg over his bike, forcing the engine to roar through the quiet.

My fingers wrapped around the helmet strap. "My car..."

He turned pained eyes on me. "I need to ride, and I need you with me." He reached his hand out to me again. "Please, Bliss."

I would have followed this man anywhere. Onto his bike was no hardship. The damn TV and paperwork

Vincent and I had salvaged from Axel's place were still in the back of my car, and Saint View Hospital wasn't exactly known for its high-tech security measures. There'd be drunks and drug addicts and plenty of other people coming through this parking lot who might see the TV and think it would be better placed on their living room wall, but what did I care? They could have the damn thing if it meant that much to them.

War needed me, and I wasn't going to say no.

I strapped the helmet on and hoisted my leg over the seat, settling behind War, but careful not to touch him. He wanted me with him, but he hadn't said in what way. He looked so highly strung he might explode. I was literally afraid of touching him for fear of setting him off.

The bike jerked forward as soon as my second foot was off the ground. "War!" Unprepared for the sudden movement, I slid right down the seat, crashing into his solid back.

He clamped his hand on my thigh possessively. "That's where you are, when you're on my bike, baby girl. Right up against me with your soft tits at my back and your arms around my waist. Every time. You hear me? That's your seat. Yours and no one else's."

I wrapped my arms around his tight stomach, flattening my palms against his abs. "I hear you."

"Every time," he repeated.

He still took my breath away when he talked like that. "Every time," I echoed back.

My words were nearly lost in the roar of the engine and the gravel kicking up behind us. We left my car, the hospital, and all its revelations behind, the night swallowing us up. I held War tighter, and tighter as he sped through the darkness, higher and higher out along the cliff roads where his Dad had met his end.

Where I had my own demons to battle, because of what had happened there with Caleb.

War turned down the dirt road that led to the lookout, his body still stiff and unresponsive to my touch. He stopped the bike with a jerk and got off, storming to the edge where a flimsy handrail warned not to go any farther.

Panic flooded me with the way he moved. It was too quick for a man just going to take in the view. I forgot everything that had happened to me in this same spot in my fear that War might not stop at the rail. "War!" I screamed, scrambling off the bike to run after him.

His fingers gripped the rail when I caught up to him, and I fisted the back of his jacket like that somehow might stop a man twice my size from throwing himself over.

He opened his mouth and bellowed into the darkness, the sound getting picked up and lost in the crashing of waves that hit the wall below us. He screamed again, and again, until the rigidity in his muscles softened and he spun to face me. "I was ready to marry her, Bliss! I nearly gave up the only damn person I have left because I was a fucking idiot and fell for Gus' lies."

I reached for him.

He stepped back, shaking his head. "I don't even deserve you. I'm not the man you need. My dad never fell for Gus' bullshit games. It was why he kicked him out in the first place and made him start his own chapter. Fancy knew what a conniving bitch Siren was, and yet here's me, dumb War, ready to marry her because I'm too fucking stupid to see what's right in front of my face."

I reached up and grabbed his face. "Stop it. You didn't lose me. I'm still here."

He closed his eyes and shook his head. "I'm not cut out to run the club. Hawk has made no secret of that."

"Then quit."

"I can't."

"Then stay and fight for it." I could feel him slipping away. Shutting himself off in a cloud of grief and self-loathing. "Stay and fight for me."

He blinked, gaze focusing on me properly this time.

I saw my opportunity and took it. "I love you."

The agony behind his eyes screamed at me to make it better. I pressed up onto my toes, kissing his soft lips. "I love you, War. You aren't marrying Siren. You aren't leaving. Nobody is. I'm here. Nash will be, too. As well as Vincent. Rebel. All of us have your back in whatever you want to do next."

His gaze searched mine, and I nodded, trying to reaffirm the promises I'd made, because I believed them. Each and every one of them. We'd be here for him, just like he'd been there for me.

Something broke inside him.

He hauled me in tight, slamming his mouth down on mine, hot and hungry and demanding.

Shock punched through me, and for the tiniest of seconds, everything that had happened here with Caleb came flooding back, burning my eyes until I closed them.

War's touch was nothing like Caleb's. Even when he held me tight, it wasn't to hurt me but to protect me. He walked me back until we hit the hard wooden trunk of a tree, and then with nowhere else to go, he pressed in, crowding me with his big body.

Not for one second did I feel trapped, like I had with Caleb. Instead, I pulled War closer, craving more of whatever made him feel better. Desperate for his touch, and to remind him who he belonged with.

"Need you, baby girl," he whispered against my lips. "Need you so fuckin' bad." His hand trailed down my side, over the curve of my hip to my thigh and then came between my legs.

I gasped at the feel of my body coming to life. "Oh God. More."

I didn't know what it was about him, but the minute he wanted me, I wanted him. It didn't matter where or when, if he said the word, I was jelly at his feet. I fumbled for his cock, freeing it from his pants while his hand slipped beneath the waistband of mine and straight into my panties.

I shouted, free to be as loud as I wanted with nobody around.

He pushed two fingers inside me without warning, knowing exactly what I needed and wasting no time in giving it to me.

I shoved his jeans and underwear down his legs then grabbed two handfuls of his muscled ass and dragged him in closer. "Need you inside me," I managed to get out while riding his fingers. Each stroke was electrifying, drawing arousal from deep within my body and making me crave the thick, blunt head of his erection.

He withdrew his fingers to take my pants off, and I whimpered at the loss while frantically trying to guide him to where he needed to be.

The head of his cock notched at my entrance, and he teased me for just a second, coating himself in the slick wetness he'd created with his fingers.

"Fuck me," I groaned, urging him on. "Please."

He shoved my shirt up and roughly groped one breast, cupping and molding it through the fabric of my bra. "I love when you talk like that." He bent his knees and buried his face in my neck, kissing and sucking, while he pushed his dick inside me.

My eyes rolled back at how big he was. He was always exactly what I needed, and I had so nearly lost him. It wasn't even just Siren's fault. It was mine. His dad's. But none of it mattered now. Only what we did going forward.

He slammed himself inside me, roaring my name into the crashing swells of the sea below us. "I'm not giving you up, Bliss. I love you. I'm going to spend the rest of my life doing this."

"Fucking me against trees?"

He laughed but didn't stop, and I dug my fingers into his biceps as the angle changed and his cock hit my G-spot.

"I'm gonna spend the rest of my life giving you whatever makes you happy, Bliss. If that's fucking you against trees, then that's what I'll do."

I stilled, catching his gaze. "I want you for a lot more than just that."

He stopped and touched his forehead to mine, both of us catching our breaths though our bodies still thrummed together. His gaze was intense when he whispered, "I want your name tattooed on my skin the same way it's already tattooed across my heart."

I kissed his sweet lips, seeing the kindness he kept

hidden beneath a bad boy exterior. "I want that too. And yours on me."

He shook his head, pressing his hand to my chest and dragging it down between my breasts. "Not that."

"You don't want me to get a tattoo?"

"I'd love watching a needle spell out my name on your skin and know it's there forever. But I'm a greedy asshole, Bliss. Completely unreasonable in what I want from you."

"Tell me."

He pushed his hand lower, until it rested on my stomach. "I want your belly swollen with my baby."

A rush of heat engulfed me, quickly followed by a wave of lust for the man who'd shown me what true love was. Vincent and Nash had too, but some part of me had loved War from the minute he'd smiled in my direction and made me think I wasn't the piece of shit Caleb had always claimed me to be.

"Don't answer now. I know we have stuff to work out with Nash and Vincent, but I'm laying claim. I want your pussy. I want your heart. I want your time, your love, and yeah, baby girl, I want your children."

I couldn't even speak. Nash had expressed similar sentiments, and I couldn't even breathe for how much I wanted to give that to both of them. War rolled his hips against mine, stroking himself in and out of my core and went back to kissing my neck until the shock turned into tingles, and the tingles turned into an orgasm.

I don't remember the words I spoke while my body clamped down around his.

But I think at least one of them was the word "Yes."

28

BLISS

*W*ar's fingers drifted over my stomach, featherlike touches filled with gentleness and affection. He'd been doing it all night, ever since we'd driven back to his cabin and made love in quiet darkness. There'd been no spanking or edging me for so long I'd wanted to scream the house down.

But there'd been us. Him and me. Face-to-face, creating a new, deeper bond that had more than just attraction and passion behind it.

I'd loved every moment, but I was scared for what the sun would bring.

War would find Siren and Gus, and if what Fancy had said was true, blood would be shed.

"Let her explain," I whispered quietly as the first rays peeked over the horizon outside War's windows. "She's been your friend since you were babies. That means something."

He pressed his lips to my shoulder, but then he rolled away, sitting up on his side of the bed to drag underwear on. "Friends don't try to kill your parents." He cleared his throat. "Sorry, I mean *succeed* in killing your parent."

I bit my lip, watching the muscles tighten across his broad back and shoulders. I put a hand to his skin, and he paused beneath my touch.

I tried again. "Whatever you're planning to do, you don't have to do it."

He shook his head. "There's a code, mama."

I knew the code. It basically boiled down to an eye for an eye. There was no love lost between me and Siren, but I didn't want to see her dead either. I didn't know how to fix what she'd done though, and if she'd been the one to kill Axel, then I probably would have been in the same shoes as War. I couldn't bear to think about it. So I concentrated on what I could control instead. "Mama?"

War glanced over his shoulder at me with a grin. "Just thought I'd try it on for size. Don't know if I can call you baby girl anymore if we're...you know." He leaned over to stroke my belly again. "Trying to have a baby girl."

My heart hammered. I'd barely slept, thinking about what we'd somehow agreed to do.

I didn't regret it. But there were things we needed to work out. "We need to talk about Vincent and Nash. Even if they're on board, how would any of that even work?"

He leaned in and kissed my lips. "I'm not asking you to give them up. I know you love them too. We'll work it out." He pulled away and went back to getting dressed.

But with every article of clothing he put on, my sense of dread grew. "Don't go," I whispered.

He paused. "I have to."

"I know. But not today. Nobody else knows what Fancy said."

War sighed. "It's not fair on anyone to drag this out longer than it has to."

"Just today," I begged. "Just give it one day for your head to cool. Last time this happened, you and Scythe..."

War swallowed thickly.

The last time War had believed someone guilty of killing his father had resulted in disaster. War had a soft spot for Siren. How could he not? He'd grown up with her. Been promised to her. Even though he denied it, he must have seen his life stretching out before him with her at his side.

I didn't want him doing something he couldn't undo. The man already lived with enough regret. He didn't need any more, and nothing would happen if he just took twenty-four hours to think it through.

"I need you today." I forced the words to sound more like a demand than me begging. "We need to talk to Vincent and Nash. One day, War. That's all I'm asking for."

His gaze met mine.

"I don't ask you for much."

His lips brushed over mine. "You don't ask me for anything."

I kissed him back. "I'm asking for this. I'm calling everyone into Psychos in an hour. My car is still at the hospital, so I need a ride."

He gave in and prowled across the bed to me again, tucking his face into my neck. "Sell that car and just ride everywhere on the back of my bike."

I laughed, his stubbly beard rasping over my skin deliciously. I tilted my head to give him better access.

"You gonna strap a baby seat on the back if I get pregnant?"

He pressed his body to mine, giving up all pretenses of getting dressed, and ground himself against my thigh. "When, not if. Vincent and Nash will be on board."

I nodded slowly and let him fit himself between my legs again. But my mind was elsewhere, seeds of doubt popping up that threatened to ruin everything.

I was still in my head when we arrived at Psychos an hour later, ready to meet the others. But instead of finding Nash and Vincent, it was Rebel bustling around. War disappeared in search of the guys, but I stopped and stared. Then burst into tears.

Rebel turned huge eyes on me and ran to my side.

She put her arm around my shoulders. "What's wrong?"

I shook my head. "Nothing. It's just I've never seen it look so good in here. Did you do all this?"

She let me go and shoved her hands in the pockets of her wide-legged jeans. "Might have. It's never a good idea for a doctor to tell me to rest and take it easy. I basically took that as a personal challenge."

I gazed around. "Did you paint?"

"Nash helped. A little."

I laughed, sniffing back tears.

Psychos looked good. Better than I had ever seen it. The usually sticky floors gleamed with new polish. The normally grubby walls were fresh and clean. I ran my fingers along the seam of a black tablecloth and glanced at Rebel. "I'm not sure half our clientele even know what tablecloths are."

She grinned back. "I thought we could teach them.

Found 'em out back in a box of random crap. Figured you might like them."

"I do. The whole place looks great." I drew her in for a hug. "I'm sorry I wasn't here to help. I was so overwhelmed even thinking about everything that had to happen here. It just felt easier to let it go."

Rebel's expression turned fierce. "You can't sell the place, Dis. We'll make it good again. I swear it."

I squeezed her hand. "I know."

War came sauntering back and slung an arm around my shoulder. "Place looks fucking A, Rebel. Nice." He held a hand out, and she fist bumped him with a grin, but then he dropped a kiss on my head. "I'm going out for a smoke, mama. Don't want to stink the place up now that Rebel has it smelling better than the bottom of an ashtray."

I watched him walk away, staring after him as the door closed behind his perfect ass.

"Mama," Rebel screeched, the second the door closed. Her fingernails dug into my skin, and her eyes went as huge as dinner plates. "Girl. You got a bun in the oven you didn't tell me about?"

I laughed and shook my head. "No." But I dragged her into the kitchen, glancing at the door over my shoulder like War might change his mind and walk back in at any second. "We did kind of somehow decide to try though."

Rebel's shriek was ear-piercing. "No fucking way!"

I clapped a hand over her mouth. "*Shhh*! We haven't even properly talked to Vincent and Nash yet—"

She yanked my hand away. "You're breaking up with them? Nash will be devastated..."

I shook my head. "I hope not. But we all need to discuss it. If they don't want to..."

"Are you joking? Vincent always talks about kids and having a family, you know that. And Nash..."

"Nash had a shitty childhood, and he's forty and probably pretty happy with his life just the way it is." I bit my lip.

Rebel frowned. "Or he'd be the best fucking father out there. I think that's more likely, don't you?"

"He did say he wanted kids with me, but it was right after we'd...you know—"

"Fucked each other's brains out?"

I laughed. "Something like that. Things said in the heat of the moment don't count. He hasn't mentioned it since..."

I swallowed hard, my nerves rising again until they were choking me. I tried to breathe around it and flatten the panic, but it came out more like hyperventilating.

Rebel's face changed from shock mixed with excitement to concern. "Hey. You've gone pale. Sit."

She steered me to a stool, and I sat gratefully, leaning forward to rest my elbows on my knees, my hair falling around me to form a protective wall.

Rebel squatted in front of me. "What just happened? I swear to you, Bliss. This isn't going to be a problem for Nash and Vincent. They're all so stupidly in love with you that this weird foursome you have going on doesn't even faze them. They're gonna be doing backflips over just the very idea of having a baby with you."

"That's the problem," I said quickly, scared War would come in and hear. "I know they're all going to say yes."

She squinted at me. "I'm not seeing the problem here, Dis. You're gonna have to spell it out for the high school dropout."

"I don't think I can have kids."

Rebel's frown deepened. "What makes you think that?"

"I tried to go on the pill when I was sixteen. Not because I was having sex, but all my friends were, and I wanted to be prepared for when it happened to me. The doctor told me I was too overweight to get pregnant."

Rebel's expression turned to one of fury. "Are you serious? How dare he!"

I lifted a shoulder. "I think he's right. I never got pregnant with Caleb."

She scoffed, "Your ex? He sounds like a jackass. Your body probably knew it and rejected his inferior sperm."

I giggled a little at that, loving that talking to her always made me feel better. She was the best girlfriend I'd ever had and had truly shown me what it meant to have a bestie. But the truth of the matter was, it wasn't just Caleb who my body rejected. I bit my lip. "I haven't been very careful," I admitted. "With any of them. It's been months…"

Rebel tilted her head quizzically. "So you're saying you've been having a shitload of sex, with three different guys for months…"

I cringed. "It's bad. I know. But everybody said they were clean…" It wasn't really any excuse to be so irresponsible, but there was something about the three of them that had always made me want to throw caution to the wind. I couldn't bring myself to regret anything we'd done.

Rebel waved her hand around. "Not what I was getting at. Are you sure you aren't already pregnant?"

I nodded. "I'd know...wouldn't I?"

Rebel shrugged. "Fucked if I'd have a clue. I've never been knocked up and never will be." She crossed her legs like that might keep her baby-free, which made me laugh even though it was kind of hysterical. She stood normally again, sobering us both. "When was your last period?"

I racked my brain. "I honestly don't even remember."

Rebel raised an eyebrow. "If it were recent, I think you'd remember."

She had a point.

"O.M.G. You're so knocked up!"

I slapped her hand. "Stop. I'm not."

"Your boobs are huge."

"My boobs are always huge."

"Fair point. I'm getting you a pregnancy test anyway." She moved for the door.

I caught her hand, ready to stop her.

She gave me a look.

She was right. I really couldn't remember the last time I'd had a period, and that wasn't good. "Okay, do it. But don't tell the guys. I need to—"

Rebel waved me off, grinning ear to ear. "I'm claiming fairy godmother right now. That Sandra bitch will have to wait for baby number two to get her shot."

She disappeared through the doors before I could even agree.

And I was left with a churning feeling in my stomach and no idea if it was hope or terror.

29

VINCENT

*T*his was the worst surprise morning tea I'd ever been to.

Across a table of little sandwiches, cakes, and other delicate foods, my mother, Jezebel, and Ophelia scowled at me. Their expressions didn't match their pretty floral dresses or the crisp white napkins on their laps. They were certainly at odds with the rest of the room, full of older country club ladies nibbling as they discussed lawn bowls or something equally dull.

"So, you're back," my mother said with the enthusiasm of a limp dishcloth.

"Your excitement over my return is astounding, Mother." I took a bite out of the corner of a sandwich and wrinkled my nose.

My mother seemed to like my return about as much as I liked cucumber sandwiches.

"I'm happy to see you, V," my sister said. "You look a whole lot better than the night we dragged your ass outta that prison. But you made a promise to Jezebel."

I eyed the woman who'd been part of my rescue team. "I'm grateful the two of you were here to help when I needed it. But I made no such promises to Jezebel." I glared at my mother. "You knew very well that was Scythe."

She shrugged. "He agreed."

"And I disagree. Since Scythe isn't coming back, whatever the three of you had planned for me, it's off."

"Vincent, be reasonable," my mother complained. "You can't just give up the business and marry that girl. She's in love with two other men, for goodness sakes!"

"And me," I said firmly. "She loves me too."

"She's a slut," my mother argued back, saying the word loud enough that the old ladies at the table next to us sucked in shocked gasps.

Slowly, I took the napkin from my lap, smoothing and twisting it into a rope shape.

Perfect to loop around my mother's neck.

Ophelia kicked me beneath the table. When I looked at her, she mouthed, "Knock it off."

Ugh. Older sisters were so annoying.

Instead of strangling the woman who'd given birth to me, I focused on Jezebel. "I'm sorry she made you believe that there could be a union between us. I do wish you the best." On paper, the two of us would have been perfect. But paper didn't account for the way I loved Bliss. Or for the fact I thought about her all day and dreamed about her all night. Or for the fact she and I had been intimate, and that in her wake, no other woman would ever compare.

I didn't need a wealth of sexual knowledge to know that.

Bliss was it for me, and this morning tea was holding me up in getting to her. I pushed to my feet, eyes narrowing at my mother. "We're done, Mother. Have a lovely life. I'm sorry I wasn't the son you wanted."

"Vincent!" she snapped. "Stop being so dramatic and sit back down."

I twisted my head, cracking my neck, then leaned down, lips to her ear. "If you ever speak about Bliss like that again, I will snap your neck, Mother. Trust me, I've already planned it out in my head a thousand times. I'm really just searching for an excuse to do it."

Her mouth dropped open.

Ophelia bit down on her lip, fighting back laughter. "See you later, little brother."

I nodded at her, and Jezebel, because that was simply good manners, and then I moved toward the exit.

"You don't control Scythe, my son," my mother called out across the room, clearly no longer worried about what the old biddies thought. "Once he's back, he'll see reason."

Seventeen witnesses. Fifteen women with silvering hair, plus two waiters wandering around with pitchers of lemonade. If I snapped my mother's neck right now, that would be a terrible amount of extra work. I'd be even later in meeting Bliss.

I shoved my hands into the pockets of my suit pants to keep from wrapping them around my mother's ancient neck. It didn't matter anyway. Scythe wasn't coming back. Ever.

Cold, bro. Super cold.

At least his voice was quieter and more easily ignored

now. It wouldn't be long until I didn't hear it at all. Everything would be better when that happened.

I drove my rental car back toward Saint View, dropping the weight of my mother's nonsense with every mile that passed beneath the tires. In Psychos' parking lot, War leaned against the wall with the Psychos' clown logo above his head, a cigarette dangling from his fingers.

"Fabulous timing," I murmured. "Thanks, Mother."

I didn't want to be alone with War.

I knew Bliss loved him. So did Scythe. But I didn't know where that left War and me. I was drawn to him, but that was Scythe's lingering influence.

That would fade as surely as his voice.

War stubbed out his cigarette as I approached. "Hey, man."

I nodded but kept walking, trying to move past him.

War's hand shot out, circling my wrist.

On instinct, I grabbed his hand, breaking the hold and slamming him up against the wall. My chest pressed to his, my hands wrapped around his wrists to pin him. My heart hammered, adrenaline rushing my veins, my flight or fight response switched firmly to fight.

We stared at each other, our gazes locking while our chests rose and fell in unison. Our breaths mingled, his misting over my lips until I darted my tongue out to swipe it away.

War's gaze dipped to my mouth and then back up to my eyes. Confusion flickered in his. "Scythe?"

I let him go.

The hope in his voice gutted me.

It was the same hope my mother held in hers. Always hoping her favorite would come back.

War was no different.

"Scythe is gone," I muttered, heading for the door again.

"Vincent, wait."

I couldn't ignore the pain in War's voice. I paused with my hand on the doorknob, wishing I could just keep going without hearing what he had to say.

"Bliss thought...I dunno. That maybe Scythe could still hear..."

I closed my eyes, but something inside me, probably something that belonged to Scythe, said that I owed this man the truth. "Say what you need to say."

War nodded, palming the back of his neck. "Just tell him...just tell him I fucking miss him."

Tell him I miss him, too. That I'll find a way.

I shut it down. I'd given away too much, and now the lines were blurring once more. Panic reared its head. I'd waited a lifetime for someone who looked at me the way Bliss did. Who accepted me for who I was, awkwardness, love of knives, and Scythe included.

I couldn't lose it again.

I opened the door and walked inside without answering him.

He didn't try to follow me.

30

BLISS

I was going to throw up. It was still before lunch, so of course, I then convinced myself it was morning sickness and not just impending pregnancy test nerves or the worry over having to meet Jerry later that night. Which I still hadn't worked out a way to get out of. It was a relief when Vincent walked in, even if his face was as stormy as a winter day.

He came straight over to me, lifting my chin and planting his lips firmly on mine.

With relief, I sank into his embrace, clutching his strong biceps, and kissing him back. "I— Missed—You—Last—Ni—" I said between kisses.

But he was insatiable, holding me and kissing me until my head spun. His tongue plunged into my mouth, surely and steadily blowing my mind and taking everything he needed all at once. He kissed me until I was confused as to who I was actually kissing, Vincent or Scythe.

But when I pulled back, the look in his eyes told me

everything I needed to know. The kiss might have felt like a blurry line, but it was Vincent steering the ship. I laid my head against his chest. "I'm really glad you're here."

He held me tighter. "Thank you," he whispered against my hair.

I wasn't sure what he was thanking me for, but then the door opened again, and Nash and War came in, laughing about something.

I was suddenly terrified War was going to be the one to spill the beans, and with the doubt in my head about whether I could have a baby, or whether I was already pregnant, I suddenly wasn't ready.

So I said the first thing that came to mind instead and hoped he'd go along with it. "I want to throw another party. A Psychos' party, to be specific. If that wasn't obvious."

Nash grinned and nudged me with an elbow. "Does this mean you're not selling the place?"

I shrugged. "I don't think so. My father won't be happy. He thinks this place is a sinking ship and he very well might be right."

"If that's true, I'm ready to go down with it," Nash declared.

War sniggered. "I'm always keen to go down."

I bit my lip from laughing and looked to Vincent. "What do you think?"

"Will it make you happy?"

I considered the question, then nodded. "I think so. I suspect my dad is right. But this bar is more than just a business. I don't think I can see it go to someone else."

"Then I'll run security. I'm well enough."

"I'll run the bar," Nash said. "As always."

"Whatever you want from me," War added, "Just ask. You got it."

The door swung open, and Rebel burst through, a pharmacy shopping bag clutched in her hands. "Got it!"

I widened my eyes at her, and she finally seemed to notice the other guys all staring at her. Nash's gaze narrowed in on the bag clutched in her hand.

"Got what?" he asked curiously.

Oh God. I was going to have to come clean, but I was so not ready to do that. Not until I knew for sure for myself.

"My herpes cream," Rebel sassed at him.

All three guys made a face.

She glared at them. "Oh, like any of you can talk. You probably don't own a single condom between the three of you. Mind your business."

I stifled nervous laughter that threatened to explode as all three guys looked awkwardly away.

"Bliss, come help me...apply this," Rebel sang out, motioning toward the bathroom.

"Ugh, damn, Rebel! That's revolting," War complained, fake gagging.

But I linked my arm through hers and let her lead me to the bathroom.

"See?" Rebel told them over her shoulder. "Bliss is a good friend. Unlike the three of you."

Nash was decidedly green. "I'm gonna need a stiff drink to remove that thought from my head."

War and Vincent quickly agreed, and Rebel and I disappeared into the hallway while the men headed for the top-shelf bottle of whiskey.

Rebel yanked me into the empty women's room and

shoved the bag at me with a glare. "You owe me so big for that one. Fairy godmother duties probably ain't gonna cut it. I think you're gonna need to just name this kid after me."

"What if it's a boy?"

"I just told those guys I have a venereal disease to cover for your pregnant ass. You owe me a baby name, Bliss!"

I couldn't keep in my laughter. She was so ridiculous but also the most beautiful soul I'd ever had the pleasure of meeting. "I love you, you know that, right?"

She shoved me toward the toilet stalls. "Yeah, yeah. You'd better, because Nash ain't ever gonna let me live this one down. I'll bet they're out there right now, thinking up horrible nicknames for me."

I smiled, but nervous butterflies took flight in my stomach as I pulled the test from the bag.

"Did you do it yet?" Rebel called. Her footsteps pitter-pattered all over the tiled floor, like she couldn't stand still.

"I need to read the instructions first!"

"Just pee on the stick. How much instruction could you need?"

She was right. I was too impatient, and it seemed pretty basic. I peed on the stick, cleaned up, and then slowly emerged from the stall.

Rebel pounced on me. "Well?"

"It's negative."

She snatched it from my hands, while I washed mine. "What? No way. Your boobs are definitely bigger."

I wiped my hands on some paper towel and turned around, leaning my ass against the sink. "I told you I couldn't get pregnant. I'm such an idiot. I can't believe I let myself get carried away last night. Imagine me, foolishly telling this beautiful man that yeah, sure, no problem, I can have kids with you."

"Bliss…"

"Vincent is going to leave me. He's so good with kids, there's no way he'll hang around now."

"Bliss, it's positive."

"And Nash…" I blinked at her. "What?"

She spun the test around that very clearly now had a second line in the positive section. I stared at it, making sure it was really there. But there was no mistaking it. "Holy shit."

Rebel grinned smugly at me. "Told you your boobs were bigger!"

I ignored her, staring down at the test that proved that asshole doctor when I was sixteen wrong.

I was pregnant.

I stared up at her, eyes wide. "I'm pregnant."

Rebel nodded. "Yes, ma'am, you sure are. Let's go tell the guys! They're gonna die."

She reached for the door handle, but a sudden terror speared through me. It left a hole shaped just like the promises I'd had to make to Jerry.

I couldn't be pregnant and work off my debt to him.

But I couldn't go back on my word either. Not when he'd threatened Verity, Nichelle, and Rebel, who was standing right in front of me, thrilled and excited for this life growing inside me.

My head spun.

I had no idea what to do.

"Not like this," I said to her slowly. "I need to think…"

"Oh! Are you going to do one of those baby announcements and film their reactions to opening a present with a onesie or something inside? That would be so funny, especially with three of them. Wow, Bliss. Who do you think the baby daddy is?"

I had no idea, overwhelmed by the sickening fear that even though it was so wanted, this little life inside me might have come along at the very worst possible moment.

Rebel came back and put her arm around me. "You okay? You look like you're suddenly freaking out. This is a good thing. Isn't it?"

I nodded because it was so damn good. But at the same time, it was so, so bad. "I don't know how to tell them." I was completely numb from head to toe.

Rebel pulled out a pen and notepad from her purse and scribbled something across the paper before she handed it over to me. "If you're too freaked out to say it, just give them this."

When I gazed down at it, the paper read: I'm having a baby.

Another wave of shock punched through me so hard I had to take a step back.

"What?" Rebel asked. "Too simple?"

It wasn't that at all.

In fact, her note had made me forget entirely that I was even pregnant.

Because the I's in her message had little hearts above them. Just like I'd seen on the note we'd found in Axel's apartment.

31

BLISS

*W*hen Rebel and I walked out of the bathroom together, she nudged me with an elbow, completely unaware that I was spinning in a whirl of turmoil over a tiny love heart on a scrap of paper pushed into my pocket.

"I'm going to go so you have some space to talk to them. Stop stressing though, okay?" She grinned. "It isn't good for the baby."

I didn't even know what to say. If Rebel had been in a relationship with my brother at any point, recent or ancient history, surely, she would have said something before this? Or Nash would have. Even War probably would have been aware. Which led me back to a sickening worry that she was deliberately keeping her relationship with him a secret.

She'd been devastated at his funeral. I'd put it down to him being like a brother to her, but now I questioned everything from the minute I'd stepped inside the bar, that very first night, when she'd been the first person I saw. Rebel was the best friend I'd ever had, and suddenly I was questioning every word she'd ever said to me.

I hated it.

Feeling like maybe she'd only befriended me in order to cover something up.

It couldn't have all been so we wouldn't suspect her. You couldn't fake the friendship we'd formed.

But Caleb and I had faked an entire relationship. He'd lied and cheated at every chance he had, and I'd made out to everyone that we were the perfect couple. I'd gone along blindly, so stupidly desperate to be loved by him that I hadn't seen the signs.

All I could think was that maybe I'd done the same thing with Rebel.

I stumbled back out into the bar where the guys were sitting around watching a game on the small TV because the big one from Axel's place was still in the back of my car. Along with the weirdly threatening non-Valentine's Day card with the hearts above the I's.

All three guys looked my way, but it was Nash who sat back, a smug grin on his face. "So. War wants to knock you up, huh?"

I gaped at War. "You told them? Just like that? In the middle of a game?"

He shrugged. "I'm a really bad secret keeper, mama. I hope the baby doesn't inherit it. All good though. They're on board."

My mouth dropped open. "Excuse me?"

"I would like a baby," Vincent said quietly, fingers clenched around his glass. "Quite a lot, actually."

I glanced at Nash. "And you? You're just going along with this?"

He stood and crossed the room, dipping his head to press his lips against mine. "More than okay. I already told you I wanted you pregnant, even though you clearly didn't believe me at the time. So hear me now, Bliss. I'm so fuckin' okay I think we should go start trying right now."

I batted him away. "Be serious!"

"I am." His palms cupped my face and drew me in so he could kiss me properly, his tongue slipping past my lips to meet mine.

I closed my eyes, my worry about Rebel, and what I had to do with Jerry and Siren and my brother's murder all disappearing in his touch, and in the knowledge that these three men wanted me and the little life I was carrying.

It was everything I'd thought I'd wanted with Caleb. Everything my body hadn't given me then because it had all been so wrong and I'd just been too stupid to see it.

I couldn't help but think this was my sign that Nash, War, and Vincent were right. So right, in every way. For me, and for the life I wanted to share with them.

I needed to find a way out of this deal with Jerry. Because now it wasn't just Rebel, Verity, and Nichelle I had to protect. I had to protect myself too.

War stood, coming to stand at my back. "I second Nash's suggestion." His tongue dragged around to the side of my neck, kissing and sucking until he whispered, "Come on."

He linked his fingers between mine and pulled me toward the doors that led to where we held the parties. I let him, because I needed time to process all of this. My head and my heart hurt, but my core tingled, knowing exactly what was on the other side of that coatroom. Nash followed easily, he and War with a common goal.

I glanced over at Vincent, still watching us from the table. My gaze met his. My heart swelled. Of the three of them, I knew how much Vincent wanted a family. This, sharing me with two other men, was probably not what he'd envisioned at all.

But I so desperately wanted him to be on board. "Will you come with us?" I asked him softly. "Please."

We needed this. The four of us. I had to see that it could work. It couldn't be me sleeping with War and Nash and never having Vincent there. He'd always be on the outside, and how long would it be before jealousy reared its ugly head and the four of us fell apart?

Vincent watched me with his dark-brown eyes. "I'm always going to give you whatever you want, Bliss."

"I want it to be what you want too."

He glanced at War uncertainly, and my heart doubled in size when War put aside his own demons and nodded. "She wants you, V. Like it or not, you, me, and Nash? We're the three musketeers now."

War laughed it off, but Vincent didn't join in.

He watched War carefully. "I'm not Scythe. I can't be him for you." He glanced at me, and Nash too. "For any of you. I don't know how. I wish I did."

War nodded. "I know. I get it. None of us can change who we truly are deep inside. I won't ask you to."

I disentangled myself from War and Nash and put my arms around Vincent's shoulders, linking my fingers at the back of his neck so I could stare into his eyes when I spoke. Because he needed to hear it. Truly hear it and believe it. "All I need for you is to be you. I fell in love with you, before I fell in love with Scythe. Whoever you are, Vincent Atwood, you're enough."

He let out a shuddering breath, wrapping his arms around me tighter. "You're the most beautiful thing I've ever seen."

I brushed my lips over his. "Then take me to bed and show me."

He lifted me off the floor, walking purposefully toward the coatroom that separated the bar from the party area. Nash jogged ahead, switching on the strip lighting that cast gentle blue light around the room.

"One of the VIP rooms," I murmured to Vincent. "The one at the back on the right. The bed..."

"Is big enough for four," Nash supplied, leading the way.

Holy shit. Four. Was I seriously going to do this? Have sex with three men? It was one thing to have a threesome, but this was basically an orgy.

With me at the center of it.

If Vincent hadn't been carrying me, I might have turned and ran in the opposite direction. But then he was laying me down on the bed, and three huge men loomed over me, each one with a hunger in their gazes that heated me right through.

"Take your clothes off, baby girl."

I shivered at the thought of getting naked in front of them. The lighting was soft, but they'd see every inch of me. Once upon a time I would have told them to turn the lights off.

But I wanted to see them too. I wanted to watch their faces, their bodies, their muscles tight and rippling beneath their skin and the lust in their eyes when they looked at me.

In the dark, it was too easy to let my head make up lies.

In the light, I saw the truth.

They wanted me as much as I wanted them.

I stood shakily on the mattress and undid my pants, pulling them down over my thighs and toeing them off.

War grabbed them, tossing them aside, but his gaze never left mine.

My shirt was next, unbuttoning it with trembling fingers, and slowly revealing my bra as I went.

Vincent stepped back, finding an armchair in the corner to settle into. I let him go because I had my own nerves to deal with. I gnawed on my bottom lip, distracted by the butterflies rioting around my stomach.

Nash reached out and swiped his thumb over my lip, popping it free from my teeth. "You nervous?"

"Yes," I admitted.

Nash pushed his thumb inside my mouth, wetting it with my saliva. "Anytime you want to stop..."

I shook my head. "I don't want to stop."

Nash caught me around the waist with one strong arm and held me while he moved his hand beneath my panties to cup me. His wet thumb massaged my clit, rubbing slow circles over it. "Good. Because I can't get enough of touching you."

War knelt on the bed and pressed a kiss to my stomach. "Reach up. Grab the straps for support."

I looked up, only remembering how this room was themed when I saw the bar installed on the ceiling, and black straps with leather cuffs on the end. Easily tall enough to reach the straps while I was standing on the bed, I grabbed on to the cuffs, not putting them on, but using them so I didn't wobble all over the bed like War had suggested.

War tongued my belly button and grabbed handfuls of my ass, while Nash continued his magic on my clit. Pleasure soared through me with every touch, but I was very aware that this was not wholly unlike how we'd found Vincent—tied up, beaten and bloody, in the prison training grounds. Though this was clearly a very different situation, I watched him carefully, searching for any signs he didn't want it.

His gaze was fire, burning over me in an inferno of heat and flames.

A tiny moan slipped from my lips, and so slowly it was almost agony, Vincent undid his belt.

But Nash and War stole my attention, Nash changing the position of his hand so his thumb slipped up inside me, instantly stroking my G-spot, while he and War worked together to strip me of my underwear.

Completely nude and on display for them, I was the center of their attention. Nobody's gaze strayed, all three of them fixated on my body and bringing me pleasure.

God, I wanted them. So badly.

I let go of the restraints, needing to be on their level so I could kiss and touch them.

War growled. "One day I'm going to cuff you to those." He toyed with a matching set of restraints that fell off the edge of the bed. "Or these."

The promise unlocked some new kink in me. One that craved that loss of control and the complete and utter trust it would take to let someone have it. I would have given it to any of these men in a heartbeat. They'd proved over and over that they'd never hurt me and were here solely for my pleasure.

But right now, I just needed them. Naked. Warm. Moving inside my body. War and Nash stripped their clothes, neither an ounce of shame nor interest in each other's bodies. They were both all about me, and War crashed down on the bed, taking me with him. He pulled me onto my side so we faced each other, his hard, thick erection between us.

He kissed me deeply, tonguing my mouth the same way he'd tongued my belly button earlier and my pussy so many times before. His kisses were like a drug, each one spinning my head and taking me higher. Nash lay down behind me, reaching an arm over my hip to touch my clit, while War notched his cock at my entrance.

"I need to make you come," he whispered between deep plunges of his tongue.

He pushed inside me, so deliciously slowly I thought I might explode. I hooked my leg over War's thigh, opening myself up to take him deeper, and he groaned when he slid all the way in. He was warm and thick, stretching me perfectly, while Nash worked my clit.

The two of them knew my body and exactly how to get me off. Within a minute, I was writhing between them, Nash's erection prodding me from behind but letting War have his turn. War cupped one of my breasts, pinching my nipple in the way I loved, his thrusts becoming deeper and harder. Nash matched his tempo, increasing the friction on my clit until I was arching my back for Nash to kiss me.

He didn't hesitate, lifting his head and meeting me

when I twisted mine to find him. I came with War's cock deep inside my pussy, and Nash's tongue in my mouth, smothering my cries.

"Fuck, Bliss," War groaned, moving slowly in and out of my body, torturing himself and prolonging both our orgasms.

I moved my hips in time with his, willing to take him as long as he could stand.

"You're going to kill me before I even get to meet this baby we're trying to make."

I drew him tight to me as he stilled and kissed him because it was on the tip of my tongue to tell him I was already pregnant.

He kissed me back but then pulled away. "Roll over, baby. Spread your legs for him now."

Listening to him talk like that only made me want to lower my head and take him inside my mouth. But he was rolling me in Nash's direction, so I went with it, mentally promising War the head job of his life as a reward for having all the words that turned me on.

Nash wasted no time, moving between my legs to make his own mark on my pussy. I was so wet with War's cum that Nash slid in easily, filling me right back up where War had left off. His gaze locked with mine, and he grinned. "I hope you don't think I'm letting you go without another orgasm."

I grinned back. "That's not your style."

"Damn right."

He reached between us for my clit again, obsessively playing with it, like he owned it. But War wasn't letting him have full ownership of my body. He groped my ass, massaging and feeling me up, which only added to the good feelings Nash was bringing to life again between my thighs.

I moaned lightly, reaching behind me for War, looking for his hip to hold on to as Nash slowly increased his pace.

My hand brushed his cock, already thickening behind me again. "That was quick," I murmured.

He pressed his full body against me and whispered in my ear, "It's the thought of coming in your ass, baby girl. Kiss him while I get you ready to take us both."

My body exploded with lust at the idea, and Nash groaned, clearly having heard exactly what War had said despite his whisper. He slowed down, barely moving inside me while he waited for me and War to catch up.

War rolled away to grab a tube of lubricant, and I took the chance to glance in Vincent's direction.

When he'd come into the bar earlier, he'd been wearing a neat pair of suit pants and a neatly ironed button-down shirt.

Now, his shirt was half undone, showing off the tanned ridges of his abs and pecs. His belt had been discarded to the floor, and his pants were halfway down his hips, fly undone, impressive cock hard and in his hand, while he watched.

He didn't stroke it, but his grip on it was strangling, and precum leaked from the tip of him, shiny and just begging to join in on the action.

War crawled back across the bed, fingers slick and glossy with lubricant. He swiped them between my cheeks, finding the star of my ass and rubbing over it.

"Oh, hell," I moaned, my eyes closing even though I desperately wanted to watch Vincent more. "War..." I reached back and clutched at his hip, knowing that his fingers weren't enough for me anymore.

A swirling sensation built low in my spine with each touch of War's hands and thrust of Nash's hips. War's fingers pushed inside, and I gasped at the sudden rush of pleasure that came from having both sensitive places touched at once.

I pulled his hip again, encouraging him to put his cock exactly where we all wanted it. Nash licked over my lips. "Kiss me, Bliss. I got you."

I kissed him. Hard and deep, and I let my head spin around with thoughts of how much I loved him, while War replaced his fingers with his cock.

"Oh!" I shouted.

Nash kissed me harder, smashing his mouth against mine and muffling my shouts, but also adding his own, that sounded something like, "Tight. So fucking tight."

War paused, letting us all adjust to his size, and I glanced at Vincent, who slowly shifted his hand up and down his cock, the sight of me taking both Nash and War clearly too much for his self-control.

I wanted him to lose it completely. I wanted him to show me what he liked. I wanted to watch him bring himself to orgasm, just like I'd done, while thinking of him.

But War and Nash had other plans, both of them in unison, withdrawing and then filling me so deeply I was sure my eyes rolled back in my head. My breath caught and then disappeared, lost somewhere in between pushes and pulls of pure pleasure that lit up every nerve ending in my body and yet begged for more.

"I need to come," Nash groaned. "You're fucking killing me. You both are."

He picked up the pace, War matching him stroke for stroke, and all I could do was hold on and scream their names as my second orgasm hit me. The world around me went black beneath the intense pleasure, the orgasm stronger than anything I'd experienced today. My lungs were starved of oxygen because somewhere along the way, I'd forgotten to breathe. My legs trembled, blood zinging around my body too fast from a heart that had had all the excitement it could take. Nash caught my eye as he shouted my name and spilled his seed inside me, mixing and joining with War's, and just the thought had my orgasm intensifying until I was sure I would pass out.

War came again, buried deep inside me, his hands full of my ass cheeks while he rode me until he was done. Every thrust prolonged my orgasm, the whole thing stretching out and lingering longer than felt humanly possible.

Except it was, because my men knew what I liked, and exactly how much I could take, even when I didn't know it myself.

Nash and War both withdrew from my body, completely limp and spent, flopping back on the bed like they'd run a marathon. I breathed heavily too, exhausted and sated and messy, but not done.

Vincent watched me slide to the end of the bed to stand in front of him. Then I dropped to my knees, moving between his legs to reward him for his patience.

"Touch your breasts," he said quietly, but there was no please or timidness in the request. It was the words of a man who knew what he wanted to see.

I wrapped one hand around the base of his cock and pinched my nipple with the other, then lowered my mouth onto him, sucking and licking his head and shaft before taking him deep into my throat.

His hand came to the back of my head, but his touch was soft, and he kept his hips still, refusing to thrust up into my mouth, even though I wanted him to. I took him deeper, working my lips and tongue as hard as I could, just because I loved this gentle side of him, that was so at odds with the way he could kill a person in the blink of an eye. With me he was nothing but kind, generous, and sweet, even when I was giving him head and full permission to fuck my mouth.

After a few more minutes, he gently lifted my head. "I want a baby, Bliss. Your baby."

"I do too." I climbed onto his lap, my knees sinking on either side of his thighs, and then down onto his hard cock.

I sat there for a moment, while he gathered me close, his gaze locked with mine. His hands trailed up the sides of my body, cupping my breasts, and I leaned down to kiss him. This terrifying, violent yet sweet man, who had helped show me what it was I'd been missing, whispered my name and so much more as he came inside me. His fingers moved to my clit, already so overstimulated that it set off a third orgasm. This one was quieter, more intense, and I rocked over his lap, reveling in the way he worshipped me, even after watching me take two other men.

Still connected, but utterly exhausted, I dropped my chest down onto his, twisting my face so I could kiss the side of his neck.

He wrapped one arm around me and trailed the other up and down my spine, a low murmur of contentment on his lips.

One of the guys rolled over on the bed, I didn't look to see which one it was, I was too blissed out to care.

"Think we made a baby just now?" War asked, voice sleepy.

"I hope so," Vincent whispered into my hair.

I forced my breathing to stay even, and not give away what I already knew. I would tell them soon. But first I had to sort out the mess I'd made. If I told them what I'd agreed to in order to clear my debt, it would end in violence.

That's not what I wanted for this little life inside me.

I would make Jerry see sense. I'd pay him off some other way. Once I was back standing on my own two feet as Bliss, and not running and hiding like Bethany-Melissa, I'd tell my guys that the universe had already blessed us with a miracle.

32

BLISS

I gnawed on a fingernail, staring up at the dark ceiling and the restraints attached to it. I wondered if it had been Axel and Nash who had installed them when they'd first started running these parties, or if they'd hired a handyman. That would have been an interesting job to explain.

"I made you an appointment."

I twisted to Vincent from my position on the bed. "Me? For what?"

"A facial, a massage, and a pedicure at that place across from the girls' school in Providence."

I raised an eyebrow. "Daffodil's Day Spa? That's not something I'll turn down. That place is amazing. But why?"

He picked my foot up, kneading the sole with strong fingers. "I like looking after you. You've been biting that fingernail for fifteen minutes, and I'm worried you're going to make it bleed."

Nash pushed up on his elbow beside me. "What's

wrong? Are you stressed about something? Did we hurt you?"

War's hand went straight to my chin, twisting my face to the other side so he could see my expression.

I forced it into something neutral that hopefully didn't give away the fact I was due to meet Jerry that night, bursting the little bubble we'd created over the past few hours.

I ignored their concerns and pulled my head away from War's searching gaze. "When's the appointment?"

"Thirty minutes."

I sat up in a panic. "What? Today? I can't go today."

"Whatever you're worried about says that today is actually the perfect day." Nash pulled my fingers away from my mouth and pressed my bitten, ragged nail to his lips. "Go to the appointment. The bar reopens tomorrow, and once that happens, who knows when we'll get a day off."

War sat up, grabbing his clothes from the floor. "Yeah, we've decided. You're going."

I racked my brain, trying to think up an excuse. "I can't. My car is still at the hospital. I need to go pick it up." Not to mention get that note and study it again for similarities to Rebel's handwriting.

But War shook his head. "Nah, baby girl. You go get oiled up and relaxed, and we'll go get your car."

"I can't ask you to do that," I protested.

But he leaned over and kissed me. "After the way you just blew my mind, you can ask for any damn thing in the world, and I'll say yes. It's my fault your car is there anyway. I should have picked it up yesterday for you."

"What he said," Nash echoed. "Give us the keys. I'll

drive the Jeep, and War can drive your car back. V, you'll come too, right? We'll make a boys' afternoon of it while Bliss is getting lathered in...I don't know, whatever they lather with at those places."

"A boys' afternoon?" I echoed. "What do the three of you have in common?"

"You," they all answered simultaneously.

Well, there was that, and I really did want them to get along. Plus, it solved the problem of how I was going to sneak away to meet Jerry. I couldn't do that with all of them hanging around.

War gave Vincent a slow look. "You in?"

Vincent seemed surprised but slowly nodded. "Yes. I'll come."

I sucked in a deep breath and forced myself to get up from the cocoon of men and the safety they oozed. "I need to go get ready then."

I had a quick shower in the bathroom off my office and dressed in the clothes I'd been wearing earlier. My phone buzzed while I was putting on eyeliner, and I instantly wished I hadn't seen the message from Jerry that popped up.

Be here by 5.30. Don't keep me waiting or I might assume you aren't coming. There ain't no sick leave either, so don't even try it.

By the time I emerged with fresh makeup, all three of the guys were waiting by the door.

With my jacket in my arms, still not quite needed even outside, we all piled into Nash's Jeep, me and Nash in the front, War and Vincent in the back. I glanced at them, barely catching a look between them that lingered a little longer than it should have.

I missed Scythe and the easy way he had with War. I didn't know how War was handling it, Vincent being so different and yet still very much the same.

We drove into Providence, passing the fancy all-girls' school that had been severely damaged in a fire a while back and still hadn't reopened. I'd heard they'd sent all the girls to Edgely Academy, the all-boys' private school a few blocks away while they were making the extensive repairs required to reopen safely.

Nash pulled up in front of the day spa, his battered Jeep drawing the gaze of a couple of men in suits, sitting at a small outdoor table at the café next door.

War ignored them, holding his hand out to me. "Keys?"

I fished them from my purse and handed them over, hoping he didn't notice the tremble in my fingers.

I moved to get out of the car, but War caught my hand. "Kiss me goodbye." He grinned, his mood so jubilant it was hard not to catch it. "And make it good, baby girl," he added. "You know how I like an audience."

I shook my head and kissed him.

Nash raised an eyebrow from behind the steering wheel. "Don't think you're leaving without kissing me like that too."

A grin crept across my face. "Those guys watching us from the café are going to sure be surprised if I do that."

Nash twisted his fingers in my shirt and hauled me in. "Let them watch."

His lips met mine, kissing me sweetly.

When I pulled away, I searched for Vincent, but he was already out of the car, holding the door open for me.

I said goodbye to Nash and War and slid out, straight into Vincent's arms.

"I'll stay with you," he said. "I can sit in the waiting room."

I glanced through the glass windows of the day spa, at the two elderly ladies inside, both gawking at us. I tried to imagine Vincent sitting in the waiting room with them, his muscled arms crossed over his chest, his eyes dark and glaring at anyone who glanced in my direction. I patted his chest. "I don't need protecting from the town gossips. I'll be fine." I glanced back at Nash and War inside the Jeep. "Will you though?"

"It was nice of them to invite me. I know they probably would have preferred Scythe."

I shook my head and kissed his lips. "They just need to get to know you like I do."

He nodded. "Call me when you're finished, and I'll pick you up." He glanced back at the car again. "Or maybe we all will."

I didn't want them coming back to pick me up when I had to talk to Jerry. "It might be a while. These things take time. I'll get an Uber and see you at home."

His fingers tightened around mine. "I'm picking you up, Bliss."

I knew better than to argue when he was trying to look after me. I wouldn't win, no matter how much I protested. I'd just have to make it work. "Okay. I'll call you."

I waved as they drove off, wishing I was a fly on the wall in that car. I had no idea how their dynamic worked without me and Scythe. It would have been fascinating to find out. But they disappeared around a bend, and the reality I'd been putting off hit me squarely in the face again. I bent over, putting my hands to my knees, suddenly feeling dizzy and nauseous at what I had to do.

"Sweetie, are you okay?" A young woman poked her head out of the day spa and then rushed to my side when I shook my head. "Oh, honey. Come on in and sit down."

I let her guide me inside, suddenly sure my chest was too tight to even breathe.

The woman rubbed a comforting hand over my back while the two older ladies watched with huge eyes from their leather recliners, their wrinkled feet soaking in foot spas.

"Do you need water? Can I call anyone for you?"

"She had several very handsome young men in the car with her," one of the ladies offered. "Very handsome indeed."

I shook my head, fighting back a laugh at their gushing. I could have kissed them for providing enough comic relief that I could breathe again. "I'm fine. Just got a bit woozy. What's the time, please?"

"Nearly five."

I had twenty minutes to kill before I needed to be in an Uber and heading back to Saint View. "I've got an appointment. I don't know what they booked for me..."

The woman went behind her desk and tapped long fingernails over her keyboard. "Bliss? That's such a pretty name. Looks like you're in for the works. Massage. Facial. Pedicure..."

"Could we just do the pedicure?" I asked. "I'm going to have to reschedule the rest." I needed something to show the guys when I got home, and even more importantly, I needed something to do to occupy the time so I didn't freak out. But I couldn't do the entire list of services they offered, which was what Vincent seemed to have booked me in for.

"Of course. Take a load off and sit right there next to Miss Georgia. I'm Opal, and we'll get those toes soaking. What sweet gentlemen you have, buying you something like this."

I dropped down into the recliner and peeled my socks and shoes off, pushing them aside. Opal filled up the foot spa on the floor, adding in some scented oils, and when she gave me the nod, I plunged my feet into the warm water.

My eyes closed of their own accord, while bubbles soaked my feet and the chair behind me whirred to life to knead the tense muscles in my back.

"You can adjust the pressure there." Opal pointed to a control panel on the side of my chair. "Make it harder, or faster, or turn it off if you've had enough."

I sank deeper into the chair; pretty sure I never would have had enough. Opal pulled up a stool at my feet to start her work, while the other two ladies in the room finally lost interest in me and fell into their own gossipy conversation.

Opal smiled at me conspiratorially. "Three men, huh? One has to be your brother or something, right? Miss Georgia's eyesight isn't what it used to be."

I shook my head, everything too complicated to come up with an appropriate lie or diversion from the truth. What did it matter if I told Opal anyway? She could think me a whore, but after having Caleb throw that word in my face a hundred times, it had lost its sting. I didn't care what people thought anymore, not when all I wanted was to be happy.

"They're definitely not my brothers."

Opal raised one perfect eyebrow. "Well, isn't that something. Good for you, honey bunch."

"Thank you." It seemed an odd thing to say, but I wasn't sure how else to reply.

"I had a threesome once," the woman said as casually as anything, "but that was a long time ago, before my daughter came along."

"You have a daughter?" I asked.

She looked younger than I did, but she nodded.

"She's five now. Best thing I ever did." She eyed me carefully. "You expecting?"

I went to shake my head but then realized I'd been subconsciously rubbing my belly and decided to just be honest. "I only just found out."

Opal pulled my foot out of the spa and dried it off on a towel. "How special. And what a lucky little baby he or she will be, with all those big men to protect her." She winked at me. "And her mama, of course."

I swallowed thickly as guilt poured in. She was right. Every word. This baby was the luckiest kid in the world to have three men who wanted to be her daddy. They'd go to the ends of the earth for her. I knew that already because they did it for me.

Yet here I was, about to put her in danger because I was so determined to prove I could stand on my own two feet. Hadn't I already done that, many times over? Caleb had knocked me down, and I'd gotten back up. I'd built Psychos into a thriving business I could be proud of. I'd taken a hit there too, and stumbled with my confidence, but I'd kept going. Kept pushing, because I wasn't the stupid woman Caleb claimed me to be. I wasn't trailer trash, or a slut, because I'd fallen for three men instead of one. They respected me. They loved me. Now they were committing to having a family with me, and I was hellbent on ruining it all because somewhere along the way, I'd lost track of what was really important.

Them. Us. This disjointed feeling I couldn't shake wasn't because Scythe was suddenly missing from the equation. It was because I was putting up barriers. Walls that would keep my heart safe from men who were never going to break it.

It had just taken me this long to realize it.

"I'm an idiot," I murmured.

I needed my guys. To fill them in on what had happened so we could work out how to deal with it together. It was too big for me to deal with alone.

Opal smiled at me. "We all are when we find our person, honey. Or people, in your case." She glanced toward the window, then back at me. "That one of your fellas, too? Looks like he's trying to get your attention." She cocked her head toward the glass windows.

On the other side, Jerry smiled and waved like we were best friends.

I froze.

"Cute little girl," Opal went on, like the entire world hadn't just self-imploded. "She his daughter?"

"No," I said softly. "That's my little sister."

Verity stared at me with huge, scared eyes and tear-stained cheeks. Her wrist was pink from Jerry's tight grasp on it. I reached for my phone, but Jerry shook his head ever so slightly. The movement was tiny, but the threat was real. I dropped my hand away from my purse and glanced at the time.

I still had ten minutes until I was supposed to meet him.

He had clearly never intended to let me come of my own free will if he'd followed me here with my little sister as bait.

I stood, taking my other foot from the water, accidentally sloshing some onto Opal's pants. "I'm so sorry," I said to her. "I need to go."

She sat back on her heels. "Something wrong, sugar?"

Jerry glared at me impatiently. I didn't dare tell Opal to call the cops in case he could read my lips. In any case, it wasn't the cops I needed.

It was my guys.

"Opal," I said quietly, never taking my eyes off Jerry and Verity for a second for fear he'd disappear with her. "Does your system record incoming phone numbers? You could look up the number of the man who made my appointment, right?"

"I don't know about that, but we take down the number of the person making the booking. Do you need to call him? You can use my phone…"

"Can you? Find his number, tell him I had to leave, and that he needs to pay you over the phone."

"Sure, but is everything—"

I cut her off, walking out of the store in bare feet.

"Honey, your shoes!"

I ignored her, letting the glass door swing closed behind me, and rushed toward my sister.

Jerry cut me off, sidestepping in front of me and

pulling Verity behind him with a sharp tug on her skinny wrist.

She let out a weak cry, barely louder than a kitten mewl, but it hit me right in the chest. I loved that girl like she was my own child, and now she was in danger because of me.

"What the hell are you doing?" I hissed at Jerry.

He put an arm out to hug me, and I flinched, trying to move away. But he grabbed me, hauling me into his thick chest roughly. "Smile nicely now so the ladies in the shop don't call the police. We wouldn't want that now, not with your sweet little sister here. I already made her cry once, I don't think you really want that to happen again, do you?"

Panic surged up my throat at the thought of what he could have done to her. I hugged him back, disgusted at the feel of his arm clenched around me. "If you've so much as laid a finger on that girl…"

"You'll what, Bliss? You're as gutless as your mother. You ain't gonna do shit. And anyway, I didn't touch the brat. Yet. She's solely here because I knew you wouldn't show."

"You didn't even give me a chance," I bit out, reaching for my sister again only to have my arm caught in Jerry's meaty fingers.

We rounded a corner, and he shoved us toward a car. "Get in."

Everything inside me screamed not to. But there was nothing I could do with Verity now crying again as he wrenched her arm. "I'll do whatever you want me to do. But let her go. You're hurting her."

Jerry shrugged and wiped Verity's tears away. "I like when they cry."

My stomach threatened to empty its contents. He was sick.

Against my better judgment but with my back against a wall, I got in the car. Jerry shoved Verity in after me, and she burst into hysterical sobs as I wrapped her in my arms.

"Bethy? What's going on?"

I only had a second while Jerry rounded the car to the driver's seat. "Does anyone know you're here?"

She shook her head. "I was on my way to soccer practice. Dad was supposed to take me, but he didn't show up. It's just on the field across the road from school, so I walked—"

Jerry yanked open the door and slid behind the wheel, and Verity clammed right up in terror.

I couldn't blame her. My heart hammered too.

Jerry started the car and drove it through the familiar streets of Providence.

My phone rang, shrill in the deathly silence, and I scrambled for it.

Jerry's hand reached back, palm up expectantly. "Don't even think about doing anything other than putting that phone in my hand, Bliss."

My gaze met his in the rearview mirror, and I knew better than to push my luck. Not with Verity in the car. Not with my own child inside me. I handed the phone over reluctantly.

"There's going to be cops everywhere any minute now, all of them searching for Verity," I warned Jerry. "You know my father has money and connections. As soon as they realize she's missing, the whole town will be crawling with cops, all hunting you."

He snorted. "You think I don't know that?"

He made two more turns, and a little of my panic ebbed away when he stopped a street away from my father's house. "She can go." He turned around and glared at my sister. "You say one word about where you've been this afternoon though, and I'll slit Bliss' throat. You want that to be your fault, pretty girl?"

She shook her head fast, but I was too busy shoving her out the door to comfort her. "Go!"

She hesitated on the sidewalk, staring back at me.

I forced a cheerful smile. "I'll be fine, kiddo. Jerry is my stepdad. He just wants to talk to me about some adult things. Go home, okay? Run fast." I very deliberately used his name, praying she'd remember it and have the courage to tell her parents, despite the threats he'd made.

Tears streamed silently down her face. Then she turned and ran, her blond ponytail flying out behind her.

Jerry watched her in the rearview mirror for a moment, then shook his head. "It's uncanny. The resemblance, you know? You and her." His gaze drifted to me, and he ran his tongue over his lips. "Tasty."

I shuddered. But anything he did to me wouldn't compare to the agony I would have felt if he'd done anything to Verity. I was so relieved to have her out of the car I almost welcomed his filthy gaze, because anything was better than him looking at her like that.

But eventually, he dragged his gaze away. "As much as I'd like to sample the produce, I've got clients waiting for you." He steered the car onto the road again and drove in the direction of Saint View. "Turns out a lot of my guys like their women with a bit of meat on them. You'll have your debt paid off in no time with how many want a chance at your fresh, virgin pussy." He laughed at me. "Dumbasses will believe anything, so if they ask, you tell him you've never been touched before, got it? Maybe cry a little while they rail you."

"I'm not doing this, Jerry."

His gaze shifted to the rearview mirror, his eyes narrowing. "You owe me, Bliss, and I always get what I'm owed. One way or another."

33

VINCENT

*W*e were halfway to the hospital before I realized Bliss' jacket was shoved down the side of the front seat, squished in by the center console. "We should go back," I said to Nash. "She'll be cold."

He glanced over but shook his head. "Nah, she's inside. It'll be warm in there, and she's gotta get naked for her massage anyway."

War groaned from the back seat. "Please don't talk about her naked. I'll get hard again."

Tell him to quit complaining. I'm the one who's really missing out here.

I squeezed my eyes shut tight, but it did nothing to shut Scythe up.

Seriously, V. I mean, sex vicariously through you is shit. I do applaud you for that foursome though. I didn't think you had it in you. And this plan to knock Bliss up? Fuck, yes. Thank God you agreed to that. But there is nothing like being inside her sweet, wet—"

"Shut up."

War grumbled from the back seat. "What's your problem?"

I shook my head, the low-level headache I'd had for weeks doubling in intensity.

If you just quit being a big fucking baby and let me out once in a while...

"No." I glanced back at War and shook my head. "I mean, sorry. I wasn't talking to you. I'm just preoccupied."

That's not the way to win him over. I can tell you what is the way though. Get down on your knees and suck his—

"Scythe!"

Nash glanced at me. "You okay?"

I looked back at War.

His gaze was trained on me intently. "He's there, isn't he?"

I sighed. "Sometimes he's quiet, but he mostly takes great delight in tormenting me."

The corner of War's mouth lifted. "Yeah, I bet he does. Mouthy fuck."

"That's one way of describing him."

"I thought you two couldn't hear each other?" Nash asked curiously. "Isn't it like a 'you're here now, so he isn't,' sort of thing?"

I shook my head. "Normally we can't." Not like this anyway. I would sometimes get flashes from him when something felt out of my control. He'd take over until the thing that made me uncomfortable passed, and then his voice would go silent again. Or at least drop back to a whisper. But now, I couldn't shut him up. He was in my head all the damn time, and no matter what I did, sometimes loud, sometimes soft, but I couldn't get him to stop.

He should have been fading and yet again today he was louder than ever.

I'd googled and come to the realization that I had more going on in my head than just the dissociative disorder I'd self-diagnosed myself with.

"I think I'm probably certifiably crazy at this point," I confessed to the other two. "I'm quite confident it's not normal to have voices in your head as much as I do."

It wasn't even *my* normal. Which was the truly disturbing thing. I'd never minded Scythe's presence when he went away quickly and wasn't always in my head. But this...this incessant chatter...

I'm really fucking annoying, huh? And you think it's me they'd all prefer?

Nash took one hand off the steering wheel and clapped a hand on my shoulder. "We like your brand of crazy, V. As long as you don't decide to stab us in your sleep, we're good."

"I probably can't guarantee that..."

Nash glanced over at me and then laughed. "You're hilarious."

I wasn't trying to be.

War had gone quiet, and I forced myself not to look back at him again.

Just 'cause you ain't looking at him, doesn't mean you ain't thinking about his big, thick cock, though, huh?

Desperate for something to do with my hands, I pulled Bliss' jacket out from the space she'd shoved it into and shook it once, trying to get the creases out.

A little piece of paper fell from her pocket, fluttering to the floor of the car. I stopped in the middle of folding her jacket and bent, retrieving the slip of paper.

I'm having a baby.

I had to read it three times to be sure I'd understood it properly.

Holy fucking shit, V. Don't be dumb. She's already pregnant. Knocked up. With child!

With War giving directions, Nash parked in the hospital parking lot and tossed Bliss' keys into the back seat. "Catch."

War plucked them from the air effortlessly and leaned between the front seats. Both men were completely oblivious to the note I'd pulled out of Bliss' pocket. But Scythe wouldn't shut up.

A baby. Holy hell, I can't believe you went and knocked her up.

He went silent for a moment.

I knew why. I'd already come to the same conclusion.

It was too soon for me to be the father. We'd only just slept together in the last few days.

But she slept with me. It could still be mine.

A storm of feeling welled inside me.

V, that baby is mine.

I shook my head.

You can't keep me from her. Not now.

The keys jingled in War's hand, and then his door slammed. I jumped when his face appeared in my window. He tapped on it twice.

Slowly, I lowered the glass.

His gaze flickered over my face, true concern in his gaze. "What do you need? Tell me, and I'll do it."

I had the sudden feeling he could see right inside my head and hear every word that Scythe shouted.

"I don't know," I said quietly. "He's never been like this."

Because she's carrying my fucking baby, Vincent!

He didn't know that. It could be War's or Nash's. But Scythe had lost it. His anger vibrated through my limbs and clouded my head.

"Do you want to come with me?" War asked tentatively. "We can talk while I drive."

Something inside Scythe broke. The yearning he had to be with War flooded me, a near physical pull in War's direction.

"I'll stay with Nash," I said quickly, closing the window.

War stepped back to avoid his nose being clipped by the rising glass. But the entire time he stared at me, his eyes piercing, and again I had that same feeling that he knew exactly what I was thinking.

Because you and I aren't all that different, V. He knows me. So he knows you.

No. We were different. I wanted out of the whole killing game. I was the one who wanted a family and a wife.

Well, you got the family. It just doesn't look exactly like you thought it would. What are you going to do? Throw it away? War fucking loves you as much as Bliss does.

He loves you.

We're the same fucking person, V. Two sides of the same damn coin. If you just stopped trying to push me out for one second...

I was so confused. My headache pounded until the pain was almost blinding.

You don't handle big news well, V. And this baby is huge. Let me do it.

A trick.

Not a fucking trick. Jesus, fuck. You make this so difficult every freaking time. I'm not going away, V. I love her. And I love him. Nash is probably okay too, in his flannel-shirt-wearing way. Still not exactly sure what Bliss sees in him. Might be the giant peen. But that's beside the point. You want this to stop? Let me in.

War moved stiffly to Bliss' car. He glanced back at me once, something in his eyes so heartbreaking I could barely stand it.

I let him go, despite every muscle in my body screaming to chase after him, draw him close, and kiss him.

They were Scythe's feelings, but they felt like mine.

I gripped the armrest so tightly my fingers cracked. Or maybe that was the plastic. I didn't know.

Nash glanced over at me. "What'd the armrest do to you? Go easy."

War drove Bliss' little white hatchback out of the parking lot and turned onto the road with Nash following. I was grateful for the distraction. I kept my gaze solidly on the car in front of me as Nash turned up the radio, singing along while we picked up speed.

My phone rang, and I answered it quickly.

"Uh, hi. Are you the gentleman who made an appointment for Bliss Arthur earlier today?"

"Oh, hello. Yes, I am."

"Oh, great. Listen, honey, she had to leave, and she said I should call you for payment."

I squinted, watching War navigate a turn. "She left? She's only been there thirty minutes. Where is she?"

Nash shot me a questioning look, and I opened my mouth to explain, but then his phone rang too, connecting through the Bluetooth to the car's stereo system.

The screen on his dashboard just showed a string of numbers, no name displayed. Nash hit answer. "Hello?"

The caller's voice came through the car speakers. "Nash? This is David Arthur. Bethany-Melissa's father. Is she with you?"

My fingers clenched around the phone. Bliss' dad's words slurred a little.

"Sugar? You still there?" the woman from the day spa asked. "I'm only going to charge you for the pedicure..."

Nash made a face, one full of confusion. "Ah, hey?" he asked, answering David's question about Bliss. "No? She's at a day spa."

I dropped the phone away from my ear at the shouts in the background of Nash's call. I strained my ears, trying to hear what was going on better, the woman needing payment on my phone forgotten.

David cleared his throat. "Are you sure? Because I have Verity here..."

Nash and I both stiffened at a wail in the background.

Nash eased up on the accelerator, the car slowing in his distraction. "David? Is she okay? What's happened?"

"I'm honestly not sure. Verity just got home from school. She's crying. She says Jerry has Bethany-Melissa and—"

The slip of paper with Bliss' pregnancy declaration crumpled in my fingers and I shoved it back into Bliss' jacket pocket. "She's not at the spa. They just called. She left."

Nash clutched the wheel again. "David, can you put Verity on the phone?"

"I can't. She's crying. Listen. I'm calling the police. Bethany-Melissa isn't answering her phone, and she's not at Psychos or with you. That's enough for me to get the police involved."

"No! No police! He said he'll slit her throat!" Verity screamed.

All too vividly, the image of Jerry drawing a blade across Bliss' perfect neck appeared in my head. I knew exactly how the blood would well and gush, a violent red as the life quickly drained from her body.

After all, it was my favorite way to kill someone.

"She's already pregnant."

Nash stared at me, his mouth falling open.

"What?" That came from David on the phone. "Bethany-Melissa is pregnant?"

I'd forgotten he was even there.

If Jerry so much as touches a hair on her head, I will kill him so slowly and painfully he'll cry for his mother.

For once, Scythe and I agreed on something.

Let me out, V. Let me out, let me out, let me out.

I felt the darkness swell and roar in my ears. It drowned out Nash frantically trying to get more information from David and Verity's cries of fear. I bent over, lifting the leg of my pants and shoved my fingers into the side of my boot.

The little knife blade I always kept hidden there was like gold in my hand.

Cold.

Hard.

Precious

Scythe's laughter echoed in my ears, joining in with the swirl of chaos he seemed to create wherever he went.

I lifted my head, ready to throw away all attempts at giving up the life I'd been born to.

But before I could say anything, through the windshield, blissfully unaware that Bliss was in danger, War's car failed to brake at an intersection and went skidding off the road.

34

BLISS

*J*erry parked the car outside a trailer, not all that far from the one I'd spent my first five years in. He put one hand to the passenger seat, using it as leverage to twist himself around to glare at me. "This is where you'll be, every Saturday night until your debt is paid off. If you don't show, you know who'll be replacing you, don't you? You saw how easy it was for me to take her tonight. I can do it again just as easily. Plenty of men like 'em young."

"And if I just pay out the debt?"

"How?" he sneered. "Everybody heard about the cops nabbing all your cash. You know they're probably snorting the drugs up their noses as we speak. Hell, one or two of them might come by and use your own money to pay me for your services. Wouldn't that be the whole damn thing coming full circle?"

He laughed like it was the funniest thing in the world.

"I can get the money." I'd borrow it from Sandra. Or get a loan. Vincent's mom had money, though I doubted she was a woman I wanted to owe any more than I wanted to owe Jerry.

His filthy gaze raked over my body again. "I need to keep my clients happy, Bliss. I promised them a big titty virgin. That's you. Now get inside and get yourself ready."

My skin crawled so bad I got out of the car just so he couldn't look at me anymore.

"Love to watch you walk away, sweet cheeks," he called out the window, though I was sure it was more a reminder that he was there, watching my every move in case I decided to run.

I hurried up the steps of the trailer, forcing my head high and clutching my purse like it was armor. Music played loudly inside, and the chatter of women drifted out between cracks and crevices in thin walls. I knocked loudly.

The door swung open, and a woman stuck her head out. She was maybe ten years older than me with foundation smeared across her cheeks, but her lips and eyes still bare of product. She eyed me with a frown.

Jerry leaned on the horn. It blared, cutting through the music. "Get her ready, Lucy! Her gentleman caller will be here in twenty."

She flashed a smile in Jerry's direction and waved. "No problem! I got her!"

She grabbed my arm and hauled me inside, slamming the door shut behind me.

Then she flipped the bird at the closed door while Jerry drove away. "Fucking asshole!" she yelled as the engine sound disappeared.

Another woman smiled and waved from where she applied makeup in a tiny bathroom mirror. I'd never met her before, but the woman who'd opened the door was vaguely familiar, and she looked at me now with a similar curiosity.

"I'm Bliss," I said eventually.

Her eyes went wide. "Kim's daughter?"

"Yes."

She let out a slew of curse words that ended in, "That motherfucking asshole! I can't believe he's doing this to you, after all Kim did to keep you out."

I exhaled shakily. "He threatened my baby sister. My stepmom. My best friend. Basically every woman I know."

She shook her head angrily. "God, he's a piece of shit. One day..."

I could fill in the silence. It was a revenge vow.

"I'm Lucy by the way."

"Rhiannon," the woman called from the bathroom, capping her mascara and walking out to the main room. "Did you say your name was Bliss?"

I nodded.

"Ain't you Nash's girl?"

I nodded quickly. "Could I use your phone? If I call him..."

The woman pressed her teeth together. "Honey, if you call him and he comes storming down here like a jealous boyfriend to rescue you, you might be swept off in his arms, but where does that leave me and Lucy? Jerry would be real mad."

"And he's as nasty as a rattlesnake when he's angry," Lucy commented, cringing.

I didn't know Nash's phone number by heart anyway. So it was useless even if they had let me use their phones.

"I miss Nash," Lucy said idly, applying blush to her gaunt cheeks. "He was my first pimp, you know that? Fuck, he spoiled me for everyone after him though. Ain't none of them ever treat us good like he did." She pointed to a makeup bag on the counter. "Better slap some more of that shit on your face, doll. Jerry likes his girls all gussied up and slutty-looking. His words, not mine. Natural makeup doesn't cut it with him."

I sat at the kitchenette, not knowing what else to do, so I focused on the mention of the man who'd always taken care of me. "You were one of Nash's girls?"

The woman nodded. "He as kind now as he was back then?"

I nodded. "He's a sweetheart. I still find it hard to believe he ever did...that."

She shook her head. "Don't you be down on that man because of the things he had to do to make ends meet. Ain't nobody blamed him for that. If Jerry was outta the picture and wouldn't come dragging me back by my hair, I'd go back to Nash in a heartbeat. If he was still doing that sorta thing. I hear he's not."

"Shame," Rhiannon chipped in.

I glanced between the two of them. "You wouldn't get out of the game altogether if Jerry wasn't forcing you?"

Lucy eyed me. "We don't got no other skills, doll."

I saw my mother in these women. Broken. Desperate. All my mom had needed was someone to give her a helping hand. I'd failed her, but I could still help her friends.

"I own a bar," I found myself saying. "Psychos? I could give you jobs..."

The two women looked at each other and then back at me. Smiles played all over their lips.

"That's real kind of you, but what does your bar pay?" Lucy asked. "Minimum wage?"

"A few dollars over. Plus tips." It had been the first thing I'd made sure of when I'd taken over the place. Everyone's pay had gone up with the success of the parties, and I'd been so proud to be in a position to pay more to my staff. They worked hard for me, and they deserved the extra money.

Lucy patted my hand. "No, thank you."

I gaped at them. "You...don't want a job? You don't need any experience..."

"We got kids to support. Food and gas, doll. It's expensive. Jerry might be a fucking asshole, but he brings us work. Regular work that pays a lot more than minimum wage plus tips."

I stared at them. "But..."

Lucy shrugged. "Yeah, we know. This work isn't for everyone. Clearly not for you. But it's what we know. It's what I'm good at. I don't want to give it up."

Rhiannon abandoned her makeup and crossed her legs to pull on her heels. "I don't either. I just want better conditions. There's places where sex work is legal and not this dirty little secret, you know. Brothels run by madams where there's protection and health checks and safety."

My brain whirred a million miles an hour, and then words came out my mouth I never thought I'd say. "If I could give you that, would you come work for me?"

Both women stared, and for a second, I saw the hope in their eyes. It was pure and innocent and fueled me in a way nothing had in a long time.

These women deserved better. My mother had deserved better than this shithole of a life she'd been forced into by a man who'd tricked her into loving him.

The little girl inside me whose past was catching up with her deserved better.

A hard knock came at the door, and all three of us jumped.

Lucy opened it a fraction, sticking her head out.

"You Bliss? Jerry promised me first dibs on ya."

My stomach churned. Ever so slowly, I stood. I glanced at the cutlery drawer, wondering if there was anything sharp enough inside to do real damage with. Because there was no way I was going with this man. I was getting out of here and finding my guys. I'd hire War's club to be bodyguards for every damn woman I knew if I had to.

Lucy followed my line of sight and shook her head, like she'd read my mind and knew what I was planning on doing. "I'm Bliss," she announced, widening her eyes at me meaningfully.

The man paused. "Jerry said you had titties."

Rhiannon rolled her eyes, but Lucy took it in stride. "Let's go and I'll show you 'em."

With a final overemphasized look at me, she slipped out the door.

When it was just the two of us left in the room, Rhiannon sighed. She reached into her purse and handed me a phone. "Call whoever you need to call. I'll tell Jerry you stole it while I was with a client."

With that, she walked out the door, leaving her phone behind.

I wasn't going to waste the opportunity. I called the

bar, because it was the only number I could search online, and prayed someone would be there. "Come on, come on," I murmured, peeping through the trailer windows. "Please, Rebel. Be there."

It rang out. "Dammit!"

I thought of calling War's clubhouse, but a second internet search showed no online presence for the club, so I had no way of contacting him there either.

Time ticked, my opportunity slowly running out. I couldn't stay here.

I opened the door and slipped out into the night, running down the steps, checking over my shoulder with Rhiannon's phone pressed tight to my ear.

It was a last resort, one I'd been trained as a toddler never to do because the police were all against us.

"Nine-one-one. What is your—"

I screamed as I tripped over something in the darkness. I fell hard into the rock and dirt, the phone skittering away when I put my hands up to break my fall. Pain radiated up through my hands and wrists and into my elbows. My knees scraped, likely bleeding beneath my jeans. Tears stung the backs of my eyes, but I scrambled for the phone, and the man on the other end, who was repeatedly saying, "Hello? Anyone there?"

"Yes! Yes, I'm here!"

A boot crunched down on Rhiannon's phone. And then Jerry's fingers were in my hair, yanking my head back. "I knew you'd run. Stupid girl, you're so predictable. All I had to do was fucking sit here in the darkness, and bang, right on schedule, here you come, sprinting like your life depends on it."

I screamed again and grabbed his hands, pain ripping

through my scalp as he dragged me through the dirt. "Help!" I screamed. "Somebody, please! Help me!"

The curtains of the nearest trailer were pushed aside, and an older woman's face appeared. I scrambled, trying to get back on my feet, but I didn't miss the way she shook her head disapprovingly and let the curtain fall back. "Please!" I shouted again, even though I already knew how useless it was.

"You really think anyone is going to come out here and help you? You've been gone too long, Bliss. You've forgotten how this place works. We mind our own business around here. We don't involve the cops. And..." he yanked my hair again so he could lean down to shout in my face, "we pay our fucking debts!"

The streets of the trailer park became more and more familiar the farther he dragged me, until I saw the hell-hole I'd grown up in.

"Home sweet home, Bliss. Back where you always belonged. Get inside." He pushed me up the stairs and into the trailer, the door slamming shut behind him.

I hit the kitchen sink and spun around, glaring at him with all the rage that had nowhere to go but onto him. "I told you. I'll pay the debt. But not like this."

"And I told you that you'll pay it in any way I see fit. Clearly you need teaching. You always were a spoiled little brat. Never fucking listened. Nothing has changed." He grabbed a chair from the kitchenette, scraping it along the floor to the trailer door before slumping down into it, blocking the only exit. "Take your clothes off."

Panic surged again. "Let me go."

"Not going to happen. You cost me money tonight.

Now you're going to start paying it back. You can start by taking care of this."

He unzipped his pants, flopping his semi-erect dick out.

Bile rose in my throat. "I'm not touching you."

"You don't get a say, bitch. I own you. So get your big fucking titties out and get on your knees and suck my dick."

"There's no way in hell—"

For a big, solid man in his fifties, Jerry moved quicker than I could have dreamed possible. He shoved me against the wall so hard I didn't even see it coming.

But I felt it. My head cracked off the plasterboard painfully, sending sparks of light across my vision. For a second, the world swam, and Jerry yanked my shirt up, exposing my bra.

I went to grab for my shirt, to pull it back down, but my head pounded, and my movements were slow. "Jerry! Stop, no!"

He didn't care. He grabbed both my hands, hauling them above my head and pinning them with his meaty fingers. With his other hand, he pushed down on my shoulder, forcing me to my knees. "Open your mouth, bitch."

I twisted away, dodging his disgusting penis that was now face height. He still held my hands above my head, so it was all I could do to twist out of the way. "You put that in my mouth and I'll fucking bite it off, asshole. I swear to God, just try me!"

"Fucking mouthy bitch, just like your mama, ain't you? Takin' the Lord's name in vain. Some guys will like it, you know that? They like the fight. Me? Not so much."

He fumbled with something on the sink. "I like my bitches nice and silent while I fuck them. Since you ain't gonna shut up, this will keep you quiet."

Jerry reared back, giving up his attempts at getting his dick in my mouth. Instead, he came at me, a dirty-looking syringe in his hands. "Your mama liked a little heroin in her veins before I fucked her. You will too."

35

SCYTHE

The moment War drove off the edge of the road was the moment I felt Vincent give in.

They need you.

Damn fucking right they did.

Nash slammed on the brakes, not caring that we were in the middle of the intersection, but I was already out the door, running for the edge of the road and sliding down the embankment to where Bliss' car lay, passenger side smashed in by a tree.

"Oh, fuck me sideways." I eyed the steam rising from beneath the crumpled in hood. A hissing noise accompanied it, but all I had eyes for was the driver. If he was fucking dead before I got to tell him how I felt, I would kill him all over again.

It opened as I skidded to a stop in front of it.

I yanked it, the metal letting out a piercing squeak of complaint. And then I was in his face, frantically searching his body for injuries.

Head laceration. Probably concussion. Check for cracked ribs. Is he breathing okay?

Vincent rattled off the list of practical things. Even in my head, his tone was laced with worry.

But all I could see was that War was alive. Mad as fuck but alive.

Nash ran up behind me and stared in at War over my shoulder. "What the hell happened? You forget where the brakes were?"

War threw Nash a glare that could have killed. "I braked, asshole. The car clearly didn't get the message." He glanced over at the ruined passenger seat, grimaced, then yanked his seat belt off. He wiped blood away from his eyes with the back of his hand. "Get out of the way, V. I need to get out before something worse happens. Like this whole car going up in flames. Shit. Bliss is gonna kill me. This is a write off."

He tried to get past me, but I couldn't move. My heart hammered with adrenaline, and my fingers shook. All I could think was that he could have fucking died, and I never would have gotten to tell him how I felt.

So tell him now.

"I love you," I yelped at him. "Just in case you die in the next thirty seconds from internal bleeding or some shit."

He froze and looked at me properly for the first time. The silence rang out between us, him staring at me in confusion. Then something changed in his eyes. "Scythe?"

I couldn't help myself. "No, Madonna. Strike a pose."

War's grin widened, and he grabbed me by the shirt, yanking me down so our faces were level. His gaze ran all over my face, searching, recognizing, and then finally, his fingers gripped tighter. "Say it again."

"Hey, nice to meet you, I'm Madonna."

He snorted on a laugh. "Say you fucking love me."

"I fucking love you."

He shook his head. "You asshole."

He slammed his lips onto mine, gripping my face with both hands and sinking into the kiss.

"Ah." Nash cleared his throat. "I'm just going to go over there while you two have your reunion..."

I barely heard him. All I could think about was getting closer, pulling War in so tight he became a part of me, one I could keep. His tongue moved with mine, his mouth warm and the stubble around his lips scratching at my skin. He groaned into my mouth, and I briefly wondered if he was in pain, but the way he held me tight said otherwise. He was strong and solid, and so fucking mine.

Scythe, there's fuel leaking everywhere. This is an entirely inappropriate place for a reunion. And Bliss...

I jerked back. Eyes wide and wild as I looked for Nash. "Bliss."

War stood, wincing, but the panic in my voice clearly got to him. "What's happened? Where is she?"

Nash answered for me because I was already getting beneath War's arm to help him up the embankment.

"Jerry has her," Nash filled him in grimly.

"What?" War roared. "And you stopped for me? Are you two out of your fucking minds?" He glanced at me. "I know you are."

I shrugged. "Fair assessment."

Nash was pissed, though. "Couldn't exactly just leave

you for dead, dickhead. You think Bliss wouldn't have killed us for that?"

War shoved my offers of help away and got himself up the embankment, abandoning Bliss' car and the small crowd of people gathering to rubberneck. He threw himself into the back seat of Nash's Jeep, and I followed, closing the door while Nash got in behind the wheel.

He gunned the engine, glancing over his shoulder at us. "Really? I'm your chauffer now?"

I raised an eyebrow. "You wanna come back here and make War feel all better?"

"Ew, no. If I hear sucking noises, I'm throwing you both out."

War laughed and then groaned, clutching his head.

Nash screwed up his nose before turning back to the road he was speeding along at well over the limit. "I'm good with driving after all."

I rested my hand on War's thigh, and he put his down on top. Slowly, our fingers interlocked. But we were both too distracted, worrying about Bliss. The miles passed too slowly, each one making me more and more antsy.

If Jerry has so much as touched her...

"I know, bro. Settle down. I got this." I'd said it out loud, but barely above a whisper.

War glanced at me but didn't say anything. I guessed he was getting used to me talking to myself. I bounced one leg up and down, too much energy to contain sitting still. The darkness inside me billowed around like storm clouds. With each mile we passed, each one taking us closer to Bliss, the angrier and darker they became. "Nash, my knife..."

Nash reached across to the passenger seat and picked

it up, but then he paused. "Should I give it to you? Vincent was pretty insistent about giving up the game..."

That was before he touched Bliss.

"We're in agreement," I told Nash.

He glanced over at me and then passed back the blade.

I let out a sigh of relief that came just from having it in my hands.

"What are you going to do?" War asked.

"Depends what he's done. If he's made her a nice cup of tea, I'll ask for a cup of my own."

War grimaced. "And if he hasn't?"

I narrowed my eyes. "Then I hope that the tea is really fucking hot, throw it in his face, and... Actually, probably best I don't tell you. You get longer in jail for premeditated murder. Better I just see where my whims take me in the moment."

War shook his head. "You aren't going back to that jail. We only just got you back."

"Ye of little faith, Warrick. Ye of little faith."

"We're here," Nash announced. "It's that trailer just ahead."

War and I leaned forward, peering through the windshield into the night outside. Beside me, War's fingers flexed into fists. Mine clamped around my knife handle. Two women banged on Jerry's trailer door, their shouts echoing back to us through the open car windows.

"Son of a bitch," Nash swore. "I know them. Don't hurt them."

The second Nash got us close enough, the three of us were out of the car and racing for the trailer.

"Lucy! Rhiannon! What's going on?" Nash shouted.

The two women spun around, gazes bouncing around the three of us before landing on Nash. They both ran to him.

"Bliss is inside!" Lucy yelped. "We've been trying to get to her, but Jerry has the door barricaded."

I was already up the steps and kicking the door.

Just like the women had reported it, Jerry had something blocking it. The door barely budged an inch.

Nash glanced at me. "Together."

"Do it."

We both sent out boots hard into the metal. The entire trailer rattled, but whatever he'd blocked it with held.

A gunshot fired out one of the trailer's windows, glass spraying everywhere.

On instinct, Nash and I both ducked. The women screamed and ran, abandoning us to Jerry's whims.

"Come out, come out, Jerry," War taunted from his sheltered spot behind a car. "We need to finish what we started.

"Should have let me kill him when I had the chance weeks ago," I muttered to War, remembering the night we'd beat Jerry up and left him on his doorstep like the piece of dirt he was.

"Didn't have a good enough reason then!" War shouted.

"How about now?" I yelled back.

"Let your freak flag fly, brother."

Nash and I looked at each other, and without saying anything, both of us ran for the door, shoulder first.

Pain splintered through my body at the contact, but the door gave way, and Nash and I both tumbled inside.

Bliss' scream pierced right through my heart. She was on her knees, half hidden behind Jerry whose dick was swinging free.

Let it loose.

Fuck, yeah.

The darkness took over.

It was like inhaling a rich, expensive cigar. It filled my lungs and my nose and seeped its way into my bloodstream until it was all I knew.

The gun went off again, and I jerked at the blinding-hot pain, but the darkness didn't care. It didn't stop until it got what it came for.

The blade drew across Jerry's neck, sweet and fast, like it had a mind of its own, not controlled by my fingers or by the voices in my head. It had nothing to do with me, and yet when Jerry dropped to the floor beside Bliss, his neck a gaping smile of blood, satisfaction rolled through me.

Nash grabbed Bliss from the floor, hauling her back and into his arms, while I stood guard over my kill and gave the darkness time to subside. It always did once blood had been spilled. It was like a peace offering, one I had no problem in providing.

Jerry's blood spread across the floor, a slow-moving puddle of crimson, his eyes fixed and staring.

Dead as a motherfuckin' doornail in seconds.

Just how I liked it.

36

BLISS

I couldn't stop screaming. Nash wrapped his arms tight around me, hauling me back from Jerry's body and the blood-soaked knife in Scythe's hand.

I'd never once been afraid of him.

Not until I'd watched him murder a man right in front of me with zero hesitation or remorse. It was only then I realized the full extent of what Scythe and Vincent were capable of.

Cold, vicious, unfeeling murder.

Jerry deserved it. There was no sympathy in my heart for him, but the pure blackness in Scythe's eyes was terrifying.

He turned our way, and Nash pushed me behind him. War made it inside the trailer, breathless with dried blood across his forehead.

He froze. "Scythe…Give me the knife."

Scythe turned to look at him but didn't loosen his grip on the deadly weapon. It was then I saw the blood, dripping down his arm, and the tear in his shirtsleeve.

Instinct to protect him took over. I pushed Nash out of the way. "He's hurt."

War grabbed for me. "Bliss, no. We don't know what he's—"

But I shook him off, ignoring the knife in Scythe's hand and grabbing the other one, inspecting the injury to his upper arm. "He's not going to hurt me." I clamped my hand to the bleeding wound. "Hey, Scythe."

And suddenly, he was the man I knew and loved again. "Hey, gorgeous. Miss me?"

I grinned at him, and at the relief that flooded the little trailer. But it was short-lived. "What exactly do we do now?" I asked. "You're hurt..."

He pried my fingers away and inspected the injury. "Nah, flesh wound. It'll be fine."

I wasn't sure, and it definitely needed stitches, but it didn't look like he was going to die from it either. So the bigger problem was the very dead body at our feet.

Nash was the one to voice it. "What are we going to do about him?"

War eyed Jerry's mutilated body. "Nothing. Just leave him here to rot. It's better than what he deserves. Piece of rapist scum. Did he touch you?"

I shook my head. "If he'd had a few more minutes..."

"You can thank War for us being late," Scythe said dryly. "If we hadn't had to pull him out of your wrecked car."

"My what? Is that why you're all bloody?"

War shook his head at Scythe. "Tattletale."

Scythe shrugged. "Been called worse."

Nash cleared his throat. "Still got a dead body to deal with, guys..."

Scythe straightened. "You all go. I'll deal with it."

"No," I interrupted loudly. "No one is leaving unless we're all leaving."

"We can't just leave the body here," Scythe complained. "That's so...tasteless."

I raised an eyebrow at him. "Really? You concerned your stabby brotherhood is going to judge you?"

"A bit. I have street cred to uphold, Bliss."

I shook my head. "Okay, I vote we take the psychopath and get the hell out of here."

"Witnesses..." Scythe warned, rubbing his hands together. "We should kill them too."

"Okay, you're done. That's about enough killing from you today." Nash shoved him toward the door.

"But, Dad!" Scythe sniggered.

War joined in.

"Don't encourage him," I scolded, but a laugh slipped from my mouth too. I clapped a hand over it, trying to shove it back in, especially because it sounded a tad hysterical.

Nash shook his head, which didn't help the fatherly vibe they were ribbing him for. "Okay, all of you are going to go get in my car, without stabbing anyone else, or making any more inappropriate jokes. Whatever was seen, these people won't talk. That's the code around here, and they all know it. Plus, I doubt anybody is going to miss Jerry. They'll probably send us thank you bouquets when they find out he's dead."

We traipsed outside, blood-covered, injured, and so traumatized it had somehow become funny.

I would later blame that high, incoherent state, for what I did next.

But really, it had been a lifetime in the making. That trailer was full of memories, and none of them were happy. From lying scared beneath the blankets on my bed, peeping out only to watch Jerry rape my mother. To the nagging, aching, and constant hunger that came with neglect. "I hate this place," I muttered, staring at it through the hate and rage and fear-filled eyes of my youth. "Nothing good has ever happened here. Nothing good ever will."

By the trailer steps, a can of gasoline sat waiting for a lawn mower or car, but just begging for me to use.

"Bliss!" Nash called from the Jeep.

I glanced over at him. He already had War and Scythe in the back, both of them suddenly looking paler and weaker than they had in the heat of the moment.

In the distance a siren wailed.

But it wasn't close enough to stop me from picking up the gas can and twisting off the lid.

"Bliss," Nash called again.

I upended the can, pouring the strong-smelling accelerant in a circle around the godforsaken trailer. "Don't try to stop me, Nash. It's not enough that he's dead. He needs to burn for everything he did to my family and all the other women whose lives he's destroyed. His body doesn't deserve a burial. He should die here in the hellhole he made."

Nash's voice was closer this time, right up behind me, his warm body against my back and his mouth at my ear. "I wasn't going to try to stop you. I just came to bring you a lighter."

He pressed the small piece of plastic into my hand,

and I stared down at it. So innocent-looking, until you realized what it was truly capable of.

A little like me.

I picked up an old, rolled-up newspaper from the ground, one Jerry hadn't bothered taking inside. And held the lighter to the tip of it.

A small flame ignited, but it was all the flame I needed. Once it was alight; I dropped it into the puddle of gas.

"Fire always burns in," I whispered.

The flames lit up the night, following the path I'd made and then racing inward, taking the trailer with its greedy fingers of fire.

Nash placed a tender kiss to my cheek and led me back to the Jeep, tucking me into the front seat and covering me with my jacket.

I didn't feel the cold.

I felt alive.

***

*B*ack at Scythe's place, Nash went into nurse mode. He dropped a blanket over my shoulders, told War he needed his head scanned, and then examined Scythe's arm, determining he had a bullet-shaped hole through it. He frowned at all three of us. "You all need to be in the hospital."

"I'm fine," I protested. "Never felt better, actually."

"That's shock talking," Scythe said dryly.

I was sure my eyes were gleaming. "Did you see how quickly that fire took hold?"

War's lips turned up. "I think we created a firebug."

But I shook my head. It was more the memories that had been released and the animal of a man lying dead on the inside that had my heart pumping.

As well as the three men who surrounded me now. "How did you know where I was?"

Scythe got up and walked to the kitchen, getting a first aid kit from the cabinet. "We put two and two together. Verity takes after you. She's a gutsy little thing. Knew to call us instead of the cops."

More of the tension seeped out of me. "She got home safe then?"

"She's okay," Nash assured me.

"She's better now Jerry can't hurt her." Scythe rifled through the first aid kit, taking out Steri-Strips that he tossed to War, and a suture kit he ripped open with his teeth.

Nash winced, watching Scythe stab a needle loaded with thread through his injured arm, pulling the edges of the wound closed. "Should I even ask how you know how to do that?"

"Probably not." Scythe grinned.

We all peered at him, like he was performing ground-breaking surgery and not just stitching up a bullet wound, which he'd clearly done more than once because his stitches were neat and precise.

"Doesn't that hurt?" I asked.

"Yes."

Sometimes he was as matter of fact as Vincent was.

He popped a couple of pills when he was done and sat with his arms propped behind his head. "So. What'd I miss? I hear we do foursomes now?"

I bit my lip to hide my smile, but War leaned over.

"Fuck, I missed you." He touched his lips to Scythe's. It started as a playful, nipping kiss, but it was only moments before they deepened it, tongues stroking together as the two of them fell back against the couch.

"Bliss," Scythe groaned, pulling away. "Get over here and join the reunion."

I shuffled over so I was sitting on his other side. Instantly, his strong arm wrapped around my shoulders, drawing me in. I lifted my head, and he dropped his mouth down onto my lips.

He tasted just like Vincent, but he kissed with an arrogance that Vincent never had. His kisses were deep and plunging, spinning my head and making my body crave more.

"I forgot what you felt like," he murmured against my mouth. "God, I don't ever want to forget that again."

War pressed his lips into Scythe's neck, kissing and sucking his way down, fingers working the buttons on his shirt so he could tug it aside and kiss over his chest. I slipped my hand inside his shirt, stroking over the hard ridges of his abs, all while he kissed me stupid.

War got to the bottom of Scythe's buttons, and I moved away from his perfect mouth so he could slip out of his shirt. It was tattered and bloodstained, completely ruined, but the man who'd worn it was anything but. He was warm and sweet and here.

"How long do we get you for?" I whispered between kisses.

War stiffened, but it was the question we were all wondering.

Scythe let out a long breath, but the corners of his mouth turned up. "I don't know. Until you need Vincent more, I guess. Or until I need him. We've come to some sort of unspoken agreement. One that feels a lot like peace." His smile widened. "You being pregnant changes things. You know, since it's my baby and all."

I froze.

War jerked his head up, glancing between me and Scythe with wide eyes and then back to me. "You're pregnant?"

I opened my mouth to answer but had no idea what to say.

Nash took pity on me. "We found the note in your jacket pocket."

"What note? Goddamn, I get in one little car wreck and suddenly I have no idea what's going on with any of you. Scythe's back. Bliss is pregnant." He turned to Nash. "Anything you want to confess?"

Nash settled down on the couch beside me, his arm warm against mine. "I'm your long-lost twin brother."

"I'd probably believe that if you weren't so much older than me."

"Ah, the 'Nash is old' jokes. I'm so pleased we're still running with those," Scythe chirped.

Nash kicked him in the shin, and the three of them laughed, but my head was still spinning. "Is anyone not at all concerned by the fact I'm pregnant?"

All three of them looked at me and in unison replied, "Nope."

"I don't know which of you is the father!"

"It's me," Scythe said. "No doubt."

War rolled his eyes. "I've had more sex with her than you have. It's definitely mine."

"Don't count me out," Nash complained. "It's all about timing, not quantity."

Scythe eyed him doubtfully. "Dude, your swimmers are so ancient, they're probably still hobbling along with walking canes." He put on an old man voice. "Does anyone see the egg? I left my glasses in the other testicle."

Nash groaned. "Can we get Vincent back, please?"

I bit my lip, heart swelling as the three of them teased each other. Except amongst that, fear and doubt crept in. Because this baby did belong to one of them. And where did that leave the other two? I took in Nash, with smile lines at his eyes, but his body cut from steel. He was warm and kind, and he'd be the best father in the world. He'd protected me when he was barely more than a boy, and now he was so much more than that. This baby would be so lucky to be his child.

But if the baby was Nash's, then it wasn't War's. War with his heart-stopping grin and single looks that made me feel seen, sexy, and wanted. I'd never had a man worship me the way he did, and I worshipped him right back. Suddenly not having him in my life was unthinkable.

I could give Scythe and Vincent up no more easily than either of the other two. Vincent for his quiet protection and deep connection. Scythe for his love of mischief and sarcasm. Both for the way I felt when I was in their arms.

A tear dripped down my face, and all three of them stopped in their laughter and turned to me.

Nash twisted my chin to search my eyes, worry all over his face. "Hey, what's wrong?"

I hiccupped, sucking in a breath to try to answer him, but Scythe beat me to it.

"Geez, Nash. I don't know. We killed a man. Set his body on fire. Not to mention, I'm back, which I know was the highlight amongst all of that. Wouldn't you be a little emotional?"

I turned to Scythe.

He grinned.

And just like I always did when he smiled like that, I smiled too. "You're awful."

"But you love me."

I really did.

"Bliss," War said quietly, picking my hand up and threading my fingers through his. "I'm not going anywhere. That baby is mine, even if it comes out wearing a flannel shirt or holding a teeny-tiny baby-sized knife. "

I snorted on a laugh. "I have to push this baby out. I'm really hoping it's not holding a knife."

"I'd be so proud," Scythe leaned back and got a far-off expression in his eyes, like he was imagining the scenario. Then he pressed a kiss to my forehead. "But same. If it has War's green eyes, or Nash's...wrinkles, it's still my kid."

We all turned to Nash, and he shook his head, but then he looked me dead in the eye. "Even if I have to listen to those two make old man jokes for the rest of my life, that baby is mine too. Just like his mama. I'm all in Bliss." He glanced at the other two. "I'm all in. Even with you two assholes."

Scythe abruptly stuck a hand out. "Hands in!"

War frowned. "What?"

"Hands in! You know, like they do on the football field. Hands in."

"All right, I'll bite." War put his hand on top of Scythe's.

I wiped a tear from my cheek, grinning ear to ear at these three men who were so damn good for me, in so many different ways. I put my hand on top of War's.

Nash added his hand to the pile.

"Okay! Now...we all yell something. I didn't play football, so I don't know what." Scythe frowned. "Go team? Awesome foursome? Why don't we have a group name? All the couples do. Like Brangelina."

"Because four names together is stupid?" War asked. "Plus you have two names, so that would actually make it five."

Nash rolled letters around on his tongue. "Blwanascvi?"

Scythe stared at him. "That's terrible."

"You try coming up with something better!"

"Family," I said quietly.

They all turned and stared at me.

Nash's fingers clamped around mine. "I've never had one."

"Family," War repeated, his gaze flicking around the circle to each of us.

Even Scythe was serious for once when all four of us repeated it.

"Family."

37

BLISS

"*I* need a shower. A long, hot one that gets all this blood out of my hair," War complained, picking at the crusted blood on his forehead.

"Use mine," Scythe offered. "It's well used to blood being washed off in it."

I crinkled my nose at him, and he shrugged. "What? At least it's not normally my blood."

I supposed he had a point.

War leaned over and planted his lips on mine. "See you in a bit, mama."

He went up the stairs to Scythe's room, and for a second, I thought about following him. But then my stomach growled, reminding me I hadn't eaten all day, and it was now very late.

Nash put a hand out, stroking it over my belly. "Baby hungry?" He grabbed his keys from the coffee table. "I'll go get us all some food."

"Baby is probably the size of a pea. But I'm definitely hungry, and I'll come with you." I stood, then glanced over at Scythe. "Stay and make sure War doesn't pass out in the shower?"

"Kiss me first and make babysitting worth my while."

I obliged, loving the way his fingers speared into my hair, even for a brief goodbye kiss.

I smiled as Nash picked up my hand, and the two of us headed out to his Jeep. He glanced at me, a similar amused grin playing around his lips. "What are you so happy about?"

I lifted a shoulder. "War and Scythe."

Nash glanced up toward the bathroom on the second floor, a yellow glow coming from behind the frosted glass. "You know what they're probably doing up there, don't you?"

"I do."

Nash tugged me toward the passenger side of his Jeep and opened the door for me. "That turn you on?"

"It does," I admitted. "But I'm mostly just happy for them to be back together."

"What about V?"

"I'm learning to just enjoy whichever one I have for as long as he's here." My stomach growled again. "Let's go get that food, please."

He kissed my hand like I was a princess about to climb into her chariot. "Your wish is my command. McDonald's, here we come."

The flashing of police lights caught our attention before either of us could get in the car. We stared down to the end of the street, and Nash grimaced. "What are the odds that's not about us?"

"Slim to none?" The two police cars came to a stop

across the road. Behind them, a tow truck had my smashed-up car.

"War did a fucking good job on your car," Nash critiqued. "I hope you have insurance."

"I do."

But the insurance wasn't going to help us with the cops who were getting out of their squad car and making their way over to us.

We'd killed a man tonight. A bad one, albeit, and the world was better off without him tarnishing it. But the cops wouldn't see it like that. I'd deliberately started a fire, not to erase our sins but to bring an end to a cycle of abuse that couldn't be rectified while that structure still stood. Both could so easily lead back to us. All it would take was one word from Lucy and Rhiannon or for a nosy trailer park resident to have looked out of their window and caught Nash's license plates. I held no regret over Jerry's death, but it had all been done in the heat of the moment. Now the moment was cooling with a very real fear that we'd be caught and I'd be having a baby, alone in a prison cell.

I clutched Nash's arm.

"Breathe, Bliss. They're only here about the accident."

It was the thing I loved most about Nash. He was always the strong and dependable one. I didn't even need to say anything for him to know that while I was keeping it together okay on the outside, the sight of those red and blue lights had me terrified.

I hadn't even washed my hands. They probably still reeked of gasoline. I shoved them in my pockets, like that might help hide my sins.

"Evening, Officers," Nash greeted them as they crossed the road.

They nodded in his direction, but their gazes quickly slid to me. "Bethany-Melissa Arthur?"

"That's me."

"That your car?"

I made a face at them. "What's left of it, yes."

"Were you driving it when it went off the road?"

"I was."

Nash made a sound of disapproval in the back of his throat but didn't say anything. I ignored him. There was no way I was going to dump War into this mess.

The officers peered at me and Nash and then at the mansion behind me. "You live here?"

"I do."

"You know it's a crime to leave the scene of an accident?"

"I do. But since nobody but me was injured, I really don't want to waste any more of your valuable time, gentlemen. I do appreciate you bringing my car back. We were organizing a pickup, but you beat me to it. Thank you."

The officer nodded and motioned for his friend to come forward. He held a bundle of familiar papers. "There was a TV in the back of the car that was in pieces, but we managed to salvage these. They looked important. Come down to the police station in the morning and make a full statement, okay?"

"Of course." I took the papers from him, clutching them tightly.

The tow truck driver had already unhooked my destroyed car, leaving it like an eyesore on the side of the pretty Providence street. The officer handed me his card, and I took it with fingers I refused to let shake.

But when they drove away, the breath I let out was wobbly.

"You okay?" Nash asked, guiding me toward his Jeep again.

"I'm angry," I admitted. "He took one glimpse of this house and made up his mind about what sort of person I was. It's the same reason Caleb isn't behind bars right now. If you have money in this town, you can do any number of unspeakable acts and the police just turn the other way."

"It worked in our favor tonight."

"But look how we were treated the night of the raid at Psychos. Like we were nothing more than mangy animals." I shook my head. "Axel's murder will probably never be solved, because he didn't matter enough in the eyes of the police."

"He mattered," Nash said quietly.

I knew he mattered to those of us who'd cared about him, but it wasn't enough. "I never truly realized how two towns that share a border could be so very different."

"Money is the difference. It changes everything."

"I hate that."

Nash pulled his seat belt across his chest, clicking it into place. "So let's do something about it."

"If you've got ideas, I'm open to them."

He shrugged, steering the car onto the main road. "You're already doing it. Or at least, you tried. Giving your mom a job and getting her away from Jerry was the first step. It didn't end the way we wanted it to, but that doesn't mean we should stop trying. We make it better one person at a time. Breaking the cycle of poverty for one family, so it doesn't repeat in their kids. You got out. We just need to find a way to get all the other little Blisses out."

"I offered Lucy and Rhiannon a job at Psychos tonight," I mused. "They both turned me down."

Nash nodded. "I'm not surprised. It's the work they know. They've had a lifetime of people telling them they can't be anything more."

Something Lucy had said kept repeating over in my head. It had sparked an idea that had hidden away in all the commotion, but now it reignited. "What if we gave them somewhere safe to work? The work they know, and want to continue, but somewhere that puts the women first, not the clients?"

He glanced at me. "That sounds dangerously like you suggesting you want to be a madam, Bliss."

"You were a pimp."

He chuckled. "I went to jail for it."

There was a risk I would too. I knew that. But this broken system was never going to change if people in the position to make it happen didn't stand up and create change in whatever way they could. "I have the room at Psychos. That building is huge, and we don't use half of it. We already run a sex club there. Would it really be much of a stretch to offer extra services? Paid services. You know the women. They trust you. They'd work for you. If we don't step in, some other Jerry-like pimp will. I don't know if I can sleep, knowing we could have done more but didn't." My mom's broken expression played over and over in my head. She was safer in prison than she was as a woman on the streets of Saint View.

But so many of her friends were still out there. If I hadn't had Axel and Nash and my father to break the cycle, then I would have been out there too. "Help me do this, Nash. Please. You saved me once. Help me pay it forward."

He glanced over at me, a small smile pulling at his lips. "You know most people would have left Saint View and never looked back. You're not like anyone I've ever met before."

"I hope that's a good thing."

He reached across the gearshift to take my hand. "It's one of the reasons I'd share you with a hundred men, if that's what you wanted. You're too good for me to keep all to myself."

"So we're doing this?" I asked hopefully.

He laughed. "What's one more illegal activity that we could potentially all go to jail for? It's never stopped us before."

I sat back, knowing even though it came with risks, it was what was right. They were risks I was willing to take, because if I didn't, who would?"

"We're going to need a meeting with Rebel and the rest of the staff," Nash mused. "Shit, Bliss. We have so much to do if we want to get this up and running. I'll talk to Lucy and Rhiannon..."

He went on, but the mention of Rebel had me searching through the stack of paperwork on my lap for the card Vincent and I had found when we'd gone through Axel's things. I ran my fingers along the red envelope with the little hearts above the I's.

"Did Rebel and Axel ever date?" I asked abruptly.

Nash stopped whatever he was talking about and glanced at me. "What?"

"Sorry. But did they?"

He screwed his face up. "Fuck, no."

"Are you sure?" The envelope burned hot in my hands. "Vincent and I found this letter a couple days ago. It's...vaguely disturbing."

"How?"

I read it out. "*Axel. You can't keep ignoring me. What we did... It meant something to me. I know it meant something to you too.*" I bit my lip. "There's no name, but the writing is distinctive. Little hearts over the I's. Rebel wrote that note for me, when I was too scared to tell you all I was pregnant. She put hearts over the I's. I think it's from her."

"No," Nash said decisively. "Couldn't be. I would have known."

"Sounds like whatever was going on between them was secret. They might have been seeing each other behind your back."

But he held firm in his belief, shaking his head. "Rebel flirted a lot, but there was never anything behind it. From day one, the two of them were like brother and sister. If they were fucking behind my back, I'm blind, deaf, and dumb."

"The writing, though..."

"A couple of hearts over I's doesn't mean definitive proof. Is the rest of the writing similar?"

I dug the note out of my jacket pocket and compared the two. Relief flooded through me. "It's not super similar. Rebel's writing is print. The writing on the card is loopy."

"Well, there you go."

I bit my lip.

"You're still wondering, aren't you?"

"A little bit."

We bumped over the McDonald's driveway, and Nash pulled into a parking spot. He picked up his phone from the center console, put it on speaker, and pressed a finger to his lips while it rang.

Rebel's chirpy voice answered, "Boss Man. What can I do for you on this fine evening at almost midnight?"

"Quick question. Who's better in bed. Axel or Fang?"

"Ew, gross, Nash. Why would you ask me that?"

Nash feigned innocence. "What? You're the only one I know who's slept with both of them, and there's a bet going..."

"What drugs are you on? Does Bliss know you're using? You know I haven't slept with Axel. I'm gagging at the thought. Like seriously, there's vomit in my mouth."

He looked at me and raised an eyebrow. "Do you always put hearts above your I's?"

"I have no idea what you've been smoking tonight, but I'm calling Bliss to do a welfare check. Hearts over my I's? They are the only thing I can draw, but what am I? Thirteen?" She paused for a second, and then there was an ear-piercing screech that made both of us wince. "Wait! She gave you the note? That's the only time I've ever put a heart over the I's because it felt like the sort of thing that needed to look fancy and my writing is chicken scratch. But whatever, you know about the baby?"

Relief poured through me, and Nash squeezed my hand. "Yeah, I know."

Rebel screamed again, but then the screams turned into muffled sobs.

Nash's eyebrows drew together. "Whoa, you okay?"

"I'm just so happy for you and for Bliss. You and Axel were always family, but you and Bliss being together and this baby...it makes it all official. You're gonna be the best dad, Boss Man. And Bliss is going to be the perfect mom. And I'm going to be a kick-ass aunty." She sniffed. "But God, if you ever talk about me sleeping with Axel again, I will puke on you. That would be like me sleeping with you. Shud-der."

Nash looked like he had to swallow hard, but he nodded. "Got it. I'm gross. Axel's gross. All understood. Will never mention it again."

"See that you don't." She hung up without saying goodbye.

Nash turned triumphantly to me.

I held up a hand. "Yeah, yeah. Okay. I get it. You told me so."

"You believe her?"

I did. "You can't fake that level of disgust."

"Agreed. Axel loved her, but not in a sexual way."

"I'm glad. I don't like the tone of that note."

"We should take it to the police."

I agreed with that sentiment. "We'll take it on Monday when we go make a fake report about my car."

My stomach grumbled, and that set off Nash's protective dad mode again. "I'm getting you some food. No more stressing about your brother's killer, or Rebel, or the women of Saint View. At least not for tonight."

I sank back into my chair. I could give him tonight, because it was late, and I was already overly emotional.

But I couldn't imagine ever just forgetting that someone had killed my brother. Or that they still roamed the streets. Free. Ready to do it all again if they so desired.

38

WAR

*M*y head pounded. I'd hit it hard during the crash, but I didn't have the fatigue or blurred vision or any of the other signs of a concussion. Nash was probably right. I should have gone to the hospital for a head scan. But I wasn't leaving my family. Not tonight.

I stood in Scythe's shower, the word 'family' wrapping its way around my heart. I had my mom and the guys at my club. But nothing had ever felt as real and tangible as the four of us with our hands joined, declaring we were a family.

One of our own choosing.

I loved Scythe and Bliss in a way I'd never loved anyone before. I loved Vincent because he was part of Scythe. And I loved Nash for the way he cared about and protected my girl.

The spray splashed down over my back, and I leaned my head against the glass. The door opened and closed, and I darted a glance in the direction of the person who sat on the closed toilet.

His dark-eyed gaze was contemplative. "Penny for your thoughts?"

"Too many for a penny."

"I've got room on my credit card for a few extras."

I sighed. "That accident…"

"Was no accident?"

"I don't think so. When the cops catch up with us, I'll get it towed back to the compound and have Fang or Hawk look it over, but I'm pretty confident they're going to find a tampered set of brakes."

"Just like your dad's car."

I nodded. "Gus lied when he told me there was nothing wrong with my parents' car. Now it makes sense why. He was protecting his daughter." I scrubbed a hand through my hair. "I don't want to do what I know I'm going to have to do."

Scythe leaned back and folded his arms across his chest. "You don't have to do it. You can show mercy. She made a mistake…"

I stared at him. "She killed my father. And she tried to kill Bliss. That's a pretty huge mistake, don't you think?"

"Then kill her. What's stopping you? The fact she's a woman?"

I shook my head. "If that were all it was, I would have done it by now."

"It's that you grew up with her then?"

I nodded. "For a long time, she and Hawk were the family I had, you know? My parents, of course, but I don't have any siblings. Hawk and Siren were kinda it for me. I always knew how my life was going to turn out. I'd make

Siren my old lady and have a couple kids. It was simple. But now..."

"Now it's messy."

"As messy as if I tornado ripped through my life."

He sighed and stood, unbuttoning his pants. They fell to the floor at his feet, and he stepped out of them.

I watched through the glass while he pulled off his underwear and then opened the shower door. I moved aside, letting him step beneath the spray. My dick kicked to attention at the sight of his hard, sculpted body and the water running over it in rivulets. Without thinking about it, I leaned in and licked one off his collarbone. "Where's Bliss and Nash?" I asked, swallowing down the taste of his skin.

"Getting food. Bliss sent me up to check on you." His fingers circled idly around the base of my cock.

"Is that what you're doing? Checking on me?"

His hand slid up and down my length. "You seem okay to me."

I pressed him back against the shower wall and found his mouth with my lips, needing the contact and reassurance that it was still him there, and that I had him right now, when I needed him most.

I smiled against his tawny skin. "I'm better with your hand where it is." I sank my teeth into his shoulder and closed my eyes. "Fuck, don't stop."

"I hadn't planned on it."

He pumped me harder and faster, his hand gliding over me, until he dropped to his knees and took me in his mouth. The hot, wet heat was a thousand times more intense than his hand, and I put a hand on the wall above his head, rotating my hips slowly to fuck into his mouth.

He stared up at me, hot gaze tightening my balls as he took me deeper with every thrust.

"I don't want to come in your mouth," I muttered. "Fuck. I want more. I want all of you."

I waited for him to say no.

He got to his feet, moving around me to switch off the water, and then opened the shower door.

My heart froze. I'd pushed him too far. "Scythe, wait. We don't have to. I shouldn't have said that."

He stopped at the bathroom vanity and opened the top drawer, taking out a tube of lubricant that he handed back to me.

I glanced down at it, heart pounding, then looked at him in the mirror. "You sure?"

"Fuck, yes. I'm dripping just thinking about it."

I groaned, moving in tight behind him and reaching around to stroke his erection. The tip of him was indeed slick with precum, and I swiped my fingers through it, sliding it over his cock and pumping his shaft. He gripped the edge of the sink, thrusting slightly into my grip, his eyes fluttering closed when I kissed the side of his neck. With my free hand, I cracked the lid on the tube of lubricant and smeared it all over my erection, transferring the extra to the hand that worked Scythe's dick.

He groaned, my lubed-up cock notched to his ass, and he pushed back, encouraging me. "War."

I pumped him harder, kissing his neck and prodding gently at his back entrance. "Yeah?"

"Fuck me before I come all over your hand."

Jesus Christ.

He leaned forward a little more, giving me better

access and opening himself up for me to press inside his ass.

My eyes rolled back as I stilled, forcing myself to stop moving so he could adjust.

But he took over, grinding back, taking all of me.

My fingers sank into his hips, holding on, and I fought the clench of my balls that threatened to explode at the tight grip he had on my shaft. Slowly, I moved, fucking him the way I'd been dreaming about for months.

Scythe let out a hiss of pleasure, dropping his head back onto my shoulder. The position exposed his throat in the mirror. I wrapped my hand around it possessively, not choking him, but stroking my thumb up the side of his neck, picking up the pace. He reached behind to grab onto my thighs, and I was glad, because I could no longer hold back.

"Need to come inside you," I whispered in his ear. "You're so fucking tight. You have no idea." I slipped my hand down to his dick again.

He moaned, and a fresh wave of his arousal coated my hand. Fuck, I wanted to lick him. Taste how hot I'd made him, but I couldn't drag myself away from how it felt to be inside him.

"War," he groaned. "Fuck. Let me come."

I jerked him faster and slammed my body into his harder. He took every punishing blow, my hips slapping against his ass now, no holding back in the way we were fucking. I licked every inch of his body that I could get my mouth to, murmuring dirty words in his ear about how hard he made me and how bad I wanted him.

He gripped my thighs so tight, bruising pain

bloomed, but I didn't give a shit. I wanted his mark on my body in any way he gave it.

Tight against me, my dick buried deep inside, he came first. His thick, white cum spilled over my hand. I used it as lube to keep him going, working him through while he shouted his release.

It was all I needed to fall over the edge with him. I came, the first spurts of release into his ass, but then pulled out, possessively marking my territory all over his skin.

He slumped forward over the sink, dropping down onto it, completely spent. I went with him, my chest to his back, my cum and still-hard dick caught between us in a mess of sticky liquid and sweat.

For a long moment, it was all I could do to rest there. To feel his body beneath me, the rise and fall of his chest, our breathing evening out and falling in sync with each other.

I pressed a kiss to his back. "Are you okay?"

"I just had my mind blown. What do you think?" He straightened, twisting his head to one side to crack his neck. "I've been thinking about you doing that for a long time."

I laughed and kissed him again. "Next time you can..."

He looked back at me. "You want me to fuck you?"

"Yeah. If you want to."

He kissed me hard, pushing his tongue inside my mouth to taste me. "I want to do everything with you. With Bliss. And Nash too. All of it."

39

REBEL

"*W*ell, that was weird," I announced, hanging up the phone.

"What was?"

I glanced to the end of the bar and did a double take at the man sitting there. He was handsome, in a clean-cut, preppy kind of way. His neat, collared shirt stood out amongst the rest of the bar's wrinkled T-shirts and ripped denim. He nursed an amber liquid in a short glass, but I hadn't served him. Lorelai must have taken his order while I was on the phone with Nash, who was clearly high. She'd disappeared onto the floor to collect empty glasses for the dishwasher, leaving me and the hottie alone.

"My boss." I held up the phone. "I think he's been smoking. Which is unlike him since he doesn't normally partake."

The man leaned forward, his smile growing. "Do you?"

My stomach did a little flip-flop at his shiny white

teeth and sparkling eyes. I cocked my head to one side. "Why do you look familiar? You haven't been here before, have you?" He certainly didn't seem the type to be hanging out in a dive bar in Saint View, but hey, we had all sorts show up on party nights. Maybe he just hadn't gotten the 'no parties right now' memo.

"We've met. In the parking lot."

I studied him for another second, still not quite placing him.

He laughed, clutching his heart. "Damn, that hurts, pretty girl. I'm that easily forgettable, huh?"

I normally would have hated the 'pretty girl' tag, but on his lips, with his gaze heating my blood, I found he probably could have called me whatever he wanted and I wouldn't have minded. "I meet a lot of people working here."

He reached a hand across the bar. "Callum. Real estate asshole, remember?"

Recognition dawned, and I eyed his hand suspiciously. "My boss decided not to sell." I'd lied to him the last time I'd told him that, but now it was the truth.

He raised an eyebrow but didn't drop his hand. "I hope that doesn't mean I can't drink here. Because I kind of like the place."

"The floors are sticky, the beer is watered down, and if you hang around long enough, there'll probably be a bar fight."

He still refused to drop his hand. "But you're here. So that makes all the rest null and void..."

Oh, he was smooth. Way too smooth for me. I liked my men rough and tumble and ready to put me over their knee for my smart mouth. This guy seemed more like he'd want a woman barefoot and pregnant in his kitchen, ready to fetch his slippers at the end of the day when he got home from his very important Wall Street job.

But I had a clit boner going on for his dimples and dirty-blond hair, and sometimes, a girl just wanted filet mignon instead of the usual grub I was served up on the regular from working in this bar. So I put my hand in his and gave him a flirty smile. "Rebel. You probably should have remembered that if you wanted to make a good second impression." I wasn't even sure if I'd introduced myself by name last time, but I sassed him anyway.

He held my hand longer than he needed to. "I'll never forget it again, pretty girl. I can promise you that."

40

SIREN

I flinched at the banging on my motel door, then ran to the window to shove aside the cheap, dusty curtains and peer around them.

My dad stared back at me impatiently.

I let out a sigh of relief and pulled aside the security latch. "Daddy," I sobbed, falling into his arms.

He stiffened, patting me on the back awkwardly. "What have you done now?"

"I screwed up."

He shook me off and kicked the door closed behind him. "You're going to have to give me a few more details than that."

"War was in a crash."

Dad focused on me sharply. "What? I didn't hear anything about that. On his bike?"

I shook my head, hysterics creeping up my throat. "No! He was driving that bitch's car!" I paced the length of the small room, ripping at my hair, though I didn't feel it. "He could have been killed! And it would have been all her fault. She was the one who was supposed to be driving."

He ran his hand through his hair. "Fucking hell, please tell me you didn't…"

I couldn't say anything. "I was angry. I didn't mean to…"

"You fucked with her brakes, didn't you?"

"What else was I supposed to do? You said you'd take care of it, and look how far that got us. He wasn't going to leave her!"

"Fuck, you're a dumb bitch, just like your mama."

"Daddy!" I gasped, shocked. "Don't talk about her like that.""

But the anger poured off him. "What? It's true. You act without thinking, just like she always did. Now look what you've gone and done."

He was right. Not about my mama. She was smart and strong and beautiful. But when War realized what I'd done, which he would, I didn't dare think about it. There was a code in this club that extended to its women as well as its men. I wouldn't get a free pass. "You need to help me."

"Help you? Fuck, no. You're going to drag both of us down. I'm going to go find War and make sure he knows I had nothing to do with this, or with his parents' accident."

My mouth dropped open. "That was your idea! You told me to do it."

He shook his head slowly. "I can't go down for that. They'll hunt me to the ends of the earth. Not just War and his boys. How do you think it would look if it got out that I'd been the one to take down not only a brother, but the founder of the entire damn club?"

"Cofounder! You started this club too. It's yours, and they stole it. From both of us. You're Slayers royalty. I am too. That's what you always told me."

He shook his head. "You need to run. Leave. Go as far away as you possibly can and never come back."

"What are you saying?" I ran to him, grabbing his arm desperately. Tears rolled down my face, partially shock, partially fear. "Where will I go? I have no one but you!"

He backed away like I had the plague. "You're a grown woman, Siren. 'Bout time you stopped riding my coattails anyway. They won't chase you. Go now, before War has time to put it all together."

Without so much as a goodbye, he walked out of my life, leaving me in tatters, alone and betrayed by every man who'd ever claimed to care about me.

41

BLISS

"This needs to be the biggest, sexiest, most out-there party we've ever thrown," I said, mostly to Rebel because despite War's, Nash's, and Scythe's presence at the meeting, we all knew it was Rebel who was the real queen of organization.

Her eyes gleamed with the challenge I'd set. "Yes, ma'am. Restrictions? Budget?"

"Go all out. The money from my car insurance will stretch to cover this party, then hopefully it will bring in enough to fund more." I eyed my best friend. "It's gotta be huge, Rebel. Like, big enough that nobody cares they can't get high."

Rebel waved a hand around like it was no big deal. "Drugs, schmugs. Ain't nobody going to need them when they see what I've got planned." Her pen moved rapidly across her clipboard, another tucked behind her ear. "I'm going to blow their minds. They're going to be high on the scent of dirty, hot sex."

Scythe wrinkled his nose. "Sounds gross."

She threw her pen at him. "Shut up or I'll give you a starring role in the show I'm planning."

He cocked an eyebrow. "Tell me more? I'm up for a bit of exhibitionism."

She laughed and shook her head. "I don't think my girl wants to share you."

He leaned back so his chair balanced on its back two legs. "Who said anything about sharing me. Bliss can be my co-star."

Rebel glanced in my direction. "It would save on performance fees..."

I widened my eyes at her. "Are you insane? Pay the performance fees."

She giggled and added it to her list.

War's hand landed on my thigh beneath the table, his lips brushing my ear. "Baby girl, you—"

I cut him off, putting my hand to his face and pushing him away. "I already know what you're going to say, Pervert McPerv Face. I'm the mother of your child!" I glanced at the other two and shrugged. "Or the mother of someone's child. We really need to work out our terminology."

"And more beautiful for it," War charmed, ignoring my slight panic over how the hell we were supposed to explain to the world what we were.

The three of them had taken it in stride, no second thoughts to the fact I was carrying a baby, with no idea of his or her biological father. They all proclaimed their sperm to be superior, of course, but no one had asked for a paternity test.

That blew my mind and gave me the warm and fuzzies all at once.

I was dying to know whose it was, though. Would I know, just by looking at the baby? It wouldn't change anything for me, I still wanted all three of them raising it with me. But how were they all so damn chill?

My phone buzzed on the table, and I smiled at my father's picture, excusing myself from the meeting to move to the edge of the room and take the call. "Dad?"

"Hey, sweetie." His voice sounded heavy.

"Everything okay?"

"Honestly, not really. It's been a week."

Worry prickled at the back of my neck. "Is it work?" I knew my father was barely hanging on by a thread. It was a constant source of anxiety for him, and every time we talked, he sounded a little more downtrodden.

But I'd tried to put my worries for him aside. He was a grown adult. And so was Nichelle. I loved them both dearly, and I would always do everything in my power to help them in any way I could, especially when it came to Verity and Everett, but finding out I was pregnant had changed the way I viewed my father's situation.

He had to stand on his own two feet and admit his failures as much as I did.

His failures weren't mine.

I had my own that I needed to come to terms with.

Never finding Axel's murderer was one of them. But I had my own family to look after and to provide for now. I had to let my dad do the same. If that meant he had to sell his mansion and his cars and live in Saint View, then they would be okay.

There were good people here. I'd learned that. Money wasn't everything, and trying to keep them in the lifestyle they were accustomed to wouldn't work forever.

And I needed to let Axel go. I wasn't a detective. I was just a woman who'd loved her brother but now needed to move on, and truly grieve him, without the constant suspicion of every person around me.

I pressed a hand to my belly. I just wanted to be happy. For her.

My father ignored my questions about his business. "Nichelle just wanted me to check that you all were still coming for dinner tonight?"

"Oh shit." I'd completely forgotten about that.

All three guys glanced over at me, concern on their faces. I pressed my phone into my shoulder. "Dinner at my dad's place tonight? Can you all come? Please? I need to tell them about the...you know what." I really needed them all there, by my side, if I was going to do that. My stomach lit up with butterflies at the very thought of telling my straitlaced, Providence-born, sixty-year-old father that I was having a baby with three men. Even Nichelle, much closer to my age, but with her sheltered upbringing, was going to have a hard time with it, and I needed the moral support.

"I shall wear a tux!" Scythe announced gleefully.

War shook his head. "You are so extra."

Scythe grinned at him. "Just because you prefer me in my birthday suit..."

Heat flared in War's eyes.

Nash rolled his as the front door of the bar opened and two women slipped in. Nash and I both raised a hand in greeting to Lucy and Rhiannon.

"We'll be there, Bliss. Of course we will. Tell your dad we'll all see him tonight and everybody will be appropriately dressed." He shot Scythe a warning look before turning back to me. "I'm going to go show the ladies around."

"Make sure you tell them that we're going to have security, and health checks, and mandatory hygiene, and safe sex practices. They can have full creative control over their rooms. Decorate them however they want…"

Nash pressed his mouth to mine, silencing my babble. "I'll tell them everything."

"I just want to make it better for them. It's our business, but our staff is a big part of that. It has to feel like a family, Nash. Tell them that. This isn't just a place to come and earn a dollar. We care…"

"Your heart is bleeding all over the floor I just mopped, Bliss," Rebel complained. Then she turned to the newcomers. "Hey, ladies. Good to have you here. I promise, we're a shitload better to work with than Jerry." She popped up from her seat and linked her arm through Nash's. "We'll show you around."

The four of them disappeared through the doors that led to the party rooms and beyond, into the rooms currently filled with junk. Soon, though, if Lucy and Rhiannon agreed, they'd be the first two rooms where people could pay for their services. Safely. No walking streets. No fear of getting attacked. No Jerry, pocketing most of the profit and leaving the women with less than they needed to survive. We'd run the place with respect and dignity, where the women were the ones in control, not sixty-year-old, aging white men with a God complex.

"Bliss? Are you coming?"

I blinked, realizing my dad was still on the phone. I held it back to my ear. "Sorry. Yes. We'll all be there. Just give us an hour to get changed. Scythe...wants to dress to impress. Or something."

Scythe gave a satisfied nod as I hung up.

War stood, crossing the floor to pull me into his arms. He wrapped me up tightly, touching his lips to my forehead. "I might be late," he said quietly.

I looked up into his face. "Why?"

"I have to deal with Siren and Gus."

I froze. I had no love lost for Gus. He'd made his bed with Jerry, and now he could lie in it for all I cared. But Siren... "You don't have to kill her," I whispered.

"Uh, yeah, he does," Scythe called out gaily. "She tried to kill you. If he doesn't kill her, I will." He clapped his hands together. "I don't know about all of you, but I'm in the mood for a good old-fashioned drowning. Take her out to sea and make her walk the gangplank!"

I wasn't sure I'd ever get used to the way murder delighted him. I loved the man, but he truly had a screw loose. "You aren't killing her on my behalf. I'm fine. War is fine. She made a mistake, and maybe instead of going straight to murder, you could try compassion."

Scythe screwed up his face. "That's a big word, Bliss. I don't have my dictionary with me, so I think I'll stick with the murder plan."

We all knew very well he knew exactly what compassion was. But there was no point arguing with the psychopath. I tried War again, pressing my fingers into the skin of his forearms. "I'm not dead. You can't avenge something that never happened."

He inhaled deeply and then let the breath out just as slowly. "I'm not killing her. I've thought about it a million times since I found out what she did, but I can't."

"I'll do it! Pick me! Pick me!"

We both glared at Scythe, and he sat back down grumpily. "Fun wreckers."

I ignored him. "What are you going to do then?"

"She'll be ended."

"That sounds like murder by a different name," Scythe called out, and this time, I agreed with him.

But War shook his head. "She'll still be breathing. But she'll cease to exist to all members of the club. Nobody will be permitted to communicate with her in any way. Shunned, I guess."

I swallowed thickly. "For a woman like Siren, whose whole life is that club, that might be worse than death. You'd be cutting her off from everything and everyone she knows."

"She tried to kill you, Bliss. She did kill my father. The other option is turning her over to the police and she spends the rest of her life in prison."

Scythe shuddered. "Don't do that. That's a worse punishment than death."

War nodded. "I agree." He stared down at me. "I'm probably going to have to step down as prez. There are rules...rules I can't follow when they come to Siren. I still remember her as the little girl with pigtails. This is the best I can do."

It was breaking him; I could see that. Torn between what he felt was his duty, and the mercy he held because he was a damn good man, despite his upbringing. I put my lips to his chest, right above his heart. "Go. Get it done, and then come back to us, okay?"

"I love you."

"I love you too."

I watched him walk away, leaving me alone with Scythe. I turned to him, crossing my arms beneath my breasts. "Did you really suggest making her walk the gangplank just now?"

"Argh, me hearties, I did. What, no good? We could toss Little Dog in with her, then you, me, and War could sail joyfully off into the sunset together."

"What about Nash?"

"We'd throw him a life vest, and he can swim behind."

I buried a snigger of amusement. "Take me home so I can find something equally obnoxious to wear to dinner?"

His eyes lit up. "You're going to dress to match my tux?"

I leaned in and kissed his mouth. "I'd do anything to make you happy."

He stared at me, frozen for a long moment, then pushed to his feet. Before I knew what was happening, I was being hauled into the coatroom, Scythe flicking the lock on the door behind him. "Take your pants off."

"What?"

"Take. Your. Pants. Off. I need to make you come."

When I didn't move, he started doing it for me. "Nobody has ever cared about indulging my whims like you do, Bliss. Not even War."

"Is this me indulging another of your whims?" I asked, stepping out of the pants he drew down my legs."

"Fuck, I hope so." He dropped to his knees and wrapped his arms around my thighs, dragging me closer so my pussy was right at his eye height. His tongue darted out, tasting between my folds.

The first touch of him there was deliciously perfect.

"This is so wrong," I moaned, spearing my fingers into his hair. "War—"

"War would be jealous as fuck that my tongue is on your clit right now. Nash, too."

"I'll make it up to them later." I grabbed his head with one hand and the wall with the other, using it for balance so I could roll my hips in time with the wicked rhythm of his tongue. In the seconds it had taken for him to get me alone, I'd fallen fully under his spell again, desperate for his touch and his body, with no regard to where we were or who was around us.

"That's so hot." He placed kisses on my inner thigh. "I'm so into watching you with them."

I could relate. "I've been thinking about you and War."

He pushed two fingers up inside me. "About us fucking?"

"Oh God," I moaned. "Yes."

He fucked me faster with his fingers. "Did you like that?"

I nodded, too breathless to speak. The orgasm he'd been promising with his fingers and tongue for the past few minutes swirled inside me, so responsive to his touch. He stood, never stopping, but crowded me back to the wall, his big body swamping mine. I gasped at my nipples hard against his chest, his fingers curving to hit my G-spot.

He brought his mouth to my ear. "Next time, I'll fuck him in front of you so you don't have to imagine."

I spiraled into my orgasm, clutching him close while I came, my head falling back to the wall and his tongue on my exposed throat. He kissed and sucked my neck, his fingers slick with my juices, prolonging my orgasm until I was sure I would crumple into a ball.

He stepped back, watching me with his devilish grin, then swiped his fingers across my lips and into my mouth. "I love how wet you get for me."

A dirty, hot thrill spun through me when I tasted my own arousal.

"I love it when you blush too."

I scowled at him. "It's dark in here. You can't see me blushing."

"You are, though, aren't you?"

I pushed off the wall, shoving a few stray jackets aside, and grabbed my panties from the floor.

Scythe snatched them from my fingers. "I'll keep those!"

I frowned at him. "Seriously? We're going back to the house to get changed. I'm just going to put on another pair."

"Not if I hid them all."

I gaped at him. "You did not?"

He tossed my pants to me. "Get your pants on, Arthur. Let's go find out."

42

BLISS

*S*cythe had indeed hidden all my panties.

      Every. Single. Pair.

I stormed around the house, desperately searching for wherever he'd stashed them, while he shouted, "Hotter!" or "Colder!" randomly, which only served to confuse me more and prolong the agony.

Eventually, he lay back on my bed, in the tux he'd sworn he was going to wear, while I pulled on an evening gown. I'd once worn it to an over-the-top, black-tie wedding between some of Caleb's friends.

Scythe had watched me shimmer into it, completely naked beneath, and groaned. "This was possibly the worst idea I've ever had. I cannot walk around your father's house, knowing you're so naked beneath that dress. Not without fucking you first." He drew down the zipper on his fly, taking out his cock.

But I saw my chance to get the upper hand and stopped him, tucking his erection away and doing up his pants with a smug grin. "Hurts when the shoe is on the other foot, huh? No time for what you were planning. We gotta go."

"Your panties are all underneath the kitchen sink. Please go put a pair on."

I lifted my skirt, flashing him my behind and skipping out of the room. "I think I like the breeze, actually."

I laughed as he chased me down the stairs, Little Dog joining in the game when we hit the bottom floor. She ran around our feet in excited circles, barking and yipping at Scythe, desperate for him to pick her up.

I used the distraction to get myself in the car, while he locked the house.

I didn't miss the kiss he dropped on Little Dog's furry head.

Scythe drove us the few blocks to my dad's house, where Nash and War were both parked outside. They were in their usual jeans, but they'd gone for button-downs instead of T-shirts. Nash's a deep blue, War's white with the sleeves rolled up.

Nash pushed off the hood of his car when we approached, his gaze sliding over my curves. "Damn, you look good." He pressed a kiss beneath my ear. "Apparently, you two weren't joking about the dress code?"

I kissed him back and played dumb. "The no underwear dress code?"

War turned to me sharply. "You..."

I winked at him.

All three men groaned in unison, and I laughed. "It's Scythe's doing. Blame him." I flounced my way up the path, while the three of them followed. I stopped at the door, waiting for them to catch up, all three of them surrounding me with hungry expressions in their eyes.

It suddenly hit me how grateful I was to them. I blinked at the sudden rush of emotion. "Thank you," I said quietly.

It was a thank-you for everything they'd brought me. Love. Laughter. A baby. A family of my own. A confidence I'd pass on to that little life, because now I knew what it was to be truly happy with men who respected me for who I was, both inside and out.

For once, even Scythe didn't make a joke.

I swallowed down the emotion and eyed Scythe with a stern look. "Behave yourself in there, okay? I want them to love you guys like I do. Nichelle and my dad have had so much stress with his business going under, I just want this to go well."

Scythe scoffed, "I'm insulted that you would think anybody wouldn't love me. I'm very lovable, you know."

"Yeah, I'm sure all your victims were full of love and appreciation for you right before you offed them," War mumbled.

I groaned. "Please don't say anything like that in front of my father. I'm worried about him enough as it is. I'd be truly concerned about his heart if we reveal his eldest daughter is dating a psychopathic serial killer."

Scythe gave an over exaggerated cough. "We prefer the term 'cold-blooded murderer,' actually. Geez, Bliss. At least try to be politically correct."

We all ignored him.

War reached out and took my fingers, squeezing them. "Let's go in."

I let out a shaky breath and used my old key to unlock the heavy wooden door. But I paused before I pushed it open and gaped up at War. "I didn't even ask how it went at the club! Siren..."

Worry swirled inside me for the woman I didn't like but somehow couldn't want dead either.

"She's fine. Very much alive. Though she's probably wishing she wasn't."

Nash blew out a low whistle. "So, none of you will speak to her again? Ever?"

War nodded. "It'll be as if she's a ghost. Completely dead to us. Punishment worse than death, if you ask me. If the three of you suddenly wouldn't even look at me..." He shook his head. "I don't even want to think about it."

Nash winced and shoved his hands deep in his pockets. "It's brutal, but at least she has the chance to start over somewhere else. After what she did to your parents, and what she tried to do to Bliss, its more mercy than she deserves. What about Hawk? He seems to like things by the book, and you went against that, showing Siren mercy. Is he gonna be a problem?"

War shrugged. "He'll get over it."

Nash didn't seem convinced, but he relented. "You know the cold-blooded killer and I have your backs if he doesn't."

Scythe just winked.

War grinned at them. "Yeah, I know."

The banging and crashing of pots and pans from the other side of the door interrupted the conversation, and I pushed the door open. Something metal clattered against the tiled floor. I winced at the ear-grating noise. "Dad? Nichelle?"

There was no reply over the din they were creating,

but it was pretty clear where the action was. I led the guys toward the dining room to get to the kitchen beyond.

"Shit, this place is even fancier than I remember," Nash said, voice full of awe as he trailed his fingers along the mahogany table that had been beautifully set. "This silverware is probably worth more than my house.

I had to give Nichelle credit for trying. She'd even got the expensive linen napkins out and had laid the table beautifully with flowers picked from the garden. She always had been better at the decorating side of a dinner party, rather than the cooking side. In her defense, she'd never had to learn, because she'd always had personal chefs and caterers.

Nash picked up a little black-and-gold card. "And place cards? Where am I sitting?" He put it back down. "That's War's."

I picked up the one closest to me.

My heart froze.

Nash peered over my shoulder. "That mine?"

I shook my head. "No. It's my dad's."

In neat, handwritten letters that looped and curled, someone had written my father's name. David.

The I had a little heart over it.

I picked up my card that had my full name, Bethany-Melissa, in the same handwritten letters, a heart over the I. Then Verity's. Hearts and loops all around.

"Ah, shit," Nash muttered. "That's familiar."

"It's the same, isn't it?" I whispered, dread filling my body. "As the letter we found in Axel's things."

"Yeah. What are you going to do?"

"I don't know."

The cards crumpled in my hands as we walked

silently into the kitchen, the four of us standing in the doorway to stare at the chaos that greeted us.

Every surface was covered with food or utensils or bowls. Flour dusted the countertops, though what Nichelle had been baking was beyond my comprehension. A slight tinge of smoke lingered in the air, like something had been burnt a while ago.

My father and Nichelle were at the center of it all, Nichelle's face like a storm cloud. "David!" she snapped. "For the love of God. Can you actually help? You're making more mess by wiping that cloth around the countertops like that."

He flopped the cloth around half-heartedly some more.

She stopped and peered at him, grasping his chin between two fingers. "Are you drunk? Great. You've been hitting those bottles you think you hid so well in your office, huh? Fantastic. Now I have three children to take care of tonight. Like I don't already have enough to do."

"Were you having a relationship with my brother?" I asked abruptly, announcing our arrival in the worst way possible. But I had no idea what else to say. I couldn't just say, "Hey, how are you?" when a polite greeting was so insignificant in the moment.

Nichelle jumped, spinning around, hand over her heart like I'd snuck up on her and not like I'd actually called out several times. "Dammit, Bethany-Melissa! You scared me!"

But she didn't answer my question.

So I said it again. "Were you having a relationship with my brother?"

She let out a laugh that sounded wholly fake. "What? Axel?"

I didn't say anything because I already knew the answer. The guilt was written all over her face. "How? When?" I glanced at my dad. He was silently staring into his glass of bourbon. My heart broke. "Oh my God. You knew, didn't you?"

"Bethany-Melissa. It's really not any of your business—"

My mouth dropped open. "Not my business? Are you being serious right now? Your wife was seeing my brother behind my back, for how long? Weeks? Months? And you knew about it and still said nothing?"

I suddenly remembered the Psychos' mask I'd found in Nichelle's makeup drawer and clapped a hand over my mouth in disgust. I knew exactly what happened at Psychos' parties. "Was this some sort of threeway..."

Nichelle's fingers clenched around the apron she'd tied over her pretty pastel-pink sweater. "No! I mean, not exactly."

Images of my dad, Nichelle, and Axel rolling around in bed filled my head, burning the backs of my eyes until I wanted to pick up the nearest fork and poke them out.

"Anybody else vomit in their mouth a little bit?" Scythe asked. "No? Just me?"

It wasn't just him. But it wasn't just the images my brain had conjured up that made me feel sick. They were grown adults, and what they did in the privacy of their marriage was between them.

It was the sense of betrayal, that of all the people in the damn world, it was my brother they'd chosen to do this with.

The silence in the kitchen hung thick in the air, growing more and more uncomfortable with every passing moment.

Scythe tugged at his collar and leaned into War. "Would it be bad of me to ask how the hell that happened?"

"Shut up, idiot," War hissed, squeezing my arm.

But I nodded. "No actually, I'd really like to know too." I stared at my dad, but he refused to meet my gaze. That only made me angrier.

"We were trying to spice things up," Nichelle admitted. "There's an...age gap between your father and I that was becoming a problem in the bedroom..."

I squeezed my eyes shut, but although I didn't want to know what went on beneath their covers, I still had to know how my brother had come to join them.

Nichelle hurried on. "We went to Psychos one night... we'd heard about the parties from some friends, and I thought it would be fun."

"It was a right royal fucking celebration," my father said bitterly.

She glared at him, anger quick to seep into her pose, like this was an argument they'd had more than once and I'd just reopened the wound. "You agreed! You said you wanted to watch me with another man. How was I supposed to know he was her brother? I'd never met him before. If you hadn't gotten so wasted, perhaps you would have realized before things went as far as they did."

My father slammed his thick-bottomed glass down on the countertop so hard I was surprised it didn't crack. Nash went to step in front of me, like he was worried my father might actually throw the glass in our direction, but

I pushed him aside, not scared of the man I'd lived with since I was five, who'd never once raised a hand to me. I needed to know everything.

"I hadn't seen the man since he was nineteen, Nichelle. It's not like he recognized me either. We were all in masks."

"I wish I had some popcorn," Scythe whispered. "This is better than those Spanish telenovelas. I bet next we find out he's really her dad…"

Nash shoved him hard enough to send him toppling into War, who gave him a warning look that I was very probably mirroring.

But Nichelle and Dad were fully into their argument, with little care that the rest of us were even in the room.

"That's beside the point," Nichelle yelled. "We had an agreement. You were the one who went and ruined it, David. You went back on your word."

My dad's eyes blazed. "I was the one who ruined it?" He pushed to his feet to tower over his smaller wife. "It was supposed to be sex. Nothing more."

"It was!"

"You fell in love with him. That was never supposed to be part of the deal."

"I wasn't in love with him. You were just being an old, jealous man, who got more than he bargained for and couldn't handle it."

"Liar," I said quietly.

Everybody turned to stare at me. I fished the red envelope from my purse and waved it in Nichelle's face. "It was more than sex, and you know it. You were in love with him."

She stared bug-eyed at the envelope in my hand. "I don't know what you're talking about…"

I pulled it out and read the words.

"*Axel. You can't keep ignoring me. What we did… It meant something to me. I know it meant something to you too.*"

Nichelle's face crumpled. "Where did you get that?"

"We found it in a pile of his paperwork. The handwriting is the same as these place cards, so don't even try to pretend you didn't write it."

She glanced around all of us, her eyes filling with tears.

"You were in love with him," I repeated.

This time she nodded.

"Like the common slut she is," my father slurred.

"Dad!" I said sharply. I didn't care what she'd done. I wasn't going to stand by and listen to a man speak to a woman like that. Not anymore.

Nichelle shook her head silently. "No, he's right."

"No, he's not." I glared at him. "Don't talk to her like that. Ever."

My father glared at me through bleary, bloodshot eyes that made me realize he was even more drunk than I'd first realized. "What? Does that hit a little too close to home, Bliss?" He ground his teeth. "I always hated that name on you. Cheap, just like your mother."

Hurt punched through me, and War pinned my father with a glare. "Watch your mouth, old man. That won't fly with me twice." But he had his hands wrapped around Scythe's biceps and his feet planted firmly on the floor, bracing himself.

Scythe had stopped making jokes. A frost rolled over him, his expression blank and vicious all at once.

I glanced at Nash, who abandoned his post beside me and took up the spot on Scythe's other side.

I steeled Nichelle with a glare that probably rivalled Scythe's. But I was cold and hollow and not at all the happy woman who'd walked into this house just moments earlier. I forced out words I never thought I'd ask my own stepmother. "Did you kill my brother?"

Her mouth dropped open. "What? Are you insane?"

I shook my head. "Everyone has been searching for someone from Saint View. They assumed it was gang-related. We assumed it was because of his drugs or his business. None of us searched for a scorned lover."

My father snorted into his drink. "As if she'd have the guts to walk up to his house and put a gun to his head then blow his brains out. She's scared of the damn dark, and there's not even streetlights around his place."

Nichelle turned a furious expression on her husband.

But it was me who spoke. "How do you know that?"

My father shrugged and took another swallow of his drink. "Followed her there a couple of times."

"You did what? You followed me, like some creepy pervert, hoping for a glimpse of what we were doing inside? Were you outside with your hand down your pants, jacking off while peeping through his windows?" Her disgust was palpable. "You're sick, David. That's disgusting."

My father shoved to his feet, knocking a mixing bowl full of something goopy to the floor in his haste. "You're the one who's disgusting, Nichelle. The entire thing is your fault. If you'd just stuck to the agreement, none of this would have happened."

"I don't love you, David. I told you that and you wouldn't let me go. So what did you expect?"

My father threw up his hands. "Oh, I know all about how you never loved me, and how you only married me for my money. That doesn't mean you get to fall in love with someone else."

A tear rolled down her cheek. "I hate when you drink. I don't even recognize you. I married you because you were a good, kind man. But apparently, you're only that when you're sober. And ever since your work went to shit, you're never without a drink. You hide it well, of course, but drinking in the middle of the night, and first thing in the mornings makes you an alcoholic, David." She tugged viciously on the string of her apron and ripped it over her head before turning to me. "I'm sorry, Bliss. I didn't mean for all of this to happen tonight. You're welcome to stay, but I'm taking the kids to my mom's."

I could only nod.

But her tears and threats to leave only angered my father further. "This is the bed you made, Nichelle. My bed. You don't just get to leave it whenever you feel like it."

She whirled on him. "Excuse me? I'm not your prisoner, David! Not then, and not now." She let out a sob. "Goddammit. I'm not even forty yet. I'm not living like this for the next forty years. We aren't happy. We haven't been for a long time."

"He wasn't going to save you from your ivory tower, princess. You threw yourself at him like a whore, and he rejected you."

"It doesn't matter. If not him, then it'll be someone else.

My father's face turned red with rage. "And I'll kill him too."

Shock punched through me so fast and fierce it was like being hit by a bus. My lungs ached, dying to take a breath, except my body had stopped even the most basic of functions while it tried to process the words that had just left my father's mouth.

All three of my guys were locked up, tense behind me, but all of them waiting on my cue to move.

I didn't give it.

I had no control over Nichelle though.

She whirled on my father in a rage. "You what?"

She took the words right out of my mouth. I trembled from head to toe, staring at my father who broke down, shoulders hunching over while he sobbed.

If Nichelle had any sympathy for the man, she didn't show it. "Say it again."

"I killed him," my father sobbed, falling to his knees on the cold tiles. "I'm so sorry. So, so sorry." Like he'd only just remembered I was there, he reached a hand out to me, grasping the hem of my dress. "Bethany-Melissa. I'm—"

I jerked away, unable to listen to his cries while tears fell down my own cheeks.

Nichelle's eyes were dry. "You took him from me."

My father shook his head miserably. "I had to. I was going to lose everything. Killing him meant you'd stay and Bethany-Melissa would inherit his business. I knew how well it was doing and how much those parties had to be making. I thought…"

I tried to clear my throat to speak, but Nash beat me to it.

"You thought Bliss would sell the business she inherited and bail you out financially." He stared murderously at my father, the man who'd taken his best friend. "You thought you could kill two birds with one stone. Save your marriage and your business all at once."

"Only I ruined it by not selling the business." I shook my head. "Is this why you forced those real estate agents on me? Because you were hoping I'd bail you out?" Which I very nearly had. Everything I'd done in the beginning was for him and Nichelle and the kids. I'd very nearly given my brother's murderer exactly what he'd wanted.

His tears fell in fat drops onto the kitchen floor. "You're such a good girl. You always put family first."

I nodded. I did. "You forgot Axel was my family too."

He didn't say anything. But the truth was out there, painful and horrible and sickening. There was nothing more to say. "Call the police," I said quietly, staring at my father.

"Bethany-Melissa, no. Verity and Everett—"

A gunshot cut him off.

There was a scream, though I wasn't sure if it was from me or from Nichelle. Through a fog of chaos, I watched Nash drop to the floor, grab a tea towel, and shove it to my father's chest to stop the bleeding. War got on the phone and started spitting out address details to the emergency operator. And Scythe grabbed Nichelle by the wrist, applying enough pressure that she instantly dropped the gun into his hand. "Thank you very much. Sorry, sweetheart, but there's only room for one psychopath in this family."

I hadn't even seen her leave the room to go to the gun safe. I'd been too wrapped up in my father's confession.

Nichelle backed away, staring wide-eyed at the scene on the floor in front of her, and then trained her big eyes on me. "I didn't... I don't know..."

I didn't know either. Nothing was right. Everything was upside down and back to front. And as the ambulance took my father away, and the police arrested Nichelle, all I could do was let my guys surround me and tell me it was all going to be okay.

I don't think I believed them, but I loved them all the more for it anyway.

43

BLISS

I stood in front of my full-length mirror in the outfit I'd picked to wear to the party at Psychos later that night and frowned at my belly.

War cocked his head to one side from his seat on the closed toilet. "Still no bump, huh?"

I sighed. "Nope."

Nash laughed, pulling dress pants on over his perfect ass and buttoning them around his narrow hips. "You're not even twelve weeks. The doctor said everything is fine. You'll have a belly in no time, and then not long after, you'll probably be uncomfortable and hating it."

I shrugged, slipping on a cover-up that I could wear to the club. "I know. But Verity is so excited to be an aunty, and I don't think Everett really even believes I am pregnant. I need a belly to prove it to him."

Scythe washed his hair in the shower, suds flying everywhere and all down his toned body, zero shame that he was completely stark naked while the rest of us were clothed. "Well, I can't wait. I have baby fever so bad.

Vincent was thinking about sneaking over to Mae, Liam, Rowe, and Heath's place. It's Ripley's birthday soon, and Mae must be due to have that baby any day now."

I frowned. As much as I really wanted to meet Mae, who it seemed was in the same situation as me with a harem of men, the idea was worrying. "Is that a good idea? I mean, you're still technically a wanted man. Rowe is a guard, and didn't you say one of Mae's friends a cop?"

"Yeah, Boston." Scythe winked. "But it doesn't matter. We have a plan for that." He scrubbed his hands through his sudsy hair. "We're going in disguise."

I held my hands up in mock surrender. "I don't think I want to know."

"We don't have time to worry about it now anyway. It's getting late, and Rebel is going to kill us if we aren't at the bar to help set up soon. Big night!" Nash's gaze was lit up like it was Christmas.

I studied him in the mirror. "You've missed the parties?"

"Haven't we all?" War complained, standing to fight for mirror space in the bathroom that was really not made for four people. "As much as I love having Verity and Everett here all the time..."

"It makes for boring, quiet, hidden-away sex," Scythe filled in.

My father had made it through the lifesaving surgery he'd needed after Nichelle's attack. The bullet had somehow missed anything vital, and the paramedics had gotten him to the hospital quick enough for them to save him.

Nichelle had been charged with attempted murder and was being held, awaiting trial.

My father's trial hadn't begun yet, but he'd sent word via his lawyer that he was sorry and was pleading guilty too.

I'd moved Everett and Verity into Scythe's house the next day, no question in my mind that those kids were now mine.

It was the guys who'd made them ours. Nash and War had both picked a bedroom each, and now all six of us were living together and raising two kids.

Soon to be three.

Little Dog was ecstatic and loving life, with children who 'accidentally' dropped half their dinners on the floor on a nightly basis, which were quickly cleaned up by the furry Hoover.

But it had been weeks of life-changing circumstances. I'd spent a lot of my mornings with my head over the toilet, at least one guy rubbing my back, and many sleepless nights, with one or both kids in my bed. Which had left very little time or desire for anything extracurricular.

But tonight was our first Psychos' party since the raid and the renovation. Everybody was excited about it. Me maybe most of all, because I was finally starting to feel better, and Nichelle's mom had taken the kids to her place for the weekend.

The bar was already packed when we got there, most people waiting around for the party room to open. War found some of the guys from his club and kissed my forehead before moving through the crowd to them. Scythe was working, so he took up his spot by the door, his gaze permanently glued to me though, as it always was when we were here. Nash peeled off in his own direction, disappearing out the back, most likely to check on Rhiannon and Lucy whose services were making their big debut tonight.

I slipped into the party room, waving to some of the performers I recognized while they oiled themselves up and pushed their performance cages into place.

I eyed one at the back of the room that wasn't being used, its fake gold bars glinting in the low light. A hot flush coursed through my body.

"You're staring at that cage like you're thinking about getting in it," Rebel said, a touch too loudly as she came up behind me.

Isabel, one of the performers, glanced over at me. "You should totally do it at least once, Bliss. You never know, you might like it."

I bit my lip, staring at the cage again, trying to imagine me inside it, my three guys doing things to my body that they knew I liked, building me up until I came. All with an entire roomful of people watching.

Months ago, that idea would have sent terror straight to my heart, and I would have set a new Olympic record for how damn fast a woman could move her jiggly ass out the door.

Now I stared at the cage with a new appreciation for my body, my men, and the way it felt to own the fact I liked sex with them. I could admit I was turned on by the idea.

Rebel's eyes went huge. "Get the fuck outta town, Dis. You're going to do it, aren't you?"

I turned to her. "If I don't do it now, when will I? Very soon, I'm going to have a pregnant belly. And then I'll have a baby. I already can't stand the thought of leaving him."

"Or her," Rebel corrected. "You don't know it's a boy."

"Either way, my life has already changed in the blink of an eye. In a few more months it's going to change again. Maybe I just want to try it." I grabbed her arm. "Am I insane? Oh my God, I am. It's the pregnancy hormones, isn't it? They've made me as crazy as Scythe."

Rebel slapped me on the ass like I was a football player and shook her nipple tassels. "It's sex, Dis. Not murder. It's supposed to be fun and exciting. If your idea of fun and exciting is getting off while a roomful of people watch…"

My core tingled at the thought.

"Which, judging by the blush on your face, it totally is, then you should do it. You don't want to be old and wrinkly and left thinking about that time you *almost* did it with regret in your heart. Do you?"

My heart hammered, and I groaned as something occurred to me. "I can't even get drunk for Dutch courage!"

Isabel shook her head with a laugh. "Trust me, once you get started, you won't need it. It's a high all in itself, completely natural and free. And safe for our sweet Psychos' baby."

I believed her. I was already feeling hyper, just from the realization that I was doing this. And proud. So very proud of how far I'd come and the woman I was now.

Rebel bumped me with her hip. "Go get ready and get in there, Bliss. Doors are opening in two minutes."

Nerves lit up inside me, but Isabel fist bumped me before climbing into her own cage, where her performance partners waited for her.

"Rebel, wait. Can you tell the guys where I am? I might need a cheer squad."

Rebel winked at me. "I'm going to record their expressions. It'll be epic!" She hurried off, weaving amongst the guests who were now filling the room.

"I'm a strong, confident, independent, sexual woman," I muttered to myself, opening the cage door and climbing up onto the raised platform that doubled as a bed before I could change my mind. "I am not going to pee my pants with nerves. Not because I'm not wearing any. That's completely beside the point."

"You're sounding as crazy as me." Scythe grinned at me from the other side of the bars.

Instantly, some of my stress melted away. "I happen to like my men a little crazy."

He put a foot on the edge of the cage, wrapped his fingers around the bars, and hoisted himself up so we were eye height. "Whatcha doing in there?"

I shrugged. "Oh, you know. Just had a small stroke which made me think coming in here and putting on a show would be a good idea."

"You want a partner?" War asked from the floor. Heat flared in his eyes.

It would have been a whole lot easier to invite them in here to do this with me, but the three of them had no problems with confidence. Something deep inside me shouted that she wanted to do this one herself.

"I think I'm good," I said. "I do really need you both to stand right there though, so I can...use you as inspiration."

They both groaned.

Nash pushed his way to their side, gazing up at me with an impressed grin on his face. "Is it April Fools'?"

I shook my head. "More like your birthday."

"Plus Christmas, Halloween, and Fourth of July all rolled into one," War added. "Fuck, Bliss. Let me come in there."

I laughed and shook my head. "Nope. Enjoy the show."

But then darkness flooded the room, and spotlights came on, each one centered on a cage. They illuminated my skin, warming through me pleasantly. But the cheers and clapping made me very aware that I was now one of the stars of the show and all eyes were on me.

I froze.

"Close your eyes, Bliss." Nash's voice was strong and steady from outside the cage. Bossy almost.

Just the way I liked it.

I closed my eyes and was instantly calmer. The music was slow and sexy, a thumping bass that reverberated through me, heightened now I'd eliminated sight. Without thinking about it, I swayed in time with the music.

The throbbing at my core increased, and I let it spread across my whole body, the beat moving in my blood until my entire being tingled with awareness.

You're so fucking beautiful.

I want you so bad.

I can't wait to taste every inch of you.

They were Nash's, War's, and Scythe's voices in my head, hyping me up. And when I opened my eyes, I wondered if they hadn't actually been in my head but spoken right from the lips of the three men who stood below, pure lust in their gazes.

Beyond them, a crowd had gathered, watching me sway on my stage in time to the music, gazes hungry and ready for more than I'd offered so far. I liked the way they made me feel.

But my gaze kept drawing back to the three who'd become my world.

I skimmed my hands over my thighs and hips, the lace of my outfit scratching gently on my palms. The corset and matching panties were pretty tame compared to what a lot of people wore here. The lace was thick to provide coverage over my pussy, and my cleavage flowing over the top of the corset but only enough to be sexy and not indecent. The boning and silk slid softly over my belly as I moved my hands over the indent of my waist and higher to cup my breasts.

They were full and heavy, spilling over my hands, and my nipples begged for more action than they were getting. They begged for Nash's mouth or Scythe's fingers or War's tongue.

I could have called them up and gotten all three at once.

But there was a sweet agony in waiting, and in the promise that before the end of the night, I'd have all three. Right now, this was for them.

And for me.

With the three of them watching my every move, I threw inhibition out the window and fully committed. I gave in to what my body wanted. I flipped down the cups of my corset, exposing my naked breasts to the room, while I swayed my hips in time to the beat. The air hit my skin, pebbling my nipples into aching points of need, and I took them between my fingers, rolling and playing with them while sparks of pleasure lit up inside me.

Nash was slowly unbuttoning his shirt, like this was a private show I was putting on, just for him, and he was reciprocating. His erection was solid behind his pants, and with my gaze on him, he slid his hand lower, closing his eyes briefly in relief when he cupped himself.

War had taken it one step further. I met his gaze and gasped when I noticed his pants undone, thick erection in his hand.

He wasn't the only one. He had his other hand around Scythe's cock, stroking both of them at the same time.

Heat slammed into me, hot and hard, all of it centering at my core.

I got wet instantly, and it took everything in me not to slam my way out of the cage and drop to my knees in front of them, giving them all the pleasure I so desperately wanted them to have.

But I could see in their eyes that they were getting off on me being up here.

If I was being honest, I liked it too.

Isabel had been right. There was a heady rush of power in knowing that it was me who did that to them, and to the couples kissing and groping around them. It was my body and the way I touched myself that had started this.

Now I was going to finish it.

I pulled the cord on my corset, the entire thing loosening and unravelling so I could remove it easily.

That just left me in panties. A tiny, wet slip of fabric that covered my modesty from the rest of the room.

Nash's hand pushed beneath the waistband of his pants, and I did the same to mine, slipping my fingers beneath the elastic of my underwear.

The relief was instant and yet not enough. I skimmed over my throbbing clit, needing to be filled.

Slick with my arousal, I plunged two fingers inside myself, moaning at the invasion.

"Fuck."

The word was so guttural and intense I glanced over at the guys. War caught my attention, motioning me over.

I danced closer to him, alternating between plunges of my fingers and dragging them back up to my clit.

His eyes were full of desire, but there was a mischief in them too. "Lose the panties, Bliss."

I shook my head, teasing, dancing right in front and staring down so he knew it was all for him and the two men who stood at his sides.

"Lose the panties and I'll make it worth your while."

My heart thundered. I didn't know what he meant by that, but I desperately wanted to find out. I shoved the soaked scrap of fabric over my hips and let it fall to the floor of the stage. They disappeared into the greedy hands of the crowd, which sent a wave of shock through me, but then War was motioning for me to get lower so I was closer to his head height.

I did, squatting in only my heels so he could tell me whatever it was he needed to say. I kept my knees pressed together.

He grinned at me wickedly. "Spread your legs, baby girl."

My eyes widened, but there was no way I wasn't doing it, because the thought of exposing myself like that to him was such a turn-on I nearly came.

I circled my fingers around the bars, using them for support, and opened up my knees so the three of them had a front-row view to my exposed, dripping-wet pussy.

War wasted no time, giving me three of his thick fingers, thrusting them deep inside my core, stretching me like his cock would have.

It was so much better than when I touched myself, and the shout I made let everybody know exactly how much I liked it.

"Bounce on them, baby. Let all these people see how beautiful you are when you come."

I caught Scythe's eye as he dropped to the floor, taking War's cock deep into his mouth, though his eyes stayed firmly on me. So did War's, even though he pushed his free hand into Scythe's hair, fisting the strands while he took the blow job with a groan of ecstasy.

Nash stroked his cock with one hand and pressed the other to my clit, coating his fingers in my slick arousal and using it to rub all over. Every now and then, he stopped to put his fingers to his mouth, tasting my sweetness.

"Hey, how come they get to touch and we don't?" a nameless voice complained above the music and general buzz of the club.

Scythe was on his feet in an instant, squaring off with the man. "Be thankful she even lets you watch her."

But I could fight my own battles. I pinned the man with a glare. "Because they're mine. And I'm theirs."

The guy grumbled and walked away, but Nash

worked my clit harder and faster, like it was a reward. It brought me right back into the moment with my guys and the barreling need to come for them.

Nash looked ready to break the damn cage apart. "You need to come, Blissy girl. 'Cause hearing you say you're ours? I need you out of that cage and on my dick. Now. Quit fucking teasing us."

I rode War's fingers faster, squeezing my nipple with one hand, adding to the sensation. War slapped my pussy.

The sparks ignited, sending a wildfire through my body. I clamped down around his fingers, gasping and yelping, dropping my head back, pleasure rocketing through me.

Below me, War shouted his own release, coming into Scythe's mouth.

I barely had time to suck in a breath before Nash was in the cage with me, picking me up from my boneless state on the stage floor and laying me out on the bed in the center. War and Scythe followed a moment later, crowding onto the bed with me, me naked, the three of them in various states of undress.

Scythe pulled the curtain around the cage, shutting us off from the rest of the club, though we still clearly heard the round of boos and disappointment as we disappeared from sight.

"No more showing off for the masses?" I asked him.

He shook his head. "We've shared you enough with them."

War grinned, lying out on the bed on his side so the two of us faced each other. "I want your tits in my mouth, Bliss. Get over here."

I inched forward, more than needing his attention on that neglected part of my body.

His erection had died after Scythe had made him come, but he wrapped an arm around my waist, dragging me flush against him and fitted his mouth around my nipple.

Idly, I played with his hair, running my fingers through the short lengths while he sucked and bit me until my nipples were pink and shiny.

Nash fit himself in behind me, and Scythe mirrored the action, tucking himself in behind War. Nash's lips dropped to my neck as his impossibly huge dick moved between my legs from behind. Without much warmup at all, because I sure as hell didn't need it, he pushed inside my pussy.

He was warm and perfect, and he started up a slow pace, spooning me, taking what I so badly wanted to give him.

Scythe watched Nash fuck me, his eyes bright with his own need and desire.

War ground back against Scythe's body, his erection slowly coming to life again.

I knew what they both needed.

I reached over War's waist, grabbing Scythe's hand. Nash pulled out of my body, letting Scythe's fingers take his place, just long enough to gather some of my arousal.

I winked at him, and he grinned, taking his hand back and pressing it to War's ass.

War let out a guttural groan, encouraging Scythe while the vibrations tickled through my breasts. Nash took up his slow roll again, content to fuck me softly from behind while we watched War and Scythe.

Scythe played with War's entrance, coating his tight hole with my arousal, until War's dick was thick against my thigh and he was writhing on the bed in need. I took his dick, pumping his shaft while he groaned into my breasts.

"Quit being a fucking asshole, Scythe. I'm done with the teasing. Fuck me."

Scythe rolled his eyes. "You're so fucking impatient."

"When it comes to you? Yeah. I am."

My heart swelled at the tender sentiment, even if it was disguised in rough, guttural words and demands.

Scythe gave War what he wanted.

War stilled when Scythe pushed into his ass gradually, giving him time to adjust. "Oh fuck," he groaned. "Don't stop."

The tip of his dick leaked precum, and he shouted as I swiped my fingers through it.

"Bliss," Nash said, lips at my ear. "Take us both."

I moaned my consent, and Nash slipped his soaked dick from my core and nudged it against my back entrance. I lined my pussy up with War's cock.

In unison, liked they'd planned it, both men sank into my body at once.

I came instantly for the second time, the intense pleasure of having them both at once too much for my body to contain. It exploded through me, sharp points of light that reached right to my toes, curling them in deliciousness.

War found my mouth with his, the two of us kissing deeply, tongues plunging together in the same rhythm the three men moved their hips. I reached one hand back for Nash, gripping his ass while it flexed beneath my touch, and held on, taking everything he and War had to give me. With the other hand, I blindly reached for Scythe. His fingers caught mine and threaded through, connecting all four of us.

"I love you," I whispered, not intending it for any one in particular, but for all of them. That love swelled inside me, mixing with them through kisses and touches and mind-blowing connections. The four of us writhed together, each stroke a promise that this was it. Each thrust a vow to be together, even though it would never be accepted as conventional.

When I fell over the edge again, they all went with me.

Our shouts mingled, theirs deep, mine a higher note that brought them all together. I came harder than I ever had, connected to all three, the world spinning around me in flashes of color and sound and voices.

But all of it centered back on them.

Them and the love they'd shown me. The pleasure they'd taught me.

And the promises I knew they'd never break.

EPILOGUE
VINCENT

*I*n my bedroom, I stared down at the Spider-Man costume, still sitting in the Amazon box it had arrived in. "I truly hope you fit," I said quietly to the spandex suit. "I have a very important boy's fifth birthday party to attend, and he really likes Spider-Man."

Little Dog yipped, which I took to mean she approved of my wardrobe choice. I stripped down to my underwear and pulled on the skintight suit.

Ripley is going to die.

I froze at Scythe's voice in my head, terror pouring through me instantly.

Of excitement, Vincent. My God. You are so literal. This is gonna be so good! Best idea ever!

Scythe felt like a can of jumping beans had exploded in my brain and were pinging off every surface. But I breathed a sigh of relief and didn't try to fight it.

We didn't do that anymore. I didn't try to shove his voice out of my head, and I let him in when I needed him.

Or when one of my family members needed him.

War opened the door, his gaze rolling over me, heat flaring as he took in the cut of my biceps, fully on show in the tight suit.

I let Scythe's lust for him filter in.

War dragged his gaze back up to meet mine, and then he grinned. "Tell Scythe he can wear that next time he comes to my room in the middle of the night."

I blinked a few times at Scythe's very explicit reply, and War laughed. "What's he saying?"

I shook my head. "It's too dirty for me to repeat. I'll let him tell you himself later."

War tossed his keys into the air. "Plan. Let's go do this party."

"You're coming?"

He nodded. "Hell, yes. We're all coming. Bliss and Nash are waiting downstairs. They're anxious to catch up with Rowe and Liam and Heath. Bliss has homemade rocky road for them all. She was up 'til midnight last night, making a huge batch. She thinks we didn't thank them enough when they helped save your ass. But I think she actually really just wants to talk to Mae—"

"Miss Donovan doesn't know that Liam and the others helped rescue me," I cut him off, rubbing my fingers along the satin-like material nervously. "They didn't want to upset her while she was pregnant. We can't let that slip."

War hustled me toward the door. "Quit worrying. Mae isn't pregnant anymore. And Bliss needs another woman to talk to."

I thought that over, but there was only one conclusion to come to. "Miss Donovan is a very kind woman. She'd be good for Bliss."

He slung an arm around my shoulders as we walked down the stairs. "You ever gonna call her Mae?"

I squinted, thinking about it, then shook my head. "I don't think so." She'd been Miss Donovan to me the entire time I'd been in her prison classroom. It was hard to just rewire my brain to think of her as anyone but my teacher.

Scythe could call her Mae, but to me, she'd always be Miss Donovan.

I stopped on the bottom of the stairs, catching sight of Bliss in a floral dress. It floated over her tiny baby bump and brushed around her ankles. She smoothed her palms over her belly subconsciously, but all I could think about was the fact that she was having a baby. A baby I'd get to call mine.

Just like Bliss was.

I really liked the way that felt.

"Do I look okay?" she asked nervously. "I really want them to like me. If you're sure it's safe, I need someone to talk to who gets what it's like to be..." She motioned to the three of us men, all crowded around her. "In the middle of all of this."

"You look beautiful." I lowered my head, needing to kiss her and remind myself that even though I wasn't always here, I still had permission to do that.

She pressed up onto her toes and kissed me instead. "I love you too."

War clapped his hands. "We're late, come on. Let's get over there before the birthday boy needs to go take a nap."

We drove over to the cabin in the woods that Rowe, Liam, Mae, and Heath shared with their children. The cabin had been extended since I'd last been here, but the spacious yard, surrounded by trees, hadn't changed. When I'd first escaped the prison, I'd hung out at the edge of it, secretly watching the perfect family, because I'd needed to know they were safe from other threats that had followed us from the prison.

There'd been no need to hang around after that threat had been eliminated. I'd had to leave them be and go find my own happiness.

Now I was bringing that happiness full circle, taking them back to meet the people who'd made me want something more than death and threats and violence.

I asked War not to get too close so I could sneak into the party undetected, and he parked down the tree-lined drive. Ahead, the party was already in full swing, a huge Spider-Man bouncy house wobbling all over the place, and a yard full of happy people, many who I recognized, gathered around.

Bliss smiled softly at me. "You nervous?"

I nodded. "A touch."

"They're your family. They'll be happy to see you."

I shook my head. "I care about them all. Deeply. Heath and Mae were the first people to ever see me for who I really was, and I'd lay down my life for them and the people they love. But my family is all here in this car."

Nash slapped me on the shoulder. "Go make a little boy happy. Come get us when you've made your big entrance. He's going to love it."

I pulled down my mask and snuck off through the trees. Spotting Ripley among his family, I sprinted out, bounding across the grass and dropping down into the classic Spider-Man crouch.

Ripley's eyes went huge as he spotted me, and he let out a shout of glee when I covered him in silly string, the can tucked beneath my sleeve.

"Which of you went way overboard and booked this?" Mae asked the three men standing with her. All three shrugged, shaking their heads.

Ripley jumped all over me, and I hugged him close. I'd missed my little friend. I couldn't wait until we gave him a little friend of his own.

A frown creased Mae's forehead as she stared at me. "Who hired him then?"

I disentangled myself from Ripley for a moment and stood to my full height in front of the woman who'd been so kind to me when I was nothing more than the quiet inmate in the back of her classroom who couldn't do basic math. "Congratulations on the baby, Miss Donovan."

Her mouth dropped open. Then slowly, ever so slowly, like she was afraid I might explode, she put her arms around me and squeezed me tight.

I stiffened, because anyone but Bliss touching me had that effect on me, but I slowly forced all my muscles to relax.

"Thank you," she whispered in my ear.

It was a thank-you for the life she had now. Because it was me who'd helped give it to her. There'd been no time for thank-yous when the heat had been on us all.

I nodded once, accepting her thanks, and then let Ripley drag me back into play. All those old memories disappeared, replaced by his happy squeals and shouts.

Ripley looked exhausted by the time the party started wrapping up. Most of his family and friends left, taking to their cars after waving goodbye. I was sweating up a storm beneath my mask, so I jogged back to the car, where my own family patiently waited for me.

Bliss put her arms around my neck and lifted my mask up enough to expose my lips. "That was sexy. All those women were checking you out." She pressed her lips to mine.

I pulled my mask up the rest of the way. "I don't think Miss Donovan would do that..."

Bliss laughed. "True. She only had eyes for her men. Can you introduce us now?" She held up her Tupperware container of rocky road. "I hope she'll like it."

I surveyed the remaining people in the yard. Colt and Perry who both worked at the prison were there, watching Colt's daughter on the bouncy house with Ripley. Their families were with them, but everybody else had left.

I hesitated. They were good people. They were Heath and Mae and Rowe's friends for a reason. But they worked within the system that still wanted me behind bars.

All it would take was one phone call and the entire world I'd built could come crashing down around me.

But Bliss's eyes were full of hope. She needed this. So I nodded. She grinned and hopped out of the car, clutching her homemade treats.

"You're good, brother," Nash said quietly so Bliss wouldn't hear as he shut the car door. "We've got your back if anything goes wrong."

War shoved his hands in his pockets, gaze bouncing over each man left in the yard. "If the cops show, I drive. I'm good in a car chase."

"I hope that won't be necessary. I can't kill any of these people, so if someone does take offense to me being here, a car chase is a possible outcome."

War winked. "I've got twenty-odd years of playing *Grand Theft Auto*. I got this."

Nash just shook his head and we hurried to catch up to Bliss. We joined her at the edge of the clearing, Bliss and I flanked by Nash and War. She linked her fingers through mine.

War leaned his arm into mine, sticking close. Nash took up Bliss' other hand, and the four of us walked in together.

Colt was the first to spot us. He did a double take, his body stiffening. "What the hell?"

Perry's mouth dropped open. "Vincent?"

But the shock didn't last long. In an instant, she reached for her partner, Tori, fear flashing in both their eyes. "I'm calling the police!"

"Please don't!" Bliss called out, squeezing my hand. "We aren't here to cause any trouble."

Mae scurried across the yard, putting a hand out in a placating gesture to Perry. "It's okay. He's not a danger to anyone here." She shot me a meaningful look. "Right, Vincent?"

I nodded.

"This is so weird," War muttered. "Everyone being scared of the man who rescues yappy puppies."

"Little Dog would be offended by that," I replied quietly. But I was on high alert, gaze trained on the phone in Perry's hand that she wielded like it was a sword. Colt didn't seem happy either, and his partners had made a protective circle around their woman and baby daughter.

Mae shot a worried glance in their direction, but then Heath stepped forward, crossing the distance between their group and mine.

He stood in front of me, a grin on his face. "Hey, kid. Come on in. Get some cake."

He was a huge man. Taller than me by a couple of inches, thickly muscled with a sleeve full of tats. He was only older by half a dozen years, but he'd been a father figure to me since the day we'd met.

Now he was doing it again, welcoming my family into his.

"This is Bliss," I said quietly.

He smiled, his eyes crinkling at the corners, and then his gaze lowered to where I gripped her hand.

"Nice to meet you officially, Bliss, now that we aren't all distracted by top-secret missions." His gaze darted to Nash's hand in hers, and War tight to my other side, but then went back to her. He pointed across the yard to Miss Donovan. "That's Mae. And you see the dark-haired woman over there, half hidden by a wall of men? That's Lacey." He smiled kindly. "I think you might have something in common with them."

Bliss nodded eagerly, and Mae pushed forward, dragging Lacey along with her. The two of them sat Bliss down, excited conversation erupting in between cooing over the baby in Miss Donovan's arms.

Rowe and Liam came over to greet me, followed by Colt, and the two other men who came with him. There were introductions all around. Me introducing Nash and War. Colt introducing Banjo and Rafe. Liam, Rowe, and Heath already knew everyone, so then we all just stood there awkwardly until Liam grinned and said, "Anyone want a beer?"

After that, the conversation flowed freely. Banjo kept Nash entertained with stories from his days serving drinks at rich peoples' parties. Rowe took War off to see an old bike he had hidden away in a shed. The women chattered like they'd been friends for a hundred years.

A peace settled over me. A sense that I was exactly where I was supposed to be, and that all the struggles had been worth it.

Heath elbowed me. "Any heat fall your way over Tabor? They found his body."

"None." We'd heard nothing about an investigation into Jerry's body either, but that hadn't been surprising. The Providence police had a long history of putting in no effort when it came to investigating the deaths of anyone who lived in a Saint View zip code. In Jerry's case, that worked in our favor. But Tabor had been in law enforcement. He probably had friends within the department who would have wanted to see someone put away for his death.

I would have been an easy target, especially if the other guards there that night had talked.

But Tabor hadn't been my kill. His blood was on Caleb's hands. And though I knew the Providence Police Department was as crooked as Little Dog's hind leg, it had given me a quiet security that the police wouldn't find my fingerprints on the murder weapon.

Heath nodded. "Rowe said they were questioned at work, but thankfully Mae was already on maternity leave by then."

"That's good. I don't like the idea of her being upset by anything right now."

Heath watched Miss Donovan smiling and laughing with Bliss. "You and me both." He fell back into step with me and studied me with the corner of his mouth lifted in a content smile. "You look happy."

"I think I am."

"A good woman will do that for you."

I cast a glance at Nash, his grin wide. And then at War, wheeling the old bike from the shed and dusting it off. My feelings for them were mostly platonic, but the love was real. I couldn't give either of them up any easier than I could have given up Bliss. "Good men too."

Heath looked over at Rowe and nodded, confirming my thoughts. "Good men too." He folded thick arms across his chest. "You okay? With everything?"

They were two tiny words, but they held a ton of meaning. He was asking if I'd healed from being captured and tortured. He was asking if I was okay with sharing Bliss with two other men. He was asking if I was okay with the baby she carried, even though it might not be mine.

The questions all hung in the air between us, heavy and haunting.

But then Nash laughed, the sound so satisfied and happy.

War caught my eye, and warmth ignited in a place that Scythe had forged.

And Bliss crossed the yard, wrapping one arm around my waist, the other resting lightly on her belly.

"I'm happy," I told Heath. "I'm very happy."

BONUS EPILOGUE 1

REBEL

I grinned down at the photo Bliss sent me. It was a group photo of her and the guys, Vincent in a Spider-Man outfit, with a blue-and-red birthday cake in their hands.

Quickly, I typed back. *Great shot! Now smush that cake in Boss Man's face.*

Bliss wrote back almost instantly. *Can't. Ate it. Omg, I'm so full. We're sitting around with some of Vincent's friends, finishing off all the kid food at a party. I've eaten my weight in chicken nuggets and candy. Everything okay at the bar? Sorry to leave you short-staffed. I thought we'd be in late, but if you aren't too busy, we're going to hang here for a while longer.*

I surveyed the bar. It was pretty quiet. Most of the crowd were the guys and their old ladies from War's MC. Fancy sat in the middle of them all, holding court. She still seemed frail after her long stay in the hospital, but that old fire in her eyes hadn't diminished one bit.

She was a badass, take-no-shit sort of woman, and I respected the hell out of her.

Stay, I typed back. *Have fun. Quiet here.*

"Who are you messaging?" Callum asked, peering over the bar to sneak a peek at my phone screen. "Got a hot date?"

I tucked my phone away and gave him a flirty smile. The real estate agent had been in here several nights now, hanging out with me while I was on shift. I suspected he might have been harboring a crush, which was kinda cute. He wasn't my type at all, with his business suits and flashy car, but he'd surprised me by not being as boring as one would think an agent would be. Every night he'd come in here when I was on shift and sat at the end of the bar, eating peanuts and chatting about nothing and everything.

I could easily admit, the man had grown on me. To the point I might have had a little crush of my own. "Wouldn't you like to know?"

He gave me a slow, devastating grin that had my panties wet. "I would actually. Is it a boyfriend?"

I opened my mouth to answer, but then an unnatural silence fell over the bar.

I peered around Callum, to where Fancy and the rest were sitting. All talk had ceased, and they'd all turned away from the door.

"You can't do this to me!"

I blinked at the screech from the woman standing in the doorway. "Ah, shit." I reached into my back pocket for my brass knuckles and came up short. "Double shit."

"What's wrong?"

"My brass knuckles have done a disappearing act. And that over there in the doorway, is a fight waiting to happen."

Callum glanced over at Siren storming across the bar to face off with her MC.

They all refused to acknowledge her.

"Hello!" she shouted. "I'm here! Right here in front of you, a flesh-and-blood person!" She stopped in front of Hawk. "Hawk!"

She had him cornered so he couldn't look away, but he stared through her like she wasn't even there.

She screamed right in his face. "You weren't ignoring me when I was sucking your dick, were you?"

I blinked in astonishment at the fact he didn't react.

"What's going on?" Callum whispered to me.

"She's been excommunicated."

"Meaning..."

"She's shunned. She fucked something up bad enough that she could have been punished by death. But War showed mercy on her because they grew up together. So now she's just dead to them. I heard about it, but this is the first time I've seen it in action."

We watched Siren drop to her knees in front of Queenie. Anguish flashed in her eyes. I knew Queenie had a soft spot for the younger woman, but then she lowered her eyes, staring down at her lap.

"Queenie," Siren begged. "Please. I have nowhere else to go."

Callum winced. "Damn. Harsh," he whispered.

I knew what she'd done, and she'd brought it down on herself. But her father, piece of shit that he was, had fled, and hadn't bothered taking his only daughter with him. I could only imagine how alone Siren felt right now, with everybody she knew and loved all turning their backs on her.

Deserved or not, it was heartbreaking to watch.

Fancy stood, like the regal queen she was. "I think we should take this party back to the clubhouse." She looked right at Siren, still slumped on the floor. "This place reeks of shit."

Nobody argued. The women all stood instantly, following their leader. The men were slower to stand, finishing their drinks first, but one by one, they all trickled out as well.

Fang was the last to rise, his eyes locking with mine.

He hadn't spoken a word to me all night, and every time I'd tried to catch his eye, he'd been conveniently busy.

I didn't make a habit of repeat performances in any one man's bed, but Fang had always been different. All he had to do was peek at me with his brooding eyes and serious expression and I wanted to climb the man like he was a tree.

"Fang!" I called out, waving him over.

He glanced in my direction, then stiffly at Callum, before putting some money down on the table. "Have a good night, Rebel."

I bristled at the complete and utter brush-off.

Siren gave me a knowing look as she pulled herself up from the floor, dusting off her leather pants. Her mascara ran in tracks down her hollowed-out cheeks, and she wiped miserably at her eyes. "Get out now, while you still can," she told me. "He'll never love you back. Take it from someone who knows."

I didn't need Siren to tell me how men were. And I was most definitely not in love with Fang. He didn't want me? Whatever. He was just another man in my lineup, and there were plenty more fish in the sea. "Time to go," I told her. "I'm shutting up."

"See you around."

Except I knew I probably wouldn't. The club wouldn't ever take her back. She'd have to move on. It would be torture living in Saint View, watching them all be a family while she was on the outside.

I could school her on how that felt.

I swallowed thickly, watching Fang's broad back disappear out the door, into the roar of motorcycle engines beyond.

"Night is still young," Callum said when the door swung closed on an empty room. "You wanna hang out?"

I eyed him. He was cute and sweet, and even though he really wasn't my type, Fang's rejection hurt a little more than it should have.

"Yeah, I do. Let's go."

I grabbed my keys and purse from the safe beneath the bar where we kept our valuables and cast an eye around the rest of the bar for my brass knuckles, giving up when they weren't in plain sight.

I'd probably left them in my other jeans that were balled up on the floor of my bedroom, with half my wardrobe because I hadn't gotten around to doing my laundry yet this week. Ugh, I really needed to tidy up. My apartment was a disaster.

"My place or yours?" Callum asked, walking me to his car.

"Yours," I said quickly. "Mine is a pigsty."

He chuckled and pulled out his phone, tapping away on it distractedly. "I know a good cleaner."

I snorted. "Like I can afford that."

"I'll pay for it for you."

I raised an eyebrow. "Uh, thanks, that's nice of you. But it's fine. I'll clean it myself."

He opened the door to the passenger side of his car and offered me his hand to help me in.

I smiled at his manners and then gaped at the inside of his vehicle. It was all leather seats and sleek wood-grain. "This is really nice," I told him as he got in. "You fancy. How much does selling businesses make?"

"Huh?"

"You must sell some properties outside Saint View too, huh? I can't imagine commission on the dumps around here would make you enough to buy this sort of car."

He tossed his phone into the center console. "Oh right, yeah. No, I sell businesses all over."

I chattered away about the expensive car while the streets outside flashed by, each one nicer than the last. Of course the man lived in Providence. Thank God I hadn't taken him back to my crummy little place in Saint View that I shared with the mice in the walls.

He pulled into a driveway, and my eyes bugged out. "Holy shit. You live here? By yourself?"

He took in my astonished expression and laughed. "I like room to move, I guess."

I let out a low whistle. "Fancy pants, aren't you?"

He shut his door, walked around to my side, and stopped in front of me. "Is that a problem?"

I shook my head. "Not at all. My bestie, Bliss. She grew up in a McMansion like this too. She's not a douchebag about it."

He linked his fingers through mine and tugged me up

the little path that led to the front door. It had a keypad to the right of the doorway, and he glanced at me as he put his finger to it.

I laughed. "You want me to look away?"

His cheeks turned pink. "Not trying to be an asshole, but I don't know you that well."

Well enough to take me home for sex, but not well enough to trust me with the code to his door. Sounded about right. I probably should have been insulted, but I wasn't about to start handing him a key to my apartment, so I figured it was fair enough. I turned away, facing the brick wall, chattering as normal because silences made me uncomfortable. "My bestie told me this story about her ex and how his entry code was the number of women he'd slept with." I laughed at the absurdity. "What a loser."

The door popped open with an electronic beep, but I hadn't even gotten a chance to turn around before Callum fit his body to mine, chest pressed against my back, his arms wrapped around my waist. He had to stoop because he was so much taller than I was, but his embrace was warm and welcome. I snuggled into him.

He kissed my neck. "I don't want to talk about your friends anymore."

I let my head drop to one side, giving him better access to my neck. "Mmm. Me neither."

He spun me in his arms and pushed me up against the brick wall again, shoving his thigh between my legs. I gasped at the contact but ground shamelessly on him. Seeing Fang tonight had got me wet and needy, and there was an ache between my thighs I couldn't get rid of until I had another man inside me. I wrapped my arms around

Callum's neck, and he hoisted me up. My short skirt rucked up around my waist, flashing the entire street my thong, but it was dark, and there was nobody around on the pretty, tree-lined road. He could have taken me right there and nobody would have noticed, but he carried me inside, our mouths fusing together as he plunged his tongue past my lips.

Inside, I dragged my mouth away from his, taking in the spacious kitchen to the left and the sky-high ceilings that made the space feel ginormous. Callum turned right though, padding across soft carpet to sink down onto a couch that probably cost more than my car.

I went to kiss him again, but he motioned me away. "Get naked."

I grinned cheekily at him. "That's very forward of you." I stood and stepped back, not pulling my skirt down, because what was the point? We *were* about to get very naked.

His gaze narrowed in on my panties. "You've been fucking teasing me all night. Take them off."

I dragged my skirt down over my hips and let it fall in a puddle at my feet, and then lifted my shirt and tossed it on the floor. I wasn't wearing a bra, because I barely had any boobs, so I generally didn't bother.

Callum leaned back and undid his fly, taking out his cock. He stroked it while I took off my panties.

"Suck me."

I frowned. "Excuse me?"

He smiled, and he was back to the charming man who'd been sitting at the end of my bar. "Come on, baby. I need your pretty mouth wrapped around my cock. I'm so hard for you."

I let it go and dropped to my knees, hoping he'd at least return the favor.

His dick wasn't as big as I'd hoped, but there was nothing wrong with it either, so that was a bonus if I was going to put my mouth on him. I circled his base with my hand and fit my lips over the head of him.

He let out a hiss. "Oh, yeah."

He yanked his T-shirt over his head, but I didn't pay attention, too busy concentrating on blowing him. I licked and sucked him, taking more of him into my mouth with each pass.

His hand fell to the back of my head. "You dirty slut. Take it all."

Oh hell, no. Fuck that. The first demand for head I could overlook. But the name-calling? Nuh. I wasn't into it, even if I knew other people were. If I let him get away with it once, he'd keep doing it, and I wasn't the sort to just sit quietly and stay sweet.

I lifted my head, but his grip on the back of my neck intensified. He thrust his hips up, slamming his dick into the back of my throat. I choked, tears springing to my eyes. I clutched his legs, digging my nails in, and he yelped, letting me go just enough that I could get away from him.

I pushed to my feet and stared at him in a rage. "What the fuck do you think you're doing?"

He laughed. "Just helping you out."

"Go to Hell."

I grabbed my clothes from the floor when my gaze snagged on the scars across his chest.

My blood ran cold.

They weren't just scars. Each one was the shape of a letter, the five of them forming a word.

Not a word.

A name.

Bliss.

"Caleb?"

"The scars gave it away, huh?"

A sick fear swarmed my stomach. I desperately racked my brain, but I couldn't remember a single instance where this man had been at the club when either Bliss or Vincent had been around.

He'd lied about his name.

His occupation.

He'd lied about everything.

"I'm leaving," I said stiffly. What I really wanted to say was a whole lot more vulgar, but I was well aware of the situation I'd put myself in.

He pumped his dick some more, getting off on my fear as I tried to sort out my clothes so I could put them back on.

Outside, lights flashed in the driveway, and an engine shut off. I glanced toward the window as heavy footsteps sounded outside, and then inside when they let themselves in. "Caleb! Where are you? You get the girl?"

I froze, my blood turning to ice while I clutched my flimsy clothes over my naked body. "What is this?" I whispered.

Caleb's grin turned slow. It was nothing short of predatory. "In here," he called, ignoring my question completely.

The two men, both dressed similarly to Caleb, in suit

pants and button-downs, stopped in the living room doorway.

One let out a hoot of laughter. "Couldn't even wait for us this time? Damn. We've got some catching up to do then."

I darted panicked looks around the room, but one of them noticed and took guard at the only other exit. Short of smashing through a wall, there was no escape.

"No." I said it loudly, my teeth bared, and staring each man in the eye. "I'm leaving."

Without trying to get my clothes on, I stormed for the doorway.

Caleb caught my wrist and yanked it so sharply pain speared through me. I let out an involuntary cry, hating that he'd gotten that out of me.

He smiled and grabbed my tit, squeezing it roughly. "You aren't going anywhere, slut. You were up for this. You came back here with me. You knew what it was for."

"Not this!" I shouted in his face, fighting against his bruising touch. "I said no, Caleb."

He shrugged. "And I said I didn't care. You and Bethany-Melissa are exactly the same. Too fucking stupid to know what you want. I can't get to her, with her army of bodyguards. But you...you little whore. You've been all over me for weeks."

I hadn't. I'd been as nice to him as I was to any regular customer. Even if I had been, I'd never consented to any of this.

But none of that mattered.

The three of them descended on me, holding me down, breaking my skin and my spirit.

Pouring hate into my heart.

It was too bad Fang had walked out on me tonight. Because I knew without a doubt, that if I survived this, I'd never look at another man again.

———

Want to know who the baby daddy is? Or find out how Scythe handles child birth? It's in the FREE bonus scene on my website here: https://www.ellethorpe.com/itendswithviolencebonus
There's even a HEA for Little Dog!

Need more Saint View in your life? Get Mae, Heath, Rowe, and Liam's story here in **Saint View Prison.** (This is where Vincent and Heath are in prison together!) http://mybook.to/LockedUpLiars

Get Lacey, Colt, Banjo, and Rafe's story here in **Saint View High.** It might be set in a high school, but there's is nothing young adult about this series! https://mybook.to/DeviousLittleLiars

THE END...for now. New Saint View coming soon!

THERE'S THREE SAINT VIEW TRILOGIES...

HAVE YOU READ THEM ALL?

Check out www.ellethorpe.com for details!

WANT SIGNED PAPERBACKS, SPECIAL EDITION COVERS, OR SAINT VIEW MERCH?

Check out Elle's new website store at
https://www.ellethorpe.com/store

ALSO BY ELLE THORPE

Saint View High series (Reverse Harem, Bully Romance. Complete)

*Devious Little Liars (Saint View High, #1)

*Dangerous Little Secrets (Saint View High, #2)

*Twisted Little Truths (Saint View High, #3)

Saint View Prison series (Reverse harem, romantic suspense. Complete.)

*Locked Up Liars (Saint View Prison, #1)

*Solitary Sinners (Saint View Prison, #2)

*Fatal Felons (Saint View Prison, #3)

Saint View Strip (Male/Female, romantic suspense standalones. Ongoing.)

*Evil Enemy (Saint View Strip, #1) - Releases in November 2022.

Dirty Cowboy series (complete)

*Talk Dirty, Cowboy (Dirty Cowboy, #1)

*Ride Dirty, Cowboy (Dirty Cowboy, #2)

*Sexy Dirty Cowboy (Dirty Cowboy, #3)

*Dirty Cowboy boxset (books 1-3)

*25 Reasons to Hate Christmas and Cowboys (a Dirty Cowboy bonus novella, set before Talk Dirty, Cowboy but can be read as a standalone, holiday romance)

Buck Cowboys series (Spin off from the Dirty Cowboy series. Ongoing.)

*Buck Cowboys (Buck Cowboys, #1)

*Buck You! (Buck Cowboys, #2)

*Can't Bucking Wait (Buck Cowboys, #3)

*Mother Bucker (Buck Cowboys, $#4) - coming early 2023.

The Only You series (Contemporary romance. Complete)

*Only the Positive (Only You, #1) - Reese and Low.

*Only the Perfect (Only You, #2) - Jamison.

*Only the Truth - (Only You, bonus novella) - Bree.

*Only the Negatives (Only You, #3) - Gemma.

*Only the Beginning (Only You, #4) - Bianca and Riley.

*Only You boxset

Add your email address here to be the first to know when new books are available!

www.ellethorpe.com/newsletter

Join Elle Thorpe's readers group on Facebook!

www.facebook.com/groups/ellethorpesdramallamas

ACKNOWLEDGMENTS AND AUTHORS NOTES

First, if you haven't read the free bonus scene on my website, please do! I just bawled my eyes out reading it again because I love Bliss, Nash, War, Vincent, and Scythe's happily ever after so much, and that scene just tops it off for me. Thank you guys for loving them like I do.

The big question I've been asked over the last few weeks is, will there be another Saint View series?

Hell yes, there will be. As long as you keep reading them, I'll keep writing them.

Rebel's story will be my 2023 Saint View Reverse Harem....BUT, I'm also writing a series of Saint View male/female romances! The first one is Evil Enemy (Saint View Strip #1), and will release in November 2022. These are all standalone stories, and a chance for me to give all the Saint View side characters stories of their own.

But in the meantime, there's people I need to thank for the vital roles they play on my team.

Thank you to Jolie Vines, Emmy Ellis, and Karen Hrdlicka who make up my stellar editing team. Thank you to Jo Vines, Zoe Ashwood, Sara Massery, DL Gallie, Lissanne Jones, and Kat T Masen for all the chats and support. Thank you to Shellie, Dana, Louise, and Sam for your early feedback. A massive thank you to my promo and review team for always being there for me. Thank you to the Drama Llamas for being my honorary extended family.

And for the first time, I get to thank Mr Thorpe as a member of my official work team! He's the one running my signed paperback store, invoicing for signings, doing my accounts, and all the other jobs I don't want to do haha! This all gives me more time to write more books!

And of course, my babies. I love you guys.

Love, Elle x

ABOUT THE AUTHOR

Elle Thorpe lives in a small regional town of NSW, Australia. When she's not writing stories full of kissing, she's wife to Mr Thorpe who unexpectedly turned out to be a great plotting partner, and mummy to three tiny humans. She's also official ball thrower to one slobbery dog named Rollo. Yes, she named a female dog after a dirty hot character on Vikings. Don't judge her. Elle is a complete and utter fangirl at heart, obsessing over The Walking Dead and Outlander to an unhealthy degree. But she wouldn't change a thing.

You can find her on Facebook or Instagram(@el-lethorpebooks or hit the links below!) or at her website www.ellethorpe.com. If you love Elle's work, please consider joining her Facebook fan group, Elle Thorpe's Drama Llamas or joining her newsletter here. www.ellethorpe.com/newsletter

f facebook.com/ellethorpebooks

o instagram.com/ellethorpebooks

g goodreads.com/ellethorpe

p pinterest.com/ellethorpebooks

Manufactured by Amazon.ca
Bolton, ON

29852490R00231